Tangled Vines, Island Crimes

MARTHA'S VINEYARD OFF-SEASON

ISABELLA STEWART

First Edition

NEWMAN SPRINGS PUBLISHING
320 Broad Street
Red Bank, NJ 07701

First originally published by Newman Springs Publishing 2020

ISBN 978-1-64801-949-4 (Paperback)
ISBN 978-1-64801-950-0 (Digital)

Printed in the United States of America

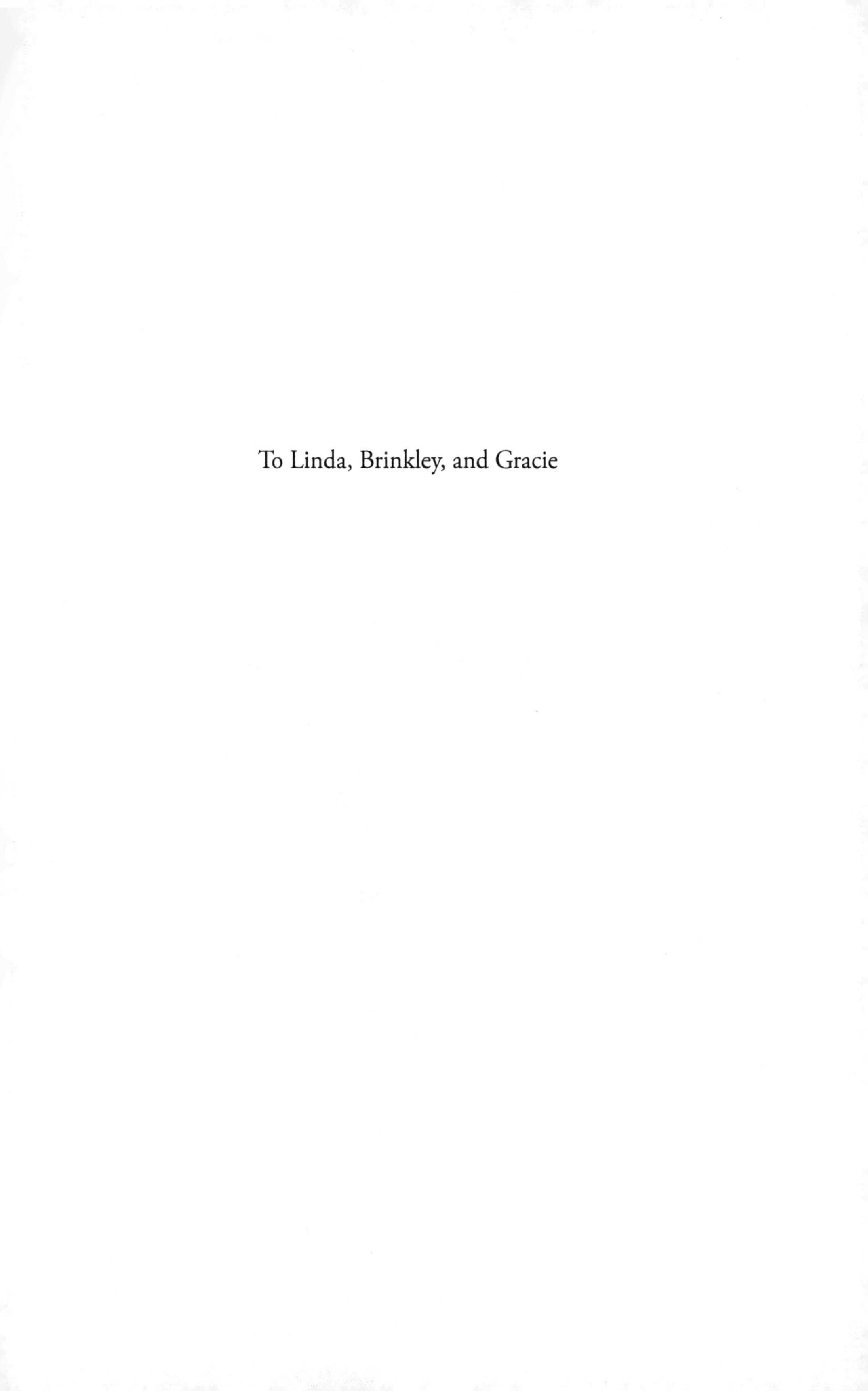

To Linda, Brinkley, and Gracie

Preface

A mostly true crime tale about racial and social castes, the drive to be accepted, unbridled greed, and, finally, murder on the resort island of Martha's Vineyard. All this takes place during the fall and early winter months, after the summer folk depart in early September. This book is the antithesis to those best sellers that take place on Nantucket's summer beaches.

In 1602 when Bartholomew Gosnold sailed around this small landmass, and landed and explored this desolate island, where rabbits and water fowl and the Wampanoag people lived, he and his men then tramped through its overgrowth, surveying the landmass as best they could. He was so taken by and impressed with the proliferation of its wild and tenacious grapevines, that he determined it was a vineyard. And this adventuresome father and explorer then gave the island to his little daughter Martha, who never did get to see her vineyard.

Today, it is a popular summer island destination whose population swells to over one hundred twenty thousand tourists and wealthy resort homeowners on a daily basis. But come Labor Day, these people all go home, leaving the seventeen thousand island people in the six towns to go about their own business. The year-rounders settle back into their routines and only occasionally get off the island to the mainland seven miles away. Unlike the mainland, where you can get into your car and travel whenever and wherever you want—on highways, into cities, among back roads, through tunnels, and over bridges—here, the only way off or on is by scheduled air or boat.

Despite the summer hoards and the number of increasing summerhouses, Martha's wild vines still run unchecked today, and much is as it originally was: enveloped in a wild and desolate beauty, proving little Martha's father was indeed discerning. Now at this time of year, these insidious and pervasive vines once again start to invade these temporarily abandoned grand houses. Gardeners won't be back until May, and the only visitors at this time of year are the caregivers hired by the owners to make sure the pipes haven't burst and rats haven't gnawed their way into the kitchen and beyond. The vines grow rapidly up the sides of the house, slowly destroying the brick foundations, choking the young saplings, and, finally, the lucky tendrils succeed in getting into the houses where they cozily spend the winters.

The other thing about the Vineyard besides its wild vines and summer people, is that here, wealth is measured by its finite landmass. On the mainland there's always room to expand. But here, there is no room to expand, except into the sea.

Land is everything—it's the only ATM available. Some year-round residents have sat on their land wealth for four hundred years (the mostly little-noticed town employees and small business owners) while others, only coming in the summer and the ones dressed in Ralph Lauren and Vineyard Vines, sit in their rocking chairs on their expansive porches overlooking the sea, preferring to count their wealth by the vagaries of the stock market rather than by their part-time land here.

The tale brings the reader into real life on this out-of-the-way island during the off-season, when summer mansions by the sea lie vacant. Would New Yorkers vacate the city for nine months leaving their jewelry unguarded in their posh apartments? Of course not. But on the Vineyard, it's different. It's safe. Nothing ever happens here. It's an old-fashioned life, a simpler one, with good hardworking down-to-earth islanders living there year-round guarding the wealthy manses. Or so the summer residents think. The proverbial cat who's away doesn't see the year-round mice begin to play. Just as children, some mice play nice and others don't.

The extreme disparity between real estate wealth obviously creates a clash of the haves and the have-nots on the island. And hidden herein is the backstory of the year-rounders' racial and cultural clashes.

Although one wouldn't imagine this small island had a variety of races (from the forever-here Wampanoags in Aquinnah to the elite black summer residents in Oak Bluffs), the imbedded racial and cultural clashes of this story involve the Portuguese-speaking people brought here in the mid-1800s on whaling ships—the white European Azoreans and the black African Cape Verdeans.

The islanders falsely assumed all the Portuguese were "the Portuguese," simply because the two groups spoke the same language. However, we soon come to understand that these are two very different groups of people—although all deemed "Portuguese" by the islanders. But these new comers—never had any sense of belonging to each other or to a common identity, despite the same language and official country of origin. The friction between the two groups was long hidden from Vineyard summer residents and only came into public view when a third group of (so-called) "Portuguese" arrived from Brazil decades later.

Almost all of this actually happened and is documented. To discuss the story further would be to venture into spoiler territory, so suffice it to say that the story has a satisfying shape in that various mysteries and crimes are solved, except for one crucial one, which becomes the subject of the next truer-than-fiction novel.

PART 1

Edgartown, 2015

Chapter 1

O what tangled vines we weave when first we practice to deceive!

Edgartown, Martha's Vineyard, September, 2015

Nestled together like the white sheep grazing on the Allen Farm's up-island pastures, down-island in Edgartown, was its own version of contented peace: pristine white houses nestled close together, side by side, on lush green lawns in town.

Of all the New England coastal tourist towns, Edgartown is the quintessential example of these picture-perfect, white-clapboard, picket-fenced villages. Visitors see only the exterior charm of this small seaside community seven miles off the Cape Cod coast: winding lanes, arching trees, picket fences resplendent with roses, and beautiful homes with manicured lawns spilling down to the harbor—reflective of the lives of those who live here. But what the visitors never see is the real Edgartown and what's hidden behind these charming and picturesque backdrops. A few hours here, strolling leisurely around town, and then they leave on the ferry and go back to their own homes, satisfied that across the sound on the island, the world is still intact and perfectly preserved.

Despite the profusion of rose-entwined picket fences that the tourists find *so* picturesque, the fences are there for another reason. They demark the boundaries between neighbors' lands, and they divide social status and wealth. In days past, islanders' and summer people's wealth and status were simply a matter of one's inheritance.

In recent years, however, things were changing. Inheritance is being superseded by made-wealth…otherwise known on the mainland as "work."

But whether or not you've had land passed down to you or you are buying land today to pass down to the next generation, land will always be the measure of wealth on an island surrounded by the sea. And unlike the mainland across the water, your wealth is not valued by your bank or brokerage account. And it's also no longer measured by your last name: the Vincents, the Nortons, the Osborns. Today land is the be-all and end-all of the Vineyard. Jeff Bezos can land his plane here, but unless he owns property, he's but a passing curiosity.

In recognition of this valuable and finite commodity, townspeople in the toniest town on the Vineyard, Edgartown, keep the outward look of their yards clipped, cared for, and maintained in uniform harmony, presenting a congenial face to passersby who stroll along their streets. The fences are there not only to safeguard one's property from a neighbor's encroachment, but also to keep prying eyes away. The rows of pickets stand there in solidarity to keep one from straying onto the front yard or from getting a peek in the windows to see what their real life is like on the inside. On the outside, everything is neat and orderly, picturesque, charming. The pickets are the townspeople's sentinels, watching, demarcating, and, above all, guarding the property, the family's wealth.

The historic white clapboard houses with dark-green shutters and their white picket fences were primarily built in the beginning of the eighteenth century, and as wealth was brought in from the faraway seas during the mid-1800s at the height of the Whaling Days, the town saw magnificent large and elegant homes along the harbor to the north, leaving behind the simpler colonials and their pickets in town. Finally, at the turn of the nineteenth century, large sprawling shingled summer homes with verandas were erected at the far ends of the harbor (the outer harbor to the north and the down harbor to the south), and instead of picket fences, one saw privet hedges with the same purpose as the pickets: keep the property private and the secrets safe. After property itself, privacy matters most on the Vineyard, as only those who have lived in small towns understand.

So, long after the summer crowd and the day-trippers leave on the Steamship ferries, popular New England summer island destinations, like Martha's Vineyard, become once again just the small, quiet coastal towns of their forefathers. With the picket fences now only sparsely covered by a few straggling late-fall roses, with the profusion of wild grape leaves turning a rusty color, with late afternoon hints of fast approaching fall crispiness, and with an intensity in the smell of salt air that only comes at this time of year, the town begins to return to normal. It readjusts. It settles in. Like an old house...a creak here and there, a little settling of the foundation, or a lightly billowing curtain from a crack in the window. Back to normal. Settled in.

And as the leaves begin to fall, and yards are a little less kept up than in the summer, walkers (and the town has many of its own) begin to notice the fading roses less and the tangled vines more. Many of the houses are vacant over the colder months until the next season, and these properties are largely unkempt. The wild grapevines have once again begun to take over the pickets where the roses had earlier flourished. And the vines, tangled masses, don't stop there. They grow insidiously on the trees, strangling them in their unrelenting ascent to reach the top, mirroring the actions of some of the townspeople.

And so, this off-season story begins...not with profusions of summer roses and breezy ocean winds, tourists and ice-cream cones, and drunken kisses in the dunes, but with the off-season's wild grapevines, dried and brittle, impatiently waiting for the spring wind and sun. For these are the grapevines that gave the island its name, so overgrown with them everywhere, that in May 1602, Bartholomew Gosnold named the newly discovered island Martha's Vineyard, after his deceased daughter and the profusion of wild grapes that overwhelmed the land.

This is the story of life in the off-season, of its land that determines wealth and status, and of its white picket fences that hide secrets. It's the story of how its prolific grapevines grow tangled and how people get caught in them, unable to extricate themselves from their snarly hold. It's the story of the haves and the have-nots, of greed and little guilt, and of determination and daring. It's the story of Edgartown's summer homes, behind all those whitewashed pickets and hedges, when their owners have left after the season, and the story of grand up-island estates, behind all those stone walls, when the real-world beckons at summer's end. It's somewhat the story of Martha's Vineyard in the off-season when owners and their cat are not here, having returned to their year-round homes until the next summer. The owners assumed their vacant property would be well cared for during these nine months, looked after by their real estate agency that had their keys. But there was one particularly cunning island broker who, like their summer home's resident mouse, had been waiting patiently all summer for this exodus. It's the proverbial story of when the cat's away, the mouse…

Chapter 2

Edgartown, Tuesday, September 8, 2015

Trey walked out of the Yacht Club at the foot of Dock Street on Edgartown's harbor and waved hello to Rick, who was standing in the harbor parking lot at the foot of Main Street. He walked over to Rick.

Trey was the darling of the Yacht Club members. He was one of them. Tall, sandy haired, and slim, he had been through the prerequisite prep school and the four-year New England college (Dartmouth). His full name was Bradford Endicott Sargent III, hence his nickname Trey—a common nickname for a boy whose name is the "III" in a family, usually a Boston Brahmin family. Trey was certainly that, and so typical of these old families, the family wealth was dwindling. So, Trey knew he had to work, but since he needed to, it would have to be a job among "his own," whether or not it paid less than a more conventional employment in a bank or other business among people he didn't know.

If you knew his family or had seen their portraits, you'd recognize the Sargent look—a squint in his left eye. It wasn't bad—it was just a trait. And he rather liked looking at his ancestors' portraits when he visited his parents in their Chestnut Hill home outside of Boston. The Sargent squint, as it was known, was a stamp of authenticity. No matter what Trey's employment future was, he always had that as he moved through life.

At the Yacht Club, he was always polite—"Yes, Mrs. MacMillan." "Of course, Mr. Griswold, my pleasure." He easily could have called them by their first names as they knew who he was and often invited him to their summer cocktail parties, but he wisely kept a formality to their relationship in the Club.

Other than his job, he was pretty much like anyone else in this snooty little summer town once frequented only by old families from Boston, New York, and Philadelphia—and, now, by newer self-made millionaires. And, even though he worked at the Yacht Club, Trey was still considered to be "one of the guys," the year-rounders who made their living there: small-town lawyers; bankers from local family-owned savings and loans; and town, hospital, or school employees. He was one of the "crossovers"; he could walk "both sides of the street," as people here said. The crossovers were the ones who had year-round employment, health benefits, vacations, and maybe even a 401(k). They didn't have to hustle to find summer housing; they had rented or even owned their places. The seasonal hotel and restaurant managers and the boutique-shop owners who had none of these benefits were lucky (or, smart enough) to "get out of Dodge," as they'd say, and bring their talents south to Florida and the Caribbean islands where they'd stay until the next summer season opened again on the island.

Unlike the seasonal residents or visitors, all of the year-rounders were working people. They lived here, even in the winter. They shopped at the Stop & Shop. They sat next the town's drunks at the Wharf Pub drinking a beer or a watered-down Pinot Grigio like everyone else, swapping comments about the weather, the fish, the most recent scandal. And there were always scandals. The most recent was the expose of one of the town selectmen whose painting company was largely comprised of illegal Brazilians who had recently arrived on the island. He'd write one large check to his chief painter, a legal Brazilian, who'd then deposit it into his own account and from there disperse cash to the workers. Everyone knew this now. But, like everyone living here, you could get away with murder, and nothing would really happen to you of any consequence.

"How's everything going, Trey?" said Rick, a wash-ashore attorney who couldn't have made it in the real world. He represented the locals with their DUIs, assaults and batteries, domestic disturbances, marking crossed lanes and left the drugs to the other attorneys from off-island. It was known that it took him nine tries to pass the Massachusetts bar exam. But it didn't matter to anyone of any consequence in the working community of the island. They didn't need anyone good. They didn't have many consequences either… perhaps a $250 fine and five days "volunteering" at Community Services. That's all.

"Better now that the Club has been pretty much put to bed for the year! Most everyone's gone. And, decommissioning in a month means I'll be a free man. We ought to go get a drink some night after work anytime now. Other than just cleaning up, I've been going through the new membership proposals and the first and second recommendations. It's such an ordeal and bound to ruffle some feathers, especially this year," said Trey.

"What do you mean?"

Trey shrugged his shoulders. "Well, we already had some problems. Barbara nominated Maria and Walter, and not everyone feels Maria—or now, rather, *they* should be members. They don't know the new husband, and although it's not said out loud, you know, it's that Maria's parents worked for many of the older members. Plus, Maria and Walter are really ostentatious and have been flinging their new wealth around, and many think it's 'unbecoming,' but they are up for vote in a couple weeks when we have the Board meeting in New York. I'm not looking forward to the showdown next summer. I really can't tell how it will play out." He kicked an old penny for luck without bending to pick it up. Perhaps he should have, he thought, as he looked at Rick to see his response.

"Well, she's certainly come a long way from her beginnings. How many Portagees could claim they were being considered for the Yacht Club! Not that I have anything against them, mind you, but it is a first. The Club could use a little shaking up," said Rick. "If they hadn't had that downturn in membership fifteen years ago, I never would have been asked to join. We need more year-rounders, and I wouldn't be opposed. But…that's just me."

Trey hunched his shoulders and said with a sigh, "We'll see, I guess." Rick nodded.

They stood for a few minutes and shot the breeze about the fishing derby beginning in a month and then parted. Trey took his black Jeep Cherokee and went home for lunch. Rick ducked into Dock Street Coffee Shop, across from the Club and parking lot, for a quick sandwich. He told Mary, "Hey, beautiful, hurry it up! I ain't got all day, you know—the criminals are waiting for me to bail them out!" he said loudly, provoking a few chuckles from the regulars.

One of them said, "Don't flatter yourself, Rick. I heard one of those clients of yours who was supposed to make bail hanged himself rather than be represented by you. Har-de-har-ha!" And then everyone laughed and hooted.

Rick laughed along with them, not realizing they were mocking him and his reputation. No matter how hard he tried, he just didn't fit in with the others. But he never realized it. Oblivious and with a smile still on his face, he chomped down on the Reuben that Mary had placed before him as the Thousand Island dressing oozed out and down his stubby fingers, which he then sucked. Dock Street was the sort of place that manners weren't important, although Mary herself noticed him doing this and shuddered at the sight. What Janet saw in him, she couldn't imagine. Janet was friendly, had done a great job getting the arts society up and running, talked to everyone regardless of their background or job, and everyone liked her—town and gown both. Mary thought about what her father had said about a few of the people in the Yacht Club who were "real." He'd say, "They walk both sides of the street. Yes, sir. Both sides of the street, they do." Rick's wife, Janet, was one of those real people.

While the Thousand Island sauce was dribbling down his fingers, Rick went over the conversation he had earlier that morning when he called Maria at Baldwin Real Estate Agency. She didn't know why he wanted to meet with her, as he wasn't representing a real estate client that she had, but nevertheless agreed to meet at her office at two o'clock.

What Maria didn't know was that before Rick had gone down Main Street to get a sandwich and had stopped to talk to Trey outside the Yacht Club, Rick had just a little earlier run into the Cape and Islands' district attorney, Charlie O'Brien. Rick was concerned with

Charlie's questions about real estate and any "deals" going down with his former officemate Owen Carson and Maria.

Rick had been in front of the Dukes County Savings Bank, in the center of this small town on Main Street, and was about to go up the three worn brick steps into the bank, when he heard his name called out. Rick had been on the Vineyard since 2000 as an attorney in his father's law firm in the Fall River factory town, home to Portuguese and Lebanese immigrants and mill workers, so most people knew him.

"Hey, Rick! Wait up!" Charlie yelled as he bounded across the street. It was Charlie O'Brien, Cape and Islands' district attorney, leaving the courthouse steps, across the street.

Rick stepped out behind the bank's picket fence and onto the brick sidewalk. "Charlie, how the hell are you doing?" he said as he smiled.

"What are you doing—going to rob the bank?" Charlie joked.

"Nope, not today, don't have my crossbow with me." Both men laughed out loud.

A few years earlier, one of the locals took a (toy) pistol, went inside the Dukes County Savings Bank on Main Street, and handed the lone teller a note saying "Give me your cash." She gave him $3,880, while sounding the alarm. He ran out the door and across the street, where his one-legged buddy was waiting in their car in front of the police station on Church Street. Off they went down Church Street, around the back of the Preservation Trust, out onto Pease's Point Way, veering right onto Upper Main Street, and then headed off on the West Tisbury Road, the road to the state forest and airport. Even though Edgartown had never had a bank robbery in its 370 years, the two policemen on duty gave chase in their cars toward the state forest. Just past the road to the airport, the robbers screeched to a stop near the forest bike path and fire road and jumped out, grabbing a bow and arrow from the back seat, and went running into the scrub oak forest, with the police just a minute behind them screeching to a stop. A few arrows flew wildly through the air, and the police fired a couple of warning shots in the sky to scare them. Within minutes, the robbers had surrendered, and by 6:30 p.m.,

Walter Cronkite, who took a particular interest in the story, being a summer homeowner who himself banked at the Savings Bank, ended his news program with the story, with the newsroom staff laughing out loud as he tried to deliver it as a straight news item. "And that's the way it is—at least on Martha's Vineyard!" and he ended shaking his head and laughing with the others in the newsroom.

Charlie and Rick shot the breeze for a moment, and then Charlie said, "What have you heard lately about your former partner Owen?"

Rick was used to this. "He's *never* been my partner, and you know that. We only shared offices when we were both starting out trying to build a law business. I see him every once in a while, leaving the courthouse, but haven't seen him recently. Why are you asking?"

"Just wondered...that's all," said O'Brien looking at a couple of young college students who were trying to see which shops were still open where they could talk to an owner about a summer job next summer. Not much was going on, but shops still stayed open at this time of year.

"I don't buy that, Charlie. I know you too well."

"Just keep your eyes and ears open and let me know if you hear anything about him or any real estate deals he's working on."

Rick looked right at him in the eyes and asked, "Are you asking about Owen or someone else?" Rick had a moment of fear until Charlie told him it was also about "a real estate broker"—perhaps both Owen and the broker working on a deal together.

"I can't say more."

Rick was relieved to learn it wasn't himself who Charlie was talking about. Rick relaxed and said he'd let him know of anything he heard. They said goodbye, and Rick went into the bank, while Charlie headed to Vineyard Haven to catch the next boat back to the Cape.

But while Rick was waiting to see the bank president, Steve Voser, he thought to himself he had to be more careful, and he also needed to warn Maria to keep her mouth shut, even though (supposedly) there was no way she could possibly know what he knew was going on in her office. It was amazing that people didn't realize when too many coincidences added up to bugging and eavesdropping, but—they didn't. They just thought it was curious Rick knew so much from his circle of acquaintances. Anyway, he had to warn Maria without letting on that he knew *exactly* what she'd been up to. He had finessed the fact that he was listening in on her office conversations by pretending "he knew" from his "sources" what was going on. That's how he had entered into "an agreement" with her about sharing some of the escrow funds she had quietly been accumulating on the sly.

One thing he didn't want was Maria dealing with Owen on any of the real estate title searches she might have in mind. Rick was going to make it perfectly clear that the only person other than Maria who was in on things was himself. No one else.

Chapter 3

Edgartown, Thursday, September 10, 2015

Owen was hardly a stable person, and he also had loose lips. He didn't understand what was private or public. To him, it was all the same.

Maria got to know him when she had worked as a young high school apprentice in Stuart Baldwin's Real Estate Agency after school during her junior and senior years at the regional high school. Owen Carson was a decidedly odd attorney with an eidetic memory, who preferred eking out a living by doing title searches rather than making real money meeting with clients or going to court.

He was tall and lanky, actually weird looking. He reminded people of a large crane with eyeglasses: long-legged and long-necked and who walked like cranes do, with necks outstretched, not pulled back. Also similar to a crane, Owen would often crouch a little to be less noticeable (so he thought), to avoid a passerby, rather than quickly walk away to the other side of the street. Definitely odd, but in some ways very endearing as he wanted to be of help to everyone, and it was so easy for him to do so with his photographic memory.

If Charlie thought there was something amiss going on between Maria and Owen, it would mean Charlie had started to nose around Maria's transactions. This could lead indirectly to Rick and his recent "agreement" with Maria.

Rick couldn't chance a thing. Plus, he didn't trust Maria 100 percent, now she had remarried that off-islander. At least with Matt, her first husband and high school sweetheart, she was just dipping into client escrow funds a little as they all did, the attorneys and brokers, and could always repay it when the time came. But now, having to keep coughing up money to keep Walter, her new husband, happy, she was becoming reckless. No one could figure out what Walter had done or how he got his money before he came to the island. Most thought he had his own money, but Rick knew better. He was a kept man, but his background still remained a mystery to everyone…even Rick. Rick didn't trust either one of them now, but the money was good; she didn't have a clue how he knew everything, and he certainly couldn't argue with that.

Rick looked at his Seiko watch (a diver's) and saw it was almost 2:00 p.m. He quickly gulped down his Coke and finished his sandwich, leaving some of it on his tie, paid and left a $2 tip on the counter, pushed himself up off the low red stools, said g'bye to Don and the regulars, and made his way up Main Street to Baldwin Real Estate Agency for his meeting with Maria. He walked slowly, with his head bent a little, reminiscent of the beginning of his mother's scoliosis, and as he passed the Paper Store and looked at his profile in the window, he realized he was beginning to also look like his portly father. Lebanese were usually taller and had finer features than most Middle Easterners, but someone's first impression of Rick was that of someone who was more Sicilian: stocky, light olive skinned, and with dark hair and eyebrows. And his nose was not aquiline but rather "squishy." One of the girls at the Dock Street Coffee Shop called him Fred Flintstone. He knew better than to make fun of their own Portagee builds, as he wasn't much better in that department. *Better start watching those Reubens,* he thought to himself. *Pretty soon they'll start calling me a Portagee.*

Rick nodded to Senna as he came in the door and saw that Maria's door was half open. Business were casual on the Vineyard—no formalities, walk right in, sit right down.

"Don't bother to get up, she's expecting me." Senna nodded, continuing her computer work. Senna barely said anything. She was there to work for her cousin, not ask questions, and to leave on time every night at four forty-five. She was smaller than Maria, but you could see the family resemblance through their father's side. Maria looked more like her mother, which was her saving grace. She was tall, and overall, she was attractive as long as she didn't smile and show her crooked teeth. She had lost some weight since remarrying and was passable. Thanks to her new second husband, she was still keeping her figure. But she had one habit that gave her away: blushing, causing her face to flush in irregular bright-red spots, almost as if she had rosacea. If you knew her, you'd know something was up that she didn't want you to know about.

As Rick lightly pushed the office door open, he saw Maria quickly putting down the phone. She looked nervous. Her round oily face looked even more flushed than usual, and her hand automatically went up to smooth her thick shiny black hair, which was a useless gesture as it was curly like all the others.

"Hello, Maria. I haven't much time," he said as he shut the door firmly, "and I *know* you're busy too. So, let's get straight to the point." He stared her in the eyes and didn't move a facial muscle. He looked intimidating, and that's exactly what he meant to be. Saying he *knew* she was busy was not just a figure of speech. He meant he had knowledge.

And, Maria knew as soon as he said he knew she "was busy too" that he had something on her again. She tried to look composed but knew her rapid blinking and involuntary tics preceded her face reddening. All this she could not control, and it was giving away her anxiety. Rick noticed it too. She readjusted her chair and placed her hands on the desk, looking at him straight in the eyes.

"What's up?" she said.

"It's about Owen. You know full well that Owen and I were officemates. Let's just say we remained friendly even though we don't work together, okay? And, let's just say that a little bird told me that you two have been working on something behind the scenes. Something you haven't told me about yet. Get the picture?" Rick then noticed the lunch residue on his tie, some sauerkraut, and flicked it off, without moving a muscle otherwise. Here was a picture of a cornered prey and its hunter.

Maria tried not to show her surprise at what he said and to get her voice under control and said, "What are you talking about, Rick?"

Rick said, "Maria. Let me be specific. I've heard that you and Owen may also be working on some real estate deals of your own. I want to remind you that we have an understanding that I am your real estate attorney. If a third person—such as Owen, just for example, of course—were to get involved with your real estate deals instead of me, they might not be so understanding about this little signature problem or anomaly as I did," referring to notarizing a "signature" of the real estate broker's widow, Peg Baldwin, who was not present and not really "with it" anymore. Rick had the signature notarized but made sure Maria paid the price. He made her agree to have him be the attorney for any real estate matters and to get a cut off the top. "You know Owen's reputation for flapping his gums. Today's visit is one good example of 'loose lips sink ships.'" He stopped and continued the stare.

Maria felt her face flush. She tried to look calm and answered, "Yes, so what? Owen's doing some preliminary title work for me, but it's by no means anything I'm ready to talk about at this time, as it's really premature and probably will go nowhere. If it starts to look as if I really have a client, I'll let you know, and you will represent me, honest." Why she had ever gone to Rick in the first place about the forgiveness loan when Peg Baldwin seemed to be slowly dying, she never knew. This was now a nightmare.

She knew she could report him for blackmail, but it would get her in just as much trouble or even more. Properties she'd been showing that weren't even for sale, forging fake purchase and sales contracts, taking down payments for these properties, delaying the closing date ("You know how slow things go on the Vineyard") until the first client screamed they had had enough of this island mentality where time *does* stand still, and they wanted their money back in full—now! So, they got their down payment back—not from their own escrow account she supposedly had set up, but hadn't, but from another person's deposit who hadn't yet screamed bloody murder. So far, it had worked.

Maria knew that unless she could keep this con up, always getting a new off-island "buyer" to plunk down money for a private sale of a property that was "not yet advertised," she'd not make her goal of getting enough money by the first of the year to live the rest of her life in Brazil. All she needed was about another half to a million dollars to reach her new life far from this windswept stagnant island, and she wasn't going to let this little chubby half-baked lawyer stop her. It was far easier to cut him in on some of this than to throw away her dream she had worked so hard for. She'd already made her escape plans—it was now just a matter of timing, which she believed was on her side for at least another three or four months. The summer people had left and wouldn't be back until May at the earliest.

All she had to do was to get another couple interested in an "off-the-market" spectacular house and plunk down new down payment—several hundred thousand dollars—that would replace an earlier client's down payment that she had already spent. It was robbing Peter to pay Paul. This medieval expression was as relevant across the ages as it was today. Ask anyone who has gambling debts or owes large amounts of money: what do they do? One simple temporary solution: check-kiting. But those who are lucky enough to hold client escrow accounts, as Maria and Rick do, have far greater capacity to delay the inevitable. In essence, unscrupulous attorneys, real estate brokers, and trust officers are professional gamblers. Just one more roll of the dice, that's all they need. Just one more real estate client who adds earnest money into the agency's escrow account will be enough money to add back to an earlier buyer's closing costs. Just one more, that's all that's needed. For now.

So far, Maria had been able to delicately withdraw one card from the shaky house she had been building and replace it with a new one. The shaky structure was still standing. But she knew it was only a matter of time before another client dissatisfied with the wait demanded another card be removed to repay them. She would then have to try again to delicately remove that and to quickly replace it with a new card. Each time she was forced to do this, her house of cards would stop growing, and it might cause the entire structure to topple. Whoever said, "Time is of the essence," should have added, "and so is skill." Building the house took skill and nerves, but the only way to win was to stop the game when the house was still standing—and walk away. People like Maria, who had already put everything on the line with her deceptive real estate practices, were greedy or cocky or desperate enough to think, "I'll add just one more card. That's all I need. Just one more card. And then I'll be fine for life."

Maria prided herself on her steady hand—that is, until Rick came along and seemed to know all about her every move as soon as she made it. Uncanny. And, unnerving. To keep the next card in play, she had to maintain her confidence and superiority to others. But he was unnerving her, and her fingers began to falter.

These thoughts all flashed through her mind while sitting across from Rick, but she knew she still had to keep going on her house until enough of her clients in her Rolodex were exhausted. Just one or maybe two more. That's all it will take.

"Maria, just remember one thing: I have my sources. And further, I don't intend to go down with any sinking ships. Watch yourself and whom you're dealing with. We both have too much at stake here. Any title searches you may be doing need only involve me. Not Owen. Even if he's cheaper. Understand?" Rick warned, as he stared coldly into her eyes.

She said, "Rick, I only used Owen for a quick check on a title I was doing when I was overloaded. I hear you. Don't worry. I'm not dealing with him. Only you."

She thought to herself, how does he know she was using Owen for a deal she didn't intend to cut Rick into that they had been doing? He knows *everything*, she thought, and she felt decidedly uncomfortable. Her stomach had been acting up recently. Maybe it was those pills that were supposed to make her less anxious that Walter had gotten from Doc Coffin. *I've got to keep my wits about me. Too much hangs on it*, she thought, trying to keep her face composed and natural.

He said, "Good. Make sure it stays that way. And don't go blabbing your mouth all over the place. Neither you nor I can afford it—literally and figuratively."

Rick left the office and quickly went down the Dr. Daniel Fisher House driveway onto Main Street and across to Tilton Way, where he turned onto Cooke Street until he reached Magnuson Way, where he entered his office. Ellen must have been in the bathroom as she wasn't at her desk. He shut his door and played the recorder. He stood there listening. Maria hadn't made or received any calls since his visit a few minutes ago. Rick sat down at his desk. He smiled. Maria was a cow—a cash cow, and he wasn't even halfway through milking it. Life is good, he thought. Life is good. And he pulled out a package of the Honey Barbeque Cape Cod Potato Chips from his drawer and munched on a couple. Even with the door shut, his secretary Ellen could hear him. *Crunch, crunch, crunch.* It was like Chinese water torture to her. She couldn't stand him.

Maria sat for a minute at her desk; she knew she was had by Rick, but there wasn't any other way getting around this one. She tried to toss off her worries about trusting him and immediately went back to work, going through her Rolodex and reading the notes she had there on each individual. She felt better and more confident doing this. Now *she* was the huntress seeking prey, and a good one at that. She quickly forgot the fear that Rick had inspired in her a few minutes earlier. She *would* prevail!

PART 2

The Vineyard and Brazil, 1950–1998

CHAPTER 4

Edgartown, Oak Bluffs, early 1950s

The Vineyard today is a contrast of names. But in Edgartown, the names are homogenous and bear their English origin. A walk through the Old Westside Cemetery two blocks from Main Street, Edgartown still clearly illustrates this. Every lane and street on the island are named after the "Natives," as they erroneously called themselves; some streets were named after their families several times over. In Edgartown, there's Norton Lane, Norton Street, and Norton Road. The most confusing street name today in this small town of four thousand people starts with *Pease*: Pease's Avenue, Pease's Pond Way, Pease's Point Road, Pease's Point Way North, or Pease's Point Way South. Their ancestors permanently staked their property by their surnames and made sure that others who followed forever knew where their property had been, whether their names be carved into granite or marble gravestones or lettered on wooden street signs and maps. Today you'd call it overkill, but they made their point, and it was indelible. It was a way to prove "I was here," even if their progeny didn't survive to keep the line going. The rest of those early ones, who arrived a little later, didn't have streets named after them. These were the people who had to settle on writing their name in the sand. At least the names of the first settlers would live on forever, no matter if there weren't any future generations still left on that clump of sand and tangled in vines in the middle of the ocean. They had staked their posterity.

But, as it turned out, many of their descendants indeed still live here today. They were wise enough not to decamp. A good number of them still live in Edgartown behind the picket-fenced yards in town or "down harbor," where the land sprawls beyond, unlike the town's neatly ordered and compact streets. Here their land is marked off only by bushes and hedges. Whether picket fences or hedges, the end result is that you knew where the property lines were. No straying here.

Some of these original English immigrant descendants preferred to live up-island in the Chilmark and West Tisbury rolling fields and farms, property there guarded not by prim pickets or well-trimmed hedges, but by the rugged stone walls placed there by their more adventuresome ancestors almost four hundred years before.

Six miles to the north of Edgartown, the town of Oak Bluffs lies. It was originally part of Edgartown although it's impossible to see how they were once joined. In 1880, this town (the only planned community on the island) became Cottage City due to the Methodist Campground's immense popularity. The Methodists prevailed then; each summer they would arrive by steamship for multiday religious camp meetings held under large tents and in the open air. As families returned to the grove year after year, tents pitched on the ground gave way to tents pitched on wooden platforms and eventually to small wooden cottages; hence, Cottage City. Curving networks of narrow streets lined with quaint Carpenter's Gothic cottages, picket fences, and tiny pocket parks. Small in scale and closely packed, the cottages grew more elaborate over time. Porches, balconies, elaborate door and window frames became common, as did complex wooden scrollwork affixed to the roof edges as decorative trim. The unique Carpenter's Gothic architectural style of the cottages was often accented by the owner's use of bright, multihued paint schemes—pinks, blues, greens, and yellows—and gave the summer cottages a storybook look. Dubbed gingerbread cottages, they became a tourist attraction in their own right in the late nineteenth century. Many houses are still family owned and passed on generation to generation, but the land itself belongs only to the Methodist association.

The Gothic cottages were the antithesis of the good breeding and respectability personified by Edgartown's homogenous and well-proportioned white clapboard houses with their dark-green shutters and rose-covered white picket fences, built in the years at the time of the American Revolution and later the Whaling Days.

The two stepsisters, Edgartown and Oak Bluffs, were like oil and water. In addition to each town's violently contrasting idea of architectural tastes, the younger stepsister, Oak Bluffs (or *OB*, as she insisted on being called), rebelled; and she became the honky-tonk, somewhat trashy, teenager of the family. Her older debutante stepsister and her friends and families would never even visit OB unless it was summertime—to bring their kids to the Flying Horses Carousel—and then rush right back home to the cool greenery of their orderly streets and white clapboard houses to have a drink on their porch, gazing out on the sailboat regattas in the harbor. It was the beginning of "class" on the Vineyard.

While the Northeasterners who favored Edgartown put down their summer roots in the quaint harbor town of Edgartown, Oak Bluffs went in the other direction and began to welcome a group (or rather two groups) of foreigners: the Portuguese. One would think that immigrants from across the Atlantic who spoke the same language would embrace each other as "long-lost cousins," but they did not socially interact, except occasionally, and then usually only for work, even though they lived together on one little island seven miles off the coast of Massachusetts.

Most people today on the Vineyard had no idea when all the Portuguese had arrived. They assumed it was in the past century but never bothered to inquire. It didn't matter to them. These people were here now, that's all, and they did pretty cheap work for whatever islanders' needs may be. Although the seventeenth century English were the first immigrants, their descendants today insisted on being called "Natives." These people never once stopped to consider that the real Natives were the Wampanoag Tribe, who, somehow, god bless them, had learned to put up with these English settlers and then their descendants named Pease, Vincent, Coffin, Norton, farmers and fishermen since the early 1600s.

To the Peases and Osborns and Mayhews, the newcomers in the 1800s from islands in the Azores and Cape Verde were all "Portagee."

True, the Mayhews and Peases observed that some of them were light-skinned and others were dark. But they were all Portuguese, they decreed. And they mostly lived in Oak Bluffs, thank the Lord.

In reality, the Cape Verdeans had nothing in common with the Azoreans except their language. They were slaves from Western Africa, off the coast of Senegal, and were brought to the Cape Verde islands in the mid-1400s by their owners, the Portuguese plantation owners. They were black.

Only a decade or so before the Portuguese had started to populate the Cape Verdean islands, they began to populate the string of islands west of Lisbon called the Azores. The Azoreans were European and had no interaction whatsoever with, or even knowledge of, their "neighbors" and countrymen 1,500 miles to the south, off Africa.

It was only in the 1800s when whaling and shipping captains from the East Coast began to pick up fishermen and farmers from these two island groups for their ships that the two "Portuguese" (speaking, that is) groups ever met on the shores of New England and on the island of Martha's Vineyard. Speaking the same language does not make a white European want to mingle with a former African slave, and their children would certainly not be allowed to interacting socially with them. But the Peases and Osborns and Mayhews thought they were all the same...granted some had different coloring...but they were all Portuguese.

So, once again, the Wampanoag Tribe had to make room for a new influx of immigrants and learn to interact with them, just as they did with the English who had come in the 1600s to farm the island. The Vineyard has long been an island of immigrants, not even counting the summer variety.

Within the Portuguese community, the Cape Verdeans were the "outcastes." That was until a well-liked Verdean who had made his way up in the island world became a constable. Behind his back, but in an affectionate way, the local year-round people called him by the nickname *Peter Pop*, and then adding *the Chocolate Cop*. They only knew him as one of the many Portuguese on the island and didn't realize he, of pure African descent but from a Portuguese-owned island, was a distinct and separate member of the Vineyard's "Portuguese community." About the only thing that brought the two disparate groups even remotely together from time to time were the occasional religious festivals and the later Portuguese American Club (the PA Club).

Although most Portuguese (speaking, that is) lived in Oak Bluffs, a small group of Azorean families lived in Edgartown, as did Maria's family, just outside the downtown area of white picket fences where the old families lived. They tended to be of a higher class and interacted daily with the Old Names and the Summer Folk, as cooks, laundresses, mechanics, gardeners, etc.

Chapter 5

Edgartown, 1970s

Maria's first language was Portuguese, and until she went to school, Maria did not speak English and didn't have to. Everyone she knew and lived among spoke Portuguese. The townspeople called her neighborhood *Rinso Heights*, named after the laundry soap at the height of popularity from the 1920s until the 1950s and which was the first mass-marketed soap powder sponsoring afternoon radio shows, hence the origin of *soap operas*.

Josie Belisle, Dodo Benefit, Lilian Silva, Valentina Almeida, Maria's mother, and other Azorean women and their families lived here. The women earned money in the season by cleaning summer-houses during the day and bringing home laundry at night, hanging it out to dry in the backyards of their compact little cottages in this out-of-the-way area of the village, off Planting Field Way. The brilliant white sheets, nightgowns, and undergarments billowed and crackled in the morning wind and sun as their children walked to school. The naughty ones would play hide-and-seek behind the drying laundry, sometimes soiling the clothes enough for their mothers to have to rewash.

What a difference the area is today! Maria could hardly remember living there growing up. In the '80s, sprawling gray-shingled summerhouses appeared farther on down the lane next to Eel Pond, where only fishermen had ventured in the past, and now this area began to be known for its large houses built for summer people who knew the value of the magnificent views of the Sound. Soon thereafter the little "Portagee" white-shingled cottages and bungalows that were still considered to be in the village were bought up, and architects and designers tripled or more these living spaces—wraparound porches, sleeping additions, even a second story. It wasn't the house itself that was desirable—it was the land. Real Estate people on the mainland cry "Location, location, location!" But anyone who has lived near or understood the value of finite resources knows it's different. On the island, they cry "Water, water, water!"

Unfortunately, the Edgartown Portuguese in Rinso Heights did not grasp the true value of their land, and they were eager to sell their little cramped abodes to put money in their pocket and get into "modern" houses. Moving away from the village itself into the outskirts of Edgartown's scrub (an area consisting mainly of brushwood and stunted forest growth) brought them into newer ranch-style homes with real Formica counters, large harvest gold or avocado-green refrigerators and separate freezer compartments, and—best of all, washers and driers. That was more than enough to please them. So, the old green and red flags of the Azores that once were affixed to their small porches in town were replaced by tall flagpoles flying the Red, White, and Blue along with the small triangular Yacht Club burgee. "Rinso Heights" disappeared, and the more genteel "Planting Field Way" took its place and name. It was an end of an era, and few people noticed it had disappeared.

Today, Maria thought her family and cousins had been fools. They had no idea of the money they could have made from their cottages if they had kept them. They were so stupid.

Chapter 6

Edgartown, 1980s

Maria's father, Miguel, was known to be a particularly good and honest hard worker. Living in Rinso Heights, he would walk the few blocks downtown to the harbor on a daily basis. He left school in the eighth grade and started off as a teenager on the Coal Wharf in Edgartown (also known as Osborn Wharf) unloading boats and hauling others in to shore. Bit by bit, he began to learn the mechanical aspects of the boating business, and eventually he became Edgartown's dockmaster, an unusual position for a Portuguese on the island. The commercial fishermen and the yachtsmen all thought highly of him and called him by his first name. He, however, no matter how young they might be, always called them "Mr. Osborn" or "Master Pease."

Largely through Miguel's work and reputation, the summer people from the Yacht Club would ask if his wife did cleaning and laundry. Soon Ana was making the daily summer trips to Edgartown's finest waterfront properties with her husband and spent the day cleaning these grandiose homes and bringing home the laundry at night. In the off-season, Ana would sew and make clothes that a small shop in Edgartown, run by Peg Baldwin, would buy from her. The Almeidas became a fairly comfortable family, for a Portuguese.

As a very young child, Maria would stay with her mother going from room to room in these huge summer homes as her mother cleaned and changed the beds from the laundry she had washed and set out to dry at Rinso Heights. Maria loved looking out at the water and the boats from the large windows on the harbor. Billowing sheer curtains blew in the breeze, and she'd pretend they were the sails to her boat, racing along the harbor with the others.

When she was about five or six, these families would often have Maria play with their kids running around outside on the manicured lawns or inside on rainy and windy days.

But as she grew older, it was different. Her mother said she "needed her help." Ana asked her to stay in the kitchen helping plate the cakes and cookies for the children's parties—her contemporaries and her former playmates. How embarrassing it was for her to be seen in the kitchen with hand-me-downs some of them had once worn. Passing the cookies and clearing the plates was the worst part of it. They knew and she knew that it was no longer the same relationships. She sensed she was now different. It's what her mother was telling her without saying it aloud.

It got worse for Maria as she got older: they in their Ralph Lauren floral design slacks, pastel polo shirts, thin gold bracelets, and blond straight hair, easily moving and laughing among the boys, making dates for the next Yacht Club dance, meeting at the Club's Snack Bar after morning sailing lessons. Maria only received a nod or "Hi, Maria, how are you?" as they sped by on their bikes to the tennis courts, with no intention of hearing her reply.

She hated it. And she began to hate her parents. She hated being born here on the island and staying behind for a dreary desolate off-season, when the others left at the end of the summer. She hated her father's and mother's names: *Miguel* and *Ana*. She hated all her island cousins, stupid and content to follow in their parents' footsteps, cleaning and gardening for the wealthy summer people, no better off than being indentured servants. She hated the festival of the Holy Ghost Association and hated Oak Bluffs. The social scene for her family consisted of the Portuguese American Club, also in Oak Bluffs. Even though she knew by then that the Cape Verdeans were the lowest rung of the Portuguese status ladder, and the European Azoreans such as Miguel and Ana were at the top, this did not make a bit of difference to Maria; she was still "Portagee," as the summer kids would call them. She hated her father's physique: a hairy Coke machine on legs. And her mother was now growing an even darker black mustache and was "settling" like old houses on a brick foundation in the town.

When she became fourteen, Stuart Baldwin, the island's most successful real estate broker, had become to know Maria a little through her parents and was impressed with her intelligence and willingness to learn. He asked Miguel if Maria might want to help out a little in the agency for the summer. Peg also had that small gift shop in town, and Maria could divide her time between the two. It wouldn't be much money, but Maria was known to be a smart girl, and it could be of help to her later. When Miguel asked Maria, she jumped at it! No more being the odd man out with the Junior Yacht Club snobs, being forced to trail around after her mother, cleaning and serving teas to their parents and politely snubbed by them. She'd now be in a downtown Edgartown business with the "right" people. How lucky could she be!

Both Peg and Stuart were pleased with how well this high school student took to the businesses—for Peg, Maria's ability with inventory and math was a godsend, and Stuart found she had a gift for remembering people's names and background. Sometimes someone would call him on the phone, and he'd mouth to Maria, "It's Jennie. Who is she?" And Maria would mouth back, "Starbuck's Neck—the old Dickinson house," and Stuart would say, "Jennie—so good to hear from you. I was just thinking of you!"

Chapter 7

Brazil, summers 1993–96

At about the same time Maria began working for Peg and Stuart, Maria learned that she would be visiting her mother's sister, Fernanda, in Brazil. She was the only member of Maria's mother's family (who came from Sao Miguel, one of the nine Azores islands) who did not end up in the United States with her other siblings, but rather in Brazil, where she had married a Brazilian she met in Sao Miguel one summer and within three weeks had married and moved to Brazil.

Fernanda and Maria's mother had always been close, despite the geographic distance between the two sisters. Maria was born soon after Fernanda's husband had been killed, and in ways, Maria became the surrogate child for Fernanda, who had now become estranged from her sons and daughters due to her decisions of how to spend her late husband's settlement.

Fernanda was the only relative Maria cared for. She loved hearing about her aunt's incredible success in Brazil real estate, and when they talked weekly by telephone, her aunt would always tell Maria about her early real estate ventures in Florianopolis that had now become an international hot spot.

The summer after Maria turned fourteen, in 1993, was the year before Maria was to start ninth grade at the regional high school. Fernanda paid for her way to Florianopolis, and Maria knew instantly that she was "home." Fernanda and she had become close, closer than Fernanda had ever been to her own children; she and Maria both shared the disdain for the lives they had been born into, and they both wanted a life that was like the jet-setters and international crowd that had started to discover Florianopolis in the mid-eighties. Not only was it Maria's first trip out of the country, but the ten days she spent there with her aunt formed her future life goals. From then on Maria knew she was *not* going to live the same life her parents had on that island where she was born, which came alive only in the summer.

She was her *aunt's* child, not her mother's. And she would devote her time with her aunt to learn how to get out of the drab life she had been born into. There was no better teacher than Fernanda, who agreed with Maria's determination and life goals.

Fernanda had been the smartest one in the Calvalho family, and she turned a settlement into a land bonanza in Brazil. Fernanda invested in real estate thirty years before anyone had heard of Florianopolis, this city in the island state of Santa Catalina. Although she had lived in the southern half of the small island, where many small commercial fishermen from the Azores had populated this area, she was different. She had a shrewd eye and nose for money, although there was little she could do to amass any sizeable amount due to her husband's job.

In the late 1970s, her husband finally gave in and decided his wife might be right that he should leave fishing for better pay in the booming construction industry. Unfortunately for him, he died in an accident on his fifth day of work while working on the construction for expanding Universidade Federal de Santa Catarina. It was a particularly ugly accident: a foreman had insisted he go out on a steel beam and inspect a section of the building. Witnesses said the foreman actually took a stick, shoving at and preventing the frightened man from coming back in. He fell to his death, impaled on some upright steel rods.

Fernanda, an entrepreneur at heart, rallied the small village for a march on the university in the name of justice. Newspapers came and took photos, and then the television station came and shot a story. By the time Fernanda and her family had finished, an attorney had come to their rescue (understanding that the theatrics she was so good at might produce a handsome settlement); and in 1979, the city agreed to pay out for his death—a princely sum then of $500,000. She took the money and invested it in vacant land where the Jurere Internacional area and along the beach where Praia Mole are.

Her children thought she was crazy at the time: her one chance to make good, and she throws it away in the north part of the island, which was useless empty land, instead of investing it in their part of the island, which was fairly prosperous and had largely preserved the culture and language of their beloved Azores. Two sons stopped speaking to her; her daughter's dream of a large wedding was halted in midair. The townswomen shunned her, and Father Paulo tried to intercede on behalf of her children. Only the attorney she found in Florianopolis thought she was smart, which indeed she was, although she had to wait for ten years before she saw the value begin to escalate. By the nineties, everyone realized Fernanda was one of the wealthiest people in Florianopolis.

The Europeans followed the wealthy Brazilians, who had become bored with Rio and jet-spots like Punta del Este in Uruguay that had lost their novelty. A mere four hundred miles—just an eight-hour drive—south of Sao Paolo lay this beautiful and unspoiled island. It was exactly the same distance from Sao Paolo to Rio, so many wealthy Brazilians preferred to head south to this new and more exclusive spot than crime-ridden Rio. Within a few years, it became a mixture of Saint.-Tropez and Ibiza but "without the attitude."

Fernanda was sitting on acres of prime real estate that had now become in vogue, and Maria was there that summer of her freshman year to see how smart her aunt had been. "Forget the banks, forget the stocks! Real estate on the coast is what will be the gold of tomorrow," her aunt said each day. "Don't be like these townspeople or your parents, as much as I love your mother, Ana. She had dreams of America, and when your father's uncle arranged their marriage, Ana had always thought she'd find a good life in America. She never thought she'd be cleaning houses to help support you all, but she did. Your father is a good man, but is content to work for others. Be smart, Maria. Plan your future. Don't work for others: work for yourself!"

Fernanda made it very clear to Maria that she, Fernanda, was Azorean and *not* Brazilian. The true Portuguese (the European mainland and the islands of the Azores) were not in any way, except for language, related to the Portuguese of the Cape Verdean islands or the majority of Portuguese-speaking Brazilians, the *Pardo*, who were of mixed race: Natives and African at their base. "We are *Europeans*, Maria, and don't you forget it." Maria returned the next summer too. Fernanda began to take her further under her wing.

Two summers later, when Maria was sixteen, and had been working for Stuart and Peg after school, Maria once again visited her aunt Fernanda. This year, Fernanda brought the young girl to the various properties her aunt owned and allowed this young girl to sit in on talks her aunt had with developers and her lawyer. Maria's Portuguese was good enough to understand everything that was said. Whatever they might think of Fernanda when she walked in the door, by the time she left, they admired her. The woman from Pantano do Sul, on the southern tip of the island, a mere fisherman's wife, had the negotiating skills of the best of them. And, she knew the value of her real estate and the boom economy that was just beginning to emerge.

Maria benefited from the time with her aunt. The next summer, she would return. When it came time for Maria to leave in late August, she already had her plan in mind. She'd stop working for Peg in her shop and work as much time as possible for Stuart in his agency. Real estate would get her somewhere, but the shop wouldn't.

She confided her plan in Fernanda, and she applauded it. But she also warned her young niece, "It will take time, Maria, it will take time. But if you stick to your plan, it will work out, and one day, you too will own real estate by the coast, just like your aunt Fernanda!"

Chapter 8

Edgartown, 1996–97

Bit by bit during her last year in high school, Maria began to gain more knowledge by being helpful—even indispensable—to Stuart, and she jockeyed her position to that of apprentice to Stuart. He was delighted in this young girl's interest in his business and was pleased to be able to talk to someone other than Peg (who made it clear she didn't want him to rehash old stories about just how great his sales abilities were). He tended to repeat himself, but Maria learned to smile sweetly and act as if this was the first time he had told her about the Wakeman property and how he got the sale and not Sotheby's Boston office.

She started performing more complex tasks: drafting purchase and sales by inserting the names of the buyers and sellers, and then she moved into preliminary title examinations where she'd spend hours in the County of Dukes County Courthouse, lugging out those oversized, heavy leather volumes of county real estate transactions and seeing how far she could get before she couldn't trace back any further in time. Stuart would take her findings to Owen Carson, that odd but invaluable attorney with the photographic memory. He and that new attorney, Rick Maron, shared an office upstairs on South Summer Street. Maria's preliminary title work both impressed Owen and allowed Stuart to get a better price on the final document that the town's usual attorney of record, Thom Osborn, would prepare for the buyer or seller and sign off on. And, Maria was smart enough to play up to Thom, so that he in fact, without even knowing it, also began teaching Maria the subtleties of clouded titles and the consequences of such mistakes or oversights. Between the two attorneys, Thom and Owen, Maria gained extraordinary knowledge of the pitfalls of real estate transactions, well beyond anything her high school education could provide. And it served her well in her career; that is, at least for many years.

"Defective documentation has created millions of blighted titles that will plague the nation for the next decade," said Owen to Maria one day when she showed him a draft of a title search she had been doing for Stuart; she had puzzled over it as it seemed to be incorrect. He explained that ownership questions may not arise until a home is under contract and the potential purchaser applies for title insurance, or even decades later, as this particular title indicated, as one title deed researcher catches errors overlooked by another. "A defective title means the person who paid for and moved into a house may not be the legal owner," summarized Owen. "And it seems as if you caught one here!"

Maria was stunned that, first, she had been able to see the inconsistencies and, second, realize that the Bassett family who had lived in their home for decades may not even be the owners. "It's a nightmare scenario," said Owen. "If they were to go to sell their house, the promissory note outlining payment obligations and a separate mortgage must both be properly conveyed to prevent competing claims. And, in this case, they couldn't sell it due to the discrepancies you uncovered."

"What if we didn't say anything?" asked Maria. "Or, what happens if we notified the heirs of the Norton family where the original errors were made and inform them that they, in fact, have a claim to the Bassett home now, even if this occurred over forty years ago?"

"It depends on how honest you are, Maria. Some people would sit on information like this plotting some profit from this knowledge. Others, like me, would notify the owners and the sellers or their heirs and see if we couldn't resolve the issues and clear the title."

On the weekends of their senior year, Maria and Matt, not a particularly bright or ambitious boy but one who was a gung-ho, gun-toting Portuguese American, began seeing each other. The

Almeidas and Matt's family, the Da Costas, were good people and knew each other from the Portuguese American Club and the Catholic Church. His father and mother were employed by the Town of Oak Bluffs, which was job security for them and also their children. Children inherited these positions.

Neither Maria nor Matt had college plans, as both sets of parents thought what possible use would a degree have for someone living on the island? Matt planned to turn his past summer's rent-a-cop job into a full-time one once he graduated from the regional high school in May. Maria, of course, would continue working for the Baldwin Agency, but on a full-time basis now, after her trip to Brazil to see her aunt Fernanda, right after graduation.

In the dunes near the South Beach town parking lot, one evening in May a few weeks before graduation, Maria lost her virginity. Both were surprised it happened. They were not planning this, and being Catholics—and on the Vineyard, they hadn't even thought of getting protection. Even if they had, where would Matt buy it? Everyone knew everyone, and the only pharmacies on the island were in Edgartown, Oak Bluffs, and Vineyard Haven. There'd be no chance of discreet purchases.

CHAPTER 9

Brazil, late June 1997

Right after graduation, in late June, when Edgartown's summerhouses were being opened and carpenters' buzz saws sounded like cicadas, Maria said goodbye to Matt and her parents and left for Brazil again to be with her aunt. But this year, Maria only wanted to spend two weeks away from the agency as summer was the biggest time of year for island agents, and she was anxious to begin working full-time on her career. She told Matt the reason she was only spending a few weeks was that she didn't want to be apart from him for any longer. Matt believed her. He kissed her sloppily on the mouth, but she turned her head and simply brushed his cheek with her lips and then walked onto the 9:30 a.m. Uncatena bound for Woods Hole, and the Bonanza Bus to Logan International Airport in Boston for her eighteen-hour flight to Sao Paolo and then to Florianopolis. In the late nineties, nonstop flights from Boston didn't exist. But she was young and excited to go, so what were two extra stops in Miami and Lima to her?

Once there the next morning, she and Fernanda jumped back right in as they had left off the summer before and talked incessantly about real estate. Maria shared with her all that she was learning and updated her aunt on discussions with Stuart about her future with the agency. During the past year, Fernanda had helped Maria plan early discussions with Stuart about joining the agency upon graduation and "buying" a fraction of the business from him each year of work there. If he agreed, and later wanted to sell the agency to another, Maria would have some small claim in it. But the game plan changed, and it was now agreed that Maria would try to convince Stuart to either sell or perhaps even to will the agency to Maria. She told her aunt she was making progress, but nothing definitive had happened yet. She hoped it would evolve over the coming year.

Maria was curious if any movement had been made over the past year bringing Fernanda and her children together. Maria had never met her cousins as the rift that began when Fernanda had taken all the settlement money from her late husband's accident and invested it in real estate had split the family permanently. After a few days, Fernanda began to hint to Maria that she might one day be her sole beneficiary of her aunt's estate. Maria pretended not to understand, in a guileless manner she had been perfecting with Stuart, but she knew exactly what was at stake here.

In the years after Fernanda had taken the settlement money and invested it in land here, and before Maria had met her aunt, wealthy Brazilians and in-the-know internationals were taking the party to the forty white-sand beaches along the thirty-three-mile-long island that makes up much of Florianopolis. Long a favorite of the surf-world, it was now South America's hottest new party destination. Mega clubs, beach bars, and a caipirinha-drinking crowd suited each personality and crowd. Jurerê Internacional, where Fernanda owned much of her land, had become a sleek resort typified by sports cars, private helicopters, large designer sunglasses, and European royalty.

The other area where Fernanda had invested was Praia Mole Beach, a strip of powderlike sand and fantastic waves that was popular with well-sculpted and tanned bikini girls and oceanfront beach bars that flocked the beach. Riotous umbrellas and tiki huts turned this former neglected spit of sand into a fun-loving paradise. It was now considered one of the world's greatest surfing spots, and people flocked there from everywhere.

Whether it was a Hollywood or Ibiza nightlife one preferred, it was all there in Florianopolis. Floripa (as the visitors were now affectionately calling it) easily earned its nickname, *Ilha da Magia*. And Fernanda was sitting on all the *magia* one could have ever hoped for in a lifetime.

So much had happened in the four years since her first visit. This year, Fernanda seemed older and more tired, and she talked more of her family losses (only Maria's mother, Ana, remained of the siblings) and her regrets about the schism with her children and her wishes to see her grandchildren of whom there were now three. Ana had earlier hinted to Maria that she stood to inherit Fernanda's wealth, and warned her not to say anything when she visited with her aunt, even if her aunt hinted about it. Maria was smart enough to pretend she didn't understand her aunt's veiled allusions.

Maria now began to worry that her plans to inherit Fernanda's wealth might not happen if her aunt continued on in this nostalgic vein. She and Matt had now become a couple, and marriage was most likely inevitable now that they had had sex, although not something Maria was excited about.

Chapter 10

Brazil, Early July 1997

Maria was only staying for two weeks this summer, and she knew time was not on her side. Fernanda had changed in the past year. She seemed wistful and at times melancholy. But she was there for Maria, and Maria knew she loved her. She was more like a mother than her own and someone in whom she could confide.

Fernanda and she had talked about Matt, and Fernanda said it seemed as if he was a good man, but was that really what Maria wanted? Maria shrugged her shoulders and said it was okay. Maria knew her aunt was right. Her aunt had made a similar mistake.

The first few days, she and Fernanda talked about the past year, Maria's foray into real estate, her boyfriend, Matt, and her plans not to go to college.

Fernanda again sighed about her children and lost family life and said to Maria to make sure any children she may have remained close to her throughout life. Maria gave her a hug and said, "You are my second mother, Aunt Fernanda. I am your daughter too." Maria gave her a hug, and although Fernanda smiled and hugged her back, there were tears in her eyes. Maria knew her aunt was looking back at her life, and this new side of Fernanda was worrisome. Maria began to panic. What happened if Fernanda changed her will in favor of her own children? Her aunt was her only hope to inherit some money and property, other than years of building up a real estate clientele on the Vineyard. Maria lived for the moment and ignored the long-term. This trait would be her downfall one day.

From that moment on, Maria knew she had to take steps to ensure her inheritance. She couldn't leave things to chance this time. Once she returned to the Vineyard, her aunt would be here alone, subject to her melancholy—regrets of having her children remain strangers, and looking ahead only to death. Maria spent the next two days thinking hard about this, and as much as she tried to find a different solution, she couldn't. She decided she would have to act. Anyway, it was the end of her aunt's life, and it had been a good one. With Maria here, her aunt would at least be happy. So the decision was made.

Chapter 11

Brazil, Monday, July 7–Tuesday noon, July 8, 1997

Maria said she had a surprise for Fernanda and was going to take her out for a "special afternoon" the day after next. Fernanda was very excited and thought what a wonderful niece she had. After Fernanda's siesta that afternoon, Maria heard Fernanda say on her bedroom phone, "I can't make it on Wednesday as Maria is taking me out. Okay, I'll see you tomorrow morning, Tuesday, at ten. I'll see you then. I apologize for all this confusion with an old lady. I'm certain now. Thank you, *senhor. Muito obrigada.*"

The next morning, Tuesday, at breakfast, Fernanda smiled and looked a little uncomfortable, or awkward, as if she wasn't being completely open, and said she was going to go look for something new to wear the next day. Maria asked if she wanted her to accompany her, but her aunt said Constanca would go with her and she had already made an appointment with the owner of her favorite shop. Constanca would make sure that she'd pick out something just right or not buy anything at all. Maria didn't protest as this fit nicely into the things she had to do that were much more important and immediate.

Maria wondered if the call she overheard the day before with a *senhor* was with Fernanda's attorney, but she pushed that out of her mind. Fernanda loved her. On the other hand, Maria still had fears that the old woman was becoming a little too sentimental. And now Maria was soon heading back to the Vineyard, and it would be another year before she'd be back. A lot can happen in a year. But she convinced herself that she was just being paranoid. A few minutes later, these same fears crept back into her thoughts. She had an idea.

Her aunt stood up to go, and Maria smiled and said, "Then you'll look even more beautiful, *Titia*, for your special treat tomorrow!" She gave her aunt a kiss on the cheek as the old lady went out the door to her hair appointment and dress shopping trip.

When the heavy wood front door had shut, and Maria was alone in the main house, she knew she had to first make sure she knew exactly what her aunt's will said now, rather than guess what it said. She knew she had to find it immediately before she could continue with the wild thought that had just come to her mind.

She began to search the house in an effort to chase that disturbing thought from her mind. If she could find the current will, she knew she'd be able to fix things. She thought her aunt was the type of person who didn't trust important documents like a will and powers of attorney to a safety deposit box, but try as she could, she couldn't locate any place where Fernanda might have sequestered these documents.

Fernanda had been gone about thirty minutes, and Maria knew time was closing in. As foolish as it first seemed, that someone would actually hide valuables under a mattress, Maria finally lifted the mattress of Fernanda's bed, felt around as far as her arm would stretch, and just as she was about to give up, her index finger touched something. She quickly stretched farther and soon pulled out a large manila envelope that Maria translated to say "To Whom It May Concern—Open in the Event of My Death." Without time to read what was in the package, she quickly smoothed out the bedspread and rushed to her room, where she put the package in her empty suitcase and locked it.

A little while later, Maria went back to her room and grabbed the envelope. She saw the will was dated a year ago, right after Maria had returned to the Vineyard. She sighed with relief. Everything was being left to Maria, except an old medal of the Virgin Mary. Maria recognized it was the identical European pink gold medal that Ana had received from her mother. As was the family tradition, Fernanda wanted her daughter to have hers and to pass it down later to her oldest granddaughter. It was called the Mother-Daughter Medal, and the Virgin promised the holder good fortune and healthy children.

At first Maria was relieved; she was inheriting everything from Fernanda—land, developed properties, and a lot of cash in the provincial bank. But what bothered her still was the sentimentality of the gold family medal given to each eldest daughter and passed down through generations. If Maria was right, and Fernanda was now getting remorse about the family schism, and was now openly talking about family members who had died, and about the regrets of the rift between her and her own children—and now grandchildren, she might very well change her mind during the coming year about leaving everything to Maria, as she actively contemplated the end of her life. And, without Maria here on a daily basis to keep Fernanda on track ("You're my second mother, Fernanda!" "We're so much alike, like mother and daughter, aren't we!"), the old woman might be swayed to reconcile with her family. With Maria back in the States and not in Florianopolis on a daily basis, Maria would never know of any change in the old woman's heart—until it was too late.

Maria tried to push out of her mind the frantic thoughts she was having of how to secure her future, but she still wasn't sure that her aunt would really change her will. She'd wait until she returned and assess things then.

When her aunt returned, Fernanda seemed a little ill at ease and said, "They didn't have anything today that I really liked. It's okay, I'll wear one of my other dresses. I have something in mind."

Fernanda didn't look directly into Maria's eyes. Something came over Maria that frightened her. Maria was more than suspicious that Fernanda was thinking of changing her will to now include her children because there weren't any purchases. If she had come back with a dress or something, Maria wouldn't have thought anything about this little outing and the telephone call yesterday setting up the ten o'clock appointment. Was that what the telephone conversation was about that she had overheard on Monday? Was Fernanda with her attorney and not the dress shop owner?

If Fernanda had gone to see her attorney, it could only mean one thing: her children were now the heirs.

Maria was not going to let this happen! She had not spent all this time and affection on her aunt without being her primary beneficiary!

CHAPTER 12

Brazil, Tuesday, July 8, 1997, midafternoon

She and Fernanda sat down for tea as usual midafternoon after Fernanda's shopping outing. Fernanda said she hadn't had time to get her hair done, giving Maria more to worry about. It was time to make a life-changing decision—Maria would either have the nerve to go through with her plan or go back to her Vineyard life and live like all the others. Anyway, her plan was only forgery, not murder.

After her decision was reached, Maria knew she had to act fast and excused herself from Fernanda and their daily teatime in the garden, saying she needed to go finalize arrangements for the next day's grand outing.

Maria had reasoned that if Fernanda changes her mind once she'd gone back to the States, she'd never know it until the will was read. It would be too late.

But, if she had a full year's worth of "originals" with different dates, and, Fernanda had changed her will to favor her children, Maria could then step forward with one of the more recent "original" versions (the one that would be dated the shortest time before her death) and say, "Fernanda sent this new will directly to me because she had not trusted that even her own attorney would follow her instructions to leave everything to me. Her attorney was a good man, but very traditional and believed children came first. Fernanda told me she had misgivings and was embarrassed to go back again to see her own attorney to, once again, change back the will, as her attorney might think she was 'losing it' and may try to have the courts step in and declare her unable to manage her own affairs. Fernanda had always been in charge of her life, and she wasn't going to let anyone take away her independence, so she went to a notary and had this new will drawn up. She then mailed it to me for safekeeping. Fernanda also told me on the phone that she felt her time was not too far away."

Reasoning with herself, Maria thought she had a good plan. By forging thirteen new wills, one dated later today and the other twelve for each month until next summer when Maria would once again return to visit her aunt, then one of Maria's new "wills" would be dated *after* her aunt's latest will, starting with the one she might have made this morning (or any other one of the ones dated thereafter), and therefore Maria's later version would prevail.

Maria had gone over this plan and convinced herself this was fail proof: "If Fernanda dies in November, five months from today, I'd come forward with the will dated mid-October. The attorney would only have the will dated July and that would be outdated. The November will would prevail. If she were to die in January, I'd produce the will dated late December, etc. She hasn't even seen her own children in years, and she loves *me* like the daughter I am to her. Everyone knows that and I'm—not Fernanda's children—going to inherit the estate. She doesn't love them. She doesn't know them. She loves me!"

Despite her aunt's love for Maria, Maria knew that Fernanda was now at a vulnerable point at the end of her life and was able to easily be swayed…and change her mind. And Maria was not going to let that happen. Period!

CHAPTER 13

Brazil, Tuesday, July 8, 1997, 4:00 p.m.

Her plan resolved, Maria went into the commercial zone of town with Fernanda's will Maria had found under her mattress. Inside the business office shop, she whited out the date, the attorney's signature, and the three witnesses' signatures on the original document, and she then made multiple copies. After several attempts, Maria succeeded in producing what looked like an original document. She then took that one copy and made a dozen new copies, tracing onto each document in ink her aunt's signature, but making it slightly shaky and smudging the ink a little so it would appear that it was her own, not a xeroxed copy.

On one version of the multiple wills, the date was today's date, Tuesday, July 8, 1997, but with a date stamp indicating 4:06 p.m. (several hours after Fernanda's morning visit to her attorney). She dated the second one the day after she was scheduled to arrive back on the Vineyard. She produced eleven others in succession. In all, she made thirteen new "wills," ready to be produced as soon as she received news that Fernanda had died. The last one was dated next June, just before Maria would come back again for her regular summer visit.

She then went to find a *notario* in one of the back streets. A sufficiently shady-looking office and a wooden sign that said, "Cambio, Vistos, Documentos: Primo Costas, Notario." She said her aunt wanted all of these notarized but didn't know why she wanted them all. She was only doing her aunt's bidding, and she would be happy to pay him $300 USD for his services, and she took out the cash and put it on his desk.

He stared at her and was surprised she kept her wits about her. She looked young, but was in complete control of herself. He thought she was one very sophisticated con artist. He took the paper currency and counted out 1,200 reais and nodded. He then told his office assistant (if you could call her that—she looked more like a *puta*, Maria thought) to get two people in from the street and gave them each twenty reais, and they signed their names as witnesses. A few minutes later, with Notario Costas having barely raised an eyebrow during the signing of the wills, and with about $300 cash in US money in his pocket (that she had brought with her from her savings and her parents for graduation presents and spending money), Maria had what she needed.

She hurried back from the commercial center toward her aunt's home. It had taken longer than she had thought. She was rehearsing in her mind exactly how she'd finesse all this, should her aunt die in the next year. One minute it had seemed like a brilliant idea, and she was pleased with her creative approach. Another minute she thought there would be some way they could tell this wasn't a bona fide will or signature. If it were contested, wouldn't there be handwriting experts? Even if this was just Brasil? Would her aunt's attorney really be thought of as crooked, willing to collude with the children for a cut in the property? By the time she reached the front door, she was in a panic, confused, hot and perspiring, and almost sick to her stomach. She ran her fingers through her hair. It was already damp and beginning to curl. She hated her hair. She always "knew" that somewhere in the past, some of her Azorean Portuguese family's background on whaling vessels was intermingled with the Cape Verdean African slaves. She shook her head and told herself to get back to the present. What should she do? There were only a few days left before she was to return to the Vineyard. She began to panic again.

She had already put the original will back under the mattress while her aunt was outside talking with Constanca in the courtyard. Maria now put the forgeries in her suitcase and locked it. She was leaving in several days, and she had to make up her mind this evening, or she'd chicken out.

She had thought her duplicate wills were a smart idea, but now she wasn't sure at all. The only sure thing was left to Fernanda's not changing her mind in the coming year. And that was impossible to know until she died.

She had thought of another idea, but wasn't sure she could do it, but she didn't want to have come so far in terms of inheriting her aunt's great fortune and then, because of an old woman's stupid sentimentality at the end of her life, risk losing it, if indeed Fernanda were to have a change of heart during the upcoming months and year when Maria would be back in the States.

Maria knew there were two courses of action to take now: one was left to chance (the series of forged wills) and the other was not.

Although Maria admitted her actions reproducing several wills were clever, it still didn't completely solve the problem. Fernanda would remain here, and Maria would be on the Vineyard, five thousand miles away. Even frequent phone calls and letters couldn't assure Maria that Fernanda would hold the course and not give in to family regrets at what was clearly becoming the end of her life. People called for the priest on their deathbeds. But Fernanda might first call for her children and an attorney then, finally, the priest.

If that were the case, no other "will" that Maria could produce would hold up. A deathbed is a deathbed. Period.

She then kicked herself and said to herself, "I just wasted $300 on that sleazebag notary! He must be laughing now. 'Some stupid little Americana wanting to pull a fast one on someone. What a fool! I've got her $300, and what does she have!'" Maria was in a real state now. "Three hundred dollars out the window, and no real solution to the problem at hand!" She kept pushing away the recurring thought of the only sure way to be certain she remained in her aunt's will.

The only other way—a sure way—was to make certain Fernanda went now, before Maria returned to the States. Although for a moment Maria did wonder if her aunt had actually gone to see her attorney earlier that morning to change her will, Maria had accepted that as a probability now. And even if her aunt might change her mind in the coming months when Maria wasn't there, she still wasn't sure her aunt had done that this morning. In fact, she couldn't be sure of anything now! For the first time in her young life, Maria did not know which way to go. She finally decided that her aunt had not changed her mind that morning, and the will under her mattress was still valid unless Fernanda was able to get to her attorney's office on Thursday to change her will over to her children. Right or wrong, she had to act now. She wouldn't be able to agonize over this question for the coming year. She prayed to act now. She wouldn't be able to agonize over this question for the coming year. She prayed to the Virgin Mary, Our Lady of Aparecida, and she heard, or thought she heard, "Do not worry. She loves you." This was the sign she was waiting for—there was no turning back now. She *had* to act. Then, what Maria should have asked was: "But, who is '*she*'?" But she didn't. It was now or maybe never. And Maria wasn't about to take any chance with her future well-being. The die was cast.

Although Maria sensed she really didn't "love" as most people seemed to, she really *did* like her aunt, genuinely like her, and they were very much alike: all business, determined to gain success, decisive, and willing to take a risk. These women, bound by maternal blood, were not going to lead the life of the women who had preceded them. These two were at home in a man's world, and that is where they belonged and would stay, regardless of others, including their own families.

By late the evening before the special outing, Maria had made a decision. It was a monumental decision for an eighteen-year-old to make, and it would determine her future forever. A minute or two of hesitation, and then the decision was made. She didn't hate her aunt or want her dead. She just wanted to be sure she would receive her aunt's inheritance. It was logical and necessary, she reasoned.

She would make the next day, Wednesday, the happiest day of her aunt's life—and her last.

Chapter 14

Brazil, Wednesday, July 9, 1997, midday

She had arranged for a hired car to come midmorning and helped her aunt get ready for the afternoon out. Maria took Fernanda to each and every property she had owned or sold, and they ended up at Bistro d'Acampora for lunch.

"Maria, this is one of the most expensive restaurants on the island. You can't take me here!" Fernanda exclaimed as the chauffer got out and extended a hand.

"Titia, you are worth every penny and more. I've tried to think of something special for you today, and a tour of all that you have owned in real estate and ending up at the Bistro is the best I can think of. I saved money this year working at the agency, and I wanted to thank you for all you have done for me. You have meant more to me than my own parents, as much as I love them. You have showed me what a woman can do and how to want to have my own real estate firm and successes in life as you have done. We are more than aunt and niece, we are tied together in all possible ways. I love you, Titia, and I want you to know this now when I'm here with you. I am not looking forward to next week when I have to return, so I wanted a special memory of a wonderful day together that you and I will always have between just us and no one else."

As they walked in the lush courtyard paved with tiles and planted with vibrant green plants alongside wooden benches in the style of the island, they entered the foyer. There, the dark polished wood of antique chairs and tables, the highly polished tile covered in places by Persian rugs, and on every inch of the wall hung large paintings done by local artists. The smell of flowers was everywhere. It was the sort of place where the bright sunlight and noise of the streets could not penetrate this luxurious haven of peace and quiet. The staff had been forewarned that Fernanda and "her favorite niece" were dining there, and Chef Zeca himself came to greet them at the table. Maria made a point to explain how Fernanda was her "second mother" and that she wanted a perfect day for them as Maria would be returning to the Vineyard in less than a week. Champagne was offered, and Maria toasted, "Mama Fernanda." The old woman had tears in her eyes. They had another glass with lunch. Two hours later, the chauffeur appeared to take them home.

Maria helped Fernanda get ready for a nap ("Maria! I don't know what got into me today! Two glasses of champagne at lunch! Never have I been so spoiled!").

"Well, then, you'll have a good nap this afternoon. We can play a game of canasta and have a light dinner if you're up to it. It's been a wonderful day. I love you," said Maria as she softly closed the door on her aunt and said a silent prayer for her aunt's soul.

Right after she heard Maria's footsteps disappear down the hallway, Fernanda called her attorney and said she wanted to revert to the original will and power of attorney and have everything go to Maria and to tear up the new will she had made the day before.

Fernanda said, "I had a moment of weakness yesterday morning when I went to sign my new will giving all my real estate, except my home, to my children. Would you mind if I go back to your office tomorrow morning and sign a new one—or rather, sign the exact same will that I had signed, before I stupidly changed it yesterday. I want to go back to the original provisions giving everything to Maria.

"It's the momentary indecision and doubt of an old woman—I don't know why I came to see you to change things yesterday in favor of my children. Maria doesn't know that, of course, she thought I had my hair done. You know me well, and you know I think of Maria as my 'real' daughter. She loves me, as I love her."

Her attorney said he understood and was happy Maria and she were so close. He said together they would destroy the new version she had signed in his office the next day when she came in and she could then resign her 'old' will. Just before hanging up, he asked her where she kept her own copy of the original will leaving everything to Maria.

She said, "Don't worry, *senhor*. It is safe and hidden way under my mattress."

"Be that as it may, it's not a safe place. But since we'll see each other tomorrow, then bring that (the original) will with you to destroy, and I'll keep the new one we sign tomorrow in my office safe from now on. A mattress is *not* a smart place to leave anything valuable. Anyone could access it in a place like that!"

Fernanda said she agreed and added, "Perhaps I haven't been smart, but no harm has been done now. And, after the wonderful day today with Maria, I am very tired now and need a nap. I promise I'll bring that with me tomorrow so we can tear it up and you keep the new one in your safe. Agreed! *Muito obrigato pela compreensao.*"

"Don't worry, Fernanda. Get some sleep. We will destroy that new will you just signed tomorrow morning in my office, and Maria will once again be your sole beneficiary. You *do* sound tired, *and* you had a big day. *Uma boa noite de soma*, Fernanda," and he hung up the phone. He shook his head a little, thinking she was really exhibiting signs of old age. It wouldn't be long now, he thought, before she met her maker, poor lady. But she had a remarkable life, and her niece was so good to her that the old woman was in good hands. Things could be worse, he thought. Things could be worse.

Chapter 15

Brazil, Wednesday, July 9, 1997, late afternoon

The one-sided conversation Maria had partially overheard between Fernanda and her attorney just as she left Fernanda for her nap was only that Fernanda said she had "made a mistake" and she "needed to change the will." Maria would have lingered longer, but Constanca had just appeared in the hallway to make sure Fernanda didn't need anything. Maria shook her head and put her finger to her lips and mouthed "She's fine." Maria had to keep on going to her own room and missed the most important words her aunt made. As Caesar, Maria cast her die and crossed the Rubicon.

Maria thought the mistake Fernanda was referring to was changing the will to favor her children. What a mistake Maria had made—and wouldn't know it until after her aunt died.

Maria had gone back to her room to try to think. She was realizing her idea of producing one of the forged "wills" immediately after Fernanda died was highly suspicious. "He won't believe the authenticity of any new will I may produce after her death. Shit! I will certainly risk criminal action for forgery and extortion. How stupid I've been, and I've wasted all that money on that stupid sleazy *notario*! What a jerk I am!"

"Bitch! Fucking old woman! Just like the others—Family! Family! Family! Stupid pigs!" She was in a fury now, and there was no turning back. "I won't be getting *anything* now that I know Fernanda is going to see her attorney tomorrow morning to change her will. Nothing!"

She'd go back and forth through her options—one minute saying, "I can't do this! I can't!" And then she'd swing back to the other extreme telling herself she couldn't possibly *not* do this. And, then she'd break down again.

She tried to calm down and get a hold of herself. "I've got to just leave this place! It holds nothing for me now that she's revising her will to favor her stupid ungrateful children! I hate everything!"

But try as she may to figure out how to salvage her future, she kept going back and forth between leaving things the way they are or changing them to her favor. And then, the answer came. She had no choice in this. She could only reach one conclusion. This awareness finally brought her peace of mind. "I know what I have to do. Period."

"She's an old woman and hasn't much time anyway. And she's the only one who can get me out of the life I was born into. I don't have any other choices. It's this or nothing. And I don't want to just 'be better,' I don't want to have to worry about money or the stupid people I'm stuck with at home on the island."

"I'd actually be doing her a favor," rationalized Maria. "It will be peaceful, and she won't have to agonize over whether or not she'd be doing the right thing by changing her mind. It's not as if she doesn't love me. I know she does."

With that, Maria got up from her bed where she had been sitting and walked to the closet. She took down her big suitcase and pulled out a small cosmetic bag and took out the vial of tranquilizers she had asked Doc Coffin for before her final exams. She had also used two before her boarding the plane for her trip. There were sixteen left.

She was trembling with fear but knew she had to follow through with her plan.

This one moment in time changed Maria forever. She had always had an indifferent attitude toward people and property, but now that she had the possibility of finally getting what she believed she was owed in life, entitled to, and not the life she had been born into, Maria became a different person. Nothing was going to get in her way again; her hated Portuguese background, her parents' degrading menial jobs, and her passionless and unexciting life on the island that she had been leading would no longer be a determinate factor in her life. She would seize the day, day after day, after day, from now on. There was no place whatsoever in her mind for long-term consequences—those doctrines were for Catholics, losers, all of them. And she'd be a loser no more.

She took the next hour pulverizing the pills and then crushing them again. They became powder.

Chapter 16

Brazil, Wednesday, July 9, 1997, early evening

When Fernanda awakened in the late afternoon, she and Maria had tea with Constanca in the garden and spent the next hour with Fernanda talking of the day's adventures. She finally said she was still tired and certainly not hungry, so would go to bed in a short while. The three continued chatting and talking about the special treatment they had received by the owner and the wonderful food they had.

"It was the best day of my life, *minha filha*," Fernanda said; she was skipping the card games as she was now ready for an early bedtime. Constanca helped the old woman to her bedroom, and Maria added, "I'll bring you a tisane with honey in just a minute, Auntie." Constanca helped Fernanda into bed and gave her a kiss on the forehead, as Maria knocked on the door, as Constanca slipped out to her own quarters.

Maria brought the tisane in to the bedroom, and as she did, she looked at her aunt and said a silent prayer, hoping that it would be quick. She gave her a kiss and put her arm around her helping her sip her warm drink. Fernanda started to close her eyes; she felt so at peace and loved. A few seconds later, she was asleep.

Maria slipped out the front door and took a stroll down to the beach as the sun began its final descent. There she sat waiting. She didn't want to be at home when Constanca discovered Fernanda's unresponsive body and called out for help from Maria.

After sitting for a while, she continued on, walking along streets lined with shops and waved to a couple of the owners she had come to know. At the end of the Praia do Forte, she sat on the beach wall and took out the empty package into which she had poured the crushed sleeping pills. She tore the package into shreds and then bought an ice-cream cone from a vendor, of which she ate a few bites. Maria shoved the pieces of package into the ice cream and then threw it into the trash barrel. She then removed the label of the empty vial of the anti-anxiety medicine, hit the plastic vial with a rock, picked up the shards, and scattered them in the road as she walked back to the neighborhood where the house stood. She left nothing to chance and felt a dreaded excitement that even she couldn't quite explain. It would be the beginning of a new stage in her life.

Early the next morning, Constanca went in to see if Fernanda wanted breakfast. It was then she saw that the old woman, her wonderful employer and friend, had passed. She immediately awakened Maria, and the two women hugged each other and sobbed and said their rosaries. After the police and the undertaker removed Fernanda's body, Maria left a voice mail for the attorney, and Maria called her mother with the sad news. She'd stay for the funeral, do whatever arrangements that needed to be made, and meet with the attorney, whom she told her mother she had met with several times before when she had accompanied Fernanda on business meetings. She'd represent the Calvalho family, and there was no need for her mother to come.

Chapter 17

Brazil, Thursday, July 10–Saturday, July 12, 1997

The attorney returned Maria's early morning call when he got in the office. He of course was shocked at the news about Fernanda and said that no one knows the wishes of God until He speaks. He was silent for a few seconds and added, "Fernanda loved you very much, Maria, I want you to know that from me personally."

He then said he'd like to see Maria Saturday, at around three o'clock, after Fernanda's service, which will take place at the *Catedral Metropolitana de Florianopolis*, and he himself would make all the arrangements with the head priest.

But Maria thought he sounded strange when he talked of the reading of the will. There was something in his voice that told her things were "off." However, he seemed to quickly regain his composure and said two o'clock would be time enough after the Mass for the greeting of friends and neighbors, and light refreshments, that would still permit the others to get to his office by three o'clock for the reading.

Others? she thought. *It's hardly worth their time as there's only the medal for the daughter. Perhaps the two boys want to be there just to make sure nothing's in it for them.*

It was surprising that this woman, who had gained so much wealth and respect, still fondly remembered her origins in the small fishing village at the southeastern tip of the island. Maria dismissed any uneasy thoughts and questions and prepared to make her return trip to the States next Tuesday morning.

Many important people showed up at the Florianopolis cathedral for the 11:00 a.m. funeral on Saturday, after the news of Fernanda's death. City dignitaries, real estate barons, hoteliers and restaurateurs, bankers, and the media. Maria sat with the attorney and Constanca, the woman who had cleaned the house and cooked for Fernanda for almost twenty years. The eulogy was given by both the attorney and Maria. If her children were there, no one seemed to know. At the end, the funeral procession left the ochre colonial building. Maria felt sure her children were there, but no one came up to say hello. She did, however, catch a glimpse of a young woman who looked remarkably like herself and who did her best to conceal her glances in Maria's direction. It was a long day—the Mass itself took over an hour.

On Saturday, after the funeral reception, she appeared in the attorney's office at 3:00 p.m. as had been requested. His secretary asked them to wait in a side office and was back in ten minutes. Maria was then ushered into the small conference room, and there she discovered Fernanda's three children and Constanca, who did not tell Maria that she also would be there, apparently invited by the attorney.

The attorney sat down and pulled out a document and read from it. At first Maria couldn't focus: he read the date, which was the Tuesday, July 8, 1997 the day before Fernanda and Maria had their afternoon outing and two days before Fernanda was found dead.

The date, Tuesday, July 8, didn't register with Maria. As the attorney continued in a professional voice, Maria gradually realized this was a brand-new will. It was *not* the one she had read that was hidden under the mattress that named Maria as her principal beneficiary—the one she had used to make those forgeries. She froze, and her heart seemed to stand still. What did the new will say? She had already dismissed the idea her aunt had slipped out on Tuesday to see her attorney, when she said she was going to try to get her hair done and find a new dress for their outing the next day. *Oh my god*, thought Maria, panicking.

The new will stated: Constanca was to be given 200,000 BRL ($50,000) and her apartment in the house, with all expenses paid, until she died. After that, the apartment would revert back to the estate. Constanca began to cry, murmuring, "*Gracas a Deus. Gracas a Deus.*"

Maria was next: she was given the house and enough money in a trust to maintain it, pay taxes, make necessary capital improvements, pay for travel and visits to the house, and have reasonable spending money as determined by the attorney. The Attorney was named trustee. Maria was also given the medal that had been intended for the oldest daughter, and Fernanda had written: "The family medal that my mother gave all her daughters was intended for the eldest daughter of each. Maria will have mine as she has, in fact, become my daughter. In this way, I will always be in Maria's heart as she will be in mine."

Maria already knew what was coming, and the attorney then looked to the three children. "The remainder of my estate will be put into a trust with the interest to be split equally between my three children. Although they did not approve of how I spent their father's settlement money, I believe now they realize that long-term goals are what make a person successful and not short-term pleasures. I regret our schism and at the end of my life wished it could have been different. Perhaps this inheritance will help you three think more fondly of your mother. God bless," said the attorney in little more than a whisper.

The room was absolutely silent. No one spoke or moved. The attorney's eyes focused only on the will held in his hand. He did not look at Maria.

In a few seconds, the daughter asked what they should do and was told papers were already being drawn up to establish the trust for the benefit of the three. They would need to speak to his secretary as to which bank they wanted the money transferred to and to verify the legal names, birth date and place, and the mailing address. He indicated they should now make an appointment to see her early the following week. They filed out speechless, leaving Maria and Constanca behind.

Maria sat there looking stunned. He got up from his chair and came around to her. He said, "Maria, I want you to know that

Fernanda had called me on Monday and made an appointment to see me in my office at ten o'clock Tuesday morning so we could change her will to favor her children. She was ashamed for you to know this, so she told me she had said to you that she was going to look for a special dress. In my office, she was crying and said she did not want to go to her grave knowing she had abandoned her children, as much as she loved you. I asked her several times if she really wanted to change her will to favor her children, and she said yes. I think it's important that you know she really loved you. What you don't know is this: her previous will gave everything to you—everything," he said, shaking his head.

"But, Wednesday, after your outing with Fernanda, she called me right before she took her afternoon nap to say that she had made a foolish decision the day before, when she came to see me, to change her will favoring her children. She sounded very tired but wanted to come back the next morning, on Thursday, to change the will back entirely in your favor, except for the gift to Constanca."

He sighed. "But as you know, she died that evening before she could get in to see me. I cannot believe that she died then. This is indeed cruel irony. Had I thought there was anything imminent, I would have come immediately to the house to draw up a new will. I have talked to several judges who are also friends. Each of us agrees that despite an affidavit I could produce attesting to her change of mind the day she died, nothing could be done. Ironically, Fernanda's remorse for having 'lost' her children over the years lasted only one day. When she called me Wednesday afternoon right before she took her last nap, she had realized it was not what she wanted to do at all. She loved you and wanted you to receive her estate. She apologized for being an 'old woman' whose unfounded sentimentality had sidetracked her for a few moments. I told her not to worry, it was understandable, and we would fix it the very next day."

"Maria, I am so sorry. Sorry for you and sorry for Fernanda, God rest her soul. But you *do* have her house, and it's worth a considerable amount of money. I'm guessing $3 million with the grounds and in its location. She set up a trust for the perpetual maintenance and improvements of the property. I will approve travel and expenses to live in or check on the property. Basically, you can do anything you want to do, and I will approve it. Although you can pass the house along to your future husband and children in your will, if you decide to sell the house, which you have every right to do, the remainder of the endowment for the house will be forfeited and distributed to her children or grandchildren. My advice now is to hold on to it. It won't cost you anything out of pocket. If you want, you can put in a pool, renovate the interior—anything you want to do. As trustee, I will make sure that anything you want for the property, you shall have. Why don't you think about this for a while? No decision needs to be made now. I'm deeply sorry, Maria. I truly am. You were the most important thing in Fernanda's life, and all of us who knew her recognize your love for her. We all profoundly appreciate what you did for her. *Gracas*, Maria." He put his arm around Maria and held her as she began to sob and sob, her shoulders shaking with what he and Constanca thought was grief, but Maria was sobbing for her stupidity for having *assumed* what she overheard her aunt talk about on the telephone Tuesday was exactly the opposite of the truth. They stood like that for several minutes while he tried to calm her. *This poor young woman,* the attorney thought to himself, *she loved Fernanda so much.* Constanca moved to embrace Maria, and the two of them drove back in silence to the house.

Maria vowed never to assume again. Whatever she did in the future to secure her well-being would be researched and verified ten times over if necessary. She knew how to do accurate title searches, and that is exactly what she told herself she would do from now on in order to live the life she deserved. Every thread examined back to its origin, every i dotted and t crossed—nothing left to chance or misinterpretation. Nothing!

Chapter 18

Brazil, Monday–Tuesday, July 14–15, 1997

That next Monday, Maria went back to the attorney's office to sign the necessary title and power of attorney. After he had his secretary notarize the papers, he handed her the medal and said, "Wear it in remembrance of your dear aunt. She loved you so, Maria." She thanked him and left the office.

When she arrived back at what was now *her* house, she took the medal and flushed it down the toilet. "Fucking family! Stupid people who think a worthless medal is actually valuable! It's just a piece of shit." She slammed the bathroom door as she went out to pack.

The next day, at ten in the morning, she said goodbye to Constanca, who was crying uncontrollably. The old woman suddenly realized she was now left alone there, without her *patroa* and friend, Fernanda, and now also without the dear Maria. Maria gave her hugs and kisses, and the taxi left for the airport for a one-thirty departure. Her LATAM flight would be a twenty-hour trip by air, through Sao Paulo and Miami, to Boston by seven the next morning. Then another three hours by bus and ferry to the island. She brought the forged wills with her as she didn't want pieces of them turning up somewhere. She'd destroy them when she reached home.

She was exhausted by the time she got off the ferry in Vineyard Haven, where Matt met her. He was both concerned about her and surprised that she did not appear to be grief-stricken. She did not tell him or anyone about her inheritance, not even her mother. She was now eighteen and didn't need to. This would be her secret.

Chapter 19

Edgartown, mid-July, 1997–February 1998

But the greater inheritance she could have received from her aunt was now water over the dam. Same thing held true with her quickie marriage to Matt when she discovered she was pregnant upon returning home from Brazil right after her aunt died. She was just two months pregnant. It wasn't what she wanted, but there it was. She married him quickly on the second of August, and the baby was "premature," but Maria and Matt had been longtime high school sweethearts, and people didn't care about counting months.

It's funny now, she thought, sitting at her desk, years later. *I didn't care then how cheap our first house was, a ranch house on Twenty-First Street, just barely three feet from the Oak Bluffs line, because it had an Edgartown address and post office box. I remember the excitement of getting my first checks printed. Leaving out 21st Street, the checks read: "Maria A. Da Costa, PO Box 137, Edgartown MA 02539." What a thrill that was! It seemed like a lifetime ago, now.*

Matt advanced in the police department in the next few months before Heather was born, and Maria continued working at the agency with Stuart. When the little girl was born, Matt's mother cared for the baby during the day but still couldn't understand why Maria had picked the name *Heather*. It was so English. And, instead of the middle name traditionally being after the baby girl's maternal grandmother, Maria had picked *Anne* and not *Ana*. That's why she named her daughter *Heather Anne*, as distinct as possible from the

Portuguese names and one that would blend in with the off-island life she intended for her daughter.

Heather Anne Da Costa was christened in late February 1998 at the age of one month at Saint Elizabeth Parish by Father Almeida, the Portuguese priest who had arrived a year before from Fall River and who was well-liked, although some rumors were circling about his being fond of choirboys. And, the christening by a Portuguese priest, to some extent, helped to mollify both sides of the extended families. But it didn't rectify the sense of betrayal. Family was family; and in this tight-knit Portuguese island family, the christening still didn't smooth over the sense Maria had abandoned her heritage—which in fact she had. And, she had done this a long time before naming her daughter.

PART 3

Baldwin Real Estate, Edgartown, 1998–2013

Chapter 20

Edgartown, 1998–2013

As Stuart began to decline over the next several years, he told her he wanted her to have his agency for a steeply discounted amount when he died. He was also willing to include Senna at a lesser ownership rate, but Maria said no. Senna could continue to work there, but Maria wanted no ownership agreement with her cousin. She told Stuart she wanted to keep the name as it always had been, his name—the Baldwin Real Estate Agency. Stuart thought it was because Maria wanted to keep his memory alive and loved her for this, especially since he and Peg had never had children. He never knew why Maria really didn't want to give up the Baldwin name: it meant too much in the Edgartown area for her to change, and it would make the Yacht Club people feel comfortable. Would they really have wanted to say to friends "the Da Costa Agency" were the agents for their house search! Although she didn't say this to Stuart, she didn't want to be known as the Portagee real estate agent, as islanders jokingly (and sometimes *not* jokingly) referred to the island Portuguese. "Swamp Portagee" was another term. She had observed the Yacht Club people all her life and knew the answer. That's why it would always be known as the Baldwin Real Estate Agency.

When he died in August 2009, he had made good on his promise, and the agency was officially sold to her. Maria still had to pay off Peg for the agency on a monthly basis, but Peg never seemed to pay attention to finances, so for the first couple of months after Stuart's death, Maria just gave Peg, from time to time, payments here and there.

Peg had begun failing and was forgetful, as most older people become, and Maria arranged for Home Services to come and take care of her, eventually on a full-time basis.

A lot had happened in the few short months since Stuart had died in Maria's life. Suddenly the island became the place for land developers building gated communities, town houses, and small houses in the woods. Some were legitimate developers with good reputations, others were like Domenic "Dom" Giuliano of the old Patriarca Providence mafia family.

Included in this disparate group of carpetbaggers was a Walter Keller from Baltimore. He arrived a few months after Stuart's death. Unlike most of the new people who were arriving on the island to make their fortune in land, he was distinguished. Walter was tall and slim, handsome with a full head of dark hair, and wore business suits and ties at any public meeting and out in restaurants. No one else dressed that way. He also carried a chestnut tan leather briefcase, which she later learned was a Maxwell-Brown.

Walter needed a place to live in town and one that showed he was "serious" and "here to stay," unlike the rest of the land developers who were here to make a buck and leave. The Baldwin Agency was the obvious choice for him. And Maria was only too eager to help him. In fact, too eager.

Chapter 21

Edgartown, Late Spring-Early Summer, 2013

Maria knew she had done very well in real estate and had upped her game even more when she met Walter. He was the proverbial knight in shining armor.

At first no one noticed. She was, after all, the best real estate broker on the island, and he looked as if he had the money to spend. She was the busiest she had ever been now that Stuart was no longer hanging around the office and talking about the good old days.

She was not sitting back as Stuart had done, waiting for the phone to ring. Instead, she was "hustling," as the summer people would say. Maria was also smart enough to realize Walter wanted money just as much as she did. She felt they were alike in this and other ways and slowly tested him out on what she'd been able to plan in terms of getting enough money and leaving the island for good. Eventually, after they had started their relationship, she included him in her plans. He was more than eager. Plus, he was an asset. He inspired confidence in others.

It didn't take long before the townspeople began talking about that "new guy in town, the one who's good-looking." At first, it was assumed the reason Maria and this guy were seen around town in her Range Rover was that he was looking for property. But then, it became apparent he was more than a real estate client. And people started having "sightings": "I saw them at the Ocean View having lunch today." "Linda saw them at the Wharf Pub last week." "They were out in West Tisbury too!"

No one said anything about this to Matt, not even any of the guys. People soon learned Maria had moved out of their little ranch house on the outskirts of town on Twenty-First Street and into a downtown rental that she managed for summer people whose father had been seriously ill and therefore hadn't spent more than a week on the island early that summer. They had left the island then for the season, and it was too late to rent out now, so Maria's offer to caretake and live there was met with approval.

Heather stayed with her grandmother "until things got settled." That's the way they handled Matt's and Maria's separation. And then, it was only a matter of weeks when Walter's Grand Cherokee was parked overnight in nearby streets from Maria's rental. No surprises here.

Chapter 22

Edgartown, Tuesday, September 3, 2013

Matt was standing at the corner of Main and South Summer streets, nodding to a few of the drivers as they drove past him. He liked the month of September when island life was slowly returning to the year-round Vineyarders. Another summer gone.

Maria and Matt had been separated in the beginning of the summer, just months after Walter arrived on the island. And, although Matt didn't like the fact that Maria had taken up with this slick off-islander, he didn't protest. Ever since he had returned from Afghanistan, he seemed to have given up on things.

It was the day after Labor Day Weekend. She and Walter had gone away for five days to the Dominican Republic, and Maria had Heather stay with Matt so as not to miss the beginning of school.

Maria had come back from the trip and called the police station to let him know she had some papers to give him. The sergeant on duty, Tim Searle, told her she could find him on Main Street, probably directing traffic around the sidewalk work, as it was really slow now that most everyone had gone.

She walked down past the Dr. Daniel House, the Old Whaling Church, and the courthouse and saw him on the next corner at North Summer and Main, waving a car through once a backhoe had moved into place getting ready to dig where the sewer line had broken. Tall, dark-brown hair, skinny, and fairly good-looking, Matt seemed to be liked by people passing by. She had a moment of hesitancy and a sharp pain of regret as to what was going to happen, but shook it off just as the ubiquitous black Labs of the Vineyard do when coming out of the water at Light House Beach after an early morning's dip, their wet wavy hair shiny and glistening in sun.

"Hey, Matt, how's it going?" said one fellow, heading to the docks with his fishing gear in his hands, his eyes covered by his beat-up, old longbill hat and his lower belly protruding under the faded Menemsha Blues tee shirt. His dirty torn sneakers were held together in places with masking tape.

"Not bad since they've gone, Ed!" Matt smiled. "What a summer! Now don't you go catching all those blues. I'm not off till three today, and the derby doesn't start for another month or so! You got to save me some!"

He didn't see Maria approach him from behind, and when he heard his name, he turned around quickly. Before he could nod hello, she thrust papers into his hands and said, "I know this will come as a surprise, and I'm sorry, but I got a divorce, and Walter and I got married this past weekend in the Dominican, and it's all valid here in Massachusetts. Thom will contact you shortly about continuing child support and custody, but it shouldn't change much. I can't speak to you directly now. I'm sorry. Call Thom."

And she quickly turned on her heels and practically ran past the Yellow House, where Wrangly and Shipley Bookstore's co-owner stood enjoying the sun in her doorway.

"Weird!" she said to herself. "What was that all about? Maria practically ran past me, and Matt is just standing there in the middle of the street looking at her race away. What is going on?"

Almost immediately thereafter, Matt started shrieking in such high-pitched anguished tones that the co-owner knew she had to immediately call 9-1-1. One of the people in the car on South Summer, trying to navigate around Matt in the middle of Main Street, jumped out of his car and ran up to Matt. Someone else came out of the Bowl and Board and did the same. The two men tried to hold him, but he was kicking and twisting his body and was so strong that he broke away and started running down Main Street toward Maria, who was already a block away just beginning to cross the street onto Church Street, between the brick County of Dukes

County Court House and the Old Whaling Church, where she suddenly turned after hearing his cries.

It took the assistant manager of Bowl and Board a second before she reacted and also called the police. Matt was smashing everything in sight and threatening to kill Maria. Several of his own officers arrived within a minute and had to subdue him and pin his hands. The call went out over the scanners in town, and Rick heard it all. His scanner was on 24-7, and it's where he gained a lot of valuable information. He was a wealth of information—from all sorts of places.

By the time the cruiser came speeding down Upper Main into town, sirens blaring, with Patrolman Edwards at the wheel, he screeched to a stop and blocked Matt at the corner from running down Church Street after her. Edwards got him pinned to the cruiser, and help was soon there. Maria, of course, had already heard his shouts and the sirens and had run for cover into the little coffee shop behind the courthouse. She was shaking.

There had been no discussion about divorce at that time, so Matt was blindsided and went nuts. She knew she should have forewarned him but couldn't. Someone came up to her and asked if she was all right. Maria nodded and said, "I've got to get back to my office. Thank you."

Later, when Matt was brought to the Martha's Vineyard Hospital, all he could remember about that noon was Maria thrusting the divorce papers in his hands and her steely pronouncement: "Matt, I'm sorry. I got a divorce while Walter and I were in the Dominican Republic. The DR's divorces are legally binding in Massachusetts, and so are their marriages. Walter and I got married there. Again, I'm sorry..." And then Maria turned on her heels and started to walk away, and that's when it all went blank on him and he went nuts.

The rest of it was a blur, but not to his island friends. Matt was later told that Tim, his sergeant, had grabbed his pistol, and the other officers had all they could do to hold him until Doc Coffin got there with tranquilizers. Heavily tranquillized, he was unaware that they brought him by ambulance on the next ferry to the Psych Center at the Cape Cod Hospital, where he stayed for four weeks.

There, the professionals talked to him about his Afghanistan experience and his team's extraordinarily high kill ratio (he was pleased to tell them theirs was as high as 150 enemy troops for only one of their Special Forces team members, who unfortunately was killed), the highly dangerous raids and ambushes and the methods of killing. He returned to the States and the island with a few medals, including the Valorous Unit Award. But the nightmarish moments and bloody butcheries that had awarded him and his unit the medals had taken its toll, and Matt suffered bad flashbacks in times of stress. And this was certainly one. They also told him he was still threatening to kill Maria when the police arrived to subdue him, and they were concerned. He ignored them and kept asking to have Doc Coffin come and see him, but Doc did not have privileges there. Matt thought of Doc as a lifesaver: Doc had a relaxed view of drugs, and if they calmed Matt down, then that's what he did.

At the Psych Center, they preferred to talk and probe about his life, past and present. At first, he refused to talk. After a few days, he realized that to get out, he'd need to play the game. And so, he relived Afghanistan there. It did not help him. But he played their game and "talked" about how to relieve pressures when things got to him. He told them this was helpful and it felt good to unload and talk to someone. He insisted he didn't have any intention of really killing Maria, and when the psychiatrists were satisfied it was a just a moment of extreme anger, they approved his return if he agreed to go to counseling at Community Services when he got back to the island. And, of course he said he would. What a bunch of assholes, he thought, but I can play their game just as well as they do. The psychiatric staff congratulated themselves on doing such a good job for Matt and thereby let him go back to the Vineyard and resume his life. But all the while, he just wanted to kill her.

PART 4

Edgartown, 2015

Chapter 23

Edgartown, Thursday, September 17, 2015

Down at the foot of Dock Street, on the old Osborn property, people were moving about in the Edgartown Yacht Club's main building. It didn't look much like what most folks would think would be a prestigious yacht club, but it was unusual. Finished in 1927, the weathered shingled Yacht Club juts out over the water, with a narrow wooden dock way surrounding the building. At the end, on the deck that offered the best views of Edgartown and Chappaquiddick, stands the flagpole. Every night during the season, the commodore goes out on the deck, the staff lowers the flag, and precisely at sunset, the small but roaringly loud cannon is shot. "As you were!" bellows the commodore, and the members once again sit down. Occasionally a small child will giggle at the noise (grandparents quickly admonishing them) or a guest will shriek (much to the embarrassment of the Club member, who had already forewarned them of the cannon's surprisingly loud boom). But it was now too late in the season for sunset canons. Still nine months to the end of May when the Club would hold its commissioning, formally opening the Club for the summer season.

Upstairs in the office, the two year-round staff members were compiling applications to present to the membership committee. The first nomination carries more weight than the next two; every candidate must have three. Many were legacy, others were "newcomers": those that had purchased a house in the "right" areas, had made good impressions at cocktail parties around town, and were "attractive."

"Attractive" seemed to be the key to membership: "They're the ones that bought the old Rowe house—they really are such an *attractive* couple." But there were also a few problematic applications each year: certain members, especially those in year-round island businesses, would sometimes promote someone who really wasn't "quite right" for the Club, whatever that term might mean. If you belonged to the Yacht Club, you knew exactly what "quite right" meant—it was indefinable but real. And this year was no exception. Even the staffer realized it as she put the application on the pile and called over Trey, the Club manager.

"I heard about ten days ago she might try, but I didn't think Barbara would actually submit her name and push for her," he said. "This is going to be a problem—a real town and gown fight that we don't need next summer. There's enough problems with the commodore and the regatta already!" Trey looked at the calendar and confirmed the meeting was next week in New York.

"Better call Lizzie and forewarn her. She'll have a fit. She really didn't want to chair the committee again this year, and now this!" He went off to his office overlooking Chappy and shut the door hard. The staffer continued opening the applications. A seagull flew by his window, shrieking, flapping hard against the late September winds, its sharp eyes looking for a flash of silver announcing a scup or sea robin. If Trey hadn't been so concerned about the phone call to Lizzie, he might have noticed the gull and made a mental note that this bird was the opposite of the harbinger of spring—it was more like a premonition of things to come this year with that application now lying on his desk. He picked up the phone and dialed Lizzie.

Chapter 24

Edgartown, Monday, September 21, 2015, late afternoon

Walter walked up School Street to the home Maria and he and her daughter were renting—the Cooke house built in 1756. It was a typical Georgian house you saw all over town, reflecting the longtime English influence on the eastern seaboard. Walter didn't care much about the architecture, except when it was featured as one of the five Edgartown homes to be open to the public during "Christmas in Edgartown" week, the second week of December. The Historical Society had already drafted the brochures and shared it with Maria and Walter. He was pleased to read,

> The Jared Cooke House (1756) is one of the island's finest examples of Georgian architecture. The center-entry facade of this symmetrical, two-story clapboard house boasts a paneled front door capped with a decorative crown and a fanlight transom. The double-hung sash windows with twelve panes are entirely original glass. Inside 11-foot-high ceiling are decorated with carved ornaments, as are the elaborate mantelpieces, paneling, stairways and arched openings. The house had been in the Cooke family for almost 12 generations and is now occupied by the owner of a successful island real estate firm, The Baldwin Agency, and her husband, an off-is-

> land entrepreneur who has just joined the firm. The house will be on the market after the first of the year.

He liked the fact they had been mentioned and the terms *successful* and *entrepreneur* used. Walter liked to be talked about in this manner.

While he sucked up to the Edgartown Yacht Club members he saw in town, privately he thought the only reason they were there was that their grandparents and parents had been born first. Remittance men, he called them. Dwindling away the last of their ancestors' fortunes. Never having done much in their privileged lives, Walter felt they were naive and ready for the fleecing. Instead of doing research on a new investment, they'd throw money at a loser, based on old boy connections. "Doug came out of Citibank in New York—one of their top people. He's starting a new fund, but it's limited to only fifteen people, and I'm one of them. His reputation is impeccable, and he's brilliant. Patty and I have known Doug and Cissy since we were kids summering here. Our parents were friends. We go way back." They deserve what they get, Walter thought. And, won't they all be surprised in a few months when Doug is forced to unveil his investment miscalculations, he mused as he entered the front door.

But he *was* happy that Maria had pushed Barbara to get them nominated. They should hear soon, and he thought the chances were good. Maria was the top real estate broker on the island, and people thought she had "married up" with him. He was careful not to devolve anything of his background, and they all just thought he had come from money as they had.

Frankly he would be a little surprised if they did make it, but nevertheless thrilled. He had a way with people with money—he seemed like one of them. Little did they know about his previous life and name. It paid to stay off that Facebook thing, and it had paid to have his name legally changed to *Walter Keller*. He had hired a Penn State computer major to search his new name or any link to it, even feeding the Geek his real name and addresses, and the guy couldn't connect the two. Perfect.

Maria was already mixing a drink. "Want a scotch or a dirty martini?" she asked with her back to him. "Dirty martini, just like us!" He smiled, and he walked up to her from behind, put his hands on her hips, and gave her a kiss on the cheek.

Boy, almost two years ago since he had met her here, and she was already getting hippy, just like her mother's side of the family. It's all that linguica the Portagees (picking up on the pejorative local term for the Portuguese) eat; you can see globules of fat floating in the kale soup when they make it. He hated going to her mother's house for family celebrations. He had never met Maria's father, but Maria's sister bought the parents' house; and almost every Sunday, the entire family was expected to be there for dinner. The house stunk of cabbage from the soup, and he couldn't stomach the greasy potatoes served with grilled linguica or the fava beans with onions. And rather than fresh cod from the docks, they had to get bacalao—that shriveled dried-up cod they had to soak for days. And then they mashed potatoes with it. It was like eating fish cream of wheat. These people were uncouth. Maria at least had ambition, even though she was beginning to look like all the women who hung out at the Portuguese American Club (known as the PA Club) in Oak Bluffs.

But Maria was his ticket. Even though some of these real estate "transactions," which she began to confide in him about, had been her ideas to begin with (and he *did* give her credit for that), he considered himself to be the real brains behind everything. However, without her access to the wealthy summer folks, he'd be nowhere on this island. And, he knew it.

On top of this, she had early on confided in him that she had inherited a large estate in Brazil from an aunt and that no one, not even her parents or Matt, knew about this. Maria also had money flowing into her real estate brokerage account here. He'd keep her for all this—it was well worth it. Right now, they had been focused on getting in to the Yacht Club. It wasn't as easy as he thought it would be, but he had remained hopeful.

Anyway, whether it had happened or not, fairly soon, in a matter of months, they'd be living in Brazil, and certainly not on this windswept Atlantic island with a bunch of inbred locals all with the same names of *Coffin*, *Osborn*, *Pease*, *Vincent* or those stocky laborers from "the old country," the Da Costas, Almeidas, and Coutinhos, along with the third group, the summer influx of New England bow-tied preps, the Smiths, Davies, and Wilsons. The Brazilians didn't count—yet.

Together they sat down in the library with their drinks: she on the Laura Ashley plum-colored chintz sofa and he in the upholstered wingback. Macadamia nuts were in a small silver bowl on the glass coffee table, with the cocktail napkins she got at Pequod, the only gift shop on the island where you could find Caspari napkins, Cuisinart products, unusual kitchen gadgets, and beautiful wineglasses: lots of things to look at and buy when you were bored—and had the money and good taste to do so. The Marticks owned the store and had earlier politely refused ("business reasons, you know") to second Walter and Maria to the Yacht Club. Actually, Walter mused, despite that, he and Nick still had a pretty good relationship—Walter would often stop in to say hello when nothing else was going on, which he had done that afternoon.

"I saw Nick today. He and Maddie have just gotten back from Vero, and the shop is going to be going through some renovations but open in time for Christmas in Edgartown. He looks the same, only tanned—I didn't see Maddie. She was out somewhere. He did mention that Gavin would be graduating from college next summer and back here to get involved with the store. By the way, we got the draft of the 'Christmas in Edgartown' brochure today—it's over on the desk for you to look at. I think we came out just fine."

"I ran into her at the Stop & Shop while I was getting a few things for dinner," she said. "They're thinking of retiring, but Nick just can't seem to break away from the store. We got caught up on a lot, and I let her know that Barbara was the one who had nominated us for the Yacht Club. I could see she was surprised at that, but said 'How wonderful,' and we moved on. I know the nominating committee just met. Keep your fingers crossed!" Maria smiled inwardly sensing they would be elected.

It was less than a year ago, Maria thought, that I had Bob and Barbara put my name up for Yacht Club consideration! Life was getting better, she thought, momentarily happy and excited. But as so often with her, her mood quickly changed and became dark. She still resented how long it had taken to get where she was today, compared to the summer people her own age. They hadn't needed to do anything except be born. Tanned, long legged and thin, confident, laughing and knowing no boundaries, except for the little white picket fences, prim and proper, that protected their valuable summertime homes. Even if she got elected into the Yacht Club, she knew she might never get a chance to use it if her plans for Brazil worked out. It didn't matter if she did or didn't get to use it; it was the thrill of "winning" that counted. While other women on the mainland talked of glass ceilings, she had succeeded in breaking through the picket fences and was now on the other side where the owners sat.

Her plans were to get them out of here, off the island for good, and she would, in another five or so months. She smiled a little at this thought and took another sip.

She had already lit the fire, and the flames were intense, their reflections flickering in the windowpanes behind her. He raised his glass and said, "Cheers, to new successes," and smiled knowingly. She smiled and said, "Cheers, may the new successes begin to materialize now," and she took a sip of the cold smooth liquid. Tanqueray and a drop of Noilly, with two of the blue cheese-stuffed olives she loved so much. He looked at her, waiting for her to speak. Her hair was her best asset. Shiny, dark, and full. Her face wasn't awful, just ordinary. She looked better when she wore red lipstick. He knew she'd pack on the pounds like all the others. But right now, there was more to her than looks.

"I spoke to the Parsons today about continuing our rental. They want to know why it is that the house isn't on the market yet. They said the cousins had called them over the weekend and want to get the estate settled. Charles even said he might make a trip to the Vineyard to see what he could do to hurry this up."

"I hope you talked him out of it!"

"Don't worry. I said I could get them some advance money now and would hope all the paperwork for the people interested in buying it at the premium price could be arranged by early summer. I pointed out that with the interested buyers being in Europe all winter that they were not ready to close until at least June, and it would be far better for the two of us to stay here through then, rather than rent it out to off-season tenants. I said, 'You've known me since I was a child, and Walter and I will care for this house so nothing will be damaged.'"

"What did he say then?"

"He agreed it was in safe hands, but was still concerned. I then said, 'We can always get another buyer, Charles, but this offer is spectacular, and I don't think you can ever match this in a thousand years.' He knows the 'offer'"—and she smiled and took another sip—"is $450,000 over any other interested party has offered. Don't worry, they need the money."

"I think you should call him tomorrow and say perhaps he's right—it may be better to sell now and not wait for six months. That should get him to shut up," said Walter with disdain. These families were so pathetic—neither Charles nor his other Parson cousins could come up with the money to buy the family property. Each one had depleted whatever they had inherited without ever adding to their own individual wealth "the old-fashioned way"—by earning it. They deserved this. How things would have been different if he had been born into these families.

"I was thinking the same thing: I'll reverse the psychology and say, 'Better safe than sorry,' and give him my best 'I understand it's more important to have the sale now rather than wait a few months for the offer $450,000 higher.' I think he'll cave in. That will buy us some more time. But then we'll have to send them some money representing the 'earnest money.'"

"Can you come up with a down payment? It's got to be big enough so they won't question it."

"I've got it in the bank, but I'd prefer to get a new client to foot the bill. It will give us more time in the house, and then we can pull out of here in the late spring, right before the 'sale' is scheduled," she answered.

"It will be worth it. By the way, have you heard back from the California couple about the Morse House?" He had finished his martini and was getting up to make another.

"Want a refresher?" he asked. She nodded her head yes.

"Actually, they called late this afternoon. Their last name is *Aznavarian.* They want to come next weekend to take a look at the Morse estate and also the Hall House. I said I'd call Tom at the airport tomorrow and speak to him about a hangar rental and then get back to the couple. Get this: they're flying in on their Gulfstream—a G650! They asked if I could look into landing and a hangar at the airport for them to make sure we can accommodate the plane."

"What—are you kidding me!" he yelled, almost dropping the glass. "They're like $50 or $60 million. You can fly six or seven thousand miles in one. You've really hit the jackpot here, my dear! I can't believe it." He walked over and planted a kiss on her forehead, handing her the drink. "A G650—they have to be loaded!"

Maria also had Stephanie Kramer in mind as a possible target, but wasn't yet going to tell Walter. She needed some more cash and didn't want him to know how tight everything was getting at the moment. If he felt they were skating on thin ice, Maria's "value" was greatly diminished, and she was smart enough to realize that.

One of the greatest assets she inherited when she took over the Baldwin Agency were the keys—hundreds of keys to the very best properties on the island. With all the wealthy people who leave the island for their year-round homes in September, Maria was entrusted to make sure their properties were safe and kept up during the nine months of the year when they weren't there. Not only was caretaking lucrative, three hundred dollars a month ("$10 a day to make sure your property is well looked after," said Maria to her new clients, and they had to agree, that was cheap), but this gave Maria "options" that otherwise would not have been possible.

Maria smiled and raised her glass. "Balls to those who think smalls!" They both laughed.

And there they might be, next Memorial Day, at the Yacht Club commissioning—full-fledged members! That is, in the unlikely event, they were still here in Edgartown. Maria was anxiously awaiting the phone call from the club. *Any day now*, she thought.

Chapter 25

Edgartown, Monday, September 28, 2015, morning

After Maria's surprise announcement of their divorce, and her remarriage, Matt had gone to live with his brother in Maine due to the imposed three-month medical leave from the Edgartown Police Force in 2013. When Matt returned to the island, he found it depressing. He was only just now slowly returning to normal, and this was almost two years later.

He still didn't like to be out in public, but two of the officers had called in sick that day, and so he had to take a few hours on Main Street that afternoon as movie crews were bringing in their production trucks, and traffic needed to be curtailed while the big trucks headed down Main Street. Matt and many of the locals hated the film people ever since *Jaws*. Loud, brassy, and drunk most of the time. Flinging around money like it was nothing. Screwing with the town's daughters. Even getting Marjorie Moflett pregnant. But the selectmen and tourist industry—the hotels, restaurants, and real estate agents—loved them, especially now in the off-season. So here they were. God help us all, Matt thought, scowling as the first one came down the street.

It was still a quiet time of year: tourists were six months away from invading the small island, so life now continued as usual. He was still reluctant, but slowly started showing his face. He needed to go to the Stop & Shop from time to time to pick up a dozen eggs, some snacks, steak, and a few household goods. He tried to go early in the morning to avoid most people; he was painfully aware of their whispers about his breakdown on Main Street, and didn't want to be an object of pity or derision. He was trying to pick up where he left off, but it was not easy with a guy like Matt, and not easy on a small island where everyone knew everything about everyone else. Or, at least it *appeared* that everyone knew everything about everybody. But it wasn't the case at all, as people including Matt later discovered.

About three weeks after Rick had that strange conversation with Charlie wherein he said "keep your eyes open," he ran into Matt at the Stop & Shop, and Rick began to talk to him. "Matt, I know it's been a long time since she pulled that on you, but I'm glad to see you getting back and out. I just want you to know that people are behind you. What kind of a bitch does that to someone?" he asked.

Matt relaxed a bit, but still felt uncomfortable. Since Rick had come to the island right after the war in Afghanistan in 2001, Matt had always known who he was. Although Rick tried to fit in as one of them—the guys at the Club and at the VFW, he never really gained the guys' complete trust and friendship. He tried too hard to be an islander, and it never worked. Matt remembered old Arnie Fischer, taking the West Tisbury town meeting floor, saying to someone who was calling herself an "islander" (as she had lived there most of her life): "Lady, my kittens were born in my oven, but that don't make them muffins." The townspeople roared with laughter for minutes before the moderator got their attention by the gavel. "Order! Order!" Fred Wilson chortled, his eyes tearing in laughter. "Order! Order!" The woman never returned to the town meetings again. Rick seemed to think he could break that you've gotta-be-born-here-to-be-a-native barrier, but he couldn't. On the other hand, he wasn't a bad guy, and they did share war experience and love of guns.

"Thanks, Rick. I appreciate it. It was a shock, and I really didn't see it coming, even though we had all but separated. I thought about coming to see you to find out if the divorce was really valid, but it has to be, or she wouldn't now be saying she was married."

"Unfortunately, I've heard that the Dominican Republic does have these crazy divorce laws and is valid, as is their marriage. I don't understand how it can be, but save your money. It's all legal," said Rick. "What's the status with your daughter now?" asked Rick. "Is she visiting with you on weekends, and is your child support established? That's maybe how I can help you."

Just then, Mrs. Thornton moved down the aisle; she was one of the town's worst gossips. "Let's pay up and get out of here. We can talk at Dock Street. Have you had breakfast yet?" Rick asked.

"I'm not sure I want to go down there," said Matt.

"Don't be foolish. I can tell you the guys are all behind you, and they'll be glad to see you out and about. Come on, I'll meet you down there. I can use some linguica and eggs about now!" said Rick, moving his way to the cash registers. Matt nodded okay and soon was driving down Main Street right behind Rick's Cherokee. It was a dark, cloudy day. WMVY had just done the local news (nothing except local high school sports scores and notice of a Community Services meeting that evening, mainly Alcoholics Anonymous and Narcotics Anonymous and some Mental Health Support groups) and the weather. It said a storm was coming later this afternoon, but at least it wasn't a hurricane.

As he found a space at the Dock Street parking lot, he noticed white caps forming in the outer harbor and Jeff leaving the harbormaster's office, going out to take a better look at the approaching weather. Jeff could tell weather better than any of those weathermen on TV, just by looking at the waves and by feeling the wind and moisture. He'd put up the flag if need be. Most everyone heeded that flag. It was only those who didn't come from here that ignored Jeff's warnings. And, nine out of ten times, they had to be towed to shore or plucked from the sea. They'd never learn, those off-islanders, he thought contemptuously.

Chapter 26

Edgartown, Monday, September 28, 2015, morning

"Matt! Good to see you!" said Larry, who was joined by a chorus of locals. "Matt, haven't seen you in ages! Looking good," said Don, behind the counter, who rarely said anything to anyone as he flipped pancakes and moved country-fried potatoes and scrambled eggs with a deftness that was quick and precise.

"Coffee?" asked Don, without turning his back. His long stringy dark hair was tied back in a ponytail; he wore the same white tee shirt winter or summer, and his four large southwestern turquoise and silver rings completed the picture. People sent him postcards from all over the country and sometimes the world. They were displayed on every available wall space, yellowed with the grease and the smoke of frying all day. In the summer, tourists would poke their heads in, take a quick look around, and duck back out. Everyone in there liked it that way.

After they had eaten and said hello to a few more of the guys, Rick said, "Why don't you come to my office tomorrow, and we can talk about your daughter and support. I know how much you care for her, but I want to make sure that what you do is fair to her, as well as you. Maria seems to have a lot of money now, and you need to make sure you have enough. Can you see me tomorrow?"

Matt nodded and shook hands with Rick. He thanked him out in the parking lot and said they'd meet tomorrow in the morning after Rick filed a few papers in the courthouse.

Matt looked down Dock Street and saw the harbormaster had just hoisted the single red flag for small craft advisory. It could get worse later, and Matt scrapped his plans for going out in the boat. He got into his Jeep, which was parked in the lot between the Dock Street Coffee Shop and just opposite the Yacht Club (people didn't seem to note the irony of how perfectly this lot was situated—the townies of the coffee shop staring directly across the lot to the gownies of the Yacht Club), and drove home. He thought about what Rick said about meeting tomorrow and discussing his child support. "That bitch! I hate her so much!" he uttered as he sped around the corner up to North Water Street and headed back to the police station.

Chapter 27

Edgartown, Tuesday, September 29, 2015, late afternoon

The next day, just before she was to leave the office, Maria was finishing an electronic deposit into her off-island account when the phone rang. It was from Trey saying she and Walter had been accepted into the Club, effective January 1. Maria couldn't believe it! What a fabulous day! She rushed out of the office to find Walter to tell him the good news about the Yacht Club. Wouldn't people like Mrs. Bliss have a cow! Her housekeeper's daughter now a member, cavorting with all the Bliss family as equals. Ha! Life *is* good!

She entered the back door to the house and burst into the kitchen, just as Walter, who was in the library, quickly hung up his cell phone. He looked startled to see her, but she didn't notice. "Walter! Darling! We've made the Yacht Club! Can you believe it!" Maria burst out. "We're in! We did it! I'm so happy! Trey just called me at the office." He *was* pleased with this news and quickly went over to give her a big hug and kiss.

"Darling, that's wonderful! We need to celebrate. Let's go to the Alchemy, we haven't been there for a while, and have dinner. I also think we should invite Barbara and Bob as they're the ones who sponsored us. I'll call them now. We can leave a note for Heather—I'm sure she won't mind," said Walter.

For a second, Maria hesitated. "I was supposed to help her with some homework tonight, but she'll understand. I'll put her dinner out, and she can reheat it. I'm going to take a quick shower and get ready. Make sure there's an ice-cold martini when I come down.

Oh, Walter. I'm so happy!" And she ran upstairs. She quickly said a prayer to Reina Santa Elizabet of Portugal (nee Queen Isabel) for listening to her prayers she began when she was about ten years old and understood that she, the daughter of a cleaning woman in the grand harbor summerhouses of North Water Street, would no longer be playmates with the residents' children when her mother was cleaning there. They were now off to sailing lessons at the Junior Yacht Club and the Snack Bar, forming their adult and lifelong summer friendships. Maria started praying that one day she too would be welcomed into the Yacht Club—and all the heretofore unattainable social advantages it held. And now, at last, years later, her prayer has been granted. "*Muito obrigada, Santa Elizabet, muito obrigada!*" And she hurried to get ready.

Meanwhile downstairs, as he was stirring the martinis, Walter thought Maria's gamboling up the front stairs was more like… thudding.

But the Club *was* great news! Life was good. He dialed Barbara to see if they were free.

CHAPTER 28

Edgartown, Thursday, October 1, 2015

Thursday was an unseasonably warm day for the beginning of October on the Vineyard. Rick had walked down to the harbor and was thinking about where to dry-dock his boat this year. He wasn't happy with Edgartown Marine's new prices. The water was calm, small fish were swimming near the docks, and for a moment, only the distant hum of a motorboat entering the outer harbor could be heard. Overhead, two gulls screamed their high-pitched call and dove into the water right off the Chappy Ferry landing. One surfaced with a good-sized fish in its beak, the other screamed again and this time got one too. Another spotted a clam washed up on the sand and dove down to pick it up and then ascended almost vertically and dropped it on the pavement. The clam broke open, and the gull then enjoyed his lunch. *Smart birds*, he thought.

The Old on Time II little ferry (affectionately called TOOT by locals) had just started to cross the short five-hundred-foot distance from the foot of Daggett Street across to Chappaquiddick Island (which wasn't really an island: it was a peninsula). It was full: three cars, and it was a little after noon, and no cars waiting on Daggett Street. Proof that ordinary life, as year-rounders knew it, was returning to the island after the summer invasion, he thought to himself.

No matter how long one lived in Edgartown, *The Old on Time* was amusing. It was a simple motorized, flat-bottomed vessel with room only for three cars and had wooden benches on each side running the length of the vessel for walk-ons. The standard procedure is that three cars, or one truck only, drive onto one end. The ferry captain places wooden chocks under the wheels of vehicles on the ferry deck, and a "safety" chain is hung across the front and back end. You shift the vehicle into park and shut off your engine; when you reach the other side, a little more than a minute later, you drive straight off. Supremely simple, a *rara avis* in today's world. First-time visitors can't get over it. Some cheap fun is to take *The Old on Time* over and right back again, hoping you will be the first vehicle in line: with your hands on the car wheel, and only water in front of you, instinct makes you attempt to use your car's steering wheel in an attempt to "steer" the ferry yourself, no matter how many times you've been on this. With passengers in the first car, and you wildly turning the wheel pretending to be out of control, the two-minute ride turns into lots of laughs.

Rick thought about the event two weeks ago and shook his head. On the last run to Chappy that night, a car driven by a summer resident of Chappaquiddick who had come to check on her cottage fell into the harbor waters as the ferry neared the landing. Not listening to the ferry master, she had left her car running, and as the little ferry landed with a bump, the car went off the flat deck into the water. She and her passenger had got out through a window and were hoisted up onto the ramp, wet and cold. Later Tommy Norton hauled the car to shore with his boat, and Davis's tow truck was brought over to bring the car to town. The driver was later accused by the police of being intoxicated and was charged with negligent operation of a motor vehicle and operating under the influence of alcohol. Not knowing any lawyers, she called the Yacht Club and spoke to Trey. He figured this was the type of case Rick handled, and why bother any of the other members of the Legal Committee; they were from bigger Boston and New York City firms and wouldn't handle anything like a local OUI. She had called Rick that next morning and asked him to represent her in court. It never hurt to get some fun publicity, he thought. Plus, he had Googled her, and she lived in Old Greenwich. She was loaded. Even better. The issue remained that the car could not have been in Park and that her field test showed intoxication. He could scare her a bit about the county judges taking a dim view of irresponsible visitors and intoxication, the danger and expense to the others who rescued the passengers and the car, plus the police and ambulance time and could garner a hefty fee. In fact, Rick knew everyone and people were laughing about the idiocy of off-islanders, so there was little chance of more than a $100 fine. But he would play it up big and then come in as the knight in shining armor, and score big. He'd charge her $1,500.

Chapter 29

Edgartown, Thursday, October 1, 2015

She hesitated and then answered the phone, "Baldwin Agency, Maria here. May I help you?" The voice at the other end was immediately familiar. "Yes, Mrs. Bliss. Yes. Absolutely. Everything is fine, and the house will be closed this week and opened well before Memorial Day. Cleaners are going in a week from today, and KT will turn off the water for the season. I'm going over there tomorrow to make sure the linens are okay and to see if anything needs replacing. Yes, I'll call you if anything major needs doing. You'll need to send some more money for the account. I'd say about $2,000 for now. Yes, I'll give your best to my mother—she always talks about you and how kind you were to her over all those years—twenty-five, it was…a long time to be with someone.

"Yes. He's fine. I'd like you to get to know him better too. Well, it was a whirlwind romance, and now, almost two years later, I've never been happier. He's a big help to me in the agency. We're already starting to get inquiries about houses that may be on the market. As you know, I've always told you, if your family ever decides to get rid of the house, you know who to call! Yours could easily get fifteen to twenty million—no, really! Bob Sharpe's house on Starbuck's Neck sold in late August for over fourteen million—a couple from California. And, they told me they have friends who could do the same."

Maria laughed. "Oh, Mrs. Bliss, even with the Sharpe commission, I could never catch up to you! But you're right. We are doing well. Did I tell you Heather will be spending a year in Switzerland after graduation this coming year! Yes, at Le Rosey! She loves riding, and that's a perfect place for her. She's also looking forward to next summer learning to sail at the Junior Yacht Club before she takes off. We just got the news about being new members, and we're so happy we decided to join. I'll be able to see more of you and Howard now." Mrs. Bliss stifled her surprise and congratulated Maria on the Yacht Club and Heather's accomplishments. "Why, thank you. We are delighted about the Club, and I know my parents would be proud of Heather too. We still miss my dad."

After a few more minutes, Mrs. Bliss hung up. Maria sat there thinking, *What a bitch! My mother cleaned for her for twenty-five years, my father did the gardening for just as long, and all we got at Christmas was a crappy poinsettia from Danny Bernard's greenhouse. How cheap can you get?* But she showed her. She could tell Mrs. Bliss could hardly believe Heather was going to Switzerland and that Maria and Walter got accepted at the Yacht Club! Now *that* turned a few heads!

Her father would have been so embarrassed by this attempt to join. Manny "knew" his place and would never have even thought of trying to climb that ladder—he was so old-school Azorean. Frankly, she was embarrassed any time one of the old families would fondly remember her parents; it would bring up the past that she so hated.

Chapter 30

Edgartown, Friday, October 2, 2015

The tall red brick austere building on Main Street named the County of Dukes County Court House (the county's name is not *Duke*, but *Dukes County*, hence *the County of Dukes County*, or *Dukes County's County*, and whoever ordered the sign thought courthouse was two words, not one, and so be it; that remained its official name, right or wrong) was where just about every local wound up—at one point or another.

It was right across the street from the Dukes County Savings Bank, in the center of town on Main Street.

Rick Maron was about to go up the three worn brick steps into the bank, when he heard his name called out. It was Owen. Rick didn't want to stop, so he just gave a wave and continued up the steps. Rick had been on the Vineyard since 2001 as an attorney in his father's law firm in the Fall River factory town, home to Portuguese and Lebanese immigrants and mill workers. Of Lebanese Maronite Catholic descent, his father was known in this ethnic community as "the Lebanese Godfather." He was a leading member of the St. Anthony of the Desert Maronite Catholic Church and the Knights of Columbus. He made his fortune not by practicing law, *per se*, but by buying up uneducated and working-class Lebanese widows' tenement properties when their husbands died. In return, he told them they could live there until they died, and their house would be maintained at his expense during that period. Although he looked very kind and was striking in appearance—his white hair contrasted with his swarthy skin tone, and he was quite handsome in terms of Lebanese features—underneath this façade, he was as ruthless as they come. He had three sons and one daughter, and the daughter worked as his bookkeeper while the other two sons did the real estate maintenance and upkeep for the family business. He had wanted this eldest son, Richard (Rick) Jr., or Junior, as his family called him, to follow in his footsteps; and when Rick, not the brightest light on the tree, finally passed the law exam, his father's law firm was renamed Maron & Maron, Attorneys at Law, and Rick took up residence and established the firm's "overseas" practice in Edgartown. Some people behind Rick's back called it "Moron & Moron."

He was particularly sensitive to his Lebanese background on this small island. At first people assumed he was Arab because his family emigrated from Lebanon. He made sure from the beginning that people knew his difference: the Maronites were Catholic, and they made up about 25 percent of the total population in Lebanon. Further, Pope Benedict was their pontiff. Since the end of the French Mandate in 1945, presidents of Lebanon have been traditionally been Maronites, the prime minister a Sunni Muslim, and the speaker of the Parliament, a Shia Muslim. Rick gave this little spiel to anyone he met for the first time. He was a regular communicant at St. Elizabeth's Catholic Church in town, and he always made a hefty donation from the law firm. In sum, people never thought of him as an Arab. No one would walk into his office if they had thought that.

Unlike a lot of Massachusetts, the island didn't have any French Canadians, Italians, Poles, or Puerto Ricans. Yes, there were a few Lebanese and Armenians and even some Jamaicans on the island, but they weren't of any significant numbers. However, new to the island were the Brazilians. And of the two longtime Portuguese groups, it was the Azoreans who didn't want to be identified with this new wave of Portuguese-speaking people who were arriving in force on the island. Even if Maria was Portuguese, she was well aware that her family was Azorean and from Europe, and *certainly not* from the Verdean islands off Africa or the jungles of Brazil.

But this new wave of Portuguese-speaking people, the Brazilians, were now inheriting the lowest rung of Portuguese speakers on the island and most of them were here just for a year or two only for the cash (under the table) before they returned home. They were interlopers and not here to learn the language and settle, as did the true Portuguese, the Azoreans, and even the Verdeans, regardless of whether or not the latter group could attain the level of the Azoreans.

The Brazilians were swarthy (*pardo*, mixed race), didn't learn English, they stuck to themselves. They were doing menial and dirty jobs, and furthermore, they didn't care. They'd soon be back in Brazil with more money than anyone in their little towns in the middle of nowhere. "Carpetbaggers, not settlers, all of them," the older Azoreans contemptuously called them. However, as for the Verdeans, they were pleased. First, the Brazilians shared a common African heritage, unlike their snotty countrymen, the Azoreans. Second, it was 'new blood' for their children to marry and to produce a better stock of grandchildren, and all right here on the island…no need to go off island to marry.

This new group formed much of Rick's clientele. It was easy money and no great legal knowledge needed: OUIs, assault and battery, disturbing the peace, exposing oneself (taking a leak coming out of the bars late at night), failure to pay rent, larceny by check over $250, possession to distribute class B substance (Percocet), operating with suspended license—the list repeated itself over and over. But that made money for the lawyers who probably couldn't get clients otherwise, for obvious reasons. Here, on the island, very little real law had to be practiced. Bail 'em out, have them pay $50 in court costs, and charge them $300 for your service.

Chapter 31

Edgartown, Saturday, October 3, 2015

Maria sat in her office on a Saturday going through client files. Although Walter was going along with her plan regarding the California couple who were finally flying in on their Gulfstream after a year of canceled appointments, and she seemed to have put his mind at rest about the Parsons cousins getting antsy about why their property hadn't yet sold, she *was* worried. Walter hadn't known all the risks she had taken—just that she would be borrowing from Peter to pay Paul—and she feared he would back off if he really knew how precariously perched was her house of cards at the moment. She *had* to get another sale—and fast.

By this time, it was a couple of years since Matt had his breakdown and he'd been long back into his daily routines and was seen around town as usual. People had forgotten this episode, even if Matt hadn't and he was still uncomfortable out and about, and now were used to seeing Maria and Walter around town, wining and dining everywhere.

She would often go from a good mood to a bad one. It usually had to do with how effortless the lives were that the summer crowd was born into. This still bothered her even if she had just been accepted in the Yacht Club. She couldn't wait to get out of here, off the island for good, and she would! She smiled a little at this thought, and went back to work.

Flipping through the lists, she came across Stephanie Kramer's name. Divorced, in her forties, attractive in her Upper East Side way,

Stephanie had money. Not only her own money, but her father was wealthy too. Their house at Green Hollow, next to the old Walter Cronkite house on the bluff overlooking the inner harbor, was unlike most weathered, rambling structures you'd see there. Her father had made it big, apparently, in West Coast IT ventures and had a taste for the modern sleek look of the LA scene. Many people scoffed at the decor and the huge picture windows he had installed. Those that had been invited inside were stunned to see sleek steel and leather furniture, glass tables and silver sconces, striking abstract black-and-white canvasses, red lacquer walls—modernist Italian said it all. It was *not* the Vineyard, and Alex Kramer full well knew it. He was delighted in his boldness and flair and his subtle way of mocking old money, old names, and old gray-haired fuddy-duddies dressed in their requisite blue blazers, Nantucket Reds (how absurd, he thought, to buy cotton canvas pants that are "guaranteed to fade"!), and boat shoes without socks. That was *le costume de riguer* for a Saturday or Sunday evening as they all headed down to the Reading Room for drinks and then the Yacht Club for dinner, some making their way in small motorboats and tying up alongside the wharf.

Maria had been invited to the Kramer house for drinks a few times, but not being a member of the Yacht Club then, she used to excuse herself before everyone left for dinner at the Club. That only further built up her resentment about her family. But, it had also built up her resolve to become a member, and she and Barbara had been working on that, and now she's showed them!

She thought about Stephanie: divorced, attractive, and wealthy—and not wanting in men. Maria thought it was worth a try and picked the phone up. Stephanie answered on the second ring and sounded surprised but pleasant when she heard it was Maria on the other end.

Maria said, "Stephanie. I know you're not in the market, but I thought I'd give you a call anyway to tell you in advance about a fabulous house that is about ready to come on the market. I realize you have your father's place, but I didn't know if you had ever contemplated getting your own home?"

Stephanie seemed surprised, but said, "I have not considered this, but tell me, what do you have in mind? I'm at least willing to listen."

"It's a fabulous, fabulous house up in Oyster Watcha—it's just now being completed after three years of construction. The developers called me this week, and I'm getting the exclusive. The final touches can be added by a new owner, but this needs to be done quickly as they don't want to wait another season before getting back their investment." Maria bit her lip and kept quiet for the response.

"Tell me more," said Stephanie. "What's the layout and acreage?"

"It's a private waterfront compound set on twenty-two acres. It has three structures nestled on the shore—main house, oversized guesthouse, and pond house—and they all have stunning panoramic water views. The main house has classic 'Vineyard character,' with its Cape Cod style, shingle exterior, bright interior, and blue exterior shutters, yet is very spacious—13,500 square feet in total—and, with seven bedrooms and nine baths. An infinity pool runs almost the length of the house that has cabanas and an outside kitchen. And, the main house is set right at the water's edge, just a few steps away by boardwalk, with a three-hundred-foot stretch of private beach excellent for swimming or sunbathing. The guesthouse alone has four bedrooms and a farmer's porch with wood decking and outdoor shower. It's situated nearby next to the pond and is truly a special place for the summertime gatherings. Farther inland, the property also offers a private Har-Tru tennis court and an artist studio set amongst the pines," Maria rattled off as quickly as possible without taking a breath.

Silence.

"Stephanie?"

"Sorry. I was just thinking. Where is it again, exactly?" asked Stephanie.

Maria stifled her excitement that Stephanie was showing some interest, and answered, "It's off the Edgartown Tisbury Road, about halfway from town to the airport. On the left, down one of those long hidden roads. You can't see anything from the road. Talk about privacy! Stephanie, I wouldn't have called you out of the blue if I didn't think it was spectacular. I'm only going to speak to you and another person right now, and if either one of you have interest, you'd need to be quiet about this as it's not on the market yet, and get up here quickly so I can take you there to see it."

"Well, I have found it rather awkward not having my own place. I love Dad, and he's great, and his house is plenty big, but when I bring a friend for the weekend, it's not my own place, and we end up in a big house party. It's fun, but…it's not conducive to having a private weekend with someone you're getting interested in." Stephanie gave a rueful laugh and said, "Not that that's critical at this point in my life! I've just been dumped by my boyfriend of six months."

"Oh, Stephanie," said Maria. "I'm so sorry to hear this! Well, maybe this is a good time to get you up here and get your mind off him and looking forward to something new? And, you can meet Walter—you know I was remarried about two years ago."

"Congratulations, Maria! I hope you are very happy. You know, maybe you're right! I could use a little time away from the city, and a trip off-season to the Vineyard might be fun. I've never been there in off-season!"

"Absolutely! You know the Charlotte Inn is open for the winter months, and I could call Laura and Jared and tell them you are coming, and I know they'd be thrilled to have you. Plus, you could look in at your dad's place while you are here. We check it each week, as you know, but I think the linens could use some updating and a few things like that around the house you could see and tell your father so I could get it all in order before he comes up this year," said Maria, excitedly now.

"Maria, I'm so glad you called today. It was not on my mind, but the idea is intriguing. My daughters might like to have their friends visit, which we can't really do comfortably at my dad's as he's always entertaining. And, it would be nice for me to be a little bit more on my own up there and make new friends, which is hard to do now. Let me call my dad and see if I can use his plane, and I'll get back to you tonight or tomorrow. He's in Europe, so he won't need the plane. Thanks again, Maria! I'm excited," said Stephanie.

"Me too! We'll talk later. Bye, Stephanie!"

Maria put the phone down and smiled. A big smile. Walter knew almost everything, but he could absolutely not know about this one. It had to be her secret. He had no idea how little she really had: only about four million stashed away. He had said although they had the house and endowment in Florianopolis, they'd still need a minimum of five or six million for their future. All he saw were the recent sales and assumed by the way she talked that she had run up a much bigger war chest over the years since she had been in business—first as Stuart's "helper" in the office when she was at the high school, and then later after Heather was born, she got her license and became his primary agent. Matt and her family were very proud of her accomplishments at such an early age, and Maria began to feel as if she was "someone" at last, but she still wasn't anywhere yet, until her business really took off and Walter came along. The Yacht Club families began to deal with her now, and her origins faded from their thoughts.

Chapter 32

Edgartown, Monday, October 5, 2015

Maria and Walter had the same goals in life, and a plan was already in progress to make it all become a reality. It involved Fernanda and Maria's inheritance, and Peg, to whom she still owed money for the agency.

As Peg continued to decline, Maria continued to visit her several times a week at home—the only person in Edgartown who did. She arranged for Home Health aides to come in and a caregiver overnight. Everyone in town said how loving Maria was toward Peg and "wasn't Peg lucky to have Maria." Meanwhile, Peg was more and more forgetful and seemed to have forgotten all about the money Maria still owed her for the agency. All she cared about were the visits from Maria. They talked about the past, neighbors, and the town; and Peg always asked about Ana, Maria's mother, and Matt, her husband.

Maria continued to see Peg regularly, but didn't "update" Peg about people who had come and gone, became ill or died—she kept her in "the past present"—and never told Peg about her surprise quickie divorce from Matt and immediate remarriage to Walter. Maria thought this news would have upset Peg—perhaps to the point that Peg's memory would be joggled enough to ask about the payments for the agency. "Let sleeping dogs lie," rationalized Maria.

Then, in late August 2015, almost six years to the date Stuart died, Peg had a stroke and was put into Windemere, the hospital's long-term care department. No one knew why it was called that. It could have been a misspelling of Windermere, the shallow but wide lake near Beatrix Potter's home in the Lake District, or a name someone tried to translate as "wind of the sea" in fractured French. As such a facility, it was nicer than off-island nursing homes. Attached to the hospital, it had every emergency service available 24-7.

But what made it stand out was its gray wooden exterior, and porches with rocking chairs, reminiscent of the Carpenter's Gothic gingerbread cottages just a mile down the road at the old Methodist Campgrounds. It had a Vineyard feel to it, and hospital visitors were encouraged to pop in and say hello to the patients. The main interior entrance opened onto the hospital corridors, and there was always a busy atmosphere with people walking by. Islanders were not sequestered away in a utilitarian rest home on the Cape where they'd rarely get island friends and family visiting. One thing you can say for the Vineyarders: they take care of their own. And Peg was one of Windemere's residents since her stroke.

In the two months that Peg had been in Windemere, Maria was a frequent visitor to Peg. She also acted as her unofficial power of attorney since no one else was as close to the Baldwins as Maria had been. The island often bent rules in instances like this. Maria would come and go freely and always say hello with a big smile to the nurses and caregivers and bring treats to them. "She's such a doll," they'd say after she left. "Just like her mother, she is," another would say. "And not stuck up, even though she's got a lot of money now. She knows her parents' roots and never got too big for them," an older aide added. What passed as genuine love and concern was just the modus operandi for Maria. She knew full well how to play the game, having studied people from a young age, and knew exactly how to get what she "deserved" in life.

After Peg's admission, Maria soon realized that if Peg didn't recover, the courts would make Maria pay what she had promised in the contract she signed before Stuart's death. No one could tell her if Peg would recover or die, but the nurses intimated that Peg could die at any time. Maria knew she had to act—and act fast. Both Matt and Walter assumed Maria had been given the agency and had no idea she was to pay it off in installments. It was another secret Maria had to keep.

She had access to Stuart's old Selectric typewriter and typed up a "Promissory Note to Be Forgiven upon Death" that read, due to the fact Peg and Stuart never had children, and Maria was in essence their "adopted daughter," as sole surviving spouse, Peg forgave any promissory notes that Stuart had written Maria regarding the sale of the agency. Maria checked when she gave the last monies to Peg, found Peg's bank deposit slip, and dated the forgiven promissory note the very next day after the deposit, back in early June, two months before Peg's stroke. Then Maria found some old correspondence from Peg to several vendors in Peg's desk, went to the Xerox machine in the office, and successfully traced Peg's signature onto the document she had just written by placing the document over Peg's signature. It was a bit shaky, but after all, Peg was too. It looked good enough.

"May I speak to Rick please?" Maria asked the receptionist.

"It's Maria Keller calling." She still wasn't completely used to speaking her name, but she liked the way it sounded.

He got on the phone, and she said, "Rick, may I come by right now? I need you to notarize something. It will be worth your while." Within ten minutes, she was in Rick's office, and they had struck an agreement. She told him that she had come across this forgiveness note as she was gathering up Peg's "Memory Box" to bring up to Windemere. Peg had told her after Stuart's death that she intended to execute such a note but apparently never got the chance to have it notarized. Rick sat back in his chair, crossed his arms, raised his eyebrows, and looked skeptically at Maria, with a smirk on his face.

"Maria," he said, "do you actually believe I buy that?"

"It's true," said Maria. "This *is* Peg's signature. I just assumed this had been taken care of by Peg, but she obviously hadn't time to get it notarized before her stroke. They often told me they wanted me to have the agency, but until Peg dies, they wanted payments to ensure she wasn't lacking in resources. I'd be happy to pay you for this, as you know it means a great deal to me that their wishes are carried out."

She was shocked by the amount he extracted, and it wasn't what Maria had expected, but he was a hard bargainer, and they needed each other, so she agreed. She signed a note for Rick's payment. Then

Rick told her to come back at four o'clock and he'd have his secretary (the one who actually was the notary) seal and sign the "forgiven" promissory note, as well as his and her promissory note.

Before she left Rick's office, Rick said, "Maria. Once again, I keep hearing you and Owen are doing some more business together. This time with a new client. I warned you about a month ago of this. I used the expression then of 'loose lips sink ships,' remember?"

"What are you talking about, Rick?" she said.

"Maria, just remember one thing: I have my sources. I'm the only one you can be dealing with regarding title searches; I better not hear about Owen and you again. I've warned you enough already. Not Owen. Even if he's cheaper. Understand?" Rick warned, as he stared coldly into her eyes.

She said, "Rick, I only used Owen for a quick check on a title I was doing when I was overloaded. I hear you. Don't worry. I'm not dealing with him. Only you." She thought to herself, how does he know she was using Owen for a deal she didn't intend to cut Rick into that they had been doing? He knows *everything*, she thought, and she felt decidedly uncomfortable. Her stomach had been acting up recently. Maybe it was those pills that were supposed to make her less anxious that Walter had gotten from Doc Coffin. *I've got to keep my wits about me. Too much hangs on it*, she thought, trying to keep her face composed and natural.

He said, "Good. Make sure it stays that way. And don't go blabbing your mouth all over the place. Neither you nor I can afford it—literally and figuratively."

Maria left Rick's office and quickly went down Main Street where she entered the Dr. Daniel Fisher House and climbed the stairs to her second-floor office. She knew she was had by Rick, but there wasn't any other way getting around this one. She tried to toss off her worries about trusting him and immediately went back to work.

When she had closed the door, and left his office, Rick sat at his desk for a minute. He smiled: life is good. *She doesn't know what hit her. I have her by the balls!* he said to himself, oblivious to the idiocy of his analogy. And he strolled down Main Street to the Dock Street

Coffee Shop, with the same smile on his face, and was back in his office in thirty minutes.

When his secretary returned from lunch, he brought her Peg's document and the new one he and Maria had just signed for his own payment of "services rendered" and said, "Maria Keller couldn't wait. I verified Mrs. Baldwin's signature, and you know this is Maria's and mine. I need you to notarize both documents," he said, looking at her in his "don't ask questions, just do it" way. She hated to be put in these circumstances, but she knew better than to question him. She pulled out her notary seal from the desk, signed, and before she could date the Baldwin document, he said, "We need to predate that. According to the wording in the document, she had this drawn several months ago. The date you should put on her document is *June 1, 2015*. Put today's date on my own document for 'services rendered.'" Ellen felt her face burn. She didn't like him, but this was one of the few good year-round jobs on the island, and she knew there wasn't anything else that was better, but she resented him and what he made her do. She didn't look up at him, but she dated them as instructed and sealed both documents. Rick asked her to make three copies of Mrs. Baldwin's and give Maria two of them, as well as give her one copy of Maria's and Rick's documents. Although Ellen couldn't see what the Baldwin document contained, as it was several pages long, she did quickly see the second document between Rick and Maria. Maria owed him a lot of money now, but Ellen couldn't see that Rick had done anything near that amount of work for her. Why did Maria agree to pay him one hundred thousand dollars over a five-year period?

He took his two copies and put them in his safe. When Maria returned at four, Rick was out of the office. Ellen handed her the two envelopes. Maria owed Rick plenty now, but it was still worth her while. "Thank you, Ellen. Please let Rick know I was by and picked up the documents and thank him too. See ya!" said Maria as she opened the back door and let herself out. Ellen didn't like her either, but she was stuck in her job. A year-round job on the Vineyard was like winning a lottery. Most days, however, Ellen thought it was more like finding a used scratch ticket.

Chapter 33

Edgartown, Tuesday, October 6, 2015

Maria met Stephanie at the airport. It was built during World War II as a coastal patrol base. Gradually it got to be two runways and then a small control tower that was manned only from six in the morning to ten o'clock in the evening. She waved to Stephanie as she descended the Gulfstream her father owned, and Stephanie smiled broadly and also waved. Within a minute of leaving Airport Road, Maria's Range Rover pulled off to the right onto a dirt road, and Maria said to Stephanie, "Hold on. Oyster Watcha Road is rather bumpy especially at this time of year." Yet, the two women did not feel many bumps, due to the Range Rover's suspension system that was now vastly improved over earlier models. All the women could see for a few minutes were thickets of scrub pine and oak and the graying sky above.

Maria said, "I really think anyone on the Vineyard needs a car like this. So many of our best properties are located out of sight from paved roads and down windy dirt ones like this. I just got this one three weeks ago. I love it!"

Stephanie had already noticed it was the new LUX model and mentally thought Maria must be making a fortune. She also thought it was good she was in Maria's hands as she'd be the one to represent the best properties.

As they pulled up to the enclave, Maria pointed out the Artist's Studio in the scrub pines, and from a distance, Stephanie could see the tennis courts. Nearing the house, Stephanie noticed how big it was—it wasn't yet finished, but she could certainly appreciate its size and its Vineyard weathered shingled rambling look. She liked it.

Maria jumped out of the Rover and stood for a moment as she pointed out to Stephanie the various aspects: the guesthouse, the infinity swimming pool, and the beautiful view of the tip of Oyster Pond and leading out to the Atlantic. Maria explained that the other pond, to their right, also leading to the Atlantic, was called Watcha Pond, and therefore the lone road leading in from the Edgartown Tisbury Road was called Oyster Watcha Road. She went on to explain that at one point, the Wampanoags had tried to connect the two ponds, to release fish trapped in Watcha Pond after a winter's storm closed the outlet to the ocean, but for some unknown reason, the project was never completed. She also pointed out the "Mohu" osprey nest pole, which last year had just become active again after a decade or so. The nest itself was only one of sixty on the Vineyard. Although Maria could not possibly know then how important the name "Mohu" was to become, in essence indelibly defining her life and career, the nest pole was also the name of an estate up-island that became the single most talked about property on the Vineyard and beyond.

Stephanie listened in awe of Maria's local knowledge and was glad she had made the trip, despite the chilly damp wind and gray overcast skies unusual for this time in October. Maria continued, "Ospreys are big, loud, gregarious, and not shy around human beings. What makes them distinct, however, are their unmistakable and striking dark masks and the dark-light pattern of their wings when seen from below. See how high the nest poles are? For most of the breeding season, these large and carelessly built nests act as beacons for the birds. Ospreys are pack rats who build their nests' sides high with everything from branches, plastic bags, old kite string to small metal objects—anything they can find and carry. Traditionally they nested in the bare branches of dead trees, but now many nest on top of poles and platforms built by bird lovers like the one here called Mohu.

"They should go in a few weeks and return in the spring," Maria said. "You won't see the young ones until late in June and early July, and they will grow to almost the size of their parents by late summer or early fall. If you can see one with a telescope, you'll notice their young ones' black-and-white feathers are checkered in appearance, and you'll see their eyes are blazing orange. Later as they become adults, the eye color fades to the adult yellow. Another strange fact is that the young will not return north until the spring of their third year. And then, they will return to the same neighborhood where they were born."

"Maria, how do you know so much about all this history!" asked Stephanie. "I'm in awe."

"I grew up on the island, Stephanie, and it's just natural you know things like this. That's all," said Maria, who tossed this off with a shrug. She never spoke of her father or mother or how they earned the pittances they did, "honorable" people or not. It was still degrading to Maria. "Come on, let's go into the house. I'll walk you through it."

They spent the next hour there, talking about how great it was the house wasn't yet finished as then Stephanie could choose the colors, countertops, fixtures, and tiles. Maria assured her the builders were first-rate and could have the property ready by next May 15. Maria knew that she could string Stephanie along for few more weeks after that if her plan to leave the island had been delayed a bit ("It's not worth it for you to come up now—the weather here has been horrible, and everyone is way behind with their work. Why not wait until you come back from Italy in late July?"). Stephanie had already told Maria that her father had already rented a large home in the Tuscan hills outside of Florence in Sesto Fiorentino next year from early June, when Stephanie's girls got out of prep school, through July, so the entire extended family wouldn't be on the Vineyard until August. Maria had also made a mental note to contact Stephanie's father to see if she could list his house for June and July.

Maria went on to say to Stephanie that she would act as Stephanie's clerk of the works and often did the same thing for others whose houses were being built. Her fee was not cheap, but she told Stephanie that this could become almost a half-time job in order to make sure it was all to Stephanie's specifications. The two women then went outside and walked the property where the pool and guesthouse were located, and then went over to the Artist's Studio and Har-Tru courts. It was all going to be one fantastic property when finished, Stephanie thought, and she was ready to sign papers on it.

"Let me drop you off at the Charlotte Inn. They're waiting for you, and I have to run up to the nursing home to give the nurses a little treat. I know them well now as I try to see Peg Baldwin several times a day. She had a stroke a few months ago," said Maria.

"Is that the person for whom your agency is named?" asked Stephanie.

"It was her husband's agency. He founded it in the sixties, and it became the best on the island. I went to work for him when I was still in high school, and Stuart and Peg practically adopted me. Stuart died in 2009, and he wanted me to run the agency. Peg's a dear. I try to visit the nurses too," said Maria.

"Oh, I wish I lived on an island," said Stephanie. "It just seems that everyone cares so much for each other, and the pace of life is so much better than the hustle and bustle of New York, with its impersonal lifestyle."

"Well, not everything is perfect here, Stephanie," Maria said. "But you're right: we do look after each other," she said with a note of irony that only she understood what it was that was meant.

Chapter 34

Edgartown, Tuesday, October 6, 2015, evening

Stephanie had dinner alone at the Charlotte Inn at The Terrace, the glass-paned conservatory dining room, the stark white linens contrasting with potted living trees and ferns, and ivy-covered lattice allowing the vines to reach and intertwine among the ceiling's high whitewashed beams. The dark green contrasted with the pristine white, and it was like dining in a lush garden setting. It made Stephanie think of the US Botanic Garden she loved to visit when she was staying with her friend who lived on Capitol Hill on that charming little street called Duddington Place. People there nicknamed it Brigadoon. She had once thought of moving to DC, but the thought of spending time with her friend also meant spending time with her friend's husband, whom she couldn't stand. Why she ended up with him was beyond Stephanie. So many women settle for so little. Stephanie sometimes regretted being single, but all she had to do was think of them, and her regrets flew out the window.

Service was unobtrusive but exacting; the wine steward had appeared as soon as she was settled and quietly asked what she would like. Stephanie took a moment deciding between a cocktail or just a really good bottle of wine she could later bring up to her room. "I think I'll see the wine list, thank you."

She took a look around the room and remarked how different the dining room was from the rest of the inn with its Edwardian decor and walls painted dark hunter green against which hung a myriad of nineteenth-century English oils. Stately mahogany furniture polished to a patina contrasted with silver writing sets and bronze hunting statues; restored and highly polished antique brass door latches were found on every door; silver bowls, writing sets on the desks, and antique silver boudoir water tumblers and carafes on the bedside tables. Goose down pillows and white duvets were on the beds, and the heavy European silk and linen floor-to-ceiling draperies lent an extra layer of comfort and peace to the room. There were fireplaces in every public and private room. In fact, Stephanie was delighted to see hers had been lit when she walked into her room, which looked out upon the gray-shingled *The Gazette* building.

The steward returned and asked if she had looked at the menu; he could suggest something if she'd like. Stephanie responded, "The Quail to begin with," and he asked if she wanted a special bottle or one from their standard cellar. In a good mood with the pleasant surroundings, and feeling proud of herself that she had taken the initiative to come up to the island and look at the property, Stephanie answered, "I'd like a special bottle tonight," and smiled in his eyes.

"I must warn you, I appreciate fine wines, and the one I'm going to first suggest may be a 'little bit too special,'" he said with a twinkle. He explained why (the price), but she agreed to it. He was astonished but didn't bat an eyelash when she nodded her head, and he said, "Perfect, I'll decant it in just a minute," and was gone before she realized it. Soon the steward poured a small amount of the wine in his tastevin and sniffed, swirled and then sipped it, and nodded his approval. He waited while she took her first sip, and she was delighted with the wine as it slid down her throat. She smiled and nodded. "This is lovely. Thank you."

There was one other couple there, and she recognized them as that attorney her father sometimes used for local matters, Rick Maron, and whom she thought must be his wife but whose name she couldn't remember. Just then, Laura, an attractive blonde with style, and Jared, equally good-looking—tanned and dressed in a crisp white button-down, came into the room together, went over to say hello to Rick and his wife, and Stephanie heard them call her *Janet*. Then they came over to Stephanie to greet her. "Welcome, Stephanie. It's so good to see you here, even though it's so late in the season. Maria called us to say you'd be here tonight. We're so glad to have you."

"I'm delighted to be here. It's so quiet in the off-season, but staying here is a treat. I love the beautiful antiques and paintings you've acquired, and the fireplace in my room is perfect for such a blustery and stormy night. The wind sounds ferocious now," said Stephanie.

"Jared said the storm advisory flags were now up—he had just been down to the harbor and saw the two red flags flapping wildly in the wind. It's a good night to be inside. I'm so glad you're comfortable. How is your dinner?"

Stephanie said it was fabulous, which it was. She continued, "The quail were perfectly seared and delicious with your cranberry champagne sauce."

Jared said, "The cranberries are some of our early ones and were picked at Katama just a week ago. The quail comes from Morning Glory Farm. Jim keeps us in stock even in the off-season. We try to locally source everything…except the wine! I see you've chosen one of my favorite wines: the Château Léoville-Las Cases '09 was a fabulous year, better than '05 in my opinion."

Stephanie responded by nodding and motioning them to sit with her. "I went with your sommelier's choice, and he was right. Please join me and share this fabulous bottle," said Stephanie. "It's much too good to drink alone."

She noticed Rick was looking in her direction, and then he quickly looked away. Jared called over the steward who brought two additional crystal goblets with a tall stem, correct for serving Bordeaux, and poured each a small amount. *At $300 a bottle, Stephanie is certainly enjoying herself,* Jared thought. *And,* I'm *glad she is.* Laura was very welcoming and chatted a bit about life on the Vineyard, while sipping a little bit of her wine. *No wonder she stays so thin,* thought Stephanie. Jared had a full glass and clearly appreciated all of it. *What a great couple to know here. I know I've made the right decision,* said Stephanie to herself.

While Jared and Laura were getting up and thanking Stephanie for the wine, Rick and his wife went over to say hello to the inn owners on their way out of the dining room. He briefly nodded to Stephanie. The two couples walked out together. Stephanie sat for another moment and then asked the steward to send up the rest of the bottle to her room.

In the foyer, Jared said discreetly to Rick that Stephanie was here visiting a big complex out on Oyster Watcha Road that wasn't yet finished, and it seemed as if she might buy it. Rick looked puzzled and said the only thing he knew about out there were the Freedman Developers, who had run into some financial difficulties and stopped the project.

Jared shrugged his shoulders and said, "Perhaps all they needed was a buyer like Stephanie to finish it? Maria told Stephanie she could move in May 15 if she acted now."

With that comment, Rick jerked his head around and said, "Maria? Maria was showing her the property today?"

Jared answered, "Yes, they spent the day together, and she's picking her up tomorrow morning after breakfast to bring her back to the airport."

Rick took that in slowly and then said good night to Jared and Laura, and Rick and Janet walked down the steps onto South Summer Street and up Cooke Street to their house.

Rick was thinking all the way and was uncharacteristically silent. He usually got so volatile after drinking. Just like all the Middle Easterners. Whatever got him quiet, Janet thought, was a blessing. *Carpe silentium!* she said to herself. When they walked the three blocks to their home, hurrying because of the stormy cold winds, he said, "I've got to go to the office," and went to the old stables on the property that he had converted to his law office. She went immediately to bed.

At the Charlotte Inn, Stephanie nestled into her soft comfy bed, plumped up the goose down pillows, and poured herself the last glass of wine. It was a perfect evening. And day. The winds blew outside the paned glass, and this only added to Stephanie's feeling of comfort and having arrived at a safe haven.

The storm had suddenly cleared in the night, and the morning was crisp and clear, not a cloud in the sky. Stephanie had earlier called Maria to say she'd get a taxi to the airport and not to bother to pick her up. She said she had a lovely dinner and evening at the Charlotte Inn, and she'd be in touch about the property when she got back to New York, as she *was* interested.

Chapter 35

Edgartown, Wednesday, October 7, 2015

Fall came late on the Vineyard. However, you could still see a couple of roses hanging on to the picket fences and a small patch of green grass here and there. The wind off the water was chilling, and a few of the fishermen stayed in their trucks at the parking lot, talking through the open windows, where they and Jon's Taxi liked to hang out and shoot the breeze after sunup. "So-and-so went off-island to Hyannis and got a new truck." "The Black Dog's opening yet another new store." "Next summer's going to be busy." "Steamship expects a record year," etc. Same old.

Matt was a regular at Dock Street again and would stop in around seven o'clock just about every morning. Don would put on the linguica when he saw him, and Mary placed a cup of coffee on the worn-out Formica countertop. Usually Larry and some of the courthouse people were there, as Bob and Terry, and they'd settle in to discuss the weather, any accidents or scanner reports that they may have heard, the ferry delays if any, and whether or not the scalloping was good this year, while eating their breakfasts.

Patterns are predictable on an island where everyone knows what everyone else is doing before it happens. Clem, the UPS driver, would not waste his time going to someone's home to deliver a package. He'd simply figure out where they were: Dock Street early in the morning for the gang, or sighting someone's car in the Stop & Shop parking lot, and, even more frequently, knowing who would be at

Al's Package Store or Your Market waiting for the 11:00 a.m. liquor sales curfew to be lifted. People on the island liked their liquor.

The following day after Rick and Janet had dinner at the Charlotte Inn, Rick was waiting in the Yacht Club parking lot across from the Dock Street Coffee Shop in his Cherokee. As soon as he saw Matt go into the Coffee Shop, he got out of the Jeep and followed him in. "Hey, fellas. Anyone got a spare dollar for a cup of coffee for a poor starving attorney?" he yelled out as he slipped onto one of the wobbly red stools next to Matt. That brought a few guffaws and stories about lawyers and sharks, and everyone slipped back into their conversations.

"As I said yesterday, I wanted to talk to you about child support," said Rick. "How's it going, Matt?"

Matt just shrugged his shoulders and said, "As good as it can be, I guess."

"How's Heather doing now? Has she settled in with her new father? I mean stepfather, sorry," said Rick, who knew exactly what he was saying.

"Hard to say. I tried to get her for the weekend but was told she had riding lessons at Scrubby Neck, and then she had some friends having sleepovers, so I couldn't get to see her," mumbled Matt.

"Riding lessons?! That costs a bundle. I looked into that last spring for Janet's niece, and it was too damn expensive. Guess they have the money now! By the way, have you had your child support adjusted since they got married? Even though she's graduating this year, she still has another year before she's eighteen, and that can add up for you. You have the money worries, they don't."

"Nah. Haven't got around to it, I guess," said Matt, stirring his coffee aimlessly and looking at his half-eaten breakfast. Little orangey globules had formed where the linguica had sat. The egg yolk was untouched and looked like a bright-yellow smiley face without the face itself. He felt like stabbing it until it squirted out, oozing life until it was a flat, empty void. He lay down his fork and looked at Rick.

"Well, don't be a fool. If they can afford riding lessons and the Yacht Club this summer, then maybe you're paying too damn much!" said Rick.

"Yacht Club?" asked Matt. "They joined the Yacht Club? Her mother cleaned for those people, and Maria said she always hated them, the way they treated her family!"

"Well, she certainly doesn't hate them now, does she? Barbara put in their names last year. It was official a week or so ago. It's sure to stir up a hornet's nest with some of the members, if it hasn't already.

"She sure got a sweet deal with Stuart and Peg, I'll tell you that," added Rick.

"She had to pay them, and it was a fair price, but it certainly wasn't a gift. I can't remember right now how much, but that was factored into child support. She owed Stuart and then Peg for the agency. She had way more debts than I did, and the judge set the child support based on that," said Matt.

"Look, I don't want to upset you, Matt, and I know I mentioned this to you recently, and I can't say anything more than what I am now, but I think it would be worth your time to go back to court and see just what debts she may have at the moment. You might be surprised, and it could be to your advantage," said Rick in a low voice. "Let me just put it this way: all women are bitches, and she's definitely a woman."

Matt quickly turned his head toward Rick. "What do you mean! Is she holding out something from me?" and his voice grew louder so that a few of the guys stopped talking and looked their way.

"Matt. Keep your voice down. I can't say more. But I have my sources. Think about what I've said," said Rick in a lowered voice. "I can't represent you, but I can suggest Bill. I can't say any more, so don't ask."

Matt looked like he'd explode. His face turned red, and the spoon in his hand started shaking on the coffee cup saucer. Larry got up from the stool several seats down from Matt and Rick and gave Rick a meaningful look as to Matt's agitated state. Larry came up behind them and put his hands on both Rick's and Matt's shoulders and said, "Hi, guys. You two cooking up something," and smiled, hoping to diffuse Matt's growing unrest. "Any interest in going over to the Rod and Gun this afternoon? There's a target practice at three.

We need to be out ninety minutes later to make the 'half-hour-before-sunset' rule. You both want to join us?"

Rick gave Larry a thank-you look and said, "Sounds good to me. Matt, are you in? It'll do you some good."

At first, Matt didn't answer. And Rick had to say, "Matt? Can you make it today?"

Matt nodded his head and then said sarcastically out of the side of his mouth, "Yeah, I've got some specific targets in mind, and I think I'll be a good shot! Just wait and see. Yeah, I'll meet you all there," and he put down his money and got up, still red-faced and trembling a bit.

Rick and Larry exchanged another look and walked out with him. Matt had parked down at the Town Dock across from the Old Sculpin Gallery and headed off in that direction. Rick and Larry lingered a bit and shook their heads. Rick told Larry that Matt had just discovered that Maria might have hidden money from him in the divorce that would have affected his child support payments. "He asked me if I knew anything, and I said I couldn't say, but that if he had any doubts or knowledge she was hiding monies, he should get in touch with Bill and see about a hearing in court."

Larry shook his head and said, "That woman is poison. She thinks she's Miss La-Di-Da now, prancing around in that Range Rover with her off-island imported husband. I know Matt was kidding about 'specific targets in mind,' but I'm worried about his state of mind. Afghanistan didn't help him at all—Jesus, I'm surprised he hasn't killed her yet. Not that we'd blame him with that bitch, but he needs to get away from all this, before he actually does kill her—or someone else—if he were to fly off the handle one day. Can you believe what her father would think if he were here today! God rest his soul. Her mother probably doesn't have a clue. Now there was a good man, Manny Almeida. The salt of the earth. How can the apple fall so far from the tree?"

Rick said all they could do was to look out for Matt's interests and try to diffuse any situation. "Perhaps the target practice this afternoon would get rid of some of his aggression today?" The two men talked a few minutes and then left, saying they'd see each other at 3:00 p.m.

Matt, meanwhile, had continued on out to the Harbor View Hotel and Starbuck's Neck. The day had become sunny, but the wind was still brisk. No one was in the outer harbor, and the Edgartown Lighthouse stood in sharp contrast to the landscape. It was an old, stocky cast-iron tower with a white base about thirty-five feet high topped off by another ten feet outfitted in a distinctively black "top hat." It had been barged here in the early 1880s. Ten years after it arrived in Edgartown, the Harbor View Hotel was built on the bluff overlooking the lighthouse. Over the years, shifting sands and storms filled in the land where the wooden walkway once stretched between the lighthouse and the mainland. It was now part of the mainland, and the beach was called Lighthouse Beach. Ironically, the Harbor View Hotel seemed to stand watch over the lighthouse, while the lighthouse stood watch over the harbor. Matt understood this watchdog relationship between the two monuments located at Starbuck's Neck and muttered, "But who is watching the townspeople?" The answer was no one at this point—although someone should have been.

Matt stood for a while looking out at the flat shoreline of Chappaquiddick and the sparkling sun on the water. He liked the peacefulness here. It spoke of time gone by when life was judged by the sea and the winds, not by greed and land and social standing.

Chapter 36

Edgartown, Wednesday, October 7, 2015, late afternoon

Within ten minutes of leaving off Stephanie at the Charlotte Inn, Maria was on Beach Road heading to Windemere Nursing Home. With her was Peg's "Memory Box." Maria showed the pretty pink-and-white box to the staff and explained this was Peg's most prized possession in the world and that it would do her a world of good to have it next to her bed in the nursing home where she could see it. She told them that inside were all sorts of old letters from Stuart, Christmas cards, an old passport, a few papers, photos, and all sorts of mementos and that Peg used to love to look at it in the quiet of her own home, as it brought back such wonderful memories. The staff thought the Memory Box was a wonderful idea and that Maria was such a caring, loving "daughter" to Peg.

In fact, Maria had found a box in Vineyard Haven at Shirley's Hardware Store, where she hardly ever went, and also had bought a glue gun, lace, ribbons, and pretty cotton fabric and had decorated it herself. She then smudged it, tore a little of one corner off, and slightly wrinkled the fabric. She foraged around Peg's bedroom for photos, letters, etc., and stuffed them inside. It looked good. It looked old. It looked authentic.

Maria put the box in front of Peg and smiled broadly. "Peg, look what I brought you! Your Memory Box!" With the nurse in the room, Maria opened the box, which now lay in Peg's lap, and began bringing out items for Peg to "see." Maria gently spoke to Peg about what each item was. Peg stared straight ahead and didn't respond, but the nurse thought it was heartwarming to see how devoted Maria was to her, regardless of Peg's comprehension level—if any. When Maria got up to go, the nurse placed the box right next to Peg's hospital bed, as Maria had suggested, where Peg might be able to see it when they turned her. No one was sure if Peg really understood anything or not, but they liked thinking she had her special box right next to her, to give her comfort. What a wonderful woman that Maria Keller was, the nurse thought. And, the other nurses agreed when they heard about Peg's Memory Box and Maria's caring nature. She was certainly a wonderful woman and a true islander.

Maria increased the number of times during the day she went to see Peg once she had the Memory Box. She now went several times a day. And all the staff saw just how devoted Maria was to Peg, visiting in the morning, afternoon, and evening, bringing out the Memory Box contents and talking to Peg. There were photos of Stuart, Peg, and Maria at Christmastime in the office or having cocktails after work sitting in their backyard under that big old elm tree, some Christmas cards, and a menu from a Paris restaurant. Maria would sit and reminisce with Peg, combing her hair, talking to her even though Peg couldn't respond. If a staff member came in while Maria was visiting, Maria would reach in the box and pull out something and say to Peg, "Remember the Collins family? They were such fun. This is a lovely Christmas card from them, Peg!" And she'd turn and show the staff the Christmas card photo of what was actually Maria's sister's family, although of course the staff wouldn't know. And, the more the staff saw how caring Maria was, the more they loved her and talked about what a wonderful person she was, and just how awful other people were to their families, others barely coming but once a month, and yet others just coming to visit on Easter and Christmas with a lily or a poinsettia, as if that was enough. But here was Maria, daily and trying to communicate with Peg about her past, not knowing if Peg understood anything, but clearly loving her.

At the end of that week, the doctor called Maria in the late afternoon and said he'd like to meet with her. They were concerned that Peg hadn't made any progress. Maria went to the nursing home the next morning right after rounds, and the doctor introduced himself. The head nurse who had the most dealings with Maria was there too. Both looked deeply concerned.

"Maria. We've asked to speak to you because of your deep relationship with Mrs. Baldwin. We know how much you each care for each other, but unfortunately, she is not making any progress, and we are not equipped to handle long-term cases like this. Peg will have to go to the Cape, and we'd like to do that as soon as possible, but wanted to tell you in person," said the doctor.

Maria looked startled and started to object, "But can't we wait just another week and see if there's improvement? Yesterday, I think I saw her move her eyes toward the card I held up. I'm sure she saw it! I know if I keep coming to see her, she'll get better. There just hasn't been time enough yet. Please don't take her off-island!"

She added, "Peg has enough money to pay for the week—it might be that it's all she needs to show signs of improvement. I can arrange to be here for most of the day during this week and really work with her. Please just give us one more chance. Please!"

The doctor was just there for a week's rotation and had never been to the Vineyard before. He was struck by this young woman and her love and concern for Mrs. Baldwin. He talked privately to the nurse for a few seconds, and then they sat down again across from Maria. "Nurse Harriman has said they could accommodate Mrs. Baldwin for another week, out of regard for your relationship with her, but after that, we need to make other arrangements. There's a good facility in East Falmouth that would take her permanently, and it's only a ferry ride there, so you'd be able to visit on weekends. But you do understand that this is only a grace period, and it cannot be extended without significant improvement that frankly we do not expect to happen."

Maria started crying and thanked them. She promised she'd try her hardest to get Peg to respond, but she understood ultimately that Peg would have to be cared for in a specialized long-term care facility. She pushed back her chair, still crying, and said, "I need to see Peg now. Thank you," and she quickly left, with them sitting there looking at each other and shaking their heads. "Isn't this pathetic? A young woman who'd do anything for Mrs. Baldwin, yet we can't keep

Mrs. Baldwin here, and it breaks my heart. That poor unfortunate woman should know just how devoted Maria is to her. I wish there were a way to let Mrs. Baldwin know that, but I'm afraid she simply cannot understand or comprehend anything," he said in a dejected voice. And the nurse sighed, nodded her head, and also excused herself from the office. She too had a tear in her eye as she walked back to the nurse's station to tell them of the decision to keep Peg here for one week only.

As Maria went down the corridor to Peg's wing and the nurse's station, she saw two of the nurses whispering and heard the Baldwin name. As soon as they noticed Maria, they stopped whispering. It was obvious they knew of the plans to remove Peg to the mainland. One of them gave Maria a hug and said, "It will be all right, dear. I'm sure she knows how much you care."

Chapter 37

Edgartown, Thursday, October 8, 2015, early evening

Maria was already dressed, and when Walter came down for his coffee, she told him about the doctors saying they'd give Peg a few more days, but after that, they had to move her off-island. Maria cried softly and said, "She was like my mother. I'm going to miss her so much." Walter comforted her as best he could, and then she said she was going to the office for a while as she had lots to do. Walter indicated he was going to Vineyard Haven for lunch with Nick at the Black Dog but that he'd see her later. He gave her a kiss and whispered to her, "Maria, Peg knows you love her even if she can't express it. You're a good woman. I love you."

When she returned home after lunch, he was still gone, so she left a note for Walter.

> I've gone to see Peg and then my mother. I'll have dinner there tonight. I didn't think you'd want to go. See you later.
>
> Love XOXO
>
> P.S. Heather is with Matt for the night and back tomorrow in time for the church supper.

She went upstairs and changed into slacks and a thick turtleneck. In the medicine cabinet, she removed a dozen pills Doc Coffin had given her with strict orders not to use with alcohol. He knew she liked to drink and made sure she understood these should only be taken four or more hours after any alcoholic drink. She put them in her pocket and went to the kitchen. In the pan, she heated up three cups of Cointreau, one cup of red wine that was opened, and a handful of spices: cinnamon sticks, nutmeg, ginger, cardamom, cloves, dried orange peel, and the pills. Then she added two cups of honey. When it had cooled, she poured out the contents of a ten-ounce Ocean Spray cranberry juice bottle, poured the mixture in, screwing on the top tightly. She then took a second bottle and unscrewed its cap, emptied the bottle of about one quarter of its contents, and then screwed it back on again. She put the full bottle down deep in her handbag and then went to the dining room, where she took a few cut flowers from the table and put them in the little basket, along with the "Ocean Spray, spice, and alcohol" mixture.

Maria hopped into her Range Rover and headed off to Windemere. She timed it so she'd get there as the daytime shift was leaving and the evening shift was coming on. Ordinarily they didn't let visitors in at that busy time, but because she was a regular and never a bother, they always let Maria come in. If dinner was ready, Maria would spoon-feed Peg the soft food she required.

"Good evening, Maria. It's a bit busy now as you know with the shift change, but Peg is in her room and has been resting—still no change, dear, I'm sorry to say," said the main nurse in Peg's corridor.

"I brought her some cranberry juice and some berry Jell-O. I'll see if she will take it for me. She normally loves a tart taste more than sugary," said Maria.

"That will be fine, dear. Do your best. You know where the nightclothes are if she spills a lot. You're such a dear. I do hope Peg knows you're here. We are still very worried about her lack of response, and we don't really think she's improving, but you know that already, dear, from your talk with the doctor."

"I know that." Maria sighed, looking forlorn but yet determined. "I'm not going to give up now," she said. "I just can't do that to Peg and to Stuart, rest his soul. There are many true-life accounts of people with strokes or in a coma who suddenly come out of them and act as if they had never been 'asleep.' I pray each day that Our Lady will revive Peg. I believe it can happen." And, she crossed herself.

"Well, no harm in believing, dear. You just go in there now and stay with her. I'm off in a few minutes but will be here tomorrow. Mary Gentle's on tonight, and she always looks in on Peg. Peg's in good hands, dear."

"Thank you, Mrs. Rebello. Tell Mary that Peg will be fine with me, and there's no need for her to come by while I'm here. I'll let the staff know when I leave. Good night, and thank you again. I'll see you tomorrow," said Maria. And Mrs. Rebello bustled off down the corridor to check in on the next patient.

"Peg. It's Maria. I brought you some juice. I'm going to help you with it. Let's tilt your head back so you can get it down your throat. There, that's a good girl."

It was a disgusting process: prying open Peg's mouth, trying to slip in the baby food before her tongue pushed it out again, and trying to wipe up the spittle as it came out. But feeding wasn't as messy as getting her to drink out of the sippy cups they used for her. Most of the liquid juices ended up on the large bib they put on her. It was a wonder she got any nutrition out of this entire process. It wouldn't matter after tonight, Maria mused. And, after all, Peg always did like a drink before dinner. Well, tonight she'd have a good stiff one and go out happy. It was more distressing than Maria had thought. Fernanda had been so much easier. There was only just so much Peg could swallow before it gurgled out of her throat and mouth. Maria had anticipated some of this and had also brought old cleaning cloths with her for a bib, but at one point, she had to stroke Peg's throat to get the liquid down. She didn't want her to choke to death—in fact drown—as that would be certainly suspicious, so it took more time than she had planned for. She nervously continued, all the while looking at the doorway in case the night nurse Judy stopped by. Within ten long minutes, Maria had got Peg to swallow most of the bottle, and she let Peg slump back on the pillow and laid her on her side. She put the bottle with the pills and alcohol back in her purse and took out a bottle of the Ocean Spray cranberry juice that she had partially emptied out at home and put that on the table next to

Peg's bed. She left the spoon in the Jell-O on the bedside table. She made sure the "Memory Box" was at her side and placed Peg's hand on it as if she had patted it. She thought maybe she should kiss her goodbye, but decided she couldn't do it after all. That whole process of force-feeding Peg was very upsetting to her, but she managed to push aside the images of her stroking the juice down Peg's throat, and she walked determinedly out into the corridor.

She found Mary tending to Mr. Bassett and poked her head in the door. "Peg didn't want the Jell-O I made, but seemed to enjoy the cranberry juice. She drank a fair bit, just about a quarter, so I also left the unfinished bottle by her bed. You might want to refrigerate it as if, tomorrow, she likes it as much as she did tonight, there will still be some for her breakfast. There's no sense in my staying any longer a she's sleeping soundly. She does seem *very* tired tonight. I've turned down the lights and made sure she's well tucked in, so you probably won't even need to check in on her now. I'll see everyone tomorrow evening again. Have a good night."

"G'night, dear. We all appreciate all the care you give Peg," said Mary. She then lowered her voice so Mr. Bassett couldn't hear and said, "I wish his family showed as much attention to him as you do to Peg. It's really a crime they don't come and visit him. He's no trouble at all and is very sweet. He just doesn't hear well, and it's frustrating to them when they visit," and she shook her head and gave Maria a pat on the back. Maria smiled back at Mary and shrugged her shoulders as if to say she didn't understand some people either.

In the Rover, on her way back to Edgartown by Beach Road, Maria looked at the stars. Her mother had always told her that when people die, they become one of the stars looking down at those of us still here on earth. Maria was a little disconcerted with the thought that Peg might now be looking down at Maria. She didn't like the thought of Peg watching her, knowing what Maria had really done. She shivered, abruptly turned off WMVY, and rode in silence to the Bend-in-the-Road. There, she pulled over and broke down, sobbing and sobbing, her voice wracking with deep guttural sounds until she could recover herself. She then abruptly stopped crying. That was enough emotion, and it wouldn't serve her well. She brushed her hair back off her forehead and pulled out onto the road again and continued straight into town without wavering.

A patrol car passed her, and Sargent Searle looked back in the mirror. That was Maria. What was she doing parked there? He was about ready to turn around but saw in his rearview mirror that she had just pulled back out onto the road. The night was beautiful: stars everywhere and the beginning of the peak moon, the best time for fishing as anyone knows.

He glanced again in his mirror, and the Rover was still slowly advancing behind him. He guessed she was okay, but it was weird. What a bitch. What she did to Matt was inexcusable. And, that new husband of hers was such a phony. He came into town like a carpetbagger and then latched on to her. *Must have realized she was rolling in dough...maybe she'd get what's coming to her one day*, he mused. And then he turned his attention to the moon again. It was so quiet and still, watching over the sea and land. It was silent, and like the stars, the moon saw everything but never said a word. He passed the Triangle and went down Upper Main, the moon following him, and turned onto Cooke Street and then right onto Pease's Point Way, where he checked his car in at the police station.

Chapter 38

Edgartown, Friday, October 9, 2015, 8:00 a.m.

Walter answered the phone. Maria was still sleeping.

"Hello. This is the Keller residence. Walter speaking.

"Yes, I can get her. She's still sleeping, but I can wake her up if you think it's important. What! When was this? She was just there last night visiting. Oh my god. Give me a minute. I want to let her know there's some bad news coming. Thank you," and Walter put down the phone and went upstairs to the bedroom.

"Maria, can you wake up please?" As she responded with a nod and then propped herself up on her elbow, Walter said, "It's the hospital. I'm afraid there's bad news." He handed her the phone and sat down beside her on the bed, with his arm around her.

"Oh no! It can't be! I was just there last night, and she seemed about the same, or almost the same—she was perhaps a bit more tired than usual. Oh, poor Peg! Was there anyone there when she passed? I hope someone was there with her," Maria cried into the phone.

"You just found her a few minutes ago? When did she pass?" she asked. They talked a few more minutes, and then Maria asked what happens next—should she call the funeral home, or is that something Windemere did? Maria nodded and said she'd be glad to do this. "I'm the closest thing Peg had to family. I want to make sure it's done the way Peg wanted. I can handle everything, but I need to call her attorney, Thom Osborn. We never talked about burial or cremation. I am so sad," she said, sobbing.

When she had stopped crying enough to say, "Goodbye, and thank you for calling," she put the phone back down on the receiver. Walter hugged her and said what so many people had said before: "Peg was lucky to have you. You were so loving to her. Whether she could express herself or not, I'm sure she knew you were there for her. If she could have talked, you would know this. She's in better hands now. And, unless a miracle happened, next week she would have had to have been moved to that nursing home on the Cape, and neither one of you would have been happy. What did they tell you?"

"It was Mrs. Rebello, my mother's old friend who works day shifts. She went in about an hour ago as that's when they usually got Peg up, but she was sound asleep, so Mrs. Rebello let her be and went to see Mr. Bassett. When she had got him up and breakfast was delivered, she went back to Peg's room and tried to rouse her. That's when Mrs. Rebello realized she wasn't sleeping but that she had passed in the night sometime. She said Peg looked so peaceful, and there was no sign of distress or fear. Her eyes were closed, and she was lying on her side, looking as if she was asleep."

"Maria, I'm so sorry. What do we need to do?" asked Walter. "I heard you say you'd call Thom. Do you want me to get him on the phone now for you?"

"Let me get up and wash my face. I must look like a mess. I'll come downstairs in a minute and call from there. Is there any coffee?" Maria went into the bathroom and looked in the mirror. She was not a pretty crier. Red eyes and nose, and her complexion was blotchy. She rinsed her face and tidied up and put on her cotton pique robe that Walter had given her last fall for her birthday. She went downstairs. All she could think of was that Mrs. Rebello had said she looked peaceful and that she died in her sleep. She was sure now there wouldn't be an autopsy. There never were on the island unless it was a clear sign of a violent or accidental death. Whichever doctor was available on the island at the time would pronounce someone dead, and if in those rare cases of accident or murder, he would act as a fill-in coroner. The last one she recalled hearing about was in the summer of 1969. Mary Jo Kopechne. Doc Coffin was going to have to perform the autopsy at the funeral home, as no one else was on the island to do this. But when he arrived at the funeral home, he learned the young woman's body had just been flown off-island by a Kennedy aide to her family's home in Pennsylvania.

The Vineyard's funeral director told Doc that when the girl's body arrived there, he himself had thumped on her chest, but no water came out. There wasn't any water in her lungs. And, the skin diver, whom she also knew, said the body was found in the back seat, her face pressed up toward the interior back window—in an air bubble—attempting to breathe the little oxygen that remained, until there was no more. In other words, she suffocated. One thing Maria always remembered: Mary Jo did not drown. But the Kennedys were powerful then, and they stepped in—moving the body and putting out the word that it was an accidental drowning. If the truth had been told, the public would know that she was alive after the accident and, if pulled out, could have survived.

Chapter 39

Edgartown, Friday, October 9, 2015, 9:00 a.m.

"Hello, Thom? This is Maria. I just had a sad call from Windemere. Peg passed sometime in the night. They thought she was sleeping this morning when they first went in, and they let her be for the moment. When they went back to get her up, she wouldn't respond, and Mrs. Rebello then realized she had passed over. They called me since I'm the one who's been visiting Peg, and they didn't know whom else to call. I said I'd let you know. I'm more than happy to arrange things with the funeral home and church, but didn't know what Peg wanted in terms of burial or cremation.

"I know. I agree, Thom. It's the last of the old-time generations we've had here. I saw her last night, and when I left, she was sleeping. She seemed more tired than usual, but it didn't seem unusual—just tired. Poor thing. It seems as if she just never woke up, so that's as much as we could wish for anyone. That at least makes me feel better," Maria said.

"I suppose you are going up there to bring a copy of her will and get the body released to the funeral home. There's also a 'Memory Box' that held all sorts of mementos Peg had treasured over the years, and there is a sealed letter 'Upon My Death' that you should look at. It must contain something about her last wishes you should know about. Just have the funeral home call me when you're ready, and I'll go pick out a casket for her. I can also notify the *Gazette* and the *Times* and contact Jack at Saint Andrews regarding a service. Please let me know if she had written something specific, and I'll make sure it's done.

"You're welcome, Thom. It gives me pleasure to do this for her."

Maria put down the phone and took a sip of the coffee. She looked awful, Walter thought. Puffy, haggard, and her wiry dark hair a snarled mess. Her bathrobe didn't help her any, either, even if it was one of those fancy hotel robes. It made her look like a lumpy bag of potatoes. It was taking all he could to put his arm around her, much less anything else. He shuddered to think of her dressing in front of him in the morning. He wondered if he should bring up a diet or "both of them cutting back a bit" at some other time. Not now, of course. He continued to stare for a few seconds, and then he brought himself back to the present.

Walter wanted to ask but didn't dare. He wondered if Peg had left Maria the house and other assets. Maria already had the agency, so at least she got that before she died. Walter began calculating the value of the house and land in today's market and thought it would bring at least two million. She must have had a lot in investments too. Not that he wanted to be lugubrious so soon after Peg died, but it could very well be that they stood to inherit a nice little bundle. Prompted by this prospect, he cheered up and gave her a kiss on the forehead and murmured, "Maria, I'm so proud of the way you treated Stuart and Peg. You were every inch the daughter they never had."

Chapter 40

Edgartown, Friday, October 9, 2015, 11:30 a.m.

Thom shook his head. He was back in his office after having been to the hospital to sign papers and find the envelope Maria had mentioned regarding Peg's last wishes. He couldn't understand why Peg hadn't come to him to execute the Forgiveness Note when she and Stuart had always used him for legal matters all these years, and, before him, his father. The trusts, the wills, power of attorney, health care proxies—everything regarding their assets and wishes had always been in Thom's hands. He waited a moment and then picked up the phone.

"Ellen, this is Thom. Is Rick around?" Rick picked up at once, knowing full well why Thom called. Thom shot the breeze for a while, talking about the upcoming Duck's Unlimited Dinner taking place next week at the Ocean View in Oak Bluffs, and then got down to business. "I hope you don't think I'm stepping out of bounds here as one attorney to another, but I do want to make sure of this and need your input. In Peg's belongings she had at the hospital was a Memory Box—you know, photos, old Christmas cards, little things that meant something to her over the years. But there was also a Forgiveness Note for the agency dated soon after Stuart died in there, and it's unusual for Peg to have put that there as she always had me keep her documents rather than rent a safe-deposit box at the bank. And, I noticed she had Ellen in your office notarize it. I hope you don't mind me asking?"

"No, that's fine, Thom. I don't mind at all. Ellen told me some time ago that Peg had Maria bring her into my office when I was off-island one day, and she asked Ellen to notarize a document for her. Ellen didn't read it, of course, but did witness Peg signing it. I can't exactly tell you when it was, but it was after Stuart's death—maybe several weeks? Do you want me to ask Ellen about it?"

Thom hesitated. "No, as long as Ellen saw Peg in person and witnessed it. Maria doesn't care much for me as you know, and she probably got Peg to stop into your office one day when they were out in Maria's car. I just wanted to make sure, that's all. I don't trust Maria further than I can see her, but it sounds as if it was legitimate."

"Was it to Maria's advantage?" Rick asked, twirling an elastic band in his hand, as he held the receiver to his ear with his shoulder. He plucked a wiry rogue hair from his nose.

"You can say that!" said Thom. "But it probably was what Peg wanted. She hadn't been going to church much recently, and Maria did take care of her. She was at Windemere daily seeing Peg, so perhaps she's not as much as a bitch as I think she is. Anyway," he said with a shrug, "it was up to Peg—not me. Sorry to bother you about this, but I just had to make sure. See you next week at the dinner, and bring plenty of money! Ha ha." Thom hung up the phone, and Rick gave a little sigh of relief.

Life on an island certainly has its advantages. It was one of the few places in a civilized world where a handshake and one's word was worth something. In fact, at times like this, one's word was worth everything. Rick pushed back his chair and looked out the window onto Cooke Street to see one of the big production trucks make its way down to the harbor. Things were looking up: plenty of new, young hotties here for a few weeks doing inside shots around town. And, it wasn't even next summer—it was still the fall! Not bad! Things could be worse.

Chapter 41

Edgartown, Friday, October 9, 2015

The Aznavarians had flown in on their Gulf—both Walter and Maria went to the airport to meet them, Walter more to see the plane than the couple. It was a beauty.

They all piled into the Range Rover and headed off to the Charlotte Inn, where they were staying. Although lunch wasn't being served at this time of year, Maria had seen to it that there would be a simple one served for them. Jared himself served as wine steward and suggested either a plate of charcuterie and Brie cheese or a Morning Glory Farms chicken tarragon salad. He apologized for the lack of luncheon service due to the season. They decided to take both entrees and a bottle of Cordier Pouilly Fuisse '08, well chilled. Jared brought the wine bucket, poured the first taste for Jack, received his nod, and then filled the others' glasses. He put the bottle back in the bucket, with a white linen napkin over it. "Jared, might as well bring another bottle out. This is wonderful. Another year or two, and it would be too old. But let's enjoy what we have now," said Jack. Jared smiled and walked away, thinking this guy knows his wines. And has the money to enjoy them. Perfect guests.

The Aznavarians, Jack and Darcie, were attractive and vibrant, telling Walter and Maria about their home in Pacific Palisades and in Le Castellet, France, near the Bandol vineyards. Both Walter and Maria were paying attention to the details: their Palisades California home of ten thousand square feet overlooking the Pacific on Chautauqua Boulevard. They described an incredible estate that was gated and walled with full-on ocean views. On the property itself was a very modern three-story glass home with an art gallery, two offices, library, huge dining room, two kitchens, wine cellar, nine bathrooms including his and her en suites, plus a famous 1950 Eames-Saarinen guesthouse with another two bedrooms. They said it was great for parties as the property was flat, and therefore the one-acre lot was fully usable for large gatherings, and they also had off-street parking for another twenty vehicles, a rarity in this area. Maria was calculating it was worth at least 15–20 million dollars.

Maria tuned in as the Aznavarians mentioned the name of their street, Chautauqua Boulevard. "How interesting! You know that's where the Clintons live in New York, don't you? What a coincidence you're here now, looking at Chapeda, and you also live on Chautauqua Boulevard in California. And, if you buy Chapeda that I'm going to show you this afternoon as your Vineyard vacation home, the four of you will have in common Chautauqua Boulevard, Chautauqua, New York and maybe even Chapeda! Wouldn't that be funny! And, I can arrange for you to meet them, as I'm once again renting them Blue Heron Farm up-island, although word isn't out yet. Just think!"

"Well, actually, Maria, the Clintons live in Chappaqua, New York. We're old friends of theirs, and in fact, Bill visited us just last week while Hilary was on a trip to the Mideast. But the two names do sound alike, don't they?" Jack said with a smile.

Maria felt her face redden. She must look so stupid, and her island insecurities came flooding back. Darcie leapt in and said, "And now we have Chappaquiddick to add to our Chappas!" And everyone laughed. *Thank God*, Walter thought. They didn't want to blow this one.

Darcie was stunning, Walter thought. Beautiful auburn hair, worn loosely. That casual air of the very rich…*insouciance* was the word he was looking for. Walter leaned in to catch her words. She was very soft-spoken. And it seemed she liked attention. While Maria and Jack were talking real estate and values, Walter and Darcie were talking traveling in Europe.

"Where is your place in France? I've only been to Paris," Walter told her.

"Oh, it's a marvelous property in the south. We bought the manor house. It's smaller than a castle, and *Le Castellet* means 'little castle.' It's in a tiny medieval walled town with a small chapel next to our property, and the town is perched on a hill overlooking vineyards and the Mediterranean. It's a few miles from Toulon and right next to Bandol. You know the Bandol rosés, don't you?"

Walter nodded.

"It's a typical Provence area—sunbaked ochre homes built practically on top of each other. The smell of lavender and thyme in the air, and lazy old dogs basking in the sun. Year-round, it's just a little bit bigger than Edgartown—around four thousand people. It's delightful," she said. "We only go there in the spring and fall. Summer, just like here, can be a zoo. Ten years ago it was only known to a few, but today—well, it's different!"

He said, "It sounds perfect! Do you have many houseguests when you're there, or do you two just like being by yourselves and unwinding?"

"There's always someone with us. It's not as big as California, but it does accommodate eight couples easily. Why don't you and Maria come join us this year! We'd love to have you," she offered, as she sipped some wine. "We can introduce you to the Bandol wines that grow just outside the gate. They are marvelous in the summer: the palest pink imaginable, with just a touch of saffron color. Crisp and cold. Delicious!"

"How generous of you, Darcie, but we couldn't impose upon you like that!" said Walter as he poured her some more wine. He looked in her eyes and smiled, as he was doing this.

She placed her hand on his and said, "Of course, you can! We'd love to have you." She squeezed his hand as she was talking.

He couldn't be sure yet, but it seemed as if this was more than a simple invitation. He'd be more than happy to find out later if she had more in mind.

She turned to Jack. "Jack, wouldn't we love to have Walter and Maria visit us in Le Castellet this year!" Jack was used to her spontaneous invitations and used to echoing her, saying, "Well, of course we would! It would be delightful. Besides the countryside and little villages, while you girls shop one day, I can take Walter up to the racetrack. If you're familiar with the Marseille anise drink Pastis, it's like Pernod—well, its eccentric magnate, Paul Ricard, built the racetrack there in the late sixties. It's one of the best in the world. A lot of the Formula One races take place there, and it's also a test facility. When we go there, we fly into the small airstrip on the property and our car is waiting for us there. It's only a ten-minute drive to the house."

Maria started to say something, most likely politely demurring from the invitation from clients they hardly knew, but Walter had already jumped in, which was uncharacteristically like him. "Well, I've been promising Maria a delayed honeymoon. And, I've never seen that part of France. Are you serious about this?" he asked.

"We'd drive ourselves crazy if we didn't have company all the time!" Jack laughed. And, Darcie rolled her eyes as if to agree, and they all ended up laughing.

Darcie said, "We absolutely insist. Right now is pretty well filled, but how about the spring? It's a lovely time of year: the tourists haven't arrived yet, the weather is perfect, and you'd have time to plan for it. To sweeten the pot, we could have our plane available for you. Do say yes!" she said and raised her glass to the others and, with a smile, looked Walter in the eyes. "Santé! To your health!"

They followed suit, and Walter said, "Okay, it's a deal! But only if we succeed in selling you a house this trip!" Everyone laughed again, and Maria noticed for the first time in real estate matters, Walter had taken the lead. She wasn't sure if that was good or bad, but anything that brought in a commission like the one she thought they'd get would be fine with her. She just didn't want him too involved in the business end of things. He thought the business had made her very wealthy over the past decade. Maria knew that a good deal of Walter's attention to her had to do with her perceived wealth. But it was only partly true, and she had no intention of divulging to him her finances, which would mean opening up to him about her debts. Looking at the Aznavarians, and their quick friendship, she realized more than ever that more money was needed to keep up with them. Walter seemed to think she had plenty, and she wasn't going to disappoint him and risk losing him. She whispered a silent prayer to herself. Maria felt enormous pressure right now, more than she had been feeling before. She excused herself and got up from the table.

"Maria, are you all right?" asked Walter.

"I'm fine, no problem. Be back in a second!" She went out into the mahogany-paneled library where discreet bronze signs indicated the private toilets. She splashed some water on her face and looked closely in the mirror. She wasn't a Darcie, that was for sure. She tried to dispel the vague feeling of jealousy she was experiencing. *Don't be silly*, she told herself. *Darcie and Jack are a perfect couple and totally devoted to each other.* And she went back to join them, still a bit uneasy. She *had* to get both them and Stephanie to "buy" now.

After lunch, Maria and Walter drove them to see several properties, including their own, where they were living until next summer (because the Parson cousins wanted to come up "one last summer" before it left the family forever), and if Darcie and Jack could wait until after then, they could have it for $1,450,000, well under what the property was actually worth.

Walter thought if they liked it, this could save their skin, but after a few minutes in their house, he could tell Jack's heart wasn't in it, so he brought them all to the Hall House, nearby them on South Summer Street and next to the Mayhew Parsonage and the Federated Church. That too didn't have the "caché" that Jack was used to. Walter tried once again to get them to go inside, but realized this wasn't up to their standards and dropped it.

The Morse House was better received. In town, on North Water Street, it commanded a spectacular view of the harbor. The water was flat calm today—very unusual for off-season months. Chappy looked a bit barren as all that appeared were the scrub oak and pines, gnarled from harsh winds and the biting salt air. You really had to get inland to find grass and real trees. They couldn't survive on the coastal edge. It wasn't an appealing view in the off-season, and that may have had something to do with the lukewarm reception the Aznavarians gave the grand house that stood tall behind its picket fence, opposite from the Chappy Beach Club, which had clear views of the harbor. A bricked driveway circled in front of the house and continued to the back. Typical of the year-round homes, it was white clapboard and had dark-green shutters, a highly glossed dark-green door located dead center in the front facade, nicely shaped boxwoods, and of course the ubiquitous white picket fence delineating the line where passersby could not trespass. Looking wasn't an issue, but trespassing was. And the picket fence made that very clear to anyone. The empty flower boxes and patchy lawn indicated summer was long over.

Maria gave them the history of the Morse House, still referred to by townspeople as the Captain Jedediah Pease House. Maria said, "This is one of Edgartown's true whaling captains' homes that is rich with history and dates back to 1836. The original owner, Captain Pease of the whaling ship *Acushnet*, is believed to be one of the inspirations behind Herman Melville's *Moby Dick* character Captain Ahab," she continued. As she opened the door, they went right into the living room. It was large for that era, had a beautiful fireplace on the driveway side, and they were surprised to see photographs of the late Patricia Neal on the mantle. Both Darcie and Jack were very interested to know that Oscar-winning actress Patricia Neal owned the property for many years.

Although it was a blend of modern amenities with a new kitchen with granite counters, central air-conditioning, and so forth, it was the typical quirky layout of historic properties. Nothing was open, but rather a series of individual rooms. Darcie said she wasn't sure the layout would accommodate houseguests and the large parties they like to give, but the additional guesthouse in the backyard, and the size of the backyard itself, did hold possibilities. They acknowledged it was a rare offering in the village's center. Maria locked the door as they went out to the Rover.

When she reached the Rover after the others had seated themselves, Darcie noticed the heavy key chain Maria carried with her. "How many houses do you have access to, Maria? I've never seen so many keys!" said Darcie. Before she could answer, Walter replied, "Oh, we have the majority of major properties we caretake for in the off-season, all over the island, as well as keys to those properties we've got exclusive listings on. If we didn't code each key, we'd never be able to manage. It's a full-time business for us in the off-season."

Maria knew the Morse House wasn't for them, but wanted to save the best for last. They drove again back down South Water Street and turned left onto Dunham Road. It curved around the inner harbor and soon was just a tangle of vines. Jack and Darcie looked at each other as if to say, "Perhaps we made a mistake using Maria. She doesn't seem to 'get' what we're like and what we're looking for." Just then, they pulled off the road and went a few hundred feet down a long private dirt driveway. Within seconds they saw the house. It was a striking modern home, low-lying and hugging the bluff on which it sat. Maria explained the family had won a zoning battle, and it was the only contemporary home in this old area. As they parked the Range Rover, Maria said to them, "You are the first ones to visit the home. It's not yet officially on the market as the owner just died a few months ago. The family wants me to begin marketing it when the estate settles at the end of this year, so we couldn't close until sometime after the first of the New Year, most likely in March, the way life moves here—slowly! However, they rely upon me, and if you are truly interested once you see this, I'm positive this house can be yours. I've got to warn you, it's significantly more than either of the other two properties we just saw."

"Now, this is more like it," Jack said. "What a magnificent view!"

Darcie was already one step ahead of the others, which Maria took as a good sign. Darcie had gone to the front of the house and stood on the bluff. To her right was the inner harbor leading to South Beach, across from her was Chappaquiddick, and to her left was the town and the Edgartown Reading Room and the Yacht Club, both old weathered shingled structures having been built out way into the harbor, long before zoning regulations came in.

Jack and Darcie gave each other an eye of approval, and as Maria opened the front door, she told them that the property represents one of the more important ones that will be offered in recent times. It had been in the same family for over one hundred years and boasts what is arguably the finest view in the harbor. "The lot is a little over an acre lot, and we're in the exclusive Tower Hill neighborhood. The main house has eight bedrooms with baths, and the separate two-story guesthouse you saw over there has three bedrooms, all with baths. You can see this is one of the island's finest compounds and—all within a short walk to town." As they were drawn to the front of the house, which was located atop a high bluff overlooking the good-sized sandy beach, Maria said, "Two years ago they put in a new private deepwater pier as the owners had a Hinckley 76 sailing yacht and named it Chapeda Hill, which is the name of this hill."

Jack exclaimed, "Chapeda?! We can't seem to get away from the 'Chappas' today! Chappaqua, Chappaquiddick, and now Chapeda! Maybe this is a sign?!"

The others all laughed, and Walter was quick to take Jack up on "the sign." "Just remember, you are the only ones to know this will be on the market in less than a year's time, so you might want to keep that in mind."

While Darcie and Jack wandered about on the first floor, Maria pointed out that there were water views from almost all rooms, and the waterfront included the one-of-a-kind sandy beach and two unique beachfront outbuildings—fondly named the Boathouse and the Beach House down below. "The Beach House is really just one big open room with beach furniture and a wet bar, and it's absolutely delightful when you're spending time on the beach," she said.

Upstairs in the main house was one big master bedroom, perched up high on the house, sitting much as widow's walks do on top of the North Water Street whaling captains' homes. "Oh my god, this is beautiful!" said Darcie. "You can see almost 360 degrees from here. Jack, look at this window bench—it must be thirty feet long."

She then noticed the floor model telescope near the harbor front window. Jack went over to view it and inspected it. He said, "This is beautiful. Do you know you can use it from a sitting level to a full standing height of at least five feet, with various stops in between? And take a look at the fine glove leather that cover the main telescope tube and base column! The Queen Anne-style legs make this one truly beautiful telescope. It also seems extremely stable at all heights," he said as he adjusted the height and focused the lens. "Does it come with the house?" Jack asked. "I used to be in the Navy, and I've collected naval and marine items. If we got the house, you'd have to negotiate the telescope, or the deal would be off!" The others laughed. Jack was like a kid. He couldn't take his eyes off the scope.

Maria said she'd make sure that was part of the deal and meanwhile was thinking of the next steps. Certainly, a hefty down payment for this house from the Aznavarians would help her keep the Parsons at bay for a while longer, while she tried to find a real buyer. Walter would know of this money, but not Stephanie Kramer's if she is as likely to buy as Maria thinks.

Jack and Darcie left the island late that afternoon—they told her they were seriously interested but needed a little more time to make the decision. Maria felt confident they would buy. Walter agreed with her assessment.

Chapter 42

Edgartown, Tuesday, October 13, 2015

The Parsons family was not stupid, and they had begun to ask about the money. Maria had told them she had put the down payment into escrow. She xeroxed one of her own bank statements, carefully cut and pasted the down payment onto the copy, and then recopied the "document." With a little adjusting of the copier light, she finally got a pretty good copy and wrote a little hand-written note indicating the $200,000 amount was the down payment from the couple "who was traveling in Europe now," proving they were serious and not backing out. She typed up a letter to herself using stationery she had put into her purse one day when she was doing business at the Dukes County Savings Bank. It came in handy.

The earlier-dated letter reflected the fact that the money had been received last spring, after her marriage to Walter, and that the $200,000 deposit was earnest money to be held in escrow in an interest-bearing account under the Parsons Family Trust, under the care of Maria Almeida, d/b/a Baldwin Real Estate Agency. She signed it "Stephen J. Vincent, President, Dukes County Savings Bank" (tracing over his real signature on the copier machine) and then made copies of the letter, her personal note, and the "escrow account" and sent everything to Mr. Parson. He was satisfied of course and thanked her and said it really hadn't been necessary to go to that trouble, but he certainly appreciated it. "My cousins, you know, are the ones I have to satisfy. They don't know you the way I do. Sorry about having to ask for this type of thing, but you know—it's my family. My grandparents thought they were doing a good thing, but it never works out with multiple heirs. Anyway, we're glad you and husband are staying there and keeping a watch over it. I know it's in good hands. I'll get back to them and tell them I saw the money in escrow, and we're better off waiting until summer with these people who are in Europe now. It's worth the extra money we'll get."

Chapter 43

Edgartown, Tuesday, October 13, 2015

She couldn't risk negative whispers now, so this plan at least kept the Parsons family at bay while giving Maria and Walter more time in the house. But she needed more liquid cash in case one of the cousins demanded a done deal. Walter had no idea of how little money there really was compared to what she had told him (he took an indifferent view of daily record keeping and trusted her). They had spent a lot of money since the marriage. Two trips to Florianopolis to the house she inherited eighteen years ago from her late aunt Fernanda Serpa, to see if Walter could adapt to life there; trips to New York and Boston for weekend getaways; and lots of spa treatments for Maria. So, cash flow was important to Maria as they still needed at least five more months before their plan would be realized. Yes, she still had $4 million (plus) socked away but knew that might not be enough for them over time. She was not going to Brazil with Walter and then run out of money. She knew he'd leave her, most likely for a younger beauty, and she had no desire to live there alone without him. She had figured a minimum of $6 million should do it (telling him they had $5 million). If things kept going as it was during the past several weeks, they'd be out of town by February or March, well before the summer folks would return for a quick weekend to check on the house before the summer.

At least she had managed to get the real estate agency in her name now, and Walter would never know that she had lied about that to him before Peg's death. Rick was still somewhat of a problem, but he would keep quiet as long as she held to her end of the deal. And, he certainly wouldn't know about how Peg died. Yes, there were some secrets she had kept from Walter, but she told herself it didn't matter and wouldn't matter in the long run. When they were ready, they would leave for Brazil permanently, and Walter would never have to know how much she was sweating these last several months on the island. If anything tripped up in the timing, she knew she could lose everything, and Walter would be the biggest loss. Never in a million years had she thought she would have been able to snag him, had she not portrayed her earned wealth the way she had.

She picked up an email from Miguel Barboza, a real estate attorney in Florianopolis, concerning her late aunt's home in the Jurere Internacional neighborhood that she had inherited. Real estate for the size of this house was climbing, and he wanted to ask her again if she wouldn't consider putting it on the market. He thought they could ask $3.8 million. Miguel had no idea that Maria planned to live there permanently as soon as she and Walter could do the last deal and quickly leave. No one—not even her mother or Matt—in the family knew Maria had inherited her aunt's house. And Maria intended to keep it just that way. Although Maria did not at first tell Walter, he understood full well they would *have* to leave, due to the "irregularities" in her real estate dealings.

Walter was happy with the plan to get off the island. He was much more of a Brazilian type than this dull old windswept spit of sand in the ocean. He'd leave today if it was possible, and technically he could, because for several months now, Walter had a new passport. Maria also had other papers for both of them, which were necessary to be legally and permanently living in Brazil when they went to formally apply for citizenship.

Chapter 44

Edgartown, Tuesday, October 13, 2015, late afternoon

After Rick and Matt had breakfast at Dock Street, and Rick indicated that he might be able to help Matt review his present child support of Heather in view of Maria and Walter's growing real estate practice, Matt walked up Main Street to Rick's office late that afternoon. He had to wait five minutes as Ellen said Rick was still in the courthouse but knew Matt was coming. They chatted for a while. Ellen had been divorced for three years; her ex-husband, Andy, like so many "professionals" on the Vineyard, had embezzled money (he from the bank where he was vice president of the Oak Bluffs branch). He served thirteen months in the satellite prison camp for minimum-security male offenders at the Federal prison in Cumberland, Maryland, where he spent his time playing cards and tennis, reading, and just relaxing with some pretty interesting people he probably never would have met otherwise.

She, on the other hand, was left with two teenage sons who were ridiculed at the regional high school, and although she still went to St. Andrew's Church each Sunday, she dropped out of the choir, as she felt awkward and exposed. There's no hiding or blending in on an island. If people don't actually know you, everyone knows someone who does know you. You are totally exposed like the seagrass on the dunes on a windy stormy January day.

Rick had arranged for Ellen's divorce while Andy had been away and for the house to be awarded to her solely. There wasn't any alimony due to the restitution part of the sentencing. Child support was on paper only. Once the divorce was final, she felt she had made her position clear to the community, and she reentered island life, feeling less and less the stigma that her ex-husband had flung at her.

As she was talking to Matt, she was struck by his love for his daughter. And, just as her husband had done to her, his spouse had wronged him and ruined his homelife. She found herself wondering what it would be like to spend time with him—he was lonely too and also appeared to be happy with a simple lifestyle. Wouldn't it be ironic if she might end up with a police chief while her ex-husband was a convicted felon? Ellen had a habit of fantasizing but pulled herself back in, just as Rick walked in the door.

The two men went in to Rick's office and within a few minutes came out, Rick saying they were going to Oak Bluffs to the Lampost for a couple of beers. Ellen noted Matt now seemed agitated, and he left without even nodding goodbye. The two men drove out the driveway together in Rick's Jeep.

Ellen decided to call it a day too and went in to Rick's office to tidy up his desk. There she saw the cause of Matt's distress: the court order specifying Matt pay $165 per week for Heather and Maria's claim of making only $27,000 per year, while Matt, then her husband, was grossing $41,000 plus benefits. Ellen knew then Rick was talking to Matt about refiling child support. But, since he already was representing Maria in real estate matters, ethically he should not give legal advice now to Matt. *Typical island good-ole-boys network*, she thought. *The boys carry on with their own ball game behind the scenes while pretending to play the official game on stage, seemingly not breaking any rules of legal conduct.* This game was played every day on the island—the batters and the catchers and the outfielders all looking like the game was real, but devoid of the encumbrance of those pesky referees.

Oh, well, she sighed, at least her own husband (now ex) got a lighter sentence than expected, largely due to Rick talking to the DA and Judge Mayhew privately, so she really shouldn't be bothered by the Rick-Maria-Matt conflict now. She locked the door and walked down Main Street to meet Sandy at David Ryan's for a glass of white wine. She didn't much like wine, but it was good to get out and see a girlfriend.

Chapter 45

Oak Bluffs, Tuesday, October 13, 2015, early evening

Finding a parking space on Circuit Avenue was easy at this time of year. They piled into the bar, taking a second for their eyes to adjust to the darkness and their noses to adjust to the smell of stale beer, popcorn, and unidentified smells embedded in the old wooden floors and permeating the woodwork, which probably hadn't been washed or cleaned in twenty-five years or more. This was a dive. A locals' dive.

Taking a seat in the corner, Linda came over and joked a bit with Rick about what they wanted. "You know what I want," said Rick, "just like you gave me last week out back along with all the other guys!" She laughed and bantered back, "You might know what you *want,* but you sure don't know how to deliver! What a joke of a little gun you carry on you! It doesn't even go 'pop'—just a lot of blanks in there. And you're a member of the Rod and Gun. Too much!" They continued joking like this for a few seconds, and then the two guys ordered a couple of drafts and got down to talking.

When she returned with the Narragansetts, she quipped, "Hi, neighbor, have a 'Gansett!" imitating the voice of the Red Sox announcer Curt Gowdy. They both smiled at her, and she winked and flounced away.

"Look, Matt, as I said earlier, this is strictly off the record. I represent Maria in some real estate transactions. But, she's a bitch, and I don't like to see guys like you get screwed. They do it all the time: women are bitches, and bitches are whores. They take advantage of any man, especially one who's down. We're the ones said to have the balls, but, my friend, it's actually them. And, I don't like what this bitch is doing to you." Rick took a long sip of the 'Gansett, the longtime favorite in this part of southern New England since the last century.

"I *hate* her," said Matt with passion. "And that phony she got married to—he's such an ass. Heather is spending the school week with them, and already she's talking about riding lessons and maybe even school off-island somewhere. I don't know if I can stop her, but I want to know what I can do."

"Matt, we've been through a lot, you and me. Anyone who served in Afghanistan like you and me are brothers, and we're brothers for life. My allegiance is to you. When we were there, you had the rough job. Yeah, I was in combat, but I wasn't in the Special Forces like you, God bless you, my good man. You lived hell there in that IED-infested desert. It reminds me of here on the Vineyard—the sand and the hidden roadside bombs that can maim and kill you. Ha!

"I shouldn't make light of this, as I know you don't like to talk about it, but we went through similar things in war, even though you had a tougher time. But, I can't stand by and see that bitch take advantage of you." He had been glancing at Matt, whose eyes were kept on the table in front of him and who had been taking large swigs of the brew.

"Linda!" said Rick holding up two fingers, nodding to their glasses.

"You know, when I was in Afghanistan and on my R&R, I chose Dubai. Got me a woman for the eight days, and we traveled all over. Now, granted she was a whore, but I tell you, they know how to make 'em! Sexy, beautiful, didn't say a lot, and was she ever-loving! So, she might have been a whore, but she sure wasn't a bitch like Maria. What a ho!" And they both gave a little laugh at the irony of this.

"When I arrived on the island in 2001, I met some of the vets, and your cousin's name was mentioned as being in the same company as I had been. I'm sorry he didn't make it back, but I was glad when you came back and took the job with the police here. I've never told you this before, but it was rumored that Maria was running around while you were over there and that her lifestyle was changing. Even her sister, who was dating Chris then, said the same things." Matt had finished his second. Rick had already nodded again to Linda; two more quickly arrived.

"And, the way she dumped you was unbelievable!" said Rick with a raised voice. "And, now, my friend, she's hiding money."

"I always thought she hid things from me," Matt whispered. "I couldn't find out, however, as all her books were in the agency. She had an aunt in Brazil somewhere and visited a couple of years in the summer with her before the old woman died. She apparently had money, but I don't think Maria got anything. At least that I know of. But she had to produce her income tax returns to the family court after showing me the divorce papers, and she wasn't earning a lot of money."

"I didn't know about her aunt, but what I'm talking about is about Maria's real estate business here. She's doing some funny business. Both with the agency and some real estate transactions," Rick said in a low voice.

"Are you sure? How do you know this?" said Matt.

"I have my sources," said Rick. "Look, if you want, I'll speak to her. I am pretty sure I can get her to voluntarily amend the family court order. She's a fucking witch, and nothing would give me greater pleasure than to help an Afghani brother and screw this bitch. Bitch with a capital *B*. She's gotten away with murder here!" And he finished the beer and held up two fingers for Linda to bring another round.

Matt had started on the third brew when the anger that he was trying to control finally exploded. He began talking in a loud voice, and a few of the regulars looked over his way.

Rick continued fueling Matt. "Last week, I was having dinner with Janet at the Charlotte Inn, and guess who was just leaving as we came in? I've noticed their car outside the inn a number of times, so this wasn't just some special occasion. Why they can't walk the block is beyond me. Maybe because they want people to see that Range Rover and know they're inside dining?"

"So, while you're paying her child support and maybe—just maybe—having enough left over to grab a burger at the Wharf, she and her so-called husband are living it up. I wonder just how much of the support Heather actually sees!"

Rick took another swallow. Matt had already finished his, and Linda brought over another round, having caught Rick's eye.

Matt continued swearing out loud, but getting louder and louder. "Slut! Bitch! Conniving whore! She'd eat her own child if she needed to. She has no boundaries. Playing with me about her income for child support. Then, having the gall to take up with Mr. Off-Island and coming back from a week's vacation with my divorce papers and her new marriage certificate. That bitch. I'll kill that douchebag if it's the last thing I do!" yelled Matt.

By this time, it wasn't the normal rowdiness the Lampost was used to. Matt was clearly flying off the handle. Linda came over to the table and said in a low voice to Rick that it was time to take him home. They could settle the bill later. Rick nodded and got up and asked Matt to tone it down. But, he didn't seem to hear Rick, and he continued all the way back to Edgartown. Rick was actually worried that he had gone too far with Matt and that he might have started something he couldn't stop.

Rick turned off the Vineyard Haven Road onto Twenty-First Street and pulled up to Matt's small house, not too far from the Rod and Gun Club. It was typical of this area: in the scrub oak woods, down a deeply potholed dirt road, rusted wheelbarrows and old cars in the front yards, a dog tied up outside barking at the sound of the Jeep, satellite dishes on some roofs, torn curtains in the windows, and most of the small one-story houses needing reshingling—a depressing neighborhood, particularly at this time of year, as the scraggly trees and bushes were losing leaves and the occasional patches of grass were already brown with pine needles.

Rick walked him inside, stayed for a while longer, feeding him more about "all women," and then left, saying he'd speak to Maria about child support. He repeated Matt couldn't let on that Rick had talked to him as he represented Maria in real estate and it would be a conflict of interest. Matt nodded he understood and shut the door with force. As Rick got in to the driver's seat, he heard something break inside the house.

Chapter 46

Edgartown, Thursday, October 15, 2015, evening

A few days later, at the Wharf Pub in Edgartown, after Rick did another round of buying Matt drinks, talking of all women being bitches, Afghanistan, and then about Maria's hidden money—Matt's Achilles' heel—Rick and Matt called it a day and walked up Main Street. Matt was not as loud as he had been at the Lampost, probably because it was Edgartown and he was the police chief.

As the two men came to the intersection of South Summer and Main, Rick pointed to the left toward Walter's Range Rover that was parked outside the Charlotte Inn. "Just like I said. While you're eating a burger at the Wharf, she's in there 'fine dining' with *your* child support money. And, you don't see your kid with them, will you! Whatta bitch! I don't know how you can take this. Everyone knows the real story, Matt. She's making a fool of you just like she did when you were in Afghanistan."

Matt could barely respond. Matt had said he had to check on something and said good night. Rick shrugged his shoulders, gave Matt a pat on the back, and also said good night and walked off up Main Street. He knew he had scored a big point tonight.

Matt stayed put at the corner of Main and South Summer, fury brooding in his eyes.

At the next corner, Rick ran into Sargent Searle. "Do Matt a favor, get him home before he goes and does something crazy. Maria and her husband are at the Charlotte Inn, and he told me he wants to shoot her. I realize it's a figure of speech, and God knows she deserves it, but I think he might do something crazy. He's that mad, and I don't blame him. The way she treated him, and now she's stiffing him with child support, when she's socking away money she's not telling anyone about. A week ago, Matt was in another one of his moods—I had to get him out of the Lampost as he was threatening to kill her. I don't want to see Matt in trouble."

Searle nodded and frowned, looking concerned, and walked quickly back toward the inn, just as Maria and Walter were leaving. Matt was outside waiting for them and started yelling at her, "You bitch, you're hiding money! I'm going to court to stop child support when you've got plenty socked away. I swear I'll fucking kill you someday!"

Searle grabbed Matt by the arm, gently but firmly, and tried to quiet him, but Matt tried to shake him off. The chief grabbed him and swung him around with a tight grip on his right arm and propelled him out onto the middle of the street toward Main Street, away from Maria and Walter. He tried to talk some calm in him, but Matt was now out of control, and he broke loose and headed back down Main Street toward the Harbor and the Wharf Pub. Searle at once called on his radio for Tommy and the cruiser. As Tommy swung the vehicle onto Main, the deputy chief jumped in, and they reached Matt just as he was entering the Wharf Pub. Both officers quietly took each arm and quickly led him into the car. Only Joy Harriman, who was turning off Dock Street onto Main, saw this. She knew of Matt's outbursts and put two and two together less than a minute later as she passed by South Summer, seeing Maria and Walter outside the inn earnestly talking. Maria looked frazzled. Walter was trying to calm her.

The deputy chief and Tommy brought Matt back to the station to cool off. While Tommy tried to talk to Matt, Searle called Doc Coffin, who came to the station to give Matt a mild sedation and told Matt he must get back on his medication. Doc waited awhile and then told Tommy he could drive Matt home but to make sure he took his other meds once there. Doc shook his head, clearly worried. Something had set him off today, but what?

Chapter 47

Edgartown, Friday, October 16, 2015

Maria was in early at the office the Friday morning. She had already brushed off Parsons' call and a meeting with Rick, as she had more immediate things to worry about. There had been another notice from the Bank of Boston of an overdraft. This time, it was their third warning, and a sharp notice came with it: one more time, and her account would be closed. She took her client escrow account book to Dukes County Savings and got a $2,000 cashier's check from Hilly's account. She'd never notice it, with all her family's money from Towle Silversmiths.

She then went down the street to the local Bank of Boston ATM and made a $2,000 deposit. The account would be flush by the 2:00 p.m. bank closing. She was near to getting Stephanie's deposit, so it was just a minor bump in the road. Walter didn't know about Stephanie, but he was very helpful with the Aznavarians.

Several times while she was out of the office, Darcie had called, and Walter had talked to her. He'd update Maria on the conversations they had had over cocktails that evening, and it was looking like they would make a good offer on the house. At first, Maria didn't think anything about the phone calls coinciding with her being out of the office, but today, Senna made a casual comment about Walter having called them.

Maria stopped and said, "You mean they called here, but Walter took the call?"

"No," said Senna, "Walter called Mrs. A. Why?"

Maria took a breath and tried to look normal as she casually replied, "No reason, I just thought I had heard you say that Mrs. Aznavarian called here for me," and she went into her office.

Although she left all the bills to Senna to pay, and never even looked at them, she picked up her phone and pushed the CID button and scrolled down outgoing calls. There were thirteen on the current list, some as many as twice a day, to Darcie's cell phone in the past two weeks. *Walter* was calling her! She thought about recently when Walter had made a quick trip to Boston—once for the dentist and another time for his orthopedist and cardiologist. He did not like any of the Vineyard doctors or dentists. But he was always back on the 6:15 p.m. ferry. Except that one time when he had called to say he had met an old friend, Tommy du Pont, from Delaware, in the lobby of the Ritz, where he had dropped in for a drink before heading for Woods Hole. They hadn't seen each other for years, and time just slipped away. If she didn't mind, he'd have dinner with Tommy and spend the night, but it was up to her. He also added that Tommy was one of the "real" du Ponts and was looking for a place on Nantucket, but that Walter had interested him enough in the Vineyard that he'd like to come visit in a couple of weeks. Maria was fine with that—if Walter knew one of the du Ponts, then that could only mean more money for them. She said, "Of course, dear, spend the night and tell Tommy I'm looking forward to meeting him. Make sure you invite him to stay with us, but mention the Charlotte Inn, as I personally think that can make the difference for off-islanders."

They talked a few more minutes, and then Walter said, "Love you. Tommy's also staying here, and he's just come down from his room and is waiting for me. See you tomorrow. Give Heather a kiss good night for me," and he clicked off his cell phone. Maria went back to the Travel Channel and poured another glass of red wine. She'd get dinner later. Heather was spending the night at Julie's tonight, studying (they said) for the big history exam.

As for Maria, there was still one nagging thing about Walter staying in Boston that night that didn't seem to balance, but she had a long day already, and after all, tomorrow is another day. She smiled. She loved Scarlett O'Hara. She just might put that DVD on tonight and have some of her mother's *Alcatra* that was left from Sunday's dinner. It was perhaps not the perfect time of year to enjoy the beef marinated in red wine and garlic, copied from the Caciola recipe that her mother had brought with her from Terceira in the Azores, but it was still a treat. Yes! That's what she'd do tonight. Reheat that with the rice and watch *Gone with the Wind* and tackle the bookkeeping issues tomorrow.

But she couldn't concentrate on the movie, and she was picking at the food. She was thinking of the type of house this Tommy guy may have in mind. "Too bad the Graham House wasn't for sale yet. Now that's a property!" she said to herself. "I might just take a swing up there tomorrow and look in on a couple of other properties we care for during the off-season months. It is a spectacular piece of land. Nothing is like it on the island. I might even call her son and see if he's made any progress with deciding to keep it or sell it. It can't hurt." She picked up the phone and dialed DC.

"No," said the young woman answering Mr. Graham's phone, "he's not in. Is everything all right on the Vineyard?" she asked.

Maria couldn't remember her name: Vicki or Ricki? "Oh, everything's fine. I just wanted to ask him a few questions. Will he be in later tonight? Sorry I'm calling after hours."

"No problem. But Mr. Graham is traveling abroad. He's had a horrendously busy summer, and this getaway is really needed. In fact, before he left, he told me he didn't even know when or if he might be able to get up to the Vineyard this fall."

"What a shame," said Maria. "It's such a beautiful estate, and to think of "Mohu" just sitting empty here. His mother would be upset. She loved this place." At the same time, she was thinking that if he wasn't even sure he'd get up this year, this might be a blessing in disguise. "Have him call me when he gets back and has a moment. Everything is fine. I wanted to ask him if he was interested in a summer rental. I know a couple that would pay top dollar. Thanks. See you!" Maria hung up the phone, thinking more and more about what a fortuitous bit of news this was.

Chapter 48

Edgartown, Saturday, October 17, 2015, noon

Walter was had been back from Boston for a few days but didn't have much to say about Tommy du Pont. A few days later he told Maria that Tommy had called him and thanked them for the invitation to visit, but he still had his eyes on Nantucket and maybe now the Hamptons. Maria kept pushing Walter to at least get him down here for a friendly visit. She thought a moment and said, "Why don't we see if Darcie and Jack could come back for a visit—we've really got to nail them down. They could pick Tommy up in New York or wherever he is. I'll call them this afternoon," said Maria. She watched Walter's face, and for a second, he looked startled, but then went back to an impassive expression and shrugged his shoulders as if to say, "Why not?"

They were finishing lunch at the Newes Pub on Kelley Street, and as Maria headed for the woman's room "to freshen up," Walter signaled for the check and made a quick call on his cell phone. He had to leave a message, forewarning Darcie that Maria would be calling.

As Maria turned the corner from the restroom, she saw him click off the phone and was handing the waitstaff a credit card. She made a note to look at whom he called tonight when he was sleeping, but she began to see the possibility that Walter and Darcie were entering into a relationship. Probably nothing to worry about at this stage, and anyway he hadn't been away, except for the night he ran into Tommy in Boston at the Ritz. So, if Tommy comes to the

Vineyard, Maria will know that there wasn't anything more than two old friends bumping into each other.

She felt a little better about her suspicions, and as they left the front door, she slipped her hand into his and flashed him a big smile. He noticed she had put on new lipstick, so that made her look better, but in the bright sunlight, he could see tiny little pockmarks from teenage acne that even Chanel makeup didn't hide in the sun. Perhaps she should look into dermabrasion.

He smiled back. Had she always had that dark spot on her upper left canine? He squeezed her hand and whispered, "It's so good to be with you, honey." She felt immediate relief and a sensation of calm. *Why do I worry so much?* she asked herself. *He loves me. And, soon, we'll be living a life without worry in a beautiful location. Where no one can get us.* They walked back up Main Street, hand in hand.

When she got back to the office, Stephanie had called and had left a message and wanted to set up a phone conference about the house they saw. Things were looking up! Her earlier worries had flown out the door and into the mid-October sunshine, with a flutter that barely rippled the air. Life was good. Life was good!

Senna thought her cousin looked more relaxed than she had in ages. Perhaps they *were* really in love? She went back to her bookkeeping tasks.

Chapter 49

Saturday, October 17, 2015, afternoon

Maria and Stephanie talked money, and Maria had to admit, Stephanie was a good businesswoman. She negotiated the purchase price down from $16 million (which Maria had said was a steal) to just over $14 million. And, on top of this was a separate allowance of $1.2 million for interior design, furniture and high-end fixtures, and plantings that Maria would put into a special escrow, keeping separate the escrow for the actual closing. Maria also told Stephanie that instead of her unusual 6 percent commission, she'd only charge 5 percent.

Stephanie said she'd pick out the fabrics, furniture, kitchen, and bath items in New York, but she agreed with Maria's suggestion of actually buying them on the island—it went a long way for island businesspeople if a new resident gave them the business. Maria assured Stephanie that she personally would make the purchases on the island at Vineyard Decorators and inspect them when they arrived. Both women were delighted! Stephanie didn't have to deal with the details and installation of what was ordered, and Maria had control of the money.

"Now, Stephanie," said Maria, "you may think you have a long time to figure out exactly what you want, but if you are leaving for Italy with your father and family in mid-June, you don't have a long time. Custom-made furniture and unusual fabrics often take six or even more months to get—especially getting it here on the island. It's really in your best interest to pick out everything you want in the next month or so. Do you have someone in New York you can work with now?"

"I know you're right. I don't have anyone at the moment, but one of my good friends here just decorated a fabulous home in Upper Brookville—it's the old Silva estate, if you can imagine!—and I'll call her. I'd need whomever it is to fly up to the Vineyard with me to see the house as it is now in its unfinished state so I can let you know in a few days."

"That's great. I can see you any time this week. I suggest you come as quickly as possible as word still hasn't gotten out that it's actively being marketed. I think we both should make a pact not to say anything to anyone at this time, even your father. Once the owner knows there's an interest even in its unfinished state, he could very easily decide to advertise and see what the market bares. Honestly, I can see him getting another $2 plus million if it were to become known," said Maria. "The same would go with your designer. I can get a confidentiality agreement drawn up for you and him or her, as well as one for you and me. How does that sound?" Maria asked.

"Makes sense. Oh, Maria, I'm so excited. It's been a hard time since my divorce and then my breakup with my boyfriend. I really thought this one would last, and I've been in a real funk. That's why, I think, Daddy suggested the Tuscan summer. It's going to be hard not even to tell him about the house!"

"I know how close you are to him, Steph (the first time she tried this out on her), but honestly you can talk to me, and it's the only way I can assure you the property will be yours. Honest." Maria paused a second hoping she'd hear Stephanie agree.

Finally, Stephanie said, "You're right, Maria. It will be such a surprise for everyone, and that's worth keeping my mouth shut for a couple of months!"

"Good girl! I know you can do it. Isn't this all so exciting? You'll be able to have a big Thanksgiving in your new home next year with everyone at your place and not at your dad's. And, as a special treat, I'll throw in the whole dinner with fresh turkey and all the vegetables from Morning Glory Farms and the pies from Savoir Fare. I'll get

Savoir Fare to do all the catering. All you'll need to do is to supply the wines!"

"It's a deal! I'll be back in touch this week and hopefully can get up there before Friday with the designer," said Stephanie.

"Super! Talk to you soon. Remember: this is our little secret!" said Maria. "Bye," and she hung up the receiver. It took her a second or two to go over all of this in her mind. It had worked! And, no one, not even Walter, knew about this...and, wouldn't. She had not been in a better mood since she and Walter had gone to the Dominican Republic to elope. What more could possibly happen to make her life better, she thought.

Chapter 50

Edgartown, Saturday and Sunday, October 17–18, 2015

He made himself a drink and sat down in the library. Things were getting messy with Darcie. When he had taken her up on her flirtation, and subsequent visits in Boston, it was fun and daring. Not to mention hot. She was a passionate woman who knew how to please him in adventurous ways that Maria and many others didn't know. Their first time in a hotel, Darcie intimated that she and Jack had a "quasi-open" relationship. He was so hot and couldn't wait to get to her that he really didn't think of what that meant—or, didn't mean. Later she told him that she had had a number of casual relationships, and she assumed Jack had too, but it was something neither one spoke of to the other. Hence, "quasi-open."

What did that matter to him? He certainly wasn't going to tell Maria! And soon, all this with Darcie, as fun as it was to sneak away, would be the end of what had been a pretty good thing. By early March or sometime in April, Maria and he would be out of Edgartown and living the good life in Brazil. He knew Darcie could always be replaced by a local Brazilian beauty—and probably as good or better. He was bored with the Vineyard. It had served his purpose, but now, with a wife with money and a beautiful home in Brazil, the sooner Maria could tie up her business this winter, the better. He knew his life there would be easy: they had plenty of money, and life was a lot looser. And, it wasn't so exposed a life as here on this island. You couldn't hide anything here. You couldn't escape the people. They were all around you, like ants. He needed to dump Darcie and maybe even get someone new, until they left for Brazil.

Walter had first gone with Maria to Florianopolis a month after they were married and returned again a year later. He really could see himself living there. She had told him of her plan for them to "make enough money" by the end of the following year and go live their lives in Brazil. The house Maria had inherited stunned him: it was absolutely beautiful. Cool marble floors, high ceilings and skylights, multicolored terra-cotta walls painted by a local artist. Brilliant blues, yellows, reds, and greens; fantastic floral paintings of indigenous plants with *tucanos*, *araras*, and other species he had never heard of, each bird and plant identified by the artist. It was like walking into a botanical garden that you never left. And, Constanca was a gem. Constanca lived in her own quarters on the property, behind the cabana and pool area, was loving and discreet, and an excellent cook. He made sure she liked him, paying her compliments, opening doors for her, standing when she came into the room. "De tal qualidade cavalheiro!" she said to Maria. "What a gentleman! Fernanda would have been so happy for you, dear Maria!"

Now that Maria and he were actively planning to leave the island, Maria had recently told him that they weren't just visiting her aunt's house, that the house was her inheritance; specifically, Constanca would live there until she died, at no cost, and Maria would have the entire house through her lifetime. Everything was paid for by Fernanda's generous trust, which would continue until Maria dies, or if she died first, then "her future husband and any children" could live in the house until they too died.

As he was sitting there in the library, he began to think Fernanda's family could very well argue that in 1997, the "future husband" in the will meant Matt. Matt was certainly in the picture; in fact, even if Fernanda and Maria didn't know it yet, he was already the father of Heather when Fernanda signed her will. But now that they were divorced, he worried the will might not extend to him if Fernanda's children objected. Walter realized that unless he could be assured that the language in Fernanda's will automatically extended to any (newer) husband of Maria's, he could conceivably be cast out of the house just like that. He'd have to fix any ambiguity—now, before they took off.

The next morning after Maria had left for the office again on a Sunday, he searched and finally found what he had been looking for in an old suitcase of Maria's. For a moment, he was confused as there were more than one will signed by Fernanda Calvalho Serpa and with different dates. They were all in Portuguese, and he couldn't decipher them. However, he thought there must be some reason Fernanda had signed what looked to him like the same will, but different dates, and he couldn't figure it out. He shrugged his shoulders and didn't waste time on it. He grabbed the earliest one dated the morning before she died.

Walter had already looked into Brazilian laws and called Maria and told her he needed to made a quick trip to Boston Tuesday. Tommy DuPont would be in town, and this might be the time to try again to get him to agree to come visit the island. Instead, he dialed the Brazilian consulate on Monday and made an appointment for 11:00 a.m. Tuesday. He took the will that Fernanda had signed earlier the day before she died, leaving everything to her family with the exception of the villa and endowment to Maria and "her future husband or children, if any," since that would be the one used in court if there were any legal proceedings needed. He left the others that were signed later in the suitcase and put it back in Maria's closet.

Chapter 51

Edgartown, Monday, October 19, 2015, morning

Rick had just finished listening to his tape recorder. Nothing much on that tape, just that Janet was meeting Sarah for lunch today in Vineyard Haven at the Black Dog.

He then picked up his phone and called Maria and asked Senna, who answered, to speak to her. Maria sounded worried and asked what he was calling about, but Rick said he didn't want to speak about it on the phone. Could she see him after lunch at her office? She said she would.

He went back to his tape recorder. Janet was soon leaving the house, and he'd go in now to announce that he "knew" she was meeting Sarah at the Black Dog.

"Oh, hi. I was just leaving," said Janet.

"I know, you're having lunch with Sarah at the Black Dog," Rick said.

"Why, yes! How did you know? I just spoke to her about three minutes ago," Janet said.

He smiled a half smile and looked directly in her eyes. "I have my sources. I know everything." He laughed and turned to go into the living room. "You may think you have friends, but I've known them longer."

Janet seemed surprised but brushed it off. *They must have just talked about some business thing,* she said to herself, *and Sarah mentioned the lunch.* She yelled goodbye and went out to her car and took a left on Upper Main Street toward Vineyard Haven.

He waited until the car pulled out onto Upper Main and then bent over and checked under the bed. He pulled out the small voice-activated tape recorder and put the one from the office with the new tape in its place. He then went to the kitchen, moved the Le Creuset casserole out from the back of the shelf, and listened to and then erased that tape and set it back on to voice activate. He did the same in the den.

The one in the den, however, was of interest; he listened for a minute and then said, “Bitch!” He'd take that tape to his office where he'd listen to the whole tape later. He put a new tape onto the machine. “That little bitch. She's telling her brother she's not happy with me and maybe thinking of divorce!” he said. “What a bitch. She thinks she's so smart. Well, I've got news for her! Guess who's smarter now, honey!”

Finally, he took the new digital audio recorder that he had just received in the mail and plugged the tiny unit into the basement telephone jack. The ad he had received from Electromax (found online under Covert Recordings) said it would record every word when any extension in the house was used. When the conversation ends, it goes into a “sleep mode,” using no battery power for stand-by functions, thus lasting almost twice as long as the other units he had. If this worked as it said, he'd buy more, as it would save him time from checking daily. On his way back to the office, he kicked their dog and slammed the door. “Bitch!”

He then walked down to the Baldwin Agency to see Senna. He knew Maria wasn't there as he had seen her drive out of town toward OB, or Vineyard Haven. Even if it were just to shop at the Shop & Stop, it would take her at least fifteen minutes. That was enough time.

“Hi, Senna. How are you? Is Maria in?” he asked as he opened the door.

“No, sorry, Rick. She just left for Vineyard Haven to pick up some dry cleaning for Walter, he's going off-island tomorrow.”

“He's off a lot recently, isn't he?” asked Rick.

Senna just shrugged her shoulders. She too had wondered what he was doing in Boston so often as of late.

"Do you mind if I get some papers off Maria's desk? I have an appointment in about twenty minutes, and it's about a deal we've been working on. I know exactly the envelope it will be in, and it will only take a minute," he said, walking toward the office.

Senna didn't mind as she'd knew Rick and Maria were doing lots of work together, and she herself had a lot of work to do if she was going to leave early today as had been planned.

He went in and quickly removed the tape recorder he had earlier put behind the Norfolk Pine in her office and replaced it with the other one he had brought with him.

"Sorry. I couldn't see it at first glance, and I didn't want to mess with her desk," said Rick as he came out into the main room. "I'll have to wing it," he said. "It shouldn't be a problem, just a little easier with the papers right in front of me."

"Should I leave her a note?" asked Senna, as she stood up and grabbed her purse. "I'm leaving early today, so I won't see her if she comes back into the office."

"No, no problem. She's got an appointment with me at two o'clock. I'll catch up with her then. No big deal. Thanks," he said as he held open the door for Senna, who was trying to get into her coat.

"It's windy today, isn't it?" he said, as Senna locked the door.

She nodded, and said goodbye again and turned to walk toward her car in one of the spots Baldwin Real Estate rented from the Preservation Trust. It was a deal: $1,000 donation that was tax-deductible. Rick knew that it shouldn't have been deductible as it was a quid pro quo, a value received and not a charitable deduction, but that new off-island old guy they had hired as executive director didn't know what he was doing. And either the board didn't care or some of them didn't know, and all that mattered to them was that he was pleasant and didn't rock the boat. He was perfect for the job.

"Assholes," he said, speaking of all of them. "Real assholes. Lucky their parents were born before them," he muttered, referring to their inherited wealth. *Remittance men, that's what they are*, he thought. "Assholes!"

The wind had picked up some more, and it was pretty raw walking back to the office.

Ellen had left a note on the law office door telling Maria she had gone to the post office and to just come in as Rick was expecting her. So, at two, Maria entered the office, where she found Rick listening to something that he immediately switched off when she knocked on his office door. It almost sounded like Janet's voice, but she realized it couldn't be. Janet wasn't sitting in the office.

Maria was really worried. The look on Rick's face was one of fury. But within a minute, she realized she didn't cause it. He wanted to speak to her about a deal. She knew it wouldn't be a good talk, whatever it was he had in mind.

Chapter 52

Edgartown, Monday, October 19, 2015, 2:00 p.m.

"Thom said something to me about the Chilton House," Rick said to Maria.

She looked stunned. "He did?" she said, trying to buy some time to respond. *Why would Thom say anything to Rick? Weren't things with a lawyer supposed to be confidential? Shit! Why me!* she asked herself. She was bothered enough because Walter's dry cleaning wasn't ready and it was a wasted trip to Vineyard Haven. "Damn! What a day!" she said to herself.

Leaning closer to her from across the desk, with an icy cold look, he said, "Look, Maria, we have a deal. You go behind my back, and you're cooked. It's that simple."

"I was going to tell you about the deal, but it wasn't yet a done deal, so I thought it was premature. Of course, we have a deal! I wouldn't double-cross you. This is what I talked to Thom about."

He noticed Maria was twisting her hands as she spoke, and that rash he had seen before on her cheeks emerged. She was sweating it, no doubt about it. He sat back in his leather armchair and folded his hands as he listened to her. *She is really stupid to think Thom would say anything to me*, he thought. *God, she's gullible. It's like taking candy from a baby.*

By the time she had finished telling him her plan, Rick was actually impressed. If she could pull it off—getting Thom to agree to "renters" until the estate was ready to dispose of the property—Maria and Rick could make a tidy couple of hundred thousand dollars right now with the down payment. Maria would write up a purchase and sales agreement telling the renters that because of the estate issues, it would probably take a year before the actual sale would go through. Maria would take the house down payment and tell them it was being put in an escrow account and that she would collect the actual rent on a monthly basis and bring it to Thom as executor of the Chilton estate. The beauty of this was that at the time when Thom *really* put the property on the market, if the current renters could meet the sales price, they'd buy it as they had always expected to do.

Maria had already got an idea of what Thom would ask for in the sales price, and all she'd have to do is to up that amount by the two hundred thousand dollars she'd have already collected. If they couldn't meet the price (and these chances were slim to none, as Thom didn't care about getting top dollar—he just cared about getting a fair price to satisfy his fiduciary duty), it would look like the tenants had given Maria a hefty down payment on what they assumed was a done deal once the estate was settled. In any case, everything Maria and he did was in cash. Chances are, it would work out, he thought. And, if the truth did come to light, and if she then tried to implicate him in the fraud, who would believe her? He smiled to himself. He was working behind the scenes on Doc Coffin, Matt, and others, implying Maria seemed to be very stressed and "not herself" recently. And, it was all falling into place perfectly.

The Chilton sisters, as they were called, lived in their parents' house at the end of Green Avenue, where Sara Piazza lived, just off Main Street and Pease's Point Way. They never married. Their father was said to have been a Harvard professor or headmaster in one of the elite boarding schools of New England. No one today could remember him or his wife, not even Sara who had lived there almost her entire life, but for as long as people could remember, the Chilton sisters, Mae and Gertie, lived in that house. It was a lovely house on the outside: typical white clapboard structure with Edgartown green shutters. The neighborhood kids now called it the Rabbit House.

When they were growing up, Mae spent the school year away from the island at a "school" to help her with basic occupational skills and language. Gertie on the other hand graduated from the regional high school at the top of her class. But, she wouldn't leave the island. Ever. She was one of the island's agoraphobics, and although she had once crossed the seven miles across the Vineyard Sound by the Steamship ferry to the mainland, she wasn't ever going to leave again. She helped her parents run the small bookstore out of their attached garage and seemed happy. After the parents died, Mae came to live year-round at home so Gertie could take care of her. Thom had been the attorney for the parents, and he was executor of their estate, which left the sisters enough money to stay in the family home. He had arranged with the Edgartown National Bank to allow Gertie to withdraw an "allowance," but he paid all the bills, having made special arrangements with the town storeowners.

Mae had a fondness for rabbits that other gardeners in town did not. She began by feeding them carrots and lettuce. Mae was a sweet woman but simple-minded. In the first summer after the parents had died, and the sisters were on their own, Mae often left the doors open, and Gertie didn't seem to mind. By the late fall, Mae knew it was getting cold, so she left carrots inside on the kitchen floor and the storm door ajar. The rabbits had figured out what to do, and they came and went freely until it became too cold. When Gertie finally had to shut the door, those rabbits inside stayed, and as rabbits do, they multiplied. But neither sister minded, and the rabbits certainly didn't either.

Gertie, who was ten years older than Mae, was getting older and probably had the beginnings of Alzheimer's, except it wasn't known as that then. The townspeople just explained her as being a "bit dotty." Gertie was seen less and less, and her store hours were so erratic that eventually people stopped coming there.

Townspeople worried that Mae would outlive Gertie, which was a problem, as Mae certainly couldn't take care of herself. Edgartown Market would deliver groceries to their house. One day last fall, for two straight days, the delivery man, Elmer, knocked on the door to say their milk and chicken were there, but no one answered the door, although he heard Mae say, "We don't need anything today, but thank you anyway."

When this happened again the next day, Elmer decided to look in on the girls himself and pushed and pushed until the simple hook lock on the door broke. He was the first person who had been in the house since the parents had bought it in the early 1950s. He stopped dead in his tracks: he was stunned, literally and figuratively. Literally because of the rabbit stench and droppings, probably five or six inches deep on the floorway path. The "path" was just a narrow opening in the books, cartons, empty tin cans, newspapers, old appliances, paintings, bicycles, broken TV sets, empty detergent boxes, clothespins, shoes, blankets, mirrors, magazines, bottles, a vintage treadle-style Singer sewing machine, clothes, fishing poles, and garbage. Rabbits ran loose everywhere.

Elmer had to go outside and take some fresh air. He went back in and yelled for Gertie. She didn't answer, but he could hear someone upstairs.

Elmer went back to Main Street and to the police station on Church Street, where he said he needed help at the Chilton sisters' house and to come prepared because they needed masks.

Matt was in the station that day, and he and Joe went quickly over there with Elmer. They couldn't believe what they saw. The house was "like something out of the Collyer brothers," it was repeated around town (since there weren't yet the television series *The Hoarders*). It was unbelievable. Matt and Elmer called out for Gertie and Mae and made their way slowly through narrow pathway amid the rubble. Mae eventually answered and was coaxed downstairs with the promise of a Hershey's chocolate bar. They asked where Gertie was, and she pointed upstairs. "She's been sleeping, but Mae made sure she's warm."

The EMTs—who had been there for some time—reported that at first they couldn't find Gertie, but they knew she was in the bedroom by the sweet odor of decay. She, in fact, was on her bed, but until they peeled away layers of clothing, newspapers, and blankets, they couldn't see the body.

Doc Coffin was called to the scene and determined it was likely a heart attack, and the EMTs took away Gertie's body. Thom was called over to deal with Mae, and he kept repeating to her that she had done a good job keeping Gertie warm, but Gertie had died anyway. Mae seemed pleased that she had done a good job and kept repeating, "Mae kept Gertie warm. Mae kept Gertie warm."

Mae went to Windemere that night and seemed happy, although at times she still went looking for Gertie. Everyone liked her. Back home, in the next year or two, the gardening neighbors around the Chiltons' house became really pleased with their flowers and small vegetable gardens. They were flourishing. The rabbits had been "disposed of," said the Board of Health.

Mae, however, once again began feeding rabbits. She asked for extra salad ("no dressing, please") and carrots at dinner and sneaked them into her room. When the patients were allowed out on the patio on sunny days, Gertie would toss the vegetables as far as she could in the tall grass. She was delighted to see rabbits and in her simple mind thought these ubiquitous creatures were the ones from home who had followed her there when they saw she was leaving. She felt happy knowing her rabbits were with her, even though Gertie was not.

Mae was there at the same time Maria had been visiting Peg, so Maria said hello to Mae a few times. Mae recognized many of the townspeople and was always happy to have someone stop by. About six months after she had arrived, and a few weeks after Peg had died, Mae had a stroke and lasted for only two weeks. It was for the best, everyone said, but whatever would they do with that house? It was then that Maria got the idea.

Thom hired professional cleaners from off-island and warned them what they would find. They took five days to do the job—dressed in hazmat suiting—everything had to be fumigated before it could go to the Regional Refuse District. ABC Trash dedicated one of the island trucks to the job and hauled one load after another during this time. They couldn't estimate the number of rabbit and rat skeletons they shoveled into the dumpster, but they said it was ghoulish.

Thom salvaged a few paintings and some china and crystal and gave it to the Boys & Girls Club Secondhand Store on North Summer Street. He had Kelleher Plumbing turn off the water and aired the house out for another ten days, when the off island cleaners came back to refumigate.

Jean Holloway, who was the Board of Health agent, gave the final inspection as fit to be inhabited, but Thom was in no hurry to deal with the estate that was somewhat of a mess. Maria ran into him one day at the post office and said she'd be glad to go in there and assess what needed to be done to turn it into a rentable or salable house, at no cost except expenses, if she could get the listing.

He didn't want to say yes immediately, so he just shrugged his shoulders. "I'll think about it," he told her and nodded and went out the door. As he walked back to his car, he thought it might not be a bad idea. It would avoid criticism if he hadn't gotten around to settling the estate, and she did know her stuff. There was plenty of money in the estate, and all bills had been paid. He'd let her wait a bit and see if, true to form, she contacted him again.

And, sure enough at the beginning of the following week, she called him. He said he'd draw up an agreement for the work, and again she reiterated she wouldn't charge him for her time if she got the listing—rental or sale.

CHAPTER 53

Boston, Tuesday, October 20, 2015

Having arrived in Boston on the early Cape Air flight, Walter then took a taxi from Logan Airport; he passed over the Bridge and was left off on Purchase Street in the Financial District. He was greeted at the door by a uniformed guard who ushered Walter into a waiting room. The people there looked like so many of the Portuguese on the island—the men were squat, swarthy with scruffy beards and beginning to bald; kerchiefs on the women, who were stocky and heavy featured, uncomfortably reminding him of Maria's family.

He was pleased to see that the assistant consul, Senhor Fernando Mauricio, was a rather charming man: tall, thin, dark shiny hair, and dressed impeccably, rather like himself. Walter quickly explained that Maria was tending to her ill mother and at the last minute could not make the trip to Boston with him, but he had a note from her asking them to give Walter the information. He told the consul that when Fernanda had written the will in 1997, Maria had been about to marry Matt, and therefore Fernanda put that clause into the will about her "future husband." But now that Walter and Maria were married, they were wondering if Walter would inherit this property if she were to die before he did. He also said the two of them intended to move to Brazil as permanent residents and open bank accounts there and needed to know what was required.

Senhor Mauricio had observed Walter and concluded that he was a successful businessman and his wife was tied to a well-to-do Brazilian family. They would be good to have there.

The assistant consul said, "Brazil bases its law on Portuguese law. As long as your wife creates a will naming you and any children she has or you may have together, her inheritance would automatically pass to you and ultimately her children."

Walter nodded and said that was their plan and they were seeing their local attorney next week on the Vineyard. "We both want to become permanent residents and understand we can apply here for a permanent residence permit that is valid for at least twelve months, and preferably longer. We want to open a bank account in Brazil and know this residency would be necessary. Can you do the permits here?"

"Yes, I can. Once I issue the permanent resident visa, then to open the account, the bank would need to see a photo ID, the documents proving your address in Florianopolis (which your wife has), a letter from the local lawyer saying he is paying the utility bills, etc., on her behalf as well as a statement by him that her income that he manages as trustee is more than sufficient for you both to maintain the bank account. It seems to me you'd have no problem."

"I have a question," said Walter. "After we knew Maria couldn't make the trip today, she gave me her passport and her attorney's contact information, along with a copy of her aunt's will showing Maria inherited the property and a letter stating its trust would maintain the house and Maria and me for our lifetimes. Here's her handwritten letter to you stating that she hopes you can start the permanent resident process today to avoid another trip as this is her busiest time of year in real estate. I also have the letter from her attorney stating the same thing. She wanted to know if you could process her application now, and then I can bring them back to the island with me tonight. Is this possible?"

"Well, it is a bit unusual, without her being here in person, but, my dear sir, I think I can arrange this. However, this may require a little more in funds than is normally the case, due to the circumstances," replied Senhor Fernando, entwining his elegantly buffed fingernails and looking up at the ceiling for a moment.

"But of course, *senhor*! We already knew this would take additional detail and work and are prepared to cover all these extra expenses. I was wondering what you might think if an additional five thousand dollars US today would be enough to start the process? It may not be fully sufficient, but if you find it requires more resources, please let me know, and I can wire the required balance from the bank account we want to open in Brazil to your personal account there. My wife and I are very grateful to you for being so kind and understanding."

Senhor Mauricio said he could also arrange to open a joint account through his brother who is on the board of directors of Banco Bradesco. "It's one of the largest banks now since acquiring HSBC's business a few months ago. It even can open some accounts in foreign currency and operate them online, so I'll talk to him personally about this. Again, it may take a little more effort to have him do this, but it will be assured," said the assistant consul, looking at Walter with an understanding smile.

"Absolutely! I understand. I'm going to take down your bank account information, and I can wire the funds necessary for you and your brother to open this account for us. Once it's opened, Maria and I can complete all our US banking transfers to Bradesco before we actually physically move there. We hope to go in the next couple of months."

"Do not worry, Mr. Keller. Let me give you my banking information, and you can wire the funds you think are necessary any time today before 4:00 p.m. our time. Then, I can start of the permanent resident permit tomorrow as well as have my brother open up your new account. Do not worry. Everything will be accomplished, and on behalf of myself and my brother, we both welcome you to Brazil," he said with a smile. He got up and shook hands across the desk.

He called his assistant, a beautiful brown-skinned thin woman with long straight hair, and gave the passports, will, attorney's letter of credit, and other documents so she could copy them. The assistant consul smiled at Walter and said, "You'll see beautiful women in Brazil. It's one thing we are very proud of. You are going to love it there." And he arched his right eyebrow and smiled knowingly into Walter's eyes, who met Mauricio's on the same playing field. "Yes, she's lovely," Walter admitted and smiled himself.

They talked a bit about how Maria came to inherit her aunt's property, and Senhor Mauricio said he knew the town very well, and it was indeed lovely. "You are indeed a lucky man, Mr. Keller. A rich wife and a new life together in Brazil in one of the most famous areas of our country. I will call you personally to let you know when the permanent residency documents are issued and will FedEx them to you on the island. I'll do the same with Banco Bradesco account information and balance, once you transfer the initial money into your account to cover these, ah, special fees required for these special circumstances. Most likely you'll receive the residency permits by Friday, and by tomorrow, you will hear from me when the bank account has been activated. It's been an honor to serve you, my dear Senhor Keller," said the assistant consul. Walter shook his hand, put the large manila envelope that held all the passports and legal documents he had brought with him, and thanked the assistant consul and took the taxi back to Logan.

As expected, on Friday, FedEx delivered the two residency permits and the information about their two Bradesco accounts. As a test, Walter immediately wired some money into his account and was pleased to see that by Monday, this transfer had been successfully executed.

A few days later, Maria and Walter both were at Thom's office and signed their respective wills, and each created a survivorship trust. He had told her that he had a small trust fund himself, and so wanted to be sure Thom inserted any trust funds either may have into their new wills. Maria agreed that until Heather was twenty-one in another six years, Walter should be the trustee of their respective new trusts.

By the time he got back to thinking about what to do with Darcie, Maria had appeared looking better than he had seen her in ages. Maybe tonight, with some more wine, wouldn't be too much of a chore after all. Recently, it was all he could do to think about having to make love to her. But she was a sure bet, and Darcie's mood swings concerned him. He had not expected Darcie to begin to say that she might leave Jack, and he was afraid she was impetuous enough to one day do just that.

Chapter 54

Edgartown, Tuesday, October 20, 2015

At the same time as she was trying to get the listing for the house from Gertie and Mae's estate, Maria took a bolder step. A death notice appeared in the *Gazette* stating that Oscar Pease, ninety-four, had died in Braintree, Massachusetts, where he had resided for eleven years at the River Terrace Nursing Home. There were no relatives, and the notice said that Mr. Pease had been cremated. Condolences could be sent in care of the nursing home. She waited a full week and then contacted the nursing home and asked if anyone had sent their regrets yet. They told her no, and she gave a fake name asking that they register her condolences for Mr. Pease.

The Pease property was all but forgotten—it was off Planting Field Way, down a dirt driveway, and barely visible from the potholed and dusty road that was private and led down to Eel Pond. She called Thom, whom she guessed was also the attorney for the deceased (she and about everyone else on the island knew Thom inherited the business from his father, who had been the only attorney in the town for most of his life). Sure enough, Thom acknowledged he was the attorney of record for Oscar Pease, but also said there were complications with the estate, and it wouldn't be put on the market for at least a year or two. She inquired about renting out the property as she "had clients" who'd be interested.

"They live off-island—in Arizona, in the Tucson area—and want to rent this summer and then buy. They could come as early as June and stay until late August when their son goes back to school.

They wanted their rent money to be applied to the purchase price, set now, in order to buy the house by next summer, and they will sign the necessary papers now. I've checked them out, and they are good people. It's similar to the Chilton estate. I'll prepare a purchase-and-sale agreement. They will rent it now, and when the estate work has been completed, we will apply their rentals to the purchase price. People like this arrangement. It locks them into the contract now, so the price won't go up, and if they really didn't want to buy the property when it becomes available, then they can walk away with only having paid a rental. It's a win-win."

Thom thought about it for a minute or two, realizing that would buy him time before he had to tackle the messy title, as so many of these old-time titles were "clouded" and difficult to research. He shrugged his shoulders, went to a cabinet and looked and rummaged around for a second, and then tossed her the keys. He said, "I don't want to spend a lot of money, so just figure out what needs to be done to fix it up enough for your renters this summer, get the estimates, and I'll decide." He motioned her out saying he had clients coming in.

Alone in his office, Thom decided Maria had a point: to buy some time with all the legal mess he'd have to uncover, or rather Owen Carson would have to decipher—this was not an ordinary title search. The property was so clouded that it would take months and months to even begin to make one's way through the tangled and convoluted property history. It was way above Thom's capabilities, and this is exactly what Owen Carson loved to do. His eidetic memory was exactly what made his title searches so reliable; he could keep all this in his head, while others just gave up.

Thom called Danny Bernard and told him what he wanted: the house would have to be brought up to code, and then he'd decide how much he wanted to sink into it. So, the basic property repairs were started. The electrical, plumbing, and foundation would all be corrected. A new roof would be installed. It was outside the Edgartown Historic District, so he didn't have to use red cedar shingles or get their approval. This group who could rule on any property in the district thought of themselves as having "good taste," but not one of them had any architectural or preservation background. He took care of the repairs out of the cash that had been in the owner's Dukes County Bank account.

Danny was one of the "Swamp Portagees"—short, squat with heavy, dark features. He was an honest man, able with his hands, even though he wasn't too bright. But that's exactly what made him so valuable: he never asked questions, and if Thom told him to cut corners a little bit here and there, he just nodded and said, "Yes, Mr. Thom," and did what he was asked to do, without making any comments or asking why.

Maria now had a reason to drive more frequently down toward Eel Pond to the Sutphin House, where she was caretaker. Maria had taken this time to quietly watch Danny's progress on the old Pease house.

A few days into the repairs, she ran into Thom at the Main Street Diner, behind the brick courthouse, one of the few brick buildings in the town with the exception of the school and library. He was leaving as she walked in, and she approached him and reiterated that the two people she had earlier mentioned to him were still very interested in eventually buying the Pease property whenever the estate was settled, and yes, they understood it might be a year or two before it would be available.

To make it look legitimate to Thom, she told him again that if they liked renting it this summer, they would be told they would have until Labor Day to sign a purchase and sale, and the date and amount would be left "to be determined."

"I know you said you'd think about it, but I really want to get this settled now", said Maria.

In addition, Maria would have an exclusive on the property, no matter who were they buyers. Maria would pay Thom a "finder's fee" and have him do all the legal work. There'd be money in it for him, in other words. But they want to move in now.

He took a minute at the cash register and gave the Bulgarian summer cashier a twenty. He knew this was a good deal as it would buy him time to settle the estate and present an offer to the heirs (whoever they might be if Owen could find out) and come out looking good. He was aware of his reputation as being slow (some would say lazy or "on island time"), and this would also help him in this direction. He was surprised at how fast Maria worked—she was good!

He waited for his change, which took a minute as the young dark-haired girl with the name tag "Penka" still wasn't familiar with American currency. He liked her. She was not exactly pretty, but businesslike and serious about work, unlike American college kids who worked on the island.

Maria went on. Because the owners lived in Arizona in the winter, and were leaving Labor Day, she assured them she could send them the necessary papers to sign if the estate was closed during the winter months, and they wouldn't have to be at the actual closing. She told Thom that Rick would represent them and that Rick would file the deeds in the courthouse etc. Over the winter months, she'd act as caretaker, and if the house still hadn't reached to "clear and free" title, they'd be able to rent the house again to this couple for the same price as this first year.

Thom finally agreed—it was a good deal all around for him. He could do the estate when he wanted, and if the heirs pushed, he could show them the signed P&S agreement and the rental terms and get them off his back.

"Okay, it's a deal. What can you get for the season?"

"I told them it would be $75,000, and they didn't bat an eye." She brushed aside her hair and made a conscious effort to look directly at his eyes. She hoped she looked confident and not nervous as she really felt inside. If he found out that she had told them it was $100,000 for the season, she'd be screwed, she thought.

"Do you think that's enough? Prices are skyrocketing," he said.

"Yes, it's fair on two counts. Danny's fixing up the house now, but it's just to be habitable—it's not at all the same condition as other summer rentals. Most important, they're paying this now to hold the house for when it's ready to be on the market. And, we have secured the buyers already. They are simply placeholders now. It's a 'two-for-oner' for us. Yes, it's a fair price, considering." She stopped talking there. She knew if she continued, she'd look too eager and he'd push back.

Thom took another second and nodded. "Okay, you can write up a lease, but only when Danny's just about done. Keep me posted on that, okay? I don't want any trouble about leasing it, if it's not near ready. We got plenty of time anyway until next June, but just let me know of any delays."

Maria thanked him and said with a smile, "We could make quite a team! This is almost exactly like the deal with Gertie and Mae's house—I get the people who agree to rent for the interim, and then, when you get the title and estate settled, they complete the purchase. We both win!"

Thom nodded, but he wasn't happy dealing with her even if it made sense. There was just something about her he didn't trust. And then, he brushed his concerns aside, and he walked across the small parking lot beside the courthouse and down Main Street, turning left onto Winter Street, where his father's office had been since the fifties.

In 1968, Thom landed his first real job as a young summer cop after his first year at Suffolk School of Law. The school was a night school established in 1906 in Boston (much to the vociferous objection of Harvard Law School) to "serve ambitious young men who are obliged to work for a living while studying law." The founder, Gleason Archer Sr., was given the money to complete his study in Boston with the stipulation that he pass on the favor to other boys if he had the opportunity. He believed that the growing waves of immigrants arriving in America should be given the educational opportunities that were then reserved for the wealthy few, but that he himself had the good fortune to receive from a wealthy benefactor. And so, several generations of Irish from Southie, followed by the Italians from the North End, and then other immigrant or working-class sons received their entry into the professional world, spending the summers between studies as "summer cops" somewhere in the Commonwealth's seaside resorts on the Cape and Islands or the North Shore. Thom was one of them. And like many of them, after experiencing seaside life, did not stay in Boston after graduation to become a prosecutor or defense attorney (a position no Harvard Law graduate would ever consider), but rather settled in small towns and became "general practitioners," a jack-of-all-trades lawyer.

As she saw him turn the corner, Maria breathed a sigh of relief and sat down at the diner's counter.

"The usual, Mrs.…um, um?" asked Penka, reddening as she could never recall Maria's married name, even though she had been coming to the island for three years on work visas.

"That's okay, Penka. It's now *Keller*. And thank you, yes, the usual."

Penka hurried off to the kitchen for the linguica and eggs and filled a cup of coffee for Maria.

"Here's your coffee, Mrs. Keller. Your order will be right out." Penka walked away to take care of another customer.

"Thank you, dear God. Thank you for this. I love my husband, and I want to keep him. Thank you," she whispered to herself. "Thank you."

Chapter 55

Edgartown, Wednesday, October 21, 2015, morning

What neither the Arizona "renters" nor Thom knew was that the renters believed they were the new owners: based on previous conversations with Maria, they had already made plans to fly into the Vineyard to meet with Maria a day after Thom agreed to Maria's plan. They signed papers that looked legitimate and paid Maria the full purchase price. They also made out an additional check directly to Maria with a memo note "Pease House/Quarterly Taxes." Maria had explained that the Town and County of Dukes County were notoriously slow filing deeds and issuing tax bills, so by prepaying the taxes in this way, they'd be ahead of the game and not incur any real estate tax penalties if the county register was at her usual slow pace getting the paperwork to the Town. So, by Maria collecting the tax monies from them now, which covered the taxes until next May, they wouldn't have to worry about whether or not the tax bill this year showed them as the new owners or if it was still in the name of old Mr. Pease. Next year in May, they would receive a new tax bill directly from the Town. Maria took the checks and the signed purchase and sale agreement and said that as part of the sale, she'd handle all the paperwork and be filing this for them as she was going to the tax assessor's office that afternoon on other business, so they wouldn't have to bother with all this and could fly right back to Boston and then on home.

The Moores told her she was wonderful: she made all this so easy, and they were so glad her name had come up when asking around for a good realtor. "Ryan said it was time to buy—we've been here so many times with friends and just by ourselves, and I'm so glad people led us to you, Maria! You've made it all so easy!" As they stood there waiting for Cape Air to taxi to a stop, Maria said goodbye, gave Cathy a kiss on the cheek, and shook hands with Ryan. She also added, "Tell Davis I'm looking forward to meeting him when he gets out of school this summer. He's going to love the weather here—not the 109°F Tucson has!" adding she'd be in touch as soon as the deed made its way through the process, but in all likelihood, that wouldn't be happening until the late spring. However, everything would be finished by the time they arrived this coming June. Maria stood there and waved as the small nine-passenger plane took off over the state forest, named after Matt's uncle, the superintendent from 1947 to 1984. She startled herself with the sound of her own enormous sigh of relief as the plane disappeared into the cloudbank.

Maria got back into the Range Rover, started off to town, waving at Jon in one of his taxis, who had just arrived, hoping to pick up a fare from the flight that just landed before the Moores took off. Jon was another Afghani vet, as were Rick and Matt. The three of them were all members of the Rod and Gun Club and Vets and marched in the parades with the black-and-white MIA flag every year. He didn't much care for Rick, but Matt was another thing. It wasn't just that he was an islander, born here, but as a Special Forces member, Matt saw things that none of the other vets on the island had ever imagined. Rick was a phony, pretending to be one of other guys, when in fact he spent his time there sitting in a JAG office, pushing orders. He flew the POW/MIA flag daily trying to have passersby believe he was a hero. He learned to shoot at his parents' lake house in New Hampshire at a Rod and Gun Club there. Jon bet he never used a gun over in Afghanistan. Matt was real. Rick was not.

Meanwhile, Maria, deep in concentration, quickly turned left out of the airport road, onto the Edgartown-Vineyard Haven Road, just barely missing hitting a car: Doc Coffin's. He leaned on his horn and shook his fist and then realized who it was. Maria seemed not to even notice.

"Boy, I should make a point to have her come in and see me. I think Walter may be right about her state of mind." Rick had also mentioned something like that to Doc.

As Doc pulled into the airport, Jon honked him, and Doc pulled over to the taxi. Jon said, "I saw that. She's oblivious to almost hitting you. A couple of people have said she's acting really erratically recently. Last week, I saw Rick in Oak Bluffs at the Lampost on his way out the door as I was coming in, and he shook his head, pointing to Matt in the parking lot pacing up and down. Rick was shaking his head and scowling, and told me that she's driving Matt crazy. Poor guy. And then Rick walked over to Matt and motioned him to get into Rick's Jeep."

Jon continued, "When Linda came over to take my order, I asked what was going on. She also shook her head and said Matt was acting up and yelling, and she had to go over and tell him to be quiet. Rick then told him to go to the Jeep and he'd pay the bill. That's when she confided to me that Rick said Matt was mad enough to kill Maria: she had been hiding money from him and making him pay most of the child support for their daughter," said Jon, shaking his head. "Maria's a bitch and a climber. I wouldn't doubt he's had it with her, once and for all. Matt is a good man." Jon added, "I don't want to see Matt go away again. I'm not the only one concerned."

"Thanks, Jon. I'll see what I can do." Doc waved goodbye, and as he waited for his family to emerge from the baggage claim area, he thought to himself to have Mrs. Anderson give Maria a call to get her to come in. He also would tell Mrs. Anderson not to refill any of the pills he had prescribed for Maria without first checking with him. *Maybe we made a mistake proposing her for the Yacht Club*, he thought. *I need to ask Barbara if she's seen Maria recently and what she thinks about all this.* He opened his car door and stepped out and waved at his daughter-in-law and the grandchildren, who had just stepped off the Cape Air from Hyannis.

"Hi, guys," he yelled, "come on over here! Gamma's waiting for you at home with her famous cookies!" And he quickly forgot his wanting to alert Mrs. Anderson and his wife about what he'd heard about Maria.

CHAPTER 56

Edgartown, Wednesday, October 21, 2015, afternoon

Back in town, Maria parked at the office and then walked downtown to the Edgartown National Bank, where she deposited about a third of the Moore funds into her real estate account and had the bank wire the rest into a new money account ("Maria A. Keller, d/b/a Baldwin Client Account") she had opened in Boston the prior week. The tellers knew Maria and that she sold some of the largest properties in town, so amounts like this were not unusual. They were polite enough not to ask why she hadn't put all the money here at their bank, but it did cross their minds.

Maria quickly phoned Stephanie and said, as a way to test her, that Walter had mentioned something about Maria having shown an unfinished property to a woman from NYC, and he wondered whom she was. Maria said, "Even though we're married, I can't even tell Walter about the deal we made. The owners want to keep the deal quiet right now, as they owe some money to local people like at Edgartown Hardware and a few other businesses. I don't want any of them to come and put a lien on your property right now: let them go sue the former owner and not screw you up. I know someone in town who can clear the title for you now, but we have to be quiet and let him work on it quietly."

Maria paused to hear Stephanie say she hadn't breathed a word to anyone.

"As you can see, there are no secrets on this island. I had to tell Walter those rumors were not true, wasn't sure what he was referring to, etc., but it's really important no one knows about this until the title is cleared. Just checking with you to make sure you might not have started or said something inadvertently to someone here or your family?"

Stephanie reassured her she had not and asked when they were starting work on the house.

"Next week will be when I meet with the contractors, and by that time, the title will have been cleared, and the property will be registered in a blind trust for you so no one knows who you are. If you like the idea, we could name it the *Block Island Trust IV*? People will think it's a real estate investment trust either based on Block Island or having started there, this being their fourth investment."

"Oh, Maria! You are so clever! Thank you so much. This project means so much to me—the start of a new life," said Stephanie.

"My pleasure, Stephanie!" Maria put down the phone, breathing easily again. It was still working. No one knew or suspected anything.

If she didn't have so much money, I'd feel bad as she's really nice, thought Maria, and then she hurried home up School Street to have a drink with Walter and say hi to Heather, if she were home.

Chapter 57

Edgartown, Wednesday, October 21, 2015, early evening

As she opened the front door, she heard talking in the house. It was Heather and Walter. She was surprised and glad that Walter was taking a great deal more of attention to Heather. He had always been pleasant, but something was different recently, and when she came farther into the house, the conversation was coming from the library. She saw the two of them discussing something. They stopped talking when they saw Maria, and she gave them each a big smile and walked over and kissed both on the cheek.

So much for Matt thinking Walter wasn't a family man or a good stepfather! She could tell Heather now thought Walter was good and a far-wiser help than Heather's own dad could ever be regarding more sophisticated (off-island) matters. In less than one year, after next summer, Heather would already have been in Switzerland for a month now, so before then, she needed advice from Walter, who had always lived in that kind of world. Of course, Heather loved her father, but Maria wondered, if Heather did bring new Le Rosey school friends to the island for vacations, what would they think of Matt being a policeman and someone who had never known anything other than life and family on the Vineyard?

Heather was already well aware of social differences between the classes, for that was what the Vineyard was all about: the haves and the have-nots. Some of her friends referred to the chasm as the town and gown. Whatever you called it, it was all the same. It boiled down to the year-rounders and the summer people, the off-islanders and the islanders. Few today used the terms *Natives* or *Native-born*, except for the older generation. But it all meant the same. And Heather knew where she wanted to end up, and, starting next fall, she'd begin her journey out of here—to Geneva and nearby Le Rosey.

Chapter 58

Edgartown, Thursday, October 22, 2015

The next day, after Maria and he had signed their wills in Thom's office, Walter was at home in the library, his favorite room in the house. Papered in slightly fading sand-colored grass cloth wallpaper, the room was lined with white bookshelves filled with books on the Vineyard and Whaling Days, novels from the '40s and '50s like *Rebecca* and *East of Eden*, and interspersed with WWII metal model airplanes. A fireplace was the central point in the room placed between the shelves on the north and south walls, facing a large window on the east. The two chairs that faced each other on either side of the fireplace were mahogany in color, and the worn leather cracks and saggy seat cushions made them all the more authentic to him. This was a man's den. They belonged here—the books, the chairs, the models, the fading wallpaper, everything. They fit in. And that's what Walter wanted to do himself. Fit in. And Maria was the key to the door to this room of his life.

His phone rang.

"Walter! I've got great news, darling. Jack is going over to Nice and then stay for a while at Le Castellet on some business, and he's agreed that it would make sense for me to come to the island for a week or so before I join him there and our guests arrive, as planned. Isn't that great!" said Darcie. "It will be so much easier for us to be together!"

Walter was floored. *What is she saying? Is she crazy!*

"Darcie, we can't do that. People here know everything. It will be impossible to keep us a secret. Tell me you're kidding." He stood in the library and thought wildly of what could happen when people started putting two and two together. Oh god, she was going to spoil everything if she persisted. He had to stop her.

"Don't worry, I'll tell Maria I'm coming with a girlfriend who wants to stay at the Outermost Inn and that I'll make a point to get together with you two a few times while I'm here. She never goes up there, you've said, in fact, no one from Edgartown ever goes up-island. It's like Noman's Island. It'll be fine, darling, don't worry so much! Think of all the fun we can have! I have to run now but will call you later. Love you."

"Darcie! Please don't hang up!" Silence. The phone went dead.

"Hi, dear! I'm home!" yelled Maria from the front hall. "Let's grab a drink. I'm dying of thirst! Ha ha," she said, coming into the library and moving over to give him a kiss. He hated to kiss her now on the lips and moved deftly to catch the kiss on his cheek.

As hot and exciting as Darcie was, he was now worried about her stability. She's the type (and has the money to do it) to be rash and cast her fate to the wind. At first this was appealing—she was so uninhibited in bed and in life, and it was delightful. However, things began to change when he realized she was beginning to fall in love with him, and she was not asking what they should do, but now taking over and telling him what they'd do. This could ruin his plans. He still hadn't decided the ultimate step, but he did know that at least he and Maria would be skipping off to Brazil in the spring, before the house of cards came tumbling down. But a lot could go wrong in the interim, like Darcie. All they needed was another million to add on to what they had "put aside" in these fake real estate deals, and off to Brazil they'd go. Or, at least off to Brazil *he* would go. He still wasn't sure he could do the ultimate…that would take guts, and he wasn't sure he had it in him. But it was on his mind, and he had done his research and had started asking Doc Nevin and a doctor in Boston for pills for his back pain, supposedly from a car accident in the late '90s.

Chapter 59

Edgartown, Friday, October 23, 2015, mid-morning

Days later, Maria's world began to tumble. The people who had "bought" the old Dinsmore property had enough of the waiting games and told Maria they were pulling out.

"We want our money back now. Pronto! Understand, young lady!" Mr. Potts screamed into the telephone. "My family has been coming there since after the war, and I've never seen such incompetency in all these years! My mother would not believe her eyes and ears if she were with us today," he said. "Further, Eleanor is right. Why tie up our money in this place that you can't even get to from any other place? One strike of lightning, one foggy day, and the airline cancels. We're better off in Newport or the Hamptons, where at least you can get there by the highway—not by steamship or rinky-dink little nine-seater airplane piloted by a twenty-five-year-old with acne and just out of the service!"

"Mr. Potts, I know how frustrated you are with the system, and it *is* taking much longer than even I expected, but I can assure you, this property is really a one-in-a-million opportunity. The Dinsmore House has been coveted by many who know its location and worth. Let me call the title examiner again and push them even more than ever. Could you give me a couple more weeks? I'd love for your mother to know that you are carrying on the Potts name here. She was such a dear. You know my mother loved her so much." Maria sounded her sweetest. It was good there was a phone between them so he couldn't see how wild-eyed she looked, sweat beginning to form on her brow, wetting the edge of her curly black hair.

"No way! Eleanor and I want our money back now. Furthermore, we're not interested at all—ever again—in any property on that island. I sold our family home there only because the Dinsmore property was exceptional and was just coming on the market. You've kept our money from the sale of my mother's house in the bank to purchase the Dinsmore property, and now we want our money back. We don't want the Dinsmore House or any other on the island. Ever!" he screamed again into the phone. "If people can't execute simple title searches and make sales happen, then you've got a bigger problem than me. You can sell all the houses you want, but you won't get buyers if they can't clear titles. No one will want to buy there! No one!"

Maria told them again she was sorry, and she'd try again with the title examiners' office, but Mr. Potts yelled into the earphone, "Don't bother! And if we don't get our money back immediately, young lady, there'll be trouble!"

If he said *young lady* once more, she'd let him have it. They were the same age. It's just that she, the daughter of their old cleaning lady, didn't have the same status as his Yacht Club friends, and hence, he referred to her as *young lady*; in other words, they were not "equal"—she was beneath him. *What a fat, inflated ass he is—he and his whole family*, thought Maria. She remembered her mother saying, "Young Master Potts is going to be trouble someday the way he treats his mother." And sure enough, what Mrs. Almeida had seen and heard, as she polished furniture and washed toilets cleaning their family summer home for those thirty summers, was proving right. He was trouble. She also hated to having call him *Mr. Potts* when they were the same age. But he had never said, "Oh, Maria, please call me *Ted*. We've known each other forever!" No, he wanted the divide.

"Mr. Potts. I'm so sorry. Could you think about it for a day or two, and I'll call you to see if we have any news, and then you can make a final decision. I could call you Monday morning. Is that okay?"

After a second, and a whispered conversation with "dear Eleanor" (the bitch), Maria heard him get back on the line and say, "Okay. We'll give you the weekend. Monday morning. And if the news is still another delay, we want our money wired to us that day! Understand, young lady?"

"Yes, sir, Mr. Potts. I understand completely. Again, I'm so sorry as this is out of my hands, but I will push and push them. And, no matter what, I'll phone you Monday morning."

"Goodbye, then!" said Mr. Potts as he forcefully put down the phone.

At this, Maria reached for a Kleenex and dabbed her face and neck. She hated when she stepped out of the shower, or when the day was humid as it was today, as her black hair, sleek and shiny after blowing it dry, became her bane—curly, black, wiry Portuguese hair. A Portuguese peasant's hair. And try as she did, she could never get completely away from her background, as these nasty tendrils showed. She hated her parents and all their people. She would never be one of them. She knew classmates from high school and family friends of her family all thought she was a snob, but she didn't care. She had almost escaped her roots, and Mr. Potts was *not* going to stop her.

She began to panic. Where were those Xanax, as she rooted through her Coach bag. She needed to do something fast.

Walter knew all about the Dinsmore "sale" as he did most of the other transactions (Stephanie was an exception, but it was a security blanket for them in case something unforeseen happened, and she didn't want to worry Walter any more than he was beginning to do). He already thought they didn't have enough put away to make the escape worthwhile in the spring, so it was impossible to tell him now of the conversation with asshole Potts, who wants his money back immediately. But what could she do?

She picked up her phone and speed-dialed Rick's number.

"Rick, can I come see you, or can you drop in on your way downtown?"

"Sure," he said, smirking, "what's up?" He already knew what "was up." Every time her office phone rang, he heard exactly what the conversations were—including those of her husband with that hot little Darcie slut. This was like taking candy from a baby. It was so easy.

He'd use the info when the time was right. He also was beginning to realize Maria was keeping some secrets from Walter. *Why* was the question. What was she planning?

"Why don't you come over here? It's easier." He hung up the phone. This will be fun, he thought, whistling a little ditty his father used to do on his boat when he was pleased with something. He soon heard Ellen welcome Maria and his door opened. He motioned Maria to sit down on the chair across from his desk.

Chapter 60

Edgartown, Friday, October 23, 2015, noon

"I'm afraid the Potts deal is not going to happen. They want their money back," said Maria to Rick.

"You'll find another buyer, don't worry," he replied.

"Well, actually, I have a little favor of you to tide me over until I find a new buyer," Maria said.

Knowing he had her, Rick let her speak and then told Maria he could get her out of the mess, but it would cost. He'd call Walter today to explain to him that there was a legal problem with the Dinsmore transaction, and although the Potts deal was off, he had another client who was interested in the Dinsmore estate. He'd produce the papers for Walter and Maria to sign the next day.

In other words, she could tell Walter that although she was withdrawing the $650,000 from the Potts "escrow," there'd be no actual loss of money because of Rick's new buyers. Because Walter assumed Rick knew nothing at all about Maria and Walter's shady Ponzi scheme, Walter would take Rick's word at face value. He had little curiosity and was lazy, so chances were excellent that he wouldn't ask Rick to see his escrow account to make sure the new money had arrived. He was an easy mark.

"Walter will believe me: there are new buyers. Period. End of discussion," said Rick. "And, his signature will be on the new P&S agreement alongside yours as broker of record. So, if anything happens, he'll be liable too."

"What kind of money are you talking that I will owe you?" said Maria to Rick.

"Well, it would have been $75,000, but just this morning, I've raised it to $100,000."

"What! Are you kidding me!" she yelled.

"$100,000 is cheap considering you will face jail time if word gets out. I'm sure you can easily make up this amount within my time frame. June first. That's when it's due. All of it."

"That's crazy!" she yelled.

"The higher amount is because I just learned something new," Rick said.

Rick looked at Maria straight in the eyes. "There's more to this than the Potts property. I know about the Pease House and the so-called 'renters' from Arizona who will sign a three-month lease for next summer along with a sale agreement that will be executed after the first of the year."

Mari looked stunned and gasped. "What are you talking about?"

"You think you're so smart, don't you? Let's just say people whom you think are your friends or are on your side maybe aren't your friends, but instead are my friends. I have my sources," he said.

She was speechless. Thom must have double-crossed her. How could he do this? He had promised to keep this quiet, and he knew full well that she didn't want Walter to know. She raised her voice again. "This is extortion! You can't do this! I can report you!"

"Maria, that's up to you. But let me say this. You, my dear, are running what's called a Ponzi scheme, and your husband is on most of this, although you are clearly keeping the Pease rental and its 'future purchase' quiet from your own husband. I wonder what Walter would think if I told him what scheme you've got going on now that he doesn't know about? Planning on skipping town without him?" Rick said calmly and evenly, not raising his voice to her.

He just kept his eyes steady on her and noticed the beads of perspiration on her forehead and her left hand that kept twitching. Her carefully blown-dry hair was now getting frizzy around her perspiring temple—just like all the Portagees. *You can dress them up, but you can't take them out*, he thought to himself. What a mess she was becoming right in front of his eyes. He was enjoying this little show.

"Maria, you don't seem to realize I'm bailing you out of this mess. And, I could be liable too. I'm not sticking my neck out for nothing. We're signing a loan right now, and Ellen will come in and notarize it. I'm not wasting any more time with you."

He picked up a paper and began typing on his letterhead. He handed it over the desk to her to read and noticed both her hands were trembling. She nodded, biting her lip and frowning slightly, trying to look composed. A bead of perspiration trickled down her left cheek. She was looking more and more like her mother. *They all look alike no matter how far they made it in life. Swamp Portagees—all of them.*

"Ellen! Can you come in here and notarize something for us? It'll just take a minute," yelled Rick through the closed office door.

God, she hated being yelled at. Why couldn't he just stand up and open the door? He had no manners, and even little things like this made her question why she was still there working for him. "I'm coming, just a minute, I need my seal."

Maria barely acknowledged Ellen. She kept her eyes down and didn't make contact. Rick handed the paper to Ellen, covering the text down to the signatures. Ellen stated she was forgoing the formality of looking at Maria's driver's license and watched as Maria signed her section, then handing it back to Rick to do the same. Then Ellen signed and dated in her place, with Rick still covering the body of the document so she couldn't read the content, and took out her seal and imprinted it on the paper. No one spoke, and Ellen went to the door. Rick tersely said, "Thank you. That'll be all. It's almost quitting time, so you might as well leave, but don't forget to take that package to the post office on your way. See you tomorrow."

Weird, Ellen thought. *The whole thing was weird. What was going on in there? Maria looked as if she could faint, and Rick was as red-faced as I'd ever seen him. Something went down between them. But what?* She put on her coat and shut off the computer. *I hate this place*, she said to herself, stepping out the door.

Rick turned back to his computer and said to Maria, "I'm emailing Walter now saying the Potts deal has fallen through but that I have a buyer. I'll show it to you in a minute before I send it. You better have the rest of that $100,000 paid to me by June first, or I'll turn you in. I'm not kidding, Maria. You can call it what you want—blackmail or anything. But the fact remains: half before 2:00 p.m. today, before the bank closes deposits, and the remainder of that money better be here by June first, or your game *and* marriage are up."

Maria said nothing but sat there in silence. Neither one of them realized Ellen had stepped back into the office to pick up the package she was to have mailed on her way home and overheard the last piece of their conversation.

Oh my god, Ellen said to herself as she backed out of the office with the package in her hand and ever so quietly shut the door again. They both were gambling with their future: a blackmailer and a crooked real estate broker.

"I've got to get a new job. I can't handle this. I'm just a bundle of nerves." She walked down the driveway towards the post office and got there just before the window closed for the lunch hour. Once having mailed the package, Ellen stopped across the street at the Square Rigger for a drink. Bart had never seen Ellen in there alone at the bar at lunch time, nor rarely any other time, for that matter. Something must be up, he thought.

CHAPTER 61

Edgartown, Friday, October 23, 2015, 1:00 p.m.

Rick was still in his office with the door shut. Ellen thought she heard voices when she entered the office and hanged up her coat, but didn't know of any scheduled appointments. She heard him chuckle out loud. As she set up her computer and unlocked the front door, the conversation stopped in Rick's office, and he yelled out "Is that you, Ellen?"

Then he opened the door. *Why couldn't he do so first, rather than always yell through the doors?* She couldn't stand his rude, uncouth behavior. *I wish I could quit today*, she thought.

"I've got a lot of work today. Just take phone messages. And, I don't care how many times Janet calls, I'm NOT available! Get it?"

Ellen didn't look at him and stared at her desk. "Yes, I understand." *What a pig. I don't understand how Janet can stand one more day with him.*

He shut the door, and she again heard the voices. He must have on his speakerphone, she thought, but went back to her work.

He continued listening to his tape recorder. The tape was running live.

"Hello, Mrs. Strock, this is Maria Keller from the Vineyard calling with some exciting news for you. Before I go on, first of all, how have you been? Wonderful! Same here. I'm very happy with Walter, and we're doing well too. What I wanted to tell you, but it's absolutely confidential. Can I have your word? Good. Now I know you will need to talk to Mr. Strock, but you must insist this is not to be mentioned to anyone else. If you can guarantee he'll be strictly discreet, I'll continue. Good. Thank you. Okay, here's my news."

Just then, the tape recorder stopped. Silence. "God damn it all! Fuck! Fuck! Fuck! I don't fucking believe this! Why me!" And he took his desk clock his father had given him and flung it across the room and stormed out of his office, right past Ellen, who didn't dare say a word, through the gate that connected his office to the house, and burst into the kitchen, where Janet was talking on the phone to someone.

"Forget me for dinner tonight! I'm going out!" He slammed the door, kicking one of the dogs as he headed for the garage.

Janet had put down the phone and looked out the window. His Jeep went screeching around the corner onto Main Street. She heard a horn blare and someone yell at him, "You crazy son of a bitch! You almost killed me!"

Why did he get in these crazy moods? His mother was unstable, and maybe he had inherited some of her problems. He was becoming more and more like this, and it scared her. She didn't know what to do. It was such a small island, and she had one of the few good jobs. Divorces were common elsewhere, but here, behind the white picket fences that lined the town's streets, you never knew what really went on inside. In this tight-lipped community, it was understood you did not air your unhappiness to others. It was the Edgartown code. Keep your property in good shape, repair the pickets, and deadhead the roses. That's all you had to do to get along here.

Chapter 62

Edgartown, Friday–Saturday, October 23–24, 2015

Maria, oblivious to the drama down the street in Rick's office, went on to describe the property as being in Chilmark, at 80 Gosnold's Way, a remote area near the Menemsha Hills Reservation. The house has fourteen bedrooms, all with en suite baths, two half baths, gourmet kitchen, dining room seating twenty-four, a media room, an indoor gym, library, and believe it or not in this age—a ballroom! Not to mention the infinity pool, dual tennis-basketball court, and fabulous views of the Vineyard Sound.

"I know you and Hal have been thinking of getting a larger place for your grown-up family and grandkids, and one that is in a secluded area with all the amenities. This would be perfect. I also know you both are staunch supporters of the Clintons and the Obamas, and you'll be interested to know this is the house each has rented in the past. It's my inside knowledge that the house was renting at $85,000 a week when the Obamas were last here, and they are coming back again this summer. This is the part that is ultrasecret: no one is to know yet the president will be here this coming summer. It will be announced in late May. More importantly, what no one else but you and I know is that I am going to be the exclusive broker for this estate when the Obamas go back to DC. We can sign papers now, but only if you can wait until after Labor Day for the closing to take place. I'm sure you know this will be the property of the year, and there'll be all sorts of people wanting to see this from all over the country and the world. The other property, Blue Heron Farm, the one that the Clintons had first rented, years ago during that awful time with that slut intern, was sold last week for $21.9 million. This one, your new one if you so decide, is bound to fetch far higher than that one. I'm thinking of putting an asking price of $38 million.

"The property you'd be looking…Middlemark…has been occupied by a high-profile European couple, Lord Henri and Lady Linda Terrevaut of Thames Bank in Great Britain.

"You don't know who they are? Lord Terrevaut is Belgian, and he's the one who designed the new Lincoln Registry, called the Bosc on Thames, as it looks like a giant pear hanging over the Thames, and Skillet Tower, the strange, round, bottom-heavy building, which sits on a plaza in downtown London. He's considered to be one of the world's most successful architects. Lady Terrevaut by birth is an Anheuser of the Anheuser-Budweiser Beer family and is also distantly related to the Mountbattens. Growing up in St. Louis, she was an accomplished equestrian and the founder of several *Horse & Hound* publications. Her maiden name is *Fritz* and will be the only name that appears in connection with the real estate transfer, the bulk of which was handled through a limited liability corporation. No one will make any connection to that name.

"Because the Obamas will be here for a good part of the summer, we'd need to visit the property right now, in the off-season, because once the Secret Service sets up camp before the family arrives, it will be off-limits to us or anyone else. Lord and Lady Terrevaut are in full agreement about their sale if we can keep it quiet until after the Obamas leave. It's important no gossip gets out, or the deal will be called off. They are personal friends of Barack and Michelle and know they don't want publicity."

"Oh, dear. I just don't know if we are ready, and we'd have to make a decision very soon, dear," said Sallie Strock. "I just don't have the time to come up there now either," she said.

"Now, Mrs. Strock, you and your husband have that little plane, and I know you could take four to five hours this weekend for a quick trip up and back. I'll meet you at the airport and whisk you up-island to see the house and take you right back to the airport again. I'd love to invite you to lunch, but if you both don't feel you have enough time, I'll get a picnic lunch for you from Savoir Fare, and you can take it back with you on the plane. It's a once-in-a-lifetime opportunity, and it has to be now," she said.

The next day, just after eight o'clock in the morning, Maria was once again at the Vineyard airport, greeting both Sallie and Hal as if they were old friends. Chatting along the way up-island, past the beautiful old stone walls built by settlers not for their "charm," but out of necessity to farm, Maria chatted about the rising real estate values, the well-known celebrities here and those coming in droves now, and the "like-minded" people they would get to know and be socializing with. This appealed more to Hal than it did Sallie, but it would be he who decided whether or not to buy.

When they pulled up to the hidden driveway—only a small stone marker near the RFD mailbox indicated it was called *Middlemark*. There was an etched horizontal mark right in the middle of the smooth stone under the mailbox. Hal particularly noticed and like this. This was "classy," and he knew it. Being in the family garment business in New York, he had almost single-handedly successfully pulled the company up and out of the lethargic state of affairs his elder brother and he had inherited. He bought his brother out, started dealing on the international level, and within a few years had established himself as one of the richest garment manufacturers in the world. He targeted up and coming designers and got to know them: hanging around their ateliers, talking to their own businesspeople they relied upon to rein the designs in if they got too far out, and most of all, chatted up the assistants who had the inside scoop. The assistants were rail thin as the models—would-be mannequins except for their rather ordinary looks—yet still hungry for the designer's world lifestyle. The assistants all looked the same—thinning hair yanked into excruciatingly sleek ponytails, black-framed eyeglasses at the tips of their nose, pens stuck behind their ear, crimson lipstick, crisp white blouses paired with pencil skirts. They were always on the prowl for coke. Five pounds too heavy, just like the models, they were kicked out of the firm, no matter how efficient and good they were at their job. Hal knew this and had some connections in the district where coke was easy to come by, sometimes at cost, sometimes free, but unlike other purveyors, Hal never hit on them and consequently became their friends. They complained to him about the infighting, the people who were not to be trusted, and told him what trends they saw. The assistants knew what were going to be the next big trends in fashion fourteen or fifteen months before the models strutted down the runway. Hal's cost of doing business—a few grams here and a few grams there—was nothing compared to the head start he got in manufacturing the right colors, the right fabrics, and the readiness to immediately provide them when the designers called for the "new look." He was there ready to go, six months before anyone else in the industry—even the Chinese—could provide the fabrics to the designer. Word had spread quickly among the fashion world that Hal was a genius in being able to "read" each designer's mind before he or she (he had to remember not to continue saying "he," a habit he couldn't seem to shake no matter how hard he tried) even started working on the new line that had been swimming around in his (okay, hers too) head for the past year or more.

"Hal. What do you think?" Sallie said excitedly. "Just look at this property! Maria, it's gorgeous!" Maria pulled the Range Rover up to the door and hopped out. "Do you need a hand, Sallie? These doors are so high! But when you're all over the Vineyard as I am, going down remote dirt roads with rain-washed potholes, you need something big like this. Jaguars don't cut it here!"

Hal was impressed as he walked into the enormous foyer, actually an atrium. The pale wood circular staircase was carved in a dazzling array of seashells and fish—immediately he thought of models descending that staircase and doing a series of "Fashion Weeks" right here on the Vineyard, featuring one designer after another, through the entire summer months. Beats those stuffy places where every celebrity is crammed into, under blaring hot lights in some city loft. Make it a vacation. And, he'd have the designer and photographer and the chief assistant and models stay right here. What publicity he'd get, and what secrets he'd learn from the assistants, with only a little snort here and a little snort there!

"Let's see the bedrooms and the public areas. I'm impressed already," said Hal. Sallie and Maria winked at each other—looking good!

Upstairs there were three wings: north and south and then a perpendicular wing heading west. The fourteen bedrooms didn't count the maids' quarters that were on the uppermost floor. Hal was now more convinced than ever that his Fashion Week Series plan was brilliant. Oblivious to this, Sallie was beginning to wonder if it all just wasn't too big. She definitely had plans for her their three kids and now five grandchildren, but realistically with today's work world and grandchildren's insane soccer, scouts, and music schedules, where would they find the time to actually come up here? Hal worked so much that he hardly knew Sallie's friends, and when they occasionally got together with some of the couples, Hal was always talking about business to the man, and Sallie was left talking with his wife. So, who else would they have to invite to even half fill these rooms in the summer?

Hal noticed that little furrow in her brow that was the sign she was having doubts.

"Ya know, doll, all those phonies in the city who invite you to their charity luncheons because they know you have money, but then will diss you the minute after the event is over? Well, doll, with this here house, you can throw your own charity luncheons, and believe you me, when I get finished with the publicity about this place with the *Post* and Fashion Week and *Vogue*, you'll have every one of those phonies up here just to see the place, and then, after they do, they'll kiss up to you to make sure they're invited again. I got a plan in mind, and all you need to do is to choose the charities. I'll fill you in later, but right now, young lady"—turning to Maria—"we gotta talk turkey."

Hal thought he had made the deal of the century: he got the asking price down by $1.8 million to a total sales price of $36.2 million including furniture. Maria again warned him not to speak about the property to anyone under any circumstances. The Terrevauts made it very clear and put it in their purchase and sales agreement that any leaks about the sale would null and void the agreement, and earnest money would not be returned. They themselves would make the announcement when it was a done deal and the time was right.

Sallie was used to Hal's big ideas, and they always worked. She felt the pressure about the bigness of this house slip away and once again was glad she had not turned him down those thirty years ago. She knew he would make it work, whatever it may be in life.

They handled everything that day in person before the Strocks took off. Maria gave him her Boston bank account information (she did not want that amount of money to hit Edgartown National as that would be sure to raise questions). Hal wired the 25 percent down payment by his phone so it would hit her account before 2:00 p.m. today, or Monday at the latest, with the next installment of 50 percent to be paid in forty-five days, and the final 25 percent in another forty-five days. He had Sallie begin to compile the A-list of charities. "Hey, doll, stick to the younger crowds too. They're the real thing now rather than these old biddies wearing Gran-mama's old pearls and jade necklaces. Young blood, that's the list I want. Trendy and into fashion."

Back in the city, Sallie sat down at her desk and started to put the list she had mentally compiled down on paper: the Estée Lauder Foundation/Breast Cancer Research Foundation, the Met, the Young Fellows at the Frick, the Young Garden Circle at the Botanical, the Art Production Fund, etc. And on and on the list grew, with Hal checking in every once and a while, crossing off one charity on the list or questioning another. When it was finished, he made the rounds with each assistant and asked them to choose the groups that they thought would attract the right people to their designer. They all thought this idea of Hal's was brilliant and said they'd help convince the designer's models if he or she balked at the idea of a series of eight "Fashion Weeks on the Vineyard." The week their designer was to be featured, they'd get to stay in Hals's mansion, have coke parties, and enjoy life away from the hot city. What more could an assistant and some of the models want? Hal was the man.

Chapter 63

Edgartown, Friday, October 23, 2015, evening

Walter sat Maria down in the library that night. He made their martinis as usual, but looked serious.

"I've got to tell you something. And I need you to be honest. Rick called me regarding the Potts deposit saying he had another buyer and needed my signature on the release of funds, so I went in to sign the document. He chatted about some real estate deals that he didn't know if I was aware of." He stopped and looked directly into her eyes.

She tried to keep her eyes steady and wide open, looking right back into his without blinking. Inside, she was panicking and trying to think of whatever she could say, before he told her what was said between Rick and him. Walter noticed the little drivel of sweat above her left ear and her carefully blown-out black hair starting to curl in a tendril or two. He knew then he had her caught in a lie. Rick was right.

"What do you know about the Pease House—the old guy who died off-island?"

Thank God, she thought. *I thought Rick had somehow got hold of news of the Terrevaut property or of Stephanie. I am still leery of Hal and a big mouth, but I can easily explain the Pease property.*

"Oh, honey! This was to have been a surprise for you, and Rick has spoiled it now! I'm *so* upset. You can't tell him anything."

Maria took a sip of the icy liquid with a hint of lemon zest and leaned closer to Walter. "I know you've been worried about whether or not we had enough cash to pull out of here before the summer and go to Brazil. So, I arranged a rent-to-buy deal with Thom and a couple I had met, and when the last payment comes in, right before your birthday in March, I'd show you our bank account and tell you this was the time to leave. I'm so sorry he spoiled it for you. I was doing this for you. Actually, for us. All we need is a few more months, and we'll be out of here and living the life in our beautiful home in Florianopolis. I love you, sweetie, and this is the only time I've kept a secret from you. But it was for us." She took another larger sip of her martini, getting more relaxed.

Walter sat back. He asked her a few questions about the transaction and noted that Thom was the attorney. Thom was principled (unlike Rick), and Walter also had a sigh of relief. Her story must be true. She was so stupid that for a second he felt a little bad that he felt this way about her. She was like a lovesick puppy that tried to get love and attention by playing with his new owner's shoelaces. She had no idea he'd be the one going to Florianopolis—alone.

Well, maybe arriving alone, but once there, the sky's the limit with beautiful women enamored with a wealthy American. And Constanca there, waiting on him hand and foot.

"Don't worry about it, dear. Rick made it sound so sinister that I had to bring it up. I'm sorry I doubted you. You know our marriage is built on truth, and we've always said we have no secrets from one another. So, now we don't. And, I like your idea of wrapping this up with more cash and as fast as we can. I've been thinking we should decide what we really want to take with us—and not a lot—and get a briefcase ready for a spur-of-the-moment exit if we need to. We can store them in the guest room for the moment. Remember: we can buy clothes and things like that there. I'm talking about personal things like photos, prescriptions, bank statements, legal papers such as wills, birth certificates, passports, and property deeds. You know the type of things. Why don't we each do that tomorrow?" He stood up and bent over and kissed her cheek.

"Another one?" She nodded, relaxing at last, sinking back into the worn leather armchair while he stirred the martini. Life was good.

Chapter 64

Edgartown, Friday, October 23, 2015, later that evening

When they finished the second martini, she said, "Let's go out to eat tonight. I can't face cooking. What do you think?" said Maria to Walter.

"Sounds fine with me. Where?" he said. "Andrea's?"

Andrea's was around the corner from Rick's house, and he frequently would go there with Janet. Maria didn't want to chance that, tonight of all nights.

"Let's go to the Dunes. We haven't been there in a while, and I haven't been out to South Beach in ages. And it closes soon for the season. I may have a listing coming up on Atlantic Drive, and we could drive by that before dinner," Maria said. "I'll get a jacket and meet you in the car."

They drove out toward Katama Road in silence until they came across Ernie Boch's house, the largest car dealer in Massachusetts, a huge white anchor standing upright to the right of the white paddock fence's gate much as a sentry stands guard. The house was set way back hundreds and hundreds of feet from the roadway. Two llamas were grazing near the road—a unique tax write-off for a New England summer resort town. Ernie missed nothing.

Occupying fifteen acres of prime real estate, from the Katama Bay side, the fifteen-thousand-square-foot home rose up at the shoreline like a beacon. With almost enough skylights and windows for every day of the year, at night from the bayside, it looks the *QEII* ran aground. It was no unconscious act that Ernie's house eclipsed the nearby Edgartown Lighthouse as the brightest spot on the horizon. You may not accept me, the house says, but you can't ignore me. That was Ernie.

Walter said, "Are you okay? You seem awfully quiet tonight. Are you sleeping better since I picked up those pills Doc said would help?"

"I don't think they are doing much. I awake frequently, and my mind doesn't stop working. Wish we could go on a vacation, but it's the busy time of the year, and I've got a lot of projects in the works."

"I'm seeing Doc Nevin tomorrow, and I'll ask him if he's got anything stronger for you. But why don't we see if we can get away to Brazil for five days—you can use a phone if anything comes up at the office, and we can totally write off the trip as we are going there 'to check on the property.' Besides, it will be good to see Constanca again. She's got to be getting on in age now, and who knows how long she'll last?"

Maria didn't respond. She was looking out the window to her right at the 160-acre FARM Institute and how barren and desolate it looked at this time of year…utterly windswept without any visible signs of activity except for a few of the almost two dozen Belted Galloways and American British Whiteparks that are bred. Now in the off-season, the cows are found closer to the barns eating hay. She didn't see any sign of the equally numerous breeding ewes, comprised primarily of Cotswolds. They must be inside the barns, she thought. She liked the summer months as both cows and sheep are grass-fed and can be seen eating the tall green grass, as they are rotated through the acres. Heather used to like coming here as a little girl, lingering to watch the three hundred laying hens pecking and the turkeys (which were raised for Thanksgiving, although she didn't know this) strutting around. Best of all was the Billy Jowl (the boar) and Peggy Sue, the large black sow.

"Maria? Are you there! Earth to Maria," teased Walter. They had just turned left on the corner of Katama Road and were about to enter Dunes Road and the restaurant parking lot. "What about a short trip to Brazil?"

"It's an idea. Let me think about it tomorrow after I get to the office. Tonight, I just want to relax, have some wine, and look out at South Beach." She put her hand on his shoulder and gave him a little pat. "Thanks for taking me out tonight. I really needed this!"

Walter wondered whom she had seen this afternoon. Whoever it was, it would let him know who seems to have a grip on her. He didn't want anyone spooking Maria at this time when he was making his own exit plans. He'd see Senna Monday morning sometime and casually ask her whom Maria had seen. He wasn't quite yet ready to make the move while Maria still had a few more projects to close on. The money was too good to pass up.

They were driving his new car and left the Range Rover at home. As he parked the dark-green Grand Cherokee, Maria slowly walked toward the Dunes' door. She kept replaying the conversation with Rick that afternoon. He had her, and she knew this would not be a one-time extraction of money from her. Yes, it was blackmail, but he and she both knew she couldn't report him. For that would be her downfall too.

And it wasn't the legal trouble that worried her the most: she realized that with the real estate and monies Rick was (and would be) exacting, her ability to keep Walter was doomed. Walter was already wary of some of her practices, and if he thought she didn't have the amount of money he thought she had, there would be no reason to stay with her.

Thank god for the Strocks this afternoon. That would make all the difference in the world. By Monday, when the check is deposited, we'd have more than enough to leave anytime now. And Walter would never know how much I've been sweating all this. Maria slipped her hand in his and felt an instant weight removed from her shoulders. Maria knew she couldn't live without Walter. She thought she could handle the situation herself. Maybe I could even do another one or two big deals that, somehow, I can keep from Rick, and then Walter and I can head for Brazil—forever. Life was good, again.

Chapter 65

Edgartown, Saturday, October 24, 2015, 1:00 p.m.

Rick drove by Baldwin Real Estate Agency and saw Maria's Range Rover in the driveway. She often worked on weekends.

Rick called Maria after lunch. "So, did Walter talk to you last night?"

"Yes, and I told him the Pease House was to have been a surprise so we could go on a vacation together to Europe. Why on earth did you tell him about this? This was to have been our secret, and it's why I'm paying you."

"I don't know why I think this, Maria, but I have the feeling you're doing another one behind my back—a much bigger one. Who was that couple that a friend of mine saw you with up in Chilmark yesterday morning? Said you picked them up at the airport and brought them back a few hours later." Rick stayed quiet and waited for her to answer.

"Oh, just some old clients who wanted to see what was available. I showed them around a couple of places. But nothing met with their approval."

"Funny. I heard there was one of those big properties where the Obamas or Clintons used to stay that is quietly being shopped around. Haven't you heard about this? You're one of the biggest brokers."

She could feel his eyes piercing through the phone. He knew something. But how! She hadn't talked about it to anyone at all. The transaction was all done at the airport before they took off back to

New York. She had the money put into her Boston account, so no banker on the Vineyard could have let him know she had deposited a huge sum of cash into her escrow account.

She concluded he was fishing, or else he would have dropped the name. "They're not in *that* league, and everyone is always saying those properties are coming on the market, but they never do. These people are probably going to stay in the Hamptons. He's a workaholic." She then changed the subject back to Matt, her ex-husband.

"He's worrying me. I've seen him outside restaurants where we go, he tells Heather he can't afford the child care payments any longer and that I'm just a bitch not to take care of her myself and that he may take an early retirement from the police due to medical reasons. If he does that, I will definitely have to pay for all of her expenses, and she's heading to boarding school in Switzerland next year. I can't afford that!" she said.

What a bitch she is, Rick thought. *Her husband, or rather ex-husband, suffers from PTSD, she causes a breakdown by throwing divorce papers in his hand on Main Street and is hiding all this money from him. I'm on Matt's side, honey. Just you wait!*

"Maria, don't get greedy. It'll ruin things for you. I'll have a talk with Matt today and get him to calm down. Don't go fly off the handle. You've got a lot riding on your being able to keep a cool head. Don't fuck things up now. And, don't forget—I've got a stake in this too. I'm not going to sit by and watch you fall apart. Get a grip!" and he slammed down the phone.

She sat in her office trembling, knowing full well he had her in his hands. She'd need to get things finalized, and then she and Walter get out of there earlier than they had originally planned. *God, what a mess! I can't believe this is all happening to me. It was going so well. Matt better stick around here as Heather would need a place to live once we're in Brazil. Tomorrow,* she said, *is another day. Scarlet was right.*

Maria got up from her desk and grabbed her sweater and made a voice message saying she'd check messages in a few hours.

As Maria opened the door to Doc's office, Mrs. Anderson looked up from her desk quizzically, and Maria said, "I don't have an appointment, Mrs. A., but was hoping Doc was in?"

Mrs. Anderson got up and motioned Maria to sit down and went down the hall to the office where Doc was sitting reading the *Gazette*.

"Doc, Maria is here without an appointment and wanted to see you for a minute. What should I tell her?"

"How does she seem?" he said, glancing up from the oversized newspaper, which he tried to fold unsuccessfully. It was so damn big, and although summer people and tourists found its size "quaint" and "peculiar to the Vineyard," most year-rounders hated its size. People's arms could not even stretch the breadth of the thirty-five-inch paper to fold it.

"Nervous and biting her nails," she answered, shrugging her shoulders a little. "Should I send her in?"

He sighed and stood up. "Might as well. People have been saying she's not been herself recently. Have her go into the exam room, and you stay there. I'll be right in."

In the exam room, Maria told him she had a lot on her mind recently: Matt was still not back to normal and resented her marriage, Heather was hearing things from Matt about her, but her business had never been better, and she and Walter were very happy.

"So, what would you like me to do, Maria?"

"Walter thinks maybe I should have a stronger tranquilizer from time to time when the stress is getting to me. Not too strong, however. Just something in between."

"I can write out a prescription but want you to see someone who's a professional to talk things through. You'll be surprised at how just talking to someone can help alleviate stress. You know Jane Norton, I believe? She's someone who is competent and discreet. You can call Community Services and make an appointment with her there. But that's up to you. However, it's what I suggest. Here's your script—take one of these in the morning for a week and let me know if this is helping. Don't forget Jane either."

She thanked him and went out the door onto South Summer Street and got in her car and headed to the Triangle to the pharmacy. She handed the script to Bettina behind the counter and waited about ten minutes.

"Here you go, Mrs. Da Costa—I mean, Mrs. Keller!" said Bettina blushing. "Have a good day!"

Maria got in her Range Rover and opened the bottle and took two pills immediately without water and drove back to the office. She left the phone on voice mail, and she shut the door. She tried to focus on the new purchase and sale agreement, but instead leaned back in her chair and went fast to sleep. When she awakened, she was astonished to see it was almost four o'clock.

Chapter 66

Edgartown and Aquinnah, Saturday, October 24, 2015, late morning

"Okay, but please don't call at home anymore! It's dangerous. I can't count on Maria not popping in whenever she feels like it. I'll meet you today, but after lunch—I can't imagine anyone I know will be there. I've never even been to the Land's End myself. I'll call you right before I arrive, and you can come down and meet me. Just don't make a scene, Darcie. That's all I want. Of course, I want to see you—it's just that I can't take a chance right now with Maria. She's off the deep end and taking tranquillizers, and people are talking about her. I don't want to push her over the edge. That's all I'd need. See you this afternoon, bye." Walter hung up.

What a mess this is, he thought to himself. *I never expected she'd talk about leaving him—it's the last thing I want—giving up a bird in the hand for another who may or may not get what she thinks is hers in alimony and property.* He couldn't even recall how it got to this. Darcie kept saying they had an open marriage and neither one cared if the other had a fling or two—they enjoyed their lifestyle and, actually, each other. *Why would she leave Jack now?*

Just when did Darcie flip and start talking about leaving Jack? Last he recalled, Maria and he were going to visit them in Le Castellet as a couple. He never once thought their trysts in Boston over the past couple of weeks and the phone sex were serious. Yes, she'd started saying she loved him, but she used that all the time: "I just love champagne!" "I just love that color on you!" "Here's the man I love!"

and then "I love you." He remembered distinctly the time she first told him that, and although it made him a little uncomfortable, he brushed it away thinking that was just Darcie's effusion. He'd have to give her a reason to back off now. Maybe telling Darcie he's starting a legal proceeding to become guardian of Maria? But that was far-fetched—she still functioned as a broker, and he couldn't have the courts look into the agency's records as he himself could very easily become a target. Right now, it looked as if Maria was making unilateral decisions, and that's the way he wanted it perceived. What a god-damn mess! He'd have to think of something and say it today. Period!

The drive to Aquinnah was refreshing. The fields were that beautiful fading russet color of late fall, the skies piercing blue and cloudless, and the stone walls were a multitude of subtle grays and darker colors. The rolling land and the stone were the antithesis of the white picket fences and houses close to each other in Edgartown. The Vineyard was beautiful, no doubt about it. No doubt it was still in its natural state is due, in the beginning, to its isolation from the mainland and, also, due to its short summer season. Most people didn't live here on the island year-round. He couldn't stand living here year-round. It reminded him when he was in Cumberland federal prison about twenty years ago for embezzling funds from his employer. Granted it wasn't a long stint, only eighteen months, but still he couldn't stand the isolation. And Cumberland was considered a country club: bridge clubs, golf, squash, studio art, and the work program was a joke. Good people there—all white-collar guys. He was still in touch with a few of them who had successfully hid the bulk of their money. His closest friend, Dennis, was a lobbyist—some said arms dealer—but who really knew about any of us? We all had our story. And none of us was guilty. That was our little joke, and he smiled.

But now that winter was approaching, he was getting that same feeling of Cumberland isolation again. And, he wanted out, sooner than later. He really didn't want to wait until the late spring. But first things first. And that meant dealing with Darcie today. What a mess.

He pulled into the Land's End, and a couple of people were just leaving the front steps. No one was in the lobby, but he saw who he guessed was Bill Baker, standing on the inn's back porch, looking at the grassy spread that rolls to the edge of the cliff. It had been raining there, but the fog was peeling off the Elizabeth Islands. Bill heard Walter's footsteps and turned, motioning to be quiet. He had spotted a deer in a cluster of trees. Above the deer were two ospreys atop a nesting platform.

Bill looked more like his brother Jimmy, but you could see the family resemblance in the eyes—piercing and crinkly around the edges. Before either man could introduce himself, Darcie came bounding down the stairs. "Hi, there! How are you? It's such a nice day now that we should go for a walk." She took his arm and started out the door, yelling back, "Bye, Bill. I'll see you later!"

"Thanks for not introducing me. Even if I don't know him, I don't want my name out there. Maria is really acting strangely, and I'm very worried," he said as they started down the path. His voice sounded strained, and Darcie picked up on it. "Maria had a real episode yesterday: she went crazy. I know she's got a lot of pressure on at work, and her ex-husband has been acting up. But I'd never seen her like that. It was frightening. She wouldn't tell me what it was, and for a minute or two, I thought she found out about us, but thank God, it wasn't. I made us a cocktail, and she finally calmed down, and that's when I realized she was slurring more than one drink could do. I called the doctor to the house, and he saw the new vial of sleeping pills he had prescribed earlier that day and realized she had already taken three or four of them. He gave her a shot to make her sleep, and this morning she apologized and said it was just a 'bad day.'"

He continued, "I really don't want to do this, Darcie, but I have no choice. I don't want Maria to find out about us and do something to herself. I talked to her doctor, and he too is concerned. He told me to keep her life and work as tranquil as possible, and he'd speak to Matt, her ex, about leaving her alone right now. I can't have a suicide hanging over my head. I just can't have it. And that's what the doctor was pointing to."

Uncharacteristically, Darcie said nothing. She looked at the ground that was still damp from the rain, and she kicked a pebble on the path. "But can't we continue to meet like we have been? How would she know?"

He stopped walking and looked directly at her. "Yes, we could, but I can't have you thinking you're going to leave Jack and marry me. And I can't take risks about seeing you because you show up out of the blue like today. I was afraid you'd say something if I didn't see you, and I can't live like this always worrying she'll find out about us if I don't show up or meet you somewhere. I need your word on this. And I want to make it clear I am not thinking of another marriage at this point of my life. If you want to keep going, then this marriage idea of yours stops cold. I'm not going to divorce Maria no matter how much I may want you. It ain't gonna happen, Darcie, while she's alive. I can't possibly support you the way Jack does, and I don't want Maria to kill herself if I did leave her. It's at a take-it-or-leave-it point between us." He stopped and looked her straight in the eyes. She looked pained, and he thought her eyes might have started to water.

"But do you still love me?" she asked and looked up into his eyes.

"Of course, I do, Darcie. We just need to see each other quietly as we have been. If Maria or Jack gets an inkling of this, it's over. Do you understand?" He looked around at the cliffs and vast expanse in front of them and then put his arm around her, bending down to kiss her on her lips, full and warm.

"Of course, Walter. I understand. As long as you still love me."

"Oh, Darcie, of course I do. Just think: next summer when you and Jack are in your new house here, we'll have lots of time to see one another, and it will seem natural. I'm asking Maria tonight if I can do the caretaking portion of her work for her, relieving her of additional stress. It's perfect timing given yesterday's meltdown, and it sets us up for next summer here. In the meantime, Darcie, we'll see each other in New York or Boston. But right now, young lady, I don't have much more time here. What is the name of your room, and I'll meet you there in three minutes. Just leave the door a little ajar."

In the Lighthouse Room upstairs, Darcie had never been more passionate, so adventuresome, and playful. He quickly finished getting dressed and bent down and kissed her goodbye. "Bye, sweetie," she said, “I love you, and it’s our little secret.” He smiled at her and squeezed her hand and kissed her once more.

A minute later, she heard the Grand Cherokee start up and heard the tires on the gravel driveway getting dimmer and dimmer until she couldn’t hear his car any longer. It worked out just right. She really didn’t want to divorce Jack—the money and the travel and the properties were just too good a thing. A toy boy is just fine.

Fifteen minutes later, he was now nearing the Chilmark General Store and about to bear right onto South Road. He thought about the afternoon, and he had done the right thing. Darcie believed him about Maria’s supposed meltdown the day before, and this might come in handy some other day. Right now, he felt on top of the world: he had Darcie eating out of his hands (as well as eating him, he chuckled) just as he had Maria. Life was good. He sped up.

Chapter 67

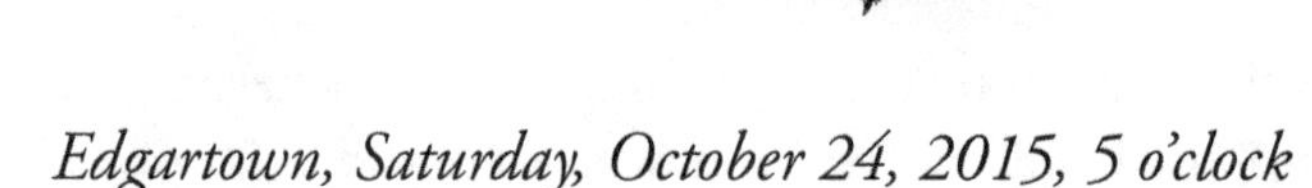

Edgartown, Saturday, October 24, 2015, 5 o'clock

"Hi, I'm home. Maria? Where are you?" Walter wandered outside in the back and saw her there in just a light sweater and said, "What are you doing here? Aren't you cold?"

At first, she didn't seem to register there was someone there, and then she snapped to. "Oh! I didn't hear you come in! Where've you been?"

He read her eyes and was relieved to see she was not suspicious. Thank God. No one had seen him up-island today.

"Just over in Vineyard Haven looking at a boat that's for sale. It wasn't that great a deal. Then had lunch at the Black Dog and drove up to West Chop. Boy, everything is really closed down now. It's dead!"

She nodded her head in agreement.

"You have a package delivered by FedEx from Brazil—some attorney's office—must be the one who did your aunt's estate. It's on the table in the foyer."

"Thanks, sweetie." She picked it up quizzically and opened it and scanned a letter and then put it back and fastened the clasp. "It's nothing—just some old files. I'll put it upstairs and be done in a minute. Thanks."

"Shall I make us a martini? Come on in before you catch a death of a cold." He noticed she seemed a bit unsteady on her feet. In a while he'd check the pills in the bottle. Right now, he had one in his pocket that was going into her drink. He had called Heather to come over for dinner and wanted her to see her mother a little "tipsy" or "under the weather," as one said on the Vineyard.

"Hope you don't mind, but I asked Heather to join us tonight for a light supper. We can have a salad and the pasta sauce we like so much that Puppy makes and have it over some linguini. I'll throw it all together, and you can sit with Heather." And he clinked glasses with her, noticing her glass was shaky and the liquid dribbling down the stem. Heather would have a real show tonight. It was all coming together, but he couldn't get cocky. Ha, that's what Darcie called him this afternoon: cocky, and he smiled and took a sip of the ice-cold drink. *Just hang in there, Walter*, he said to himself, *just be patient.*

By the time they all finished dinner, Maria was barely standing and slurring badly. Walter could see Heather was concerned, and on the way out, he said to her, "Don't worry. I'll take care of her. She's under a lot of stress recently with business, and your father is giving her a lot of grief, and there's a lot of other things, but she'll be okay. I talked to Doc Coffin the other day, and he's aware of what's going on with her, so between us, we've got her back. Don't worry, honestly!" And he gave her a kiss on the cheek as she went out the door.

"Walter, I am grateful you're here with her. It was upsetting at first when she told me how you two were married, but I can see you're taking care of her. Thank you."

He closed the door and went to look in the bedroom. Maria was out cold on the bed, not even bothering to take off her clothes. Sure enough, she had already taken two pills from bottle that he checked after breakfast. With the pill he put in her martini tonight, that made three pills. Three times the recommended daily dose.

"Good," he said to himself, looking at her with her mouth open and snoring. *After this afternoon with Darcie, I couldn't possibly do anything with Maria tonight.*

He finished the dishes and went to bed. He thought of Darcie this afternoon and moved over farther away from Maria, who had an annoying habit of trying to snuggle up to him. She was now snoring and, every now and then, snorting—as if she was in the very early stages of suffocation. *If only*, he thought, and drifted off to sleep.

Chapter 68

Edgartown, Sunday, October 25, 2015

By chance, Rick ran into Matt downtown. "How are you? I was thinking we should go up to the Rod and Gun today—get in some practice before deer season starts. You interested?"

Matt stood there a moment and finally nodded his head. "I don't get off to three. Is that okay?"

"Fine with me. Come over to the house, and we'll take my Jeep. It's beginning to turn cold, and I'd like to stay for a couple of hours. I'll bring some beer too. Maybe we can grab a pizza later at the *Lampost*. I haven't been there since you and I were last there. Whattaya say?"

Again, Matt nodded his head, and Rick continued toward downtown. "See you then!" He passed in front of the large brick building with the strange sign over the doorway: County of Dukes County Court House. Most people didn't notice it, but occasionally someone would ask, "Why is courthouse spelled 'Court House'? Second, why is it called the *County of Dukes County* Court House? Why doesn't it just read *Dukes County* Courthouse? It's redundant and doesn't make sense." Most year-rounders would simply answer, "Because that's its name." But if you served on a jury, the sheriff would start off each new jury session with the real explanation. The 1695 incorporation statute created a county by the name of *Dukes County*, as opposed to the standard form *the county of Dukes*. Some people got it, but most people, even if they heard the legal name was *the County of Dukes County*, still didn't get it. They just went along with it like everyone else.

Having bought the Sunday paper at the paper store, and back at the house, Rick left the gate open and the basement bulkhead door so Matt would know where he was. In the basement, he was choosing the pistols and the rifles he'd use today. Most weren't invited down there—just his good friends and an occasional gun aficionado like Dick LaPierre, one of the three state police assigned to the island who loved guns as much as Rick did. Like Matt, but unlike Rick, Dick also saw ferocious combat, but much earlier in Nam, and used the M60 machine guns in the Battle of Hue, one of the longest and bloodiest of the war. Rick had three of the M60s. He also had an Uzi submachine gun, two AK-47s, thirty-seven pistols (including Glocks and Berettas), forty-six rifles (some antiques and a few that his father had hunted with), and other assorted hunting rifles from which he was choosing this afternoon. He selected a Sendero and a Sako Finnlight and then decided on a third, a Marlin. By then, Matt had poked his head down the cellar and yelled, "Are you down there?" Rick told him to come take a look. It was the first time Matt had seen that gun collection, but a lot of people had talked about it.

"Wow. This is something!" Matt said. He stood there in awe. "How many do you have altogether?"

"With a new one I'm getting next week, that will make 132 total, all kinds. Take a look. You'll see some from Afghanistan and a new one from Israel. Just keep quiet about them, that's all I ask. But if you ever want to borrow any, feel free if I'm not around to come down and take one. Janet's been told not to come down here—this is my space. And she knows it! She won't bother you."

Matt was like a kid at the penny candy store—he couldn't get over the display. "I used this SPR 5.56 mm sniper rifle and so did the Rangers and Special Forces in Mohmand Valley when I was in Afghanistan. It saved my life more times than you know."

He then picked up an AK-47—they were much better than the M60s. "The only good things the Congs ever had." He then moved over to the rifles, but his eye stopped on a Beretta APX Combat 9 mm pistol and picked it up. "This is a beauty. I've always wanted one." He handled it and turned it over. "You can pretty much reach twenty-five yards with this one—not bad."

"Let's bring that one along with the others. We better get going before it's too dark," said Rick. They stayed at the range until four thirty and decided to leave then before the last light. In Oak Bluffs, at the Lampost, Linda saw them and came over to the table. "Hi, guys, haven't seen you two for a while. What's up?" she said.

Rick answered, "My wife wouldn't want me to answer that at this moment. Ha ha." He winked at her. Matt chuckled. Linda gave an exaggerated eye roll and smiled. "Okay, guys, more 'Gansetts? Or something stronger?"

Rick said to Matt, "I don't know about you, but I really feel like a couple of Maker's Marks tonight. How's that sound?" Matt nodded, and Linda hurried off.

After they took their first couple of sips, Rick said to Matt, "I've been meaning to talk to you."

After Rick finished telling Matt about "things he had heard" about Maria's real estate deals that could land her in jail if any of this proves true, he added, "I've heard the last deal she pulled off a week ago put over $200,000 in the bank. It was from some couple from New York City in society. And she's now insisting you up Heather's child support? Really?!" And he pushed Matt's second empty glass to the edge of the table and caught Linda's eye and mouthed "another one." Linda raised her eyebrow, but Rick ignored her and went on talking.

"You can do three things: sit there and do nothing, let her know you're on to something, report her to the police and let them investigate. The first and the third options aren't smart. You don't get a cut of the action. Option number two—letting her know you know—gives you the opportunity to make some cash. Call it blackmail if you want, but I'd think of it as 'payback.' She owes it to you after all she put you through. In fact, she couldn't pay you enough to make sure you'd keep quiet about this. Not only because she could face jail time, but just as important, she'd lose dear old Walter for good, not to mention her standing in the community. But that's up to you. It's your call. And if you ever said anything to her that I tipped you off, Matt, I don't need to tell you what I'd do and deny everything and throw you under the bus. I think you know I'm serious about that." Rick took another swallow and then stared directly into Matt's smoldering eyes. He saw the raw hatred there, no mistake about it. *It's working*, he thought.

"Matt? Earth to Matt," said Rick. "Hello!"

Matt heard the "hello!" and shook his head and said, "Sorry, I was thinking."

"Where is it that you've been going to in Maine?" asked Rick.

"I camp out near Birch Point Beach Park—it's way in the middle of nowhere. Just how I like it," he answered.

"What county is it in?"

"I dunno."

Rick pulled out his cell phone and Googled the state park. "It says it's there in Waldo County. Does that sound familiar?

"Yeah, come to think of it, I guess it does. Yeah, the paper there is called the *Waldo Chronicle*," said Matt. "Why?"

"Just listen. And I need you to pay full attention. I'm sticking my head out here, and I can't take a chance that you're not following exactly what I'm about to tell you.

"I don't want you to go do something foolish like taking the 9 mm to her head. I know you're pissed off, believe me! Play it smart: stay out of prison and get the money. Easy-peasy wins the race. My idea is for you to go to her office when Senna's at lunch one day. Be polite, get into Maria's inner office space, and like a businessman, don't stand in the doorway like you'd usually do, but sit down directly across from her at the desk, and first, before you say anything, just look her directly in the eyes for a second or two. Then take a deep breath and say: 'Maria, I know what you've been up to recently with real estate deals—any officer of the court like I am wouldn't hesitate to add the word *fraudulent* before *real estate.* But I've come to make you a deal because you are the mother of our child, and I don't want Heather hurt by a mother who goes to prison. I want $100,000 put into my account at Dukes County Savings Bank, and I want it noted that this is 'repayment' for marital assets, a home 'bordering Birch Point Beach Park Maine, as recorded in the Waldo County Registry of Deeds.' You can then add you're planning on leaving the island and settling there, so you'll be out of her hair before long…assuming—*ahem*—you have enough to buy a small place there. Further, you want her to sign a notarized document relieving you of all child support. I can draft that for you, but don't let on I've done it for you. If she asks, just say, 'I've got people.'

"Then, when she starts protesting and saying you're crazy and she doesn't have that kind of money, get up from your seat. Walk to the door. Turn around slowly. Look her again straight in the eyes and say, 'You heard me. You have forty-eight hours before I proceed.'" And don't say another word as you walk out of the office, as if you had all the time in the world, which in fact you do."

"Oh, by the way, I almost forgot. Here's my cell phone number. Give me a five-minute notice before you go see her. Don't call the office, just my personal cell."

Matt sat there for several seconds. Rick asked, "Do you think you can do it exactly as I just said?"

Rick nodded again at Linda and put two fingers up. Linda didn't know why, but even though Matt was drinking tonight, he was quiet and not acting up as he had the last time they were in here. *Progress*, she thought, and hurried over with the two Maker's and the bill.

On the way to the Jeep, Rick said to Matt, "Hey, if you want to borrow my 9 mm for a few days, go for it. I can see how much you like it."

"That's really nice of you, Rick. Are you sure?" asked Matt.

"Just don't use it on Maria, hear?" and Rick laughed.

Matt just grinned. "Nope, I'm going to play it cool as you said. She's probably never seen me like that. She'll be shocked. Don't worry, I won't use the gun, as much as I'd like to. It's a different ball game now. Thanks, brother. Thanks."

Chapter 69

Edgartown, Monday, October 26, 2015

The next day around 12:30 p.m., Rick's cell phone rang. "I'm heading over there now. I just saw Senna get in her car to go to lunch, and Maria's still in her parking space at the Fisher House. Don't worry. I'm cool. I got it." He hung up.

Rick poked his head out of his office door and said to Ellen, "Better take lunch now. Be back at one thirty as we've got a lot to do this afternoon."

She got up and took her purse. *Wow. First time in a long while he actually opened the door rather than yell through it! Will wonders never cease?* Ellen thought as she walked out the door to her car.

Rick settled in at his desk. In less than a minute, he heard the sound of the voice-activation tape recorder and Maria's voice. "Matt! What are you doing here?"

"Let the fun begin," said Rick to himself. Three minutes later, Matt had finished. Rick was impressed. He held it together. When he heard the door shut, the next sound was Maria crying.

"What is happening to me? What?"

Chapter 70

Edgartown, Monday, October 26, 2015, early evening

He was downstairs and making dirty martinis for both of them. Just as he finished shaking them, Maria walked in the door.

"Hello, darling, I'm in here making drinks," yelled Walter.

She was visibly nervous, and he made sure she had icy cold refills and talked lovingly to her.

"Sweetie. I've been thinking. I know we said we'd wait until after the New Year and go sometime in the spring, but I think we should go now to Brazil. We've got enough saved up. And, I'm tired of it here. Winter's coming, and I know you hate it so much. What do you think?" she said as Walter topped off her martini glass.

"Are you serious? What made this change of mind? There isn't anything wrong, is there?" he said.

"No, sweetie, no, nothing like that at all. I was just thinking out loud, but there's really nothing to keep us here now. I just got another down payment—unexpectedly from that family from Arizona I saw recently. You know, the ones I told you were just wasting my time. Well, in fact, they called today!"

"What about Heather?" he asked.

"Oh, she'll be fine. Matt is still going to be here, and I bet the Belisles will take her in until next summer. She can come visit us there, and then she'll be boarding in Switzerland. In fact, she'd probably love it! Janice and Eddie are great people, and Julie's her best friend. What teenager wouldn't like this arrangement!"

"Are you really serious? Really? How much do we have now? We need at least $3–5 million, even with all our living expenses paid for by Fernanda's estate." She didn't tell him that the Strock down payment made it into her Boston account on Friday, and at 3:00 p.m. today, when she looked online, the "pending" had already been lifted. The bank had obviously called Strock's bank and learned he was good for it and had approved it. Nine million dollars was more than enough now. She'd surprise him with the news when they were settled in Brazil. But she had wanted to make sure he was okay with leaving for Brazil with less money than Walter had hoped. It was the proof he loved her. Wait until he found out how much more she had!

He got up and went to the bar and poured what was left in the shaker into her glass, while making a new one. She seemed serious. This was too good to be true, but it meant he'd have to act sooner than he had thought. *Keep your head on straight, Walter*, he said to himself, vigorously shaking the martini until crystals formed on the shaker. *Keep your head on.*

And he went over to fill up her glass that was already empty; he pretended to knock it, and it spilled.

"Oh, honey. So sorry! Let me take this over to the sink and wipe the stem and bottom for you. I'm so clumsy!" He had his back to her and put the prescription pill into the blue cheese-stuffed olive. She was really drinking heavily now, and this was perfect for what he'd had in mind. He came back and handed her the glass and leaned over and kissed her on the forehead. Thank God it wasn't perspiring like it usually was. *Talk about gag*, he thought to himself.

"If we really do this, we'd need to get out of here quickly. Did you pack that little briefcase I told you to do, with all your papers—passport, birth certificates including Heather's, divorce papers, our marriage papers, a list of your bank accounts and their passwords, computer passwords, driver's license information, etc.?" he asked.

"Yes, they're all there except for my driver's license, of course, which I need until we leave. The other stuff is up in my closet. Where's yours?" she asked.

"I have it in the study. I'll double-check both cases tomorrow to make sure everything we need is there. As I said, we're not bringing clothes or other personal effects. We'll just leave as if we were going to Boston for the theater and an overnight. No one will be the wiser. But let's sleep on it tonight and make sure it's what we want to do."

"Okay, sweetie, but I'm sure. I want to do this no later than the day after tomorrow. The longer we wait, the easier it will be to mess up and let something slip," she said, thinking of Matt's last words: "You have forty-eight hours in which to transfer the money into my account."

He turned on the news while she went over in her head how to get the $100,000 to Matt within the forty-eight-hour ultimatum in case their own plan fell through before they could get off to Boston in time. She figured it out. She'd have to use her Boston account that she had kept hidden from Walter, but that was an easy transfer into the Edgartown National's account, where Matt and she had set up a joint account the year after Heather was born. Matt had forgotten all about it, as it was Maria who received the statements. If Walter learned of this account, she'd explain she hadn't mentioned it, as it wasn't really hers—it was both Matt's and her own money held for Heather. So, she couldn't use it by herself.

Doing all of it would fulfill her obligation ("blackmail and extortion") to Matt with a check from the bank, and keep the remainder of the money for her and withdraw, as she needed it. It was good Matt had entirely forgotten about it, and Walter didn't even know if its existence. She reminded herself she'd have to pull out the Boston bankbook and not add it to all the other documents upstairs in her briefcase that Walter was going to "double-check" tomorrow during the day. That was her secret stash. She felt better already. Life was good.

The commercial went on, and Walter turned to her and said, "You've got enough to do tomorrow. I'll make the plane reservations for the day after tomorrow, Wednesday night. We'll go business class. There's a LATAM Airlines that's nonstop to Sao Paolo that leaves around 6:00 p.m. Once we get in the air, being nonstop, there's no way we can get stopped. Don't forget, I still need to run over to Hyannis tomorrow morning, so I'll still do that. I'll be back tomorrow on the five if traffic isn't bad. You just carry on as usual. We'll have dinner out and not give any indication of what we're planning on doing the next day—no hints, even to Heather. Anything that looks out of the ordinary can tip people off."

She was slurring now. "Schweetie. You're so schmart. Love you!" While Walter was on the phone, she made it up the stairs to retrieve the Boston bankbook and put that in her purse, along with her driver's license, the only two documents she kept aside. All the other documents were in her small briefcase that she placed next to Walter's, in his study, and she made it back down the stairs to the dining room.

She felt her eyelids get heavy, and when she barely could finish the dinner of leftovers, he suggested she go watch TV in the library and he'd clean up. As he surmised, when he later went in to check on her, she was out cold. He put a throw over her and turned out the lights.

"This was easier than I had expected." He sighed and quietly crept up the stairs.

When she awakened, she was on the couch with a pillow under her head and a blanket over her. She was so lucky to have him—she looked at the grandfather's clock, and it was 12:30 a.m. Plied with alcohol and the thought of escaping before the inevitable apprehension happened, she nestled in and thought to herself, *It's going to be fine, going to be fine…*, and drifted off again to sleep on the couch.

He was actually panicked that she wanted to leave right away, but was adept at masking his feelings. He never would have made it this far had he worn his heart on his sleeve. His con games had always worked. He knew he was in control—always—even if there were surprises like Maria's sudden desire to leave the island now. He said to himself, "What the fuck happened today? She must have learned something today that tipped her off that a complaint from one of their clients had been filed." Walter cleaned up in the kitchen, and after he put the blanket on her, he went directly upstairs to examine her carry-on bag to make sure she had all the documents she would have needed to leave, if she was going to leave. Anything pertaining to him and her, he'd take.

As he was sorting through the documents, he became even more concerned: he knew her well enough to realize something made her realize she was near the end of their scheme. Someone must have talked to her to give her this impetuous thought of leaving now for Brazil, rather than waiting another month or two as they had been planning. He had to protect himself now, or it would be never. But right now, it was important to locate all their documents, papers, and bank accounts; and he started in on the process, very methodically sorting them into two piles—one was Maria's and the other was his, while he was trying to work out the final plans in his head.

He'd call Doc in the morning from the Steamship terminal before he left. He'd say he thought she might be really depressed, but was watching her carefully; and if anything changed and became really worrisome, he'd call Doc immediately. He was planning to take the 5:00 p.m. ferry back home so he should be in the house a little after 6:00 p.m. He'd add that the pills Doc had given her were working, and he was probably just nervous about leaving her alone, but "better safe than sorry." Walter would thank Doc again for keeping quiet about Maria's depression, as it was a small island and an even smaller town.

Walter realized that if word started getting around that she was having some sort of psychological issues, or that clients had been complaining about their new house not moving forward, he knew it would be the end of the road. He needed to distance himself from her immediately and not hang around waiting for the ball to drop.

If her sudden desire to leave in two days was due to the law, he knew he would also be implicated and, given his own background, would not be granted any leniency. He again started to panic and then recovered himself. He realized tomorrow was enough time to get out of here forever.

He had everything he needed now in his briefcase, then he checked her case, and except for her driver's license that she had said she was keeping on her, he found everything in order, and he shut off the bedroom light.

Chapter 71

Edgartown, Tuesday, October 27, 2015

Maria didn't hear Walter go out—he must have left earlier than expected, she thought, but he had left a note near the coffee maker that said, before he went to Hyannis, for the midday meeting, he was also doing last-minute errands: haircut and prescription refills at the Stop & Shop Pharmacy, including refills for her own that Doc had prescribed. He'd be home around 5:00 or 6:00 p.m. and to make reservations somewhere, perhaps the Harbor View for seven thirty?

What Walter didn't say was that there was a second note, he left on the floor, almost totally under the couch. He knew she wouldn't find it in the morning when she awakened. But others might…later. She couldn't believe she had slept as long as she had, and, on the couch too. Probably just the weight of everything in the process of being lifted, she thought to herself. Tomorrow night they'd leave, and the day after, Thursday morning, they'd have already landed in Brazil, with enough money for their future and alone with each other, immune from any US attempts to extradite them. Thank God for the US and Brazilian treaties.

She called Senna to let her know she'd be late and she would have a busy day finishing up some "office work." Rick didn't think anything was wrong with what he overheard on her calls, so he went down to the courthouse to check on a deed. The day was unseasonably warm for the fall, and everyone was in a good mood.

The County of Dukes County's Court House was unusual for the Vineyard. It was tall like many of the Main Street buildings, but it stood out glaringly here, as it was made of red brick, not clapboard, and just plain didn't fit in. Although the first and second-floor front windows were flanked by four flat white pilasters, awkwardly placed there for "decoration," they served no purpose except to remind people that at the time of construction, the Commonwealth didn't have enough money to install real columns, so they plastered these fake things (Janet called them *plastered pilasters*) on the façade and called it a courthouse. Or maybe the real issue wasn't money, after all. Maybe it was because Boston had no interest in this remote outpost seven miles off Cape Cod, with only a few thousand voters living there year-round, and therefore settled on this cheap structure, rather than give the Vineyard a true courthouse as almost all of the other courthouses were: impressive Greek Revival structures. Even though Nantucket's courthouse was also brick, it was proportional and didn't stand out as naked and "in your face" as this county property.

Rick stood for a second on the steps watching the landscapers mow the front lawn and then clip around the two granite war memorials and a much smaller rock containing the names of the town's sons (and a few daughters) who had served in wars in times past. One was in honor of those who served in WWII, and it was surprising how many there were for such a small town. The small rock plaque named those killed in Viet Nam. The other large granite slab was for those who served in Viet Nam. The Town and County were still considering whether or not to add Afghanistan and Iraq but had not yet decided. He had petitioned them to do so and to also add anyone's name that lived year-round on the Vineyard, but his suggestion was turned down. They responded that *if* they were to erect a new monument for these recent wars, his name would not be included. He wasn't born here. He wasn't a son. He was still upset about this and actually thought of not carrying the Viet Nam POW/MIA flag in next year's Fourth of July parade but then realized if he did, no one would know he had served.

Rick was once again reminded of what Arnie Fischer had said to the woman who introduced herself as "an islander" because she had lived here ever since she was a young girl and attended local schools. "Lady, my kittens were born in the oven, but that don't make them muffins." People never got tired of telling that story! The lady who considered herself "an islander" because she had lived here all her life was simply "living *on* the island." She wasn't ever and never would be "an islander." Birthplace made that clear. You could be voted in as a selectman, but never be an islander. You could be a volunteer firefighter, but never be an islander. You could be anything in life, but the only thing that mattered here on this land surrounded by water was your birth certificate. No matter what you had done, only this piece of paper defined who you were—an islander or not. Those who thought of themselves as an islander because they had lived there for decades were rather like those who said they were a "little bit pregnant." You couldn't be. And Rick scowled at the insular insult that he took as personal. He didn't like being told he was an outsider, but he was.

Rick made his way back to the office and saw that Ellen wasn't there. *Must be at lunch*, he thought. *Good time to call Matt.*

Chapter 72

Edgartown and Boston, Tuesday,
October 27, 2015, mid-afternoon

Later that afternoon, around 4:00 p.m., Maria was at work and getting ready to leave to go home and get ready for dinner before Walter got back from the Cape. Tomorrow was a big day, and she was both excited and scared about their escape. It would be a brand-new life for them.

Meanwhile, in Boston, around the same time, Darcie was still in her room at the Four Seasons, after Walter had left saying he was on his way back to the Vineyard. He had seemed ill at ease when he first arrived around one o'clock, later than he had anticipated. Something about banking and a little trouble getting the bankers to accept his documents, but, in the end, they did, and now he was free to be with her until midafternoon. She had already ordered room service as he called to say he didn't have a lot of time after his meetings that morning.

They embraced, and he hugged her longer than he usually did. She asked him, "Are you okay? You seem a little on edge. Maria hasn't caught on, right?"

"No, she still doesn't have a clue. But, boy, is she drinking and popping those pills. I told her last night she really needed to see someone other than Doc Coffin and get a handle on things. I had already started to suggest she take a few weeks and get to Canyon Ranch at Tanglewood, I mean Lenox, but she wouldn't hear of it, until last night when we sat down and had a serious talk. She made the decision to go tomorrow morning after I get back tonight. I called with her there, and they are expecting her in the early afternoon. Granted it's not a detox, but it should help her anyway just to get away from business. I'll drive her, of course, and then I told her I'd take advantage of that time she's off there to visit my cousin in Destin for a couple of weeks and go fishing for some amberjack or marlin."

"I've been to three of the Canyon Ranches for R&R, and I liked Lenox even better than the first one in Tucson. Ever since Mel and Enid started letting go of their management there, it just doesn't hold up to the other properties. You know, family and all that. Maria should go to Lenox, yes. It could help. I'm sorry you have to go through this with her, it can't be much fun," Darcie said, slipping her hand into his and giving him a kiss on the cheek. They were sitting at the portable table draped in white linen and eating their lobster salads and sipping an icy cold Vouvray.

"Speaking of how busy she is now, has Maria told you how our own property is coming? Jack asked me about that the other day. I told him I'd find out and see when Chapeda will be ready," she said. "So, how far along are we? I don't know if you were aware, but Maria asked for some more money about a week or ten days ago. She said it was for the initial landscape design. Have you heard?"

"I don't really get involved with the business end of it. I'm more of a facilitator. But she did mention it a few days ago, and apparently, it's coming along just fine. When I get back tonight, I'll make a point of asking and get back to you in the next day or two. And, speaking of 'getting back tonight,' don't you think we have a little unfinished business to attend to before I have to leave?"

With that, he grabbed her and tossed her on the bed, lifting her skirt and pulling down her stockings. She was the only one he had known who still used silk stockings and a garter belt—black, lacy, and see-through. He had a fleeting thought that he would miss her, and then he forgot all as they began passionate lovemaking.

"I'll call you as soon as I can, but please don't call me on my cell. Tomorrow's going to be a tough day for her and me, and I don't want her changing her mind. I can't run the risk of her finding out about us. It was wonderful as usual, Darcie. I'll miss you," and then he stopped and recovered himself.

"The way you said that, it sounded as if it were permanent." She laughed and reached up to kiss him on the lips one more time.

"Ha ha. You know, I mean I'll miss you tonight and until we see each other again," and he smiled and went out the door. He felt a little nervous but good. He had set the story about her alcohol and narcotics abuse, and if anyone checked on it, Canyon Ranch would say they don't divulge information on any of their clients.

Darcie was spending the night and seeing her old friend Lexa and her husband. She went into the bathroom and drew a hot bubbly bath and brought in a glass of the Vouvray to enjoy while she soaked. She had the best of both worlds: a lover and a rich husband.

Chapter 73

Boston, Tuesday, October 27, 2015, late-afternoon

As Darcie was taking her bath, Walter was heading down Boylston Street toward the North End and the Callahan Tunnel. He had already researched the locations of the farthermost long-term parking lot. When he left the tunnel, he took the first exit into East Boston. He then turned left at the first traffic light where Santarpio's Pizza was located, and he followed Chelsea Street over the bridge and made a right onto Eastern Avenue. PreFlight was on the right. He pulled in, gave the attendant the Capital One "Virtual Number" card that he had prepaid online and which created a new card of unique virtual numbers good only for that merchant. The card was linked to his "real" Capital One credit card account. But Preflight only receives the number printed on the virtual physical credit card he carried on himself. It did not link to his real credit card. It was the same concept as a cell phone burner. Therefore, neither the name on the virtual card and receipt said *Walter Keller*. This was ingenious.

By the time everyone realized Walter was not on the Vineyard or in Boston, nor anywhere they could think of, and they started tracing his credit cards usage, they wouldn't discover the Virtual Number payment at the parking for ages. He had prepaid the parking for two months, so that would give plenty of time for him to get settled and hire Brazilian international attorneys of the first order. He didn't think he really had anything to worry about as he was legally married to Maria; they jointly held all assets, including the agency, and all of their joint assets would be safely in his hands in Brazil. When Maria realized he had split, she would also realize the law would be after her, alone.

He had taken all of Maria's documents she had placed into the small overnight case she thought was being prepared for their flight to Brazil. These included bankbooks, statements, passwords, deeds to her aunt's property, and Fernanda's trust—which would take care of him for life, and quite bizarrely, what appeared to be numerous wills written on different dates from her late aunt. He couldn't understand why she had them, why they all had different dates, nor did he know what they said as he couldn't read Portuguese, but he would have his lawyers figure those out.

He double-checked the Cherokee for any papers that said his or her name, looked again in his briefcase and checked off the documents, one by one, until he was satisfied he had forgotten nothing. He took his carry-on bag, the little briefcase, and hopped on the red preflight shuttle bus and got off at the Terminal E, the international departure point for international flights in Boston. He checked his watch. It was just after 4:00 p.m. He breezed through TSA and through all the steps and went to the wine bar near his gate for the 6:05 p.m. flight on LATAM Airlines. As the departure hour neared, more and more dark-haired people arrived, babbling in Portuguese and trying to corral their bratty little kids. The older women looked just like Maria's mother: moles, wavy black hair pulled back in a tight bun; the younger ones looked more American. Tight leggings and loose sweaters and wearing the latest Comme des Garcons low-top sneakers and backpacks bulging with clothes and toys. Most of them shouldn't be wearing the leggings. Fat thighs and bulging asses. Just like Maria's.

He was flying on a new Boeing 767 in premium business on the ten-and-a-half-hour flight to Sao Paolo. So, most of these people wouldn't be near him. He had been careful to remove his SIM card and not use his iPad or laptop. He didn't want anyone tracking him down when Maria finally realized he wasn't coming home.

The next time he looked at his watch, it was 5:10 p.m. Announcements were being made regarding priority boarding (those obnoxious parents with their babies in these enormous convertible strollers were always first. Why weren't they put last?). By 5:20 p.m. he had boarded and was sitting in a wide comfortable aisle seat with a console on his right and on his left. No one to bump his arm or elbow. No one to spill a drink on his lap. Perfect. He lowered his seat and leaned back a bit. The attendant had already brought him an icy cold dirty martini, like the ones he and Maria had almost every night. He gave her a passing thought and concluded she deserved whatever she'd get when her clients contacted the police: it was her idea long before she confided in him about her Ponzi schemes. *Not only it wasn't my idea to begin with, I barely had anything to do with these fake transactions, except to be the charming husband in front of clients.*

Thirty minutes after he settled in and had his first martini, he felt the roar of the engines and…liftoff! He felt immediate relaxation and peace. If all went well, he'd land in Brazil in about ten hours and be out of the hands of the American jurisdiction. He felt genuinely pleased about how he had gotten away. First, she wouldn't even begin to worry until a little later this evening, probably around 7:00 p.m. His notes left this morning while she was passed out and the subsequent voice mails during the day made it sound as if he'd be back in time for dinner this evening. She hadn't even budged this morning when he left in his car. If she didn't get hold of her drinking and pills, she could end up in real rehab. And, he added, he didn't feel guilty about encouraging her drinking and taking sedatives. She was a grown-up and could have said no to both. *She's weak, that's all,* he thought as he took the last sip of his first martini.

Looking at his wristwatch (since he wasn't using his iPhone any longer), he smiled a little at the irony of just having flown over the Vineyard while she was down below on land expecting him momentarily to walk through the door.

Having prepared Doc Coffin, Rick, Matt, Darcie, and Heather for her increasing drinking and pills, I'm certain they would think she alone had brought all this reckless behavior and greed upon herself. And, further proving the point with her pills and drinking well established, when Charlie eventually finds out from Darcie what I had told her today, they would also believe Maria was ready to check in to Canyon Ranch. Who knows, perhaps her addictions would help lessen the sentence she's bound to receive? I will look like a husband who has had it and took off, plain and simple. And, it would take a while before they figure out where I am. Voila! he said to himself, and he went back in his head over all the day's events.

The *piece de resistance* was the note he had left downstairs partially hidden under the couch she had passed out on last night:

> Maria,
>
> I didn't have the heart to wake you this morning—I'll call you from Hyannis later today. I'm glad we had that talk last night. I think we need a little time off so you can get the treatment we talked about. Don't worry. I love you. The reservations have been made, and you have all the information and brochures to look at—it is a beautiful setting. We'll go over on the boat tomorrow and should get to Lenox about noontime. Once I get you settled, I'll head to Logan and from there fly to Destin. I love you and am so proud that you are doing this. I'll see you tonight around 7 if the boats are on time.
>
> Walter

The attendant brought him another martini, and he was soon asleep without having dinner. She thought he looked attractive and obviously well-to-do. *When he wakes up, I think I'll strike up a conversation. He's not wearing a wedding band.* And she shut off the overhead light, removed the glass, and put a blanket over him.

Chapter 74

Edgartown, Tuesday, October 27, 2015, early-evening

Rick tried several times, but Matt wasn't picking up his phone. However, Maria got back on her phone several minutes later. Rick settled back in his chair and turned the volume up a bit.

"Hmm. Interesting," he said to himself. "She actually made the $100,000 transfer to Matt earlier today, just as she said she would. She was on the phone with the bank's automated system checking on her transfer. I'm amazed. She must be scared shitless. I didn't know she had an account in Boston, but it doesn't surprise me. We all do." He left a voice mail for Matt to call him.

It wasn't until 6:30 p.m. when Matt called back. "What's up, Rick? I've been at an all-day conference in Hyannis for police chiefs. They read us all the new laws that help criminals and make road-blocks for us. I'm about at the point where I can't take this liberal shit anymore. The way I was brought up, someone did something to you, you took care of it yourself. No mediators, no social workers, no anyone except you and the asshole who acted against you. Just like in Afghanistan. No one asked if you couldn't have used 'less force,' 'more compassion,' or 'understanding.' Shit! If we had done that, they'd be throwing plastic flowers on our graves over at West Side."

"Well, my boy, I have some news for you. And, for once, it's good. I think she's actually going to pay you that $100,000 after all. I'm amazed, but she is definitely s-c-a-r-e-d! Good work, bro!"

"Why do you think that? I don't trust her at all," Matt replied.

Rick couldn't say anything about what he had just heard Maria confirm by phone, but asked if Matt had heard anything about secret accounts off-island. Matt said no, he didn't think she had any. They just had a child support hearing about three months ago, and nothing was produced that would show money elsewhere. "What makes you think that?" asked Matt.

"Oh, I have my sources. That's all I can say. But I think you'll hear from her real soon. Congratulations!"

"I don't understand where this money is coming from? When I was in court for Heather's child support hearing, Maria showed us her client accounts, which she can't touch, and then the small checking and savings she and that phony husband of hers have. It really wasn't that much money. Not even the $100,000 you say she's going to turn over."

Rick continued, "Let's not assume what she showed you at the hearing is all she has. And it may not all be here on the island."

"What? Are you saying she's been hiding money? I actually believed her when she said she was up to her eyeballs in debt when I went to the child support hearing. She always did the banking for us, and I stupidly never paid attention to it. She paid the bills, and that's all I ever cared about. What an asshole I've been!"

"Matt, it's not your fault. She's just a bitch, as I've said to you before. You wouldn't have had any clue what she was doing behind the scenes. She's kept it all secret, including the surprise with that new husband of hers and their lah-de-dah lifestyle. *Lifestyles of the Rich and Famous* with Robin Leach. What a bitch! I don't know how you can stand it. Frankly she deserves a bullet in the head—think of her as a Nammer. That's what she is! Killing us in her own way, while you were in that fucking Battle of Wanat going through hell and more. And what was she doing then? Quietly taking over Stuart Baldwin's business, acting sweet and cute and oh so grateful—and meanwhile, socking away all that money from you to an off-island bank you never knew about.

"You know, just like our older brothers who came back from Nam, none of us ever got a hero's welcome or parade when we got back. And now you learn that Maria was stabbing you in the back the whole time you were doing reconnaissance in the most dangerous place on earth. How many of your buddies did you find blown to bits there, with their arms and legs ripped off, shrapnel in their skin as they screamed in agony? Did she care? Did she say, 'Please, dear God, if Matt gets back, I'll make that horrible time all up to him'? Or did she say, 'As soon as he gets back, I'm outta here! Stupid jerk. I can do much better than him!'?"

Matt was silent. He had had a rough night. Flashbacks were still with him and probably always would be when he became upset and agitated. As Rick talked about the jungle and some of the guys he came across, he remembered one poor son of a bitch who begged him to put a bullet in his head. The Taliban wanted to attract other Special Forces into an ambush and so had stuffed his severed hand in his mouth, and he was still except for gagging and softly moaning. When he saw Matt creep by, his eyes begged him to do him in right there. He just couldn't take it anymore. But Matt had to steel himself and just creep by him, as a bullet sound would attract Taliban attention. His flashbacks often centered on that soldier, left in agony to die, in the middle of fucking nowhere, to be entirely forgotten by his countrymen.

"Matt, are you still there?" said Rick. Maybe he had pushed Matt too far, but he had to push him as far as he could, just short of another breakdown, if he got what he wanted out of Matt. He'd never be convicted given his mental state. He could go live in Maine and leave this rats' nest, or rather, to be more precise, leave the island, which is still covered by the same uncultivated, tangled, and barren vines that prompted Bartholomew Gosnold to sardonically name this his daughter's Vineyard. Had Rick been brighter, he could have made an analogy between the vines and the island's people.

If the people had actually tended to these vines and cultivated them, they could have produced acceptable wines over time. Instead, the only wine produced here for about thirty years was from Chicama Vineyards, which closed the year before, and when they actually tried featuring it in local restaurants and bars, the locals would jokingly ask for a glass of "Vineyard Vine." The other phrase was, "I'll have a glass of Vineyard *Vine*-egar, please."

"Matt?"

"Yeah, sorry. I got distracted."

"Look, buddy. I'm sorry to say this, but people like her always win. We are the ones who always lose. You and I don't have the slightest idea how much she's socked away, but you're the one who's left holding the bag and paying 35 percent of your salary for Heather's support. I know what you make—we all do. Even though you're now chief, you don't come close to making even two-thirds of what she's now being pressured into giving you to keep you quiet about her little real estate shenanigans. I've said it before, and I'll say it again, she is a bitch with a capital *B.* A real shit. Trash. A crook. And who's her victim? You!"

"My advice, Matt. Don't say a thing about what I just told you. Play it cool and wait. She has 'til tomorrow to get the money actually transferred safely into your account. It's in process, that I can tell you, my man. We'll know soon enough, and you don't want to screw it up now. I'll let you know when I think it's a done deal, and I'll tell you how to get our hands on it. But insist on a cashier's check. Not a personal or business one. I won't ever trust her, even if she follows through on this with you. Remember: cashier's check *only.*"

"Thanks, Rick. I won't believe it until I see it. What a fucking day. I'm so sick of assholes everywhere I go. You should see some of the other Cape and Islands chiefs. They can't chew gum and clap their hands at the same time if they tried. Can you imagine them in Kandahar with the Taliban all around them, and they're standing there wondering how to aim their gun? And now my wife—sorry, I mean ex-wife—squirreling away money and making me pay even more out of my crappy pay when she's been the one hiding the money. Jesus Christ. I really want to kill her. It'd be so easy. I just wish I could. Has she ever thanked me for serving our country in Afghanistan? Has she ever said, 'I admire you so much, Matt. Everyone said the job you had was the most dangerous of them all. You did such a good job. I'm so proud of you!' Did she! The answer is NO—not once. Not even fucking once! Bitch! If she had been in the valleys there, I would have put a bullet between her eyes. Right there.

Between those fucking eyes. Fucking bitch. Fucking fucker. God, I hate her! I'm going out. Need a drink, and try to forget all this."

"I understand, man. You've got a lot to deal with, and it's not as if you ever had to deal with anything before in your life...like what you went through over there by yourself. It's a miracle you came back. You've been through hell, and here it is again. Right in your own hometown. Shouldn't this be a place where you can find some peace? Huh? Or is your own hometown now just another Taliban village where every step might be plastic packs containing a dozen batteries or pressure plate booby traps blowing you up? Boy, Matt, I can understand how fuckin' mad you are now—who would blame you if you really killed her? You know I don't really mean it, Matt, but goddamn it! You've had enough! Wish I could join you at the Wharf tonight, but Janet has some event I'm forced to go to. Remittance men. That's all they are. Lucky their grandparents were born first. Gotta go. Talk to you tomorrow to see where we are with your $100,000. Take it easy, pal."

Matt bumbled something like "Yeah," and the line went dead.

Rick turned off the office lights and went inside his house for dinner.

Matt had parked across from the Edgartown National Bank and sat there looking at his lap for a while. He then opened his glove compartment and took out the Beretta APX Combat 9 mm pistol Rick had lent him and picked it up. He stared at that too, fingering the smooth surface, flicking his index finger over the trigger, and pushing a little. The ammo was in the glove compartment. He wasn't stupid. He sat there for another five minutes and then shook his head as if to clear his mind. He put the gun back in the glove compartment. He walked in and sat at the bar, down toward the kitchen.

"Hi, chief. What can I get you now?" said Brian, thinking it was a bit early for the chief to come in.

"Maker's. Straight up. Ice. Thanks," and he stared off at the television. It was after the evening news, and although he wasn't really watching the television, he realized it was a game between the Celtics at the Lakers. He went into his "deep hole," as he sometimes referred to the lost time when he's absorbed in things. Sometimes it was the war, sometimes his life, but tonight it was only Maria. "Another," he said. And he continued blankly staring at the television, deep within his own thoughts of revenge and hatred.

"Hey, you gotta eat. We got a special tonight. Burger with all the fixin's—how about it?" asked Brian. He had been watching Matt and had seen his mood. He didn't want to have any trouble here tonight, especially when it concerned the chief whose PTSD was well-known in town. He just didn't like his look. Something was bothering him—greatly.

Matt nodded. He had another Maker's.

"Last one tonight, chief," said Brian. "I don't want you to close us down for overserving you. Ha ha ha. And, it's on me tonight. Don't worry about it. You've done enough for everyone in this country and our town. Drive safe."

Matt got up and walked out across the street to his car. He opened the glove compartment again and put the gun on the passenger seat and drove off up South Water Street, before turning onto High and then down School Street to Maria and Walter's rental home, the one the Parsons were supposedly going to put on the market someday. It was now about 7:00 p.m.

He sat there and saw her take another drink (it was the second he had seen in the twenty minutes he was parked there) and make yet another call on her iPhone; she had been practically speed-dialing and looked frantic. Maria was still watching TV, drinking, and it looked like she was getting really sloppy with the glass. Her head bobbed, and she appeared to have finally dropped what was left of her drink, and her head flung back against the sofa. He couldn't of course hear her, but with her mouth agape and remembering her snoring, he was sure she was out of it. He kept fingering the gun, rolling it over and over in his hand, just feeling the strength of it, the cool metal in his hand. He closed his eyes and drifted off into a field of dreams someplace, somewhere long ago, over in Kandahar. He didn't know how long he had been out when he snapped to and looked at his watch. It was just after midnight. Maria was still passed out on the sofa; it looked as if her mouth was wide open, and her eyes were closed. She was slouched against the armrest. She seemed to be a heavy drinker now.

Matt felt this urge come over him from somewhere deep inside him—built up rage from the war and what it made him do, what was done to buddies, the nonexistent homecoming, the way he had to pick up where he left off in town, Maria's demanding ways and always wanting more than what he could do or even wanted to do to climb "up the ladder" she kept talking about. If he had heard her say on the phone one more time, in that fake saccharine voice, "Why, hello, Mrs. Bliss. No, it's not too late in the evening. Why, of course. I'll see to it first thing in the morning. Yes, he's fine and so is she. Yes, thank you again for calling. It's always a pleasure talking with you. Don't worry about the time. I'll see you tomorrow!" And then they'd get back to the sex, but by this time, it was too late. The spell had been broken. And he didn't care.

He was awake now and out of his dark mood. He put the gun back in the glove compartment and started the car. He drove down the Edgartown–Vineyard Haven Road to Twenty-First Street and turned down the bumpy dirt road to his house.

The leaves were falling off the trees, and the moon was out—it had the eerie landscape-look after a strafing of moondust on those Nammers.

I hate them all. Never could trust them, no matter how sweetly they smiled and nodded and pointed to where they indicated the Taliban were hiding. Then, came the ammo of their AK-47 knockoffs. They had been sitting and waiting for the "beekeepers" to lead us to them—just one more deadly hoax by these inscrutable bitches. More of our men died at their hands than they did in actual battle. One day, they loved Americans; and the next day, they were setting them up for slaughter. God, how I hate them all! And now they're here living among us, like everyday Americans—which they're not. I'd never trust any of them, no matter what they say. They're dogs. And they shouldn't be allowed in our country.

He snapped out of his thoughts and realized it was getting chilly. He'd have to turn the stove on tonight. He thought about his surveillance outside Maria's home and realized how easy it was at this time of year to take aim and put a bullet through the window. So easy!

He should have done it. Goddamn! Why didn't I do it…there was enough time, and at this time of year, the street was vacant. All the summer folk had left for New Jersey, Connecticut, and Maryland. Assholes. All of them! God, he hated this place now and everyone in it. He lit the stove and went to bed, descending again into a dark place. He knew himself well enough by now to know he needed help. He just couldn't make himself go see Doc. He was afraid he'd really open up about how much he wanted to kill her, and that might be just enough for them to send him back to Hyannis for another three-month stint. He didn't want that. He wasn't going to speak to Doc. He'd call Rick in the morning. He'd understand. They could relate. *He gets how I feel, and I'm okay with him. He's not going to send me back there. He hates her too.*

"Goddamn bitch!" he suddenly screamed out loud. "Goddamn bitch!" He went to sleep almost immediately after screaming this out, dreaming horrific scenes of the enemy and his patrol. Horrifying noises, split images of grotesquely decapitated faces, the knowledge that he was being tracked by the enemy, and then…blackness.

Chapter 75

Sao Paolo, Wednesday, October 28, 2015, 4:30 a.m.

Having arrived in Sao Paolo on time at about 5:30 a.m. (4:30 a.m. Boston time) on Wednesday the twenty-eighth, Walter sped through customs. He had taken the flight attendant's cell phone number saying he would contact her in a few weeks, as soon as he got a new phone here in Brazil and got settled. He figured that Maria might be still be sound asleep at this early hour, despite being distraught and frantic that he hadn't arrived home the night before.

He asked the limousine service desk how long it would take to get a driver and was told it would only be a half-hour wait. He was not taking any chances of being tracked by Interpol by using his old cell phone and laptop that he had he ditched in Boston. He bought a prepaid Vivo 4G SIM card and new cell phone and received information on where to add credit in various prepaid card machines around the country. However, even though he had to show his passport to get the SIM card and phone, something he wished he could have avoided, he felt chances were slim that anyone on the Vineyard could trace the new phone to him, here in Brazil. He then returned to the limousine desk and hired a limousine driver. He had given a false name to Royal American Limousines, and no one there seemed bothered to check that his name was valid, mainly because 1,000 BRL or about $250 US, on top of the fare, would guarantee this. *Money talks while the rest walk,* he thought to himself and then smiled.

While he waited, he stopped to have a coffee and a roll, called a *pão francês*. He had slept well and didn't mind the nine hours it would take to get to Florianopolis. The driver opened the door for him, and he got into the comfortable back seat. The driver's colleague sat in the passenger seat, and Walter noticed him carrying a semiautomatic under a coat draped across his lap.

After they said hello and welcome, the employees were professional and did not "chat," as do many annoying US chauffeurs. All they were paid to do was to drive and, if necessary, use the gun on those who wanted to kidnap rich foreigners. Walter had read all about crime in Brazil, and Sao Paolo was counted as being one of their most dangerous cities.

In the back seat, he found a full bar, the international edition of the *New York Times*, a television preset to CNN and the Fox Business Network, a silk eye mask, toiletries, and pillows and a light blanket. He removed his shoes and put on the slippers they also provided, glanced at the headlines, and put on his mask and leaned back, cradled by the lush leather seats and headrest. He was fast asleep in a minute.

Chapter 76

Edgartown, Wednesday, October 28, 2015, 8:45 a.m.

In his office that next morning, Rick was able to pull out the tape recorder, and he listened to a series of voice messages from Maria's home machine the day before that were making Maria frantic.

The first message was from Walter early in the morning, the first call of that day. He had already listened to that and other morning ones and knew that Walter was off-island on the Cape for the day and was due back early last night. The first one said: "Hi, sweetie, I tried the house, but guess you were already on your way from home to the pharmacy and then the office. I'm just about getting out of Falmouth, and the traffic on Route 28 is horrendous—as usual. Just wanted to let you know that last night was fabulous—I'm so lucky to have someone like you who likes it as much as I do. You are one fantastic you-know-what, sweetie! I'll probably have my phone off most of the day during these meetings. They actually take them from us when we enter the conference room! But I'll call later this afternoon to let you know what boat I'm on."

The next one, Rick hadn't yet heard. It was at 5:30 p.m. and again from Walter. "I left Hyannis later than I expected, so think it will be too late for going out tonight. I'll grab something along the way and will try for the 8:30 p.m., but it may end up being the 9:45 p.m. Either way, get yourself dinner and just know that everything is on schedule. I managed to get everything done. Don't worry. Love you, bye." And the phone clicked off.

The following messages were from this morning.

"Maria? This is Charles Potts calling again. It's just after eight-fifteen in the morning. If you don't answer me by noon today, I'm going to the police. As I told you on the phone, we want our earnest money from those buyers you say you have who are in Europe—and we want this right now! There's no reason for you to keep it in escrow, now that they haven't made a second payment, which is stipulated in the P&S agreement. When I had to call you again, yesterday, because we didn't hear from you on Monday as you had promised, you said you'd call by 8:00 a.m. this morning. I just called the bank, and they have no record of you making an attempt to wire the first earnest money lump sum into our account as you had promised you'd do on Monday, before the bank closed. Well! Today is now Wednesday! We've had it! There's been NOTHING wired into our account! Hear me, young lady! And, assuming you can spell, I said N-O-T-H-I-N-G! We want our earnest money NOW! TODAY! So, don't even bother to make excuses about why it's late even if you collect the second payment from them now. The P&S says if they are delinquent in any scheduled payments, we get to keep the money, and the sale is off. We're not selling the house to these people, whoever they are, no matter how much they are offering over the market price, unless you get us the both payments in our bank, right away! We want a closing date set and the rest of the money ready then. If not, we're going to call the Cannon Agency and have them represent us!" The phone slammed down.

The next one was again from Charles Potts. "Maria! Where are you! I want you to call IMMEDIATELY! You know what this is about—our money! I don't believe you and your little schemes anymore. CALL!" Again, Rick heard the slamming of the receiver before the call went dead. Wow, things were certainly heating up.

The next call was a Stephanie. "Hi, Maria. This is Steph calling. Just wanted an update on the work at the house out at Oyster Watcha. I know you want some more money wired in, but my private banker said I should get something in writing from you showing the invoices paid to date and the estimated amount of work to be completed. Don't think I don't trust you, of course I do! It's just something they want before I can release the next $200,000, you'd like now. Hope all is well with you and Walter! Don't worry: I haven't told anyone about the house—just as you said. It's just our little secret, but I can't wait 'til Daddy finds out after our trip to Italy this summer! He'll be proud of me and how I, or should I say we, did this all without him. I think he'll understand how much I've grown and can handle my affairs now! Ha ha. I meant 'business affairs,' not the other kind. Ha ha. Bye, love ya. Steph."

So, this was the woman he had seen having dinner at the Charlotte Inn a while ago, when Jared said she was buying some place out at Oyster Watcha. Now he understood. It must be the Freedman place as it was unfinished. And, Rick knew it had not been sold to anyone. Maria must have conned Stephanie into believing it was for sale. *What a conniving bitch*, he thought.

The next call was again from Steph. "Hi, Maria, it's me again. I forgot to say, the banker wants the following information: the full legal name of the owner, I think you said it is Freeland or Freedman or something like that; the address of the property (book and deed number) and their primary legal address; the amount I gave you that you are holding in escrow for the closing; the amounts I've advanced so far for the construction and interior decorating and each vendor. If I'm not wrong, the escrow was $350,000, and to date, I've also sent about $250–275,000 for the various vendors. Sorry to be such a pest, but you know how these people are—they want to cover their asses and get everything documented. If it were just between you and me, I wouldn't bother you about this. Bye again! Love ya."

That was the last message on the machine, made about fifteen minutes before Rick started listening.

So, it *was* the Freedman property—the one he thought it might be when Jared had told him it was out at Oyster Watcha. He'd have to drive out there this morning and see if there was any work going on out there, whether at the Freedman property or another. Maria had pulled another fast one but of course didn't know that Rick was wiretapping and recording her calls. "Hmm," he said, "this should be worth another couple hundred in my pocket for hush money." Maria was smart, he thought, but ultimately, just another stupid Portagee. She lived in the moment.

He was running through all these possibilities as fast as his mind would work. "One of these people, and it sounds as if it'll be that Potts guy, will be calling the police anytime now. Once that's done, I won't have any more access to her schemes, so if there's money to still be had, I have to get it now."

He continued trying to think the whole thing through. It was a crazy situation. Maybe Matt wouldn't have to be driven to pop her off. He was getting close, and Rick knew full well that he had been egging him on, but if Maria got arrested first, then Rick wouldn't have to give Matt that final push over the edge, and the poor guy could get the $100,000 Rick had blackmailed Maria into paying him, in return for not spilling the beans on her. He liked Matt and was sure he could get off a murder rap because of his documented PTSD and his service to his country and to his hometown. Still, if this could all be avoided, because Maria trips up herself, it would be best for everyone.

"I just need to get some more money out of her before I call Charlie at the Cape and Islands DA's office," he said to himself.

Rick left a note for Ellen that he'd be out for a couple of hours and walked out the backdoor to the office driveway and got in his Jeep. He headed up West Tisbury Road toward the airport, and before Barnes Road, he turned off to the left down the dirt road with a small handmade wooden sign saying Oyster Watcha. He went down almost to the end and came across the deserted Freedman property—construction halted by the owners' bankruptcy that was still tied up in court, thus halting any future sale of the property until this was all settled. He walked around the property, and there was no sign of anyone having been there recently. No tire tracks, no cigarette butts, no nothing. No one had been here recently. He now understood the extent to what Maria had been up to—this was a new one he hadn't heard of. He wondered just how many more of these scams she had hidden. He smiled. There would be plenty more money for him if he could get to her before the inevitable happened and she was reported to the DA. He'd have to move fast today and have "a little friendly chat" with her about some more hush money. She was in way deeper than he had originally thought. He wondered just how much Walter knew too. Was she keeping secrets from him, just as she had been with Rick?

About halfway out the road, Rick pulled over as a pickup truck kicked up sand, barreling down the road. The truck came to an abrupt stop. It was Glenn, one of the local caretakers on the island.

"Hey, Glenn! How the hell are you? Haven't seen you in a long time. How's it going?"

"Not bad. And you?" Glenn was a typical island wash-ashore from the '70s. That's when all of hippiedom descended on the island. Dropouts become carpenters, housepainters, house cleaners, bartenders, scallopers, whatever. Anything to make a subsistent dropout existence. Plaid flannel shirts, unkempt beards, dirty fingernails, smelling faintly of the musky odor of weed.

"What are you doing down here?" Glenn asked, his eyes squinting in the bright sunlight. "Hardly anyone ever comes down here off-season."

"Oh, not much, except that I had heard there was some construction going on here on some big property that was just quietly sold, and I wanted to see which piece it was. Know anything about it?"

"Nope, nothin's been sold, and there's been no movement out here. I o'tta know as I'm staying at the Wilcox House this winter, and I have most of the houses out here and check on them every once in a while. None of my people have told me their house was going to be for sale or even looked at by people, and no one is doing any construction. You must have it wrong. I'd know, believe me."

"Okay, thanks, Glenn. Have a good one. See ya.'" Rick continued out to the main road while Glenn's pickup sped down the bumpy, potholed, dirt road kicking up clouds of reddish dust.

Chapter 77

Edgartown, Wednesday, October 28, 2015, 10:00 a.m.

Matt ran into Rick at the Dock Street Coffee Shop. He slid onto a stool beside him and said in a very low voice, "I almost took one to her last night. But I came to my senses. I just hate her so much!"

Rick jerked his head up from taking a bite out of the Reuben he had ordered. A caraway seed from the sauerkraut landed on his chin that he didn't seem to notice. He often ordered that instead of breakfast. His fingers were already greasy, and he sucked on one to dry it.

"Jesus Christ, Matt! Don't do anything foolish, no matter how much you've got to hate her. Look, do me a favor. Just sit tight for another day or two. I just learned something, and I wouldn't be surprised if she gets into a big shitload of trouble. If my sources are right, and they are almost always right, she will be in deep shit, mark my words. As we say, the long arm of the law reaches everywhere."

Matt perked up. "What d'ya mean? What's going on? Can't you tell me?"

"Sorry, pal. My sources are confidential. And I don't want you going around enquiring and sticking your nose in things. That could be the kiss of death. All I want you to do is to keep quiet. I promise you'll be the first to know if you keep calm, cool, and collected. You know the drill." He took another chomp out of the grilled sandwich, getting sauerkraut and Russian dressing over his stubby chin. No matter how hard he tried to shave closely, his Lebanese ethnic background wouldn't give him a break. His older brother, Mark, looked even worse. The family genes seemed to be more closely related to primates, hirsute little beasts, than most anyone on the Vineyard, with the exception of a few black Menemsha fishermen whose ancestors came from Cape Verde. He wiped his chin and sucked his fingers and crumpled up the cheap paper napkin and tossed it on the plate right on top of the ketchup-laced cold fries.

"Look, I gotta go. Promise me you won't do or say anything."

Matt looked down at the counter and barely nodded his head. Rick got up and patted Matt on the back and went up to the cash register to pay Mary.

"Bye, Don. Bye, girls. Have a good day, and don't do anything I wouldn't do, ha ha!" That was one of Rick's signature sayings. He never got tired of saying it. Everyone got tired of hearing it.

And the coffee shop's red door opened and closed, and he went across the street to where he had parked his Jeep in the town parking lot near the Yacht Club. "Jesus. If Matt had done something to her last night, what a waste these recordings would have been this morning!" He'd have to get in contact with Charlie O'Brien as soon as he had got hold of Maria to put one last squeeze on.

Chapter 78

Edgartown, Wednesday, October 28, 2015, 11:00 a.m.

Rick pulled into the back driveway of the Dr. Daniel Fisher House and pulled up toward the Porte Cochere, where off to the right, Maria's Range Rover wasn't in its usual "Baldwin Clients Only" space.

He opened the side door and climbed quietly up the stairs to the Baldwin Agency. He wondered if she was there, hiding and not answering phones, and he didn't want to alert her that someone was coming to see her. He reached the top of the stairs and listened, his ear to the door. He was struck by how quiet it was. Eerie, he thought. Three knocks on the door told him either no one was in the office yet or she was keeping absolutely quiet.

"Maria! It's Rick! Open up! I need to talk to you right now! It's in your best interest to open the door now!" He knocked again, louder and louder. "Okay, Maria! You had your chance. I'm going to see Charlie now and tell him what I've found out about you. Are you there?"

No sign whatsoever of her, and he admired her for not budging and keeping absolutely still. He didn't think she had the resolve to hold back.

"Maria, I'm leaving now. Good luck, honey, 'cause you're going to need it!" And he thumped down the stairs and crossed the gravel driveway, making a crunch-crunch-crunch noise under his weight and got in his car and drove the few blocks back to his office.

He'd have to find her before that Potts guy called the DA. Rick wanted that last bit of money from her before she took the tumble. He went inside and called her office but didn't leave a message, and then her house, but still no answer; and he hung up before the recording began. He also tried her cell, but she also wasn't answering that either.

He went back to his car and drove up Pease's Point Way and then down School Street, pulling over in front of their house. The driveway was empty. The Range Rover was there, so that must mean Walter had taken the Cherokee off-island. Everything looked quiet, and it didn't seem as if anyone was in the house. Where was she?

He didn't want to give up yet. Another $200,000 or so in his pocket was worth keeping quiet until Potts actually made the call to the DA. He picked up the phone again, and the man who answered said, "District attorney's office, Charles O'Brien speaking."

"Hey, Charlie! It's Rick. Wanna go grab a sandwich—my treat. How about David Ryan's? I could go for a fish sandwich about now. How about it?"

"Oh, hi, Rick. I'm not sure. It's really busy here today, and I'm working on something pretty big. Don't know if I can take the time."

"Oh, come on, Charlie—we'll just take an hour. Why don't I give you some more time now, and I'll walk down and get you at the courthouse about eleven thirty. We'll be back by twelve thirty. A man's gotta eat!"

Charlie paused a minute and thought about talking once again to Rick to see if he knew anything further about what he'd been working on. All he had told Rick a while ago was that it involved some real estate, so he could find out pretty easily today if he dropped a new hint or two.

"Oh, screw it all. You're right! I need a break, and the fish sandwich sounds right up my alley. See you when you get here. I'm working today downstairs where the grand jury sits when it's in session. Just between us, they might be sitting again...soon. Don't even ask, you know I can't say anything more as it's all a secret with a grand jury. You'll find out soon enough. See you in a while," and he clicked off.

If it's about Maria, I've got to get hold of her immediately if I have any hope of getting more. Where the hell is she? Rick said to himself.

He reached Senna at home. She was taking a day off as her mother was having day surgery, and she had to pick her up at the hospital around two o'clock. Senna was surprised that Maria wasn't in the office too but had no idea where she might be unless it was showing property up-island somewhere.

He then tried Espresso Love, where he knew she frequently went in for a morning cappuccino and a croissant. No one there had seen her either, nor across the parking lot at the Edgartown Diner.

He pushed his chair back from his heavy oak desk and got up, reached for his woolen scarf, and headed out the front door past Ellen. "I'm having lunch with Charlie O'Brien. Be back about twelve thirty. If Maria calls here, get her number and let me know immediately." He shut the door and walked down to Main Street. Ellen settled back in her chair and took out her knitting. The only sounds in the office were the grandfather's clock quiet and steady tick-tocking and her knitting needles, clicking. It was so soothing. She loved these moments. He was such an asshole.

Chapter 79

Edgartown, Wednesday, October 28, 2015, 11:20 a.m.

As Rick was walking down Main Street to pick up Charlie, he ran into Matt coming out of the town hall and stopped for a minute.

"Today should be your lucky day! You should get your $100,000 today. It should post by two p.m. Call me right after you see that money in that joint account of yours. And go tell Ed Voser that if and when the money is there, you want them to remove it immediately and put it into your own personal checking account. You don't want her reversing it later. By the way, my man, you scared the shit out of her! That was your finest hour yet! You played it cool and said exactly as I told you. And it looks like it's going to work!" Rick said, slapping him on the back. "Don't go trusting that woman. Transfer that amount immediately. Be vigilant just as you were in Afghanistan. Think she's a Taliban 'beekeeper.' That's what she is—a dirty Afghan bitch."

Matt nodded that he understood and thanked him for helping in this way, giving Rick a pat of solidarity on his arm.

"Don't worry, Rick. I'll do exactly what you said. Gotta be going. I'm going to check in at the bank now to let Ed know to call me when the transfer hits my account. Talk to you later." Matt walked down the street past South Summer Street and the Edgartown Deli toward Edgartown National Bank. Rick went across the street to the courthouse to pick up Charlie.

Chapter 80

Edgartown, Wednesday, October 28, 2015, noon

They had just ordered their fish sandwiches and were waiting for them. Rick didn't know the new waitress, but she looked pretty damn good. *Maybe I should tell her, if she ever needs a good lawyer, to call me, and I'll slip her my card on the way out.* She came back with the sandwiches and refilled their iced teas, and he said that to her.

Charlie laughed. "That's right. If you want a lawyer, call Rick. But if you want a good lawyer, that's another story!"

"Har har, hardy har har." Rick laughed, and he smiled at her pale face framed by thick wavy red hair as she put down their drinks. "Allow me to introduce ourselves. This is Charlie O'Brien, district attorney, and I'm Rick Maron, an attorney in town. Here's my card," and he gave her a wink. She laughed and said she hoped she wouldn't ever need a lawyer, now that she's moved here. "But, just in case," and she took his card.

"Clever move, Rick, you old dog you. Aren't you ever afraid Janet will find out?"

"No, she's too busy with the arts society and all those lah-de-dahs she has to kiss up to. She doesn't have a clue, and I want to keep it that way, understand, Charlie?" he said with a smile.

"So, what's up, Charlie? I know you can't say exactly, but...," Rick said, wiping tartar sauce off his chin with the back of his hand. A piece of its pickle fell on his tie.

"It's about ready to break, and it's about real estate. It's big," said Charlie as he bit into his sandwich.

Rick took a second to respond and then said, "If I had to guess, it might be Maria. But I know you can't say if I'm correct," and he took another bite.

Charlie looked at him. "What would make you think that?"

"She came to me to represent her in some 'real estate matter' but wouldn't tell me what it was. I said I would but only for a hefty retainer…in the six figures. I thought it was way over what she would ever consider, but lo and behold, she gave it to me. It was then I wondered if there wasn't something fishy going on, but, as I said, she hasn't told me yet. And, even when she does, I can't break attorney-client privilege as you know.

"But it is funny we'd bring her up now, as this morning I tried calling her and even went to her office. I really needed to find out why she needed me and for the amount I told her it would cost her. I went up the stairs and knocked loudly on the door, yelling out her name, but she didn't answer. It was eerily quiet, and I heard nothing inside. Senna was out today. I called her when I noticed her car wasn't there. She thought Maria would be in the office too. As I was about to give up, I did hear the phone ring and the voice mail kick in. I couldn't hear the words themselves, but I tell you, it was a man, and he was yelling at the top of his lungs. Whoever he was, he was NOT happy!"

Rick continued, "She also hadn't been out for coffee either, as I checked. No one had seen her, so she must have gone out with a client who was driving her to some place. The opposite of what usually happens." Rick ran his finger through the little bit of tartar sauce that was left on the plate and then sucked his finger off, before taking the paper napkin to his mouth, a gesture Charlie noted by involuntarily cringing a bit.

"Have you seen her new husband around?" Charlie asked.

"Oh, here and there. They got into the Yacht Club and eat out at the Charlotte Inn, while poor Matt is still dealing with PTSD and having to fight her demanding more child support. Matt tells me the kid is going to spend next year at a ritzy boarding school in Switzerland next year. Can you believe that bitch? All while she's been hauling him to court for more child support, while she and her new husband are living it up like the Rockefellers!"

Rick looked at Charlie and said, "I've had to step in and calm Matt down several times. He hates her and would love to see her dead. Seriously. But I did just help him recover some money she had owed him from a long time ago, and that might calm him down. At least I hope so. In fact, I just saw Matt on his way to Edgartown National to see if the money had been wired into his account. Maybe on my way back to the office, I'll try to find him and see if it came in. I hadn't thought of asking him this morning if he had seen Maria today, but it's not a bad idea. I really want to nail down this so-called problem she hired me for."

"Well," said Charlie, pushing back from the table and standing up, "let me know if there's anything fishy that you can tell me about, given your client privilege. I'd be interested."

Even if Rick wasn't the brightest light on the tree, he knew that it was Maria who was going to be indicted, and it looked like it was imminent. It would be too late now to get the extra money out of her, but at least he had covered her first payment to him, saying it was a retainer for some case she thought she'd need him for.

The two men walked back up Main Street and said goodbye in front of the courthouse. "Keep me posted when you can, Charlie, and if I can get anything out of her that I can share with you, I'll let you know. But my guess is that's going to be impossible in that she's already hired me."

Charlie nodded and waved and said as he walked up the stairs, "Stay tuned and fasten your seat belt!"

Chapter 81

Edgartown, Wednesday, October 28, 2015, 12:45 p.m.

Rick quickly walked back to his office on the corner of Cooke Street and Magnuson Way and looked at his Rolodex. Somewhere he had Walter's original business card when he came into town with his condo development group, and his mobile phone number was on that. Bingo! He found it. He dialed. "Hello, this is Walter Keller. I'm sorry I can't take your call now. Please leave your name, phone number, and the reason you called, and I'll get back to you as soon as possible. Thank you for calling." Rick put the phone down before it connected to the voice mail.

A few minutes later, Ellen told Rick that Matt was on the phone. "Okay, I'll take it right now. Thanks."

"Rick," said Matt, "wanted you to know the transfer was made, and she put it in my personal checking account. I really want to thank you. I never thought she'd actually follow through. It's still hard for me to believe."

"Well, Matt, I have my sources, and they are always correct. I really didn't doubt it myself, and I had inside knowledge that she'd do it, but I couldn't be too cocky until you actually confirmed it with me. I'm glad, m'boy, you deserve this, and I was happy to help in any way I could," Rick responded. "I'm glad you called. I forgot to ask you this morning, but I've been trying to get in touch with Maria today, and I can't seem to find her. By any chance, do you know where she might be? I tried calling the office and actually went up there, but no one answered the door."

Matt said he didn't have any idea where she was. "Last I saw of her when I was outside last night was that she was getting pretty drunk and speed-dialing her phone and looked frazzled. Maybe she's sleeping it off this morning?"

Rick stopped talking, and he paused. "How would you know, unless you saw her? Huh? Were you outside their place spying on them? God, you could get in a pile of trouble doing anything like this, innocent or not. What's going on?"

Matt quietly said, "I had a bad time last night. Yah know, more anger again, spurred on by some bad flashbacks I've been having recently. I just hate her so much. I was at the Wharf and decided to drive by and just sit there. I'll tell you but no one else, for a while, I was thinking of taking a gun to her for all she's done. I sat across the street and saw her getting drunker by the minute, and she had her phone in her hand and was frantically calling someone. Probably her asshole husband as I didn't see him there. She then fell asleep or passed out."

Matt was shuffling back and forth on his feet, looking down at the sidewalk. "Look, I know it was stupid. I was close but don't think I'd really do anything. Don't worry about me, buddy. I believe in Karma, and she'll get hers someday. I'm cool, don't worry about me. Honest. It was just a bad night.

"When I left, she was passed out on the couch. Bet he's had it with her. So much for that whirlwind romance, huh?"

"Was the Cherokee still in the driveway last night?" Rick asked.

"Actually, no. It was just the Range Rover, Maria's."

"As I said, I was over at the agency a little before noon, but the Range Rover isn't parked in her regular space. And, the agency's door was locked, and she didn't respond when I knocked and knocked. I also had called out to her too. She's not answering anyone," said Rick.

"Where's Senna?" Matt asked. "She wasn't at the agency?"

"No, I called Senna at home, and her mother's having day surgery, so she had taken the day off. She guessed maybe Maria was showing property up-island, and, you know, the cell phone service sucks up there.

"I also called Walter's cell phone but hung up as it was going into voice mail. I vaguely remember I heard he was going to somewhere on the Cape for the day on business or something," said Rick, covering his tracks about tapping her phones.

"Yeah, phone service up-island does suck. But she'll show her ugly face before too long. Heather told me she was spending the night with the Belisles, so she won't know anything either. What a mother! Always pawning her daughter off on someone. And I'm still stuck paying child support! For what!" He started getting agitated again, raising his voice.

"Matt. Keep it down. You don't want to attract attention. Leave it alone for now. You have your money."

Chapter 82

Edgartown, Wednesday, October 28, 2015, 2:00 p.m.

"Rick, this is Charlie. I've got to talk to you. Can I come to your office?"

"Sure, what's up?" said Rick, getting concerned.

"I'll tell you when I get there. Be there in five. Thanks."

A few minutes later, Ellen opened the office door and ushered Charlie in. He sat down opposite Rick and began. "I don't know where Maria is, but am guessing she's still at home as no one has seen her today. You probably guessed, but she's the one under investigation now, and we've just called the grand jury back to sit again. When did you say you went to her office? And, did you ever get to talk to Matt as you said you'd try after our lunch?"

"Oh my god," said Rick. "I sorta figured that about her, but of course wasn't sure. I went there about eleven, right before I called you for lunch, and yes, I just talked to Matt. He assumed she must be up-island somewhere with a client, and the cell phone service was spotty or nonexistent. He did say something strange, but if I tell you, I don't want him getting in any trouble."

"You have my word," said Charlie.

"He almost blew it last night. He had a gun and sat outside their house across the street for quite a while. He told me he was having flashbacks and just hated her guts. Luckily, he didn't act. He saw her make a couple of drinks, and then she went to sleep, or she passed out, however you want to call it, with her head on the back of the couch with the TV on in front of her. Matt hadn't seen Walter, who was probably already upstairs in bed and must have thought it was easier to leave her there rather than to lug that load of shit up the stairs. Matt also wondered if Walter was there as he only saw her Rover, and not his Cherokee, and jokingly said maybe he had left her?

"Anyway, Matt said he continued to sit there for a moment and then put the gun back in the glove compartment and went home. End of story. Oh, I forgot, and that Heather was spending the night at the Belisles and that Maria had been frantically dialing her phone before she passed out," he added.

"Yeah, but really has anyone actually seen Walter today? Who else would she have been speed-dialing last evening if what Matt says is correct? This strikes me as funny," Charlie asked.

Carefully, Rick said, "I think I heard somewhere that he might have been off-island yesterday, but I'm not exactly sure. His Cherokee was not in the driveway this morning."

"What do you think is going on?" Rick asked.

"I don't know," said Charlie, "but I need the sheriff and me to go over to the house and present the facts to her and that she is being arrested. I doubt very much that she would have heard of the indictment and skipped town. This all has been kept strictly under wraps."

Rick picked up the phone and called Huck Manter. "Hello," said the sheriff, "can I help you?"

"Huck, it's Rick Maron. I'm here in my office with Charlie O'Brien. I'll put him on the phone."

While Charlie was explaining the indictment and the fact Maria wasn't at her office when Rick had gone by, Charlie looked at the grandfather clock. He also asked for the sheriff to check with the ferry to see when Walter had gone off yesterday and what time he returned home. It was almost three o'clock.

"Okay, Huck. Thanks. We'll meet you at their house. It's number 60 School. It's the Parson House. They've been renting it from the Parsons this fall. See you in a minute or two." Charlie handed the phone back to Rick. "I hope I'm wrong, but I need to arrest her now in case she's getting ready to flee. Let's go." The two deputies followed him, leaving Rick behind.

When Huck was driving over to Maria's house to meet Charlie, his office called him. Woods Hole had called back with the information on Walter. "What? He didn't have a return reservation yesterday? What about today? No? When did he leave yesterday morning? Yes? The seven o'clock? Are you sure he didn't have a return yesterday afternoon or evening? Okay, thank you." Huck hung up the phone.

Arriving at the house, he jumped out of his car and ran up to Charlie, who was waiting for him there. "He left on the seven a.m. ferry yesterday, but had an open return ticket. It's strange, but at this time of year, it's slow enough that you usually can get on any ferry you want. And, they had no return at all yesterday with his Cherokee—they checked all the records."

The two deputy sheriffs had just arrived and got out of their car. The three men—Huck, Charlie, and the first deputy—went to the front door, and the second deputy did the same to the back door. The deputy knocked loudly several times. No answer. They moved over into the bushes and peeked in at the living room. They saw her asleep or still passed out on the couch, exactly where Matt had told Rick she was when he left in his car the night before.

Huck moved back to the front door and yelled more urgently, "Maria Keller? This is Sheriff Manter. Please open the door now!

"Let's get in by the side door, it's less noticeable than us breaking in on School Street where we're sure to cause a commotion."

Huck told the deputy to go get the Halligan bar from the cruiser, and Charlie and Huck hurried around to the side where they met the other deputy. The two deputies used the Halligan and gained entrance to the kitchen. Within a second they were all in the house moving quickly into the living room where they had just seen Maria on the couch. Huck felt for a pulse and shook his head. "She's dead." Charlie gasped. The deputies looked stunned. While on duty, they had never seen a dead person before. She looked awful in death, and the smell of urine was overpowering. Looking at the glass near her hand and the bottle on the table next to her, it seemed clear she had not been to the bathroom for some time before she died.

Chapter 83

Edgartown, Wednesday, October 28, 2015, 3:00 p.m.

Meanwhile, Rick's curiosity had got the best of him, and he walked over to School Street. Huck had just come out the side door and waved Rick over. He told him how they had found Maria dead, on the couch, and there was no sign of foul play. The glass she had been drinking from was on the floor, and there was a vial of pills on the coffee table.

Huck and Charlie filled Rick in on how they had to break through the side door and run through to the living room calling her name without any response. They told him it was obvious that there was no need to even feel for a pulse. Pallor mortis was more than evident as it occurs almost immediately, generally within fifteen to twenty-five minutes, after death. But rigor mortis generally sets in about three to four hours after death and peaks at about twelve hours later.

"Looking at her body, and I'm no doctor, mind you, but I did have some basic medical training when I was elected," said Huck, "I'd say she died around midnight. There are four stages of death: pallor mortis, algor mortis, rigor mortis…and I can't remember the fourth one. But, if she died sometime after Matt left last night, which he told Rick this morning was around 11:30 or 12:00 p.m., pallor would have been within minutes, but no one was here to see this. Again, assuming that she died around midnight, then rigor mortis would peak around four o'clock this afternoon, and it still hasn't quite peaked by the feel of her, but it's close. She also has those purple splotches on her legs and feet, but this time, only a medical examiner or coroner will be able to determine the exact time of death by studying these blotches. The medical people will but have confirm this, but it looks like an accidental overdose to me and no sign of foul play."

They had called for an ambulance and notified the medical examiner's office on the Cape, in Sandwich. It would take a while for one of them to be assigned and to get to the ferry terminal in Woods Hole, the forty-five-minute ride over, but the sheriff would have one of his vehicles meet the boat and take the examiner the short distance to the Martha's Vineyard Hospital. In the meantime, Doc Coffin could give a preliminary noninvasive assessment while waiting for the medical examiner.

But what bothered them all was not the cause of Maria's death, but rather where Walter was. The only thing for sure was that he didn't come back on the ferry last night. "Therefore," Huck added, "Walter could not have killed her. It's another reason I believe she OD'd."

Rick was shocked. He couldn't believe she was dead. "Jesus Christ, who would have expected that? Not any of us!" he said to Huck and the deputy. "I can't believe it!" They all stood there in the driveway, shaking their head and looking down at the peastone.

Just then the ambulance arrived followed by Doc. Huck spoke to Doc and told him the details and what he thought about her death and added, "Of course, you'll know better than I, but anyway, it's my two cents' worth." Doc nodded and went inside with a frown on his face. Huck followed and came out a minute later and joined Rick and Charlie in the driveway.

Rick thought for a moment and then said, "Huck, you know I was just thinking. We need to get in touch with Walter, so you might want to call Senna to meet you at Maria's office as perhaps Walter had left a message there about his return?"

"Good idea, Rick," and he called the police to get Senna's home phone. The third deputy went with Huck to Maria's office. Within twenty minutes, Senna arrived and unlocked the office door and immediately left. They didn't tell her yet about Maria. If she thought it was strange the sheriff was there, she didn't ask.

Within two minutes, Charlie, Huck, and the deputy were listening to the messages. The one from Walter later in the day before was normal—he was trying to make the 5:00 p.m. boat, but traffic was heavy. However, the other two voice mails had Charlie bothered. Charlie looked at Huck and said, "Look, I don't think this is strictly confidential anymore, but I had just reconvened the grand jury to determine whether or not Maria had set up a real estate Ponzi scheme. We are confident she'd be indicted. The Kramer lady and the Potts man on these two messages had already been identified as being duped. They didn't know it yet, but things were heating up as you can tell by Mr. Potts's message. There are three more Ponzis that we know of and also one who is deceased, old Oscar Pease, whose house she was pretending was for sale. I had to make a decision today whether or not to include Walter. We finally decided at the last minute that we had more on her being the principal than on her new husband, but believe you me, we firmly believe he was in the know. However, indicting her alone and assuming we'd get a conviction at trial, which we know we would, given all the evidence we had collected, we figured she'd make a deal and implicate him too. She is, I mean *was*, facing a twenty-year-plus prison sentence. And, at MCI-Framingham—not the county jail down the street! However, she wouldn't have to spend more than a year and a day at Framingham if we gave her 'an offer she couldn't refuse,' believe me. The offer was implicating her husband and testifying against him. You think she'd go quietly to prison while her new lover boy was loose on the streets? I don't think so! She'd cave, and we'd get them both, as we should."

"I don't get why you're saying *Ponzi scheme*?" said Huck.

"That Stephanie Kramer tape you just heard is one example," said Charlie. "Maria had hundreds of off-islander homes she'd caretake for in the off-season months and, of course, had to have all of their keys. When the real owners weren't here, she'd show wealthy summer people, like this Stephanie woman, very desirable properties that weren't yet officially on the market. Maria would say she'd already privately and very quietly arranged this incredible purchase price with the owners, who were old friends of Maria's, and the purchase price was considerably under the market price—close to $200,000 under. The 'buyers' could check this all out on Trulia or Zillow to verify the real market value, and they would see Maria's offer really was a fantastic deal. Maria made it very clear to the prospective buyers not to say a word to anyone because other agents would immediately try to convince the owners not to sign and, instead, give them the listing at the online market price at an additional $200,000."

Charlie continued, "She'd also say the property wouldn't be ready until the spring, as the county was notoriously slow in processing the deeds, and the owners needed time to remove their furniture and belongings, along with any other excuse she could come up with. So, the closing date was set, for example, May first, nine or ten months from the date they signed the fake P&S. She'd have already forged the owners' signatures, and at the time of the signing, she'd collect the buyers' earnest money, and in a few days after the check had cleared in her account, she'd fax them a doctored bank statement showing their money had been deposited into the Baldwin Real Estate Agency clients' escrow account.

"Very often they would give her additional money to oversee renovations or interior design changes they wanted, and she'd pretend to hire contractors and oversee the work. Remember I said old Oscar Pease? He went to a nursing home off-island several years ago and died there. She even 'sold' his property although he's been dead for a couple of years. In this case, we also added *uttering* onto her forgery and fraud charges. You *forge* someone's signature while that person is alive, but when you write a deceased's name on a legal document, you are *uttering*."

He continued, "If the new 'owners' became anxious about the amount of time that was passing without photos of the changes to the property they had asked her to oversee, or for some other reason, she'd show them fake photos of contractors on some other job. For example, guys working on a new pool, landscaping, painting—any images that didn't identify the property itself, but rather photograph real work being done on some other unidentifiable property.

"I gotta hand it to her," Charlie continued. "She thought of everything. When someone would start complaining it was going too slowly and they wanted to get their money back, Maria would take 50 percent of their earnest money deposit from the pool of her fake escrow accounts and repay the complainant, with the stipulation the remainder of the 50 percent, less expenses, would be returned when a new buyer was secured and have them sign a nondisclosure agreement. If they talked or complained, they'd lose the remainder of their money. People were just happy to get out of the deal itself and wouldn't want to forfeit the hundred thousand or more that was still being held by her, so they gladly complied and did not talk about it. After several months, and she had secured another victim, she'd return the remainder—less, of course, 'expenses.'

"She was a pro. I give her that.

"I've just filed the complaint charges with the court. The grand jury is ready to go Monday, but they need an arrest first. We don't need anything more for the moment," said Charlie, with a sardonic laugh, *except for a live person*, he thought to himself.

The sheriff's deputy was told to call Senna and tell her she could not come back to work until further notice. Charlie and Huck walked back to Maria's house and went inside. Her body had been removed, and Huck told the deputy to stay outside and keep people away. Huck told the deputy to put a sheriff's seal on the door and a small sign saying, "Do Not Enter. By order of the Dukes County Sheriff's Department."

Chapter 84

Edgartown, Wednesday, October 28, 2015, 4:00 p.m.

Back inside the house, the sheriff and Charlie (whom the sheriff had just deputized as Charlie suggested) started looking around. Huck picked up a paper that had fallen on the floor. It was scribbled by hand and had "Edg. Nat'l # 011304478—100K" and showed it to Charlie. "Hmmm," Charlie said. "This could be important."

Near to where Maria had been lying, and almost hidden under the couch, they saw the note Walter left yesterday morning and read he'd hoped to be back on the five o'clock ferry. They also noticed that she had agreed to go to "cleanse" at Canyon Ranch. Not exactly a real rehab but at least she recognized she had a problem.

Charlie said, "Too bad she hadn't survived the night of 'one last drink' before she was to have gone to rehab. Some people came so close to being able to straighten out and then fail at the last second. Irony is nothing but fate played out." He shook his head and stared at the empty couch; the pillows were still visibly stained by her urine. "There's no dignity in dying," he said under his breath.

Huck didn't quite get what Charlie meant by fate and irony but had other things on his mind. He asked Charlie, "Where is Walter? There wasn't any sign he had been here, so he obviously didn't get back last night as planned. To all intents and purposes, it had looked as if he was headed back to take her this morning to Canyon Ranch, just when she had made this big decision. It just doesn't make sense?"

Both men knew they could only gather whatever might be evidence that was in full sight, until they got a search warrant.

"In any case, we've got to alert Walter, as well as Matt. I prefer to wait a bit on Matt," said Huck. "I'll call the Steamship Authority again and have someone else find out if he made a boat last night or if he's on a boat today. I want to make absolutely sure of what was told me earlier."

Looking at his deputies, he said, "You two guys call the state police and check all the Cape hospitals. Maybe he got into an accident last night? But why would he plan to drive her to rehab today and not come back? It just doesn't make sense. I'll call and put an APB on his car, and we'll get him here."

"He's not in the clear by any means, yet," added Charlie. "She was our prime target, but I don't believe he's unaware of her schemes."

Charlie said, "I'm going to get the search warrant. It's strange Walter is nowhere to be found. I'll be back as soon as I can, but you all carry on. Remember: touch only what's in full sight. I'll be back shortly with the warrant."

Chapter 85

Edgartown, Wednesday, October 28, 2015, 4:45 p.m.

In the hospital, on a gurney, even for a dead person, Maria looked like hell: her now waxy white skin contrasted with her black hair, a mass of unkempt and matted curls—not the usual blown-dry sleek shiny hair she was known for. She was completely disheveled. All that planning and scheming and chutzpah—for what? A lump of putrefying flesh about to be exposed under the bright lights of the operating room, the hospital's makeshift morgue, and then hauled back on the ferry as freight, not a passenger, inside the medical examiner's Suburban to the new medical examiner satellite offices in Sandwich, a twenty-five-minute drive. There, in one of the two autopsy rooms, the body will be manhandled (by a dispassionate stranger who went to medical college and became a physician), sliced into, fluids extracted and carried to the laboratory, her parts weighed on a scale, and then sewn up again and covered by a sheet. End of a life. Poof.

And Maria, only by the grace of God (certainly not by his omniscience), hadn't—officially, that is—died as a felon. Her family could hold their head up at St. Elizabeth's, and Father Almeida could say prayers for the dead in her name, offer communion, and pass the basket. What he did with the money in his baskets has often been the source of conjecture in town, as sometimes were his private catechism lessons for young boys.

Chapter 86

Edgartown, Wednesday, October 28, 2015, Just before 5:00 p.m.

Charlie had met with Judge Mayhew in his chambers just before the courthouse closed and explained the situation. For a judge who had seen and heard just about everything, Mayhew seemed astonished at what he just heard, shaking his head in disbelief. "Of course, I'll issue the search warrant or warrants right now. I assume you want three: one for the office and one each for the home and car?"

"Exactly, Your Honor. Thank you," said Charlie. He went back to Maria's house with the warrants. Three other men had arrived from the sheriff's office, and they went upstairs and looked in closets. It appeared that both Walter's and Maria's clothes were all there as well as what appeared to be a complete set of suitcases. In the bathroom were toothbrushes and half-used tubes of toothpaste. It looked like all of Walter's prescriptions and some of hers were in the medicine cabinet; the pills she was taking for anxiety were next to her on the couch, although the vial was almost empty, along with a martini glass. There were absolutely no signs that Walter wouldn't be back last night, or, at the latest, today. They then went on into the storage in the attic and the basement, every inch of space; and an hour later, they reported back to Huck. Nothing seemed abnormal or suspicious.

In addition, the deputies whom Huck had asked to go to the office and search it thoroughly, further reported that Maria's desk also looked normal as if someone had been working there recently and would be coming back. They also reported that Walter had left another message at the office, about 5:00 or 6:00 p.m. from the day before, that had been erased, presumably by Maria herself, saying he was running late but still thinking they could do the dinner plans, but it would be closer to 8:30 p.m. when he'd get back that evening.

They couldn't figure out where the heck Walter was and why they couldn't reach him. It sounded as if everything was perfectly normal yesterday.

By this time, Huck had contacted the Massachusetts State Police and asked for an APB on a 2012 Jeep Grand Cherokee (WK2), black, Massachusetts license plates—BLDWN2, and driver—Walter R. Keller; DOB 06-28-70. Reason: family emergency.

Simultaneously, Rick told Huck that he and Matt were friends, and he'd go find Matt and tell him and then drive him to the Belisles, where Heather was staying.

Chapter 87

Edgartown, Wednesday, October 28, 2015, 5:30 p.m.

Rick reached Matt—he was on his way home on the Vineyard Haven road and told him about Maria. He warned Matt not to say too much about sitting outside the house last night. He added, "If and when they learn about the $100,000 transfer, just say this was the last part of your divorce agreement, and ironically it was done yesterday, completed the day *before* she died. Today was simply the bank lifted the "pending" status. You should right now open a new account in Waldo or wherever that place is we talked about, ya' know, where you said you'd like to go live, and put all of that in there. Don't keep it in Edgartown."

Rick continued, "At this point, you could say something like: 'If she hadn't made the transfer yesterday, I would never have received the money at all.'"

Matt started to say something, and Rick cut him off. "Listen up! The police need to look at everyone, and people in town know that you hated her. You should expect the police to question you, especially since it's now known you were sitting outside her house last night and perhaps even thinking of putting a bullet through her head. However, the real point is you weren't stupid enough to kill her then, as you hadn't yet received the last of the money she owed you from your marriage assets. In a way, the divorce was only 'finalized' today as of the transfer into your Edgartown National Bank account. Remember: you only had confirmation *today* that the money she deposited to your account yesterday, was approved by the bank today and made available to you as of 2:00 p.m. She had already wired it yesterday when she was alive and was already dead by the time the money was officially made available to you in your own personal account. You were just in one of your moods last night, and that was all. Nothing happened. End of story."

"I've gotta see someone now, but meet me at my office around 7:00 p.m., and I'll take you over to the Belisles, where Heather is hanging out with Julie. You can tell Heather then about her mother then. I've already called Janice to give her a heads-up, and she's making dinner for the girls now. Better get bad news on a full stomach, Ma always said."

Chapter 88

Edgartown, Wednesday, October 28, 2015, 6:00 p.m.

A little before 6:00 p.m., Huck, Charlie, and Rick were still together, having gone to get a burger at the Wharf Pub. Technically, Rick wasn't part of the investigation, but being a small town, and the fact that he had had conversations with Matt and Maria in the last couple of days, Huck and Charlie had let him stay with them.

Huck told the other two that fifteen minutes beforehand, he received the final call from the Steamship Authority. They had double- and even triple-checked their manifest and surveillance cameras. No walk-on passenger resembling Walter, nor his vehicle, came on board, but they did see him leave that morning in his Jeep. Huck then called the state police, and they too said no one had seen Walter. Huck told them to check Logan, Amtrak, Boston car rental agencies, Peter Pan, and any other bus lines and hotels from Boston to the Cape for any sign of Walter and/or his car. The deputies who had called all the Cape hospitals reported the same: no one fitting Walter's description was treated there.

"There's nothing more we can do right now, guys."

Charlie and Rick nodded their head in understanding. "You can't trust half these turkeys on the island if you start asking around about Walter and what they might say. Huck is right," said Rick, standing up and wiping his chin one final time. He had a red smear on his shirt over his stomach from his fries and ketchup.

Charlie gave them each a handshake and went to get his car behind the courthouse. Huck gave Rick a ride back to his house next to his office on Cooke Street.

"Don't say anything about Walter disappearing, Rick, okay? Technically you shouldn't have been with Charlie and me this afternoon, and I don't want any trouble from anyone, especially the *Gazette* and the *Times*. Nor from Walter or, if he needs one, his attorney." Huck put on his blinker and waited until Rick responded affirmatively, and Rick got out with a wave of his hand.

"Just give me a call when you get some information about Walter, will you, Huck? I had some recent business with Maria, and she was supposed to fill me in on the details today. Of course, that never happened! I can't believe this happened. Without us saying it, I'm sure the three of us are wondering by now if Walter disappeared. And, if so, who has the money? Time will tell. If Matt hadn't received his last portion of the divorce this morning, and if the other day I hadn't received her retainer for future services, neither one of us would have the money today. If Charlie is right about her, it sounds like all her assets will now be tied up until complete restitution is made to her victims. And, we can guess that complete restitution will be impossible, given the way she and Walter have been spending. Thanks for the ride, Huck."

"I'll call you, but I can't run the risk of anyone, not anyone, knowing of the time we spent together today, so I'm not emailing you. I don't want any trace. So, I'll call you," Huck said.

"Understood. Use my office number—it's a secure line. I don't want Janet intercepting a call from you on the home phone. My cell phone sometimes drops calls, and since I'm the only one who can listen to my office voice mail, that's where to leave a message. Ellen can't even access my voice mail. So, play it safe. Have a good day, see ya," and he walked in his back gate into the back of the house.

"What a crazy day," Huck said, as he put his vehicle in drive and went to the jail and his office.

Chapter 89

Edgartown, Wednesday, October 28, 2015, 7:00 p.m.

Charlie went back to the courthouse to resume his work, after he had asked the superior court judge, who was on the island for the next two weeks and needed to stay late due to the extraordinary circumstances, what he'd like for dinner in his chambers. Judge Mayhew listened in amazement at how they found Maria, but the husband was missing.

"I think you're right, Charlie, to modify the indictment you had prepared naming both of them as coconspirators, but now that Maria is dead, there is no way she could implicate her husband to try to get a more lenient sentence, such as just a little time in the county jail followed by probation. It's too late for that, that's for sure."

"Right now, a bird in the hand is worth two in the bush. Except, the one we held in our hand just died on us, and of the two in the bush, one has apparently flown away when we weren't paying attention." They should have carried their analogy further and paid attention to the second bird in the bush; it was still there. But it wasn't of any interest to them…yet. Go ahead and rewrite the indictment and just put his name in place of both of theirs. You got all the facts assembled, and we can assume he was in the know."

He paused and seemed to be thinking over something. "You know, there is such a thing as a *trial in absentia*. It's decidedly rare, but these trials can be held for a variety of reasons, including the legal declaration that the defendant was the one who committed the crime—to provide justice for society of family members of the victims or to exonerate a wrongfully convicted person after their death. Due to the heavy cost, they are usually held only under extraordinary circumstances. But this is one of those times," the judge said. "I'll call one of my colleagues in Boston and get his opinion, but keep this possibility in mind. I can get back to you within a couple of hours. This is really an interesting case—a Ponzi scheme, irate clients, the subject who maybe attempted suicide but certainly OD'd, and a husband who's a coconspirator and vanished."

Charlie said, "I think it's time now to call back the sitting grand jury. We convened them in early October, and they're good for about another six weeks of service before their three months is up. We only met once, the day they were selected and elected their foreman, but they haven't been presented with any case yet. I was about ready to call them back today anyway, based on what we've uncovered with Maria's real estate fraud, and then Maria up and dies and Walter disappears.

"As to calling your colleague regarding a trial in absentia indictment, is that something you could see to right now, Your Honor? We're running really late as we asked Maria's cousin to meet us in the office, and she's been waiting for us there now. She works for her as her secretary—I mean, she *worked* for her, and no, we don't think she's in on anything. She's a quiet and unassuming middle-aged woman, and I'm sure that's exactly why Maria hired her. She'd never ask any questions, and she keeps to herself."

Judge Mayhew nodded and got up from his chair. "I'll go down and start the ball rolling. We should be able to get the grand jury back in Monday morning if you're set. What do you say?"

"That's fine. I'm not handling the question about *in absentia* at this time, but we can start the ball rolling with the real estate side of things. All I have to do is to change Maria's and Walter's names on the original documents we'd already prepared, *in absentia*. The rest remains the same. I'll do it now. Thanks, Your Honor. This will save us some time. I'd like to get this underway. I'm sure there's more to discover, once we start in," said Charlie.

Chapter 90

Edgartown, Wednesday, October 28, 2015, 7:15 p.m.

Senna sat in the office, still stunned with the news of her cousin. Huck and Charlie had called her at home earlier that morning to say they were coming in to meet with her and not to touch anything. They had told her about Maria and the fact that Walter was nowhere to be found, although they were looking for him. No one had an idea if she tried to overdose or if she just got drunk. One thing they wanted her to know was that she would be under investigation given her relationship to Maria and the fact she, Senna, worked side by side with Maria. Huck and Charlie both told her they believed that she had nothing at all to do with the real estate fraud, but it was no longer a matter for local authorities, and the FBI had been called in. They would be giving her a hard time, as they didn't know the islanders as they both did.

"Look, Senna, they're going to be tough on you. All I can say is tell them anything you know or heard and don't hold back," said Charlie. Senna started crying and trembling. She was unable to even grasp Maria's arrest, much less this talk about her selling people's property without their knowledge. It made no sense to her. Huck went up to her and patted her on the back in a fatherly way.

"Senna. It won't be easy on you, we know. Just try to remain as calm as you can. If you want us to get you a lawyer, we'll do that. Rick might be available, but we're not sure yet if he represents Matt, so it may be a conflict of interest. My advice is just let the FBI ask you questions, and if you feel they are getting too rough on you, say you want a lawyer and call Rick. In the meantime, we'll see if he's able to represent you, and if not, we'll have him get someone else for you if you call him. You'll be fine, my dear. You'll be fine. It's been a shock for everyone. The FBI should be here around noon."

Chapter 91

Edgartown, Thursday, October 29, 2015, 8:30 a.m.

Word on an island travels faster than the Internet. There's an old island expression, "If you want to find out what you've been doing, just step outside."

The day after the discovery of Maria's body, Janice Belisle had more phone calls than she ever had had. "Yes, I was here when unexpectedly Matt came to the door yesterday. He told me not to call down Heather and Julie yet and then told me about Maria. I can't believe it! They don't know yet, but he said she might have tried to commit suicide, overdosed, but you can't say. But she and Walter don't hide their drinks when they go out."

"Well, what happened when you told Heather her father was here?" came the voices at the other end of the phone.

"He told her that her mother was found dead. Just like that. She stood there, stunned. Julie and I both went up to her and put our arms around her. She didn't cry. She just kept saying, 'Are you sure?' And of course, Matt nodded his head. He's not a demonstrative guy as we all know, and he didn't quite know what to do, so I said to him, 'If you and Heather want to go talk in the living room, Julie and I will be here in the kitchen.'

"Julie whispered to me she thinks Heather would want to stay here instead of going up to Matt's place on Twenty-First Street, which she doesn't like at all. So, when Matt and Heather came back into the kitchen, I suggested that, and Heather jumped on it. I felt a little badly for Matt, but told him that at this age, girls feel that they can talk more to each other than to us adults."

"Oh my god!" they all responded. "Oh my god! And, then what happened?"

"Well, Matt went to his house. Huck and the DA said to keep Heather until they could locate Walter and that they'd get back to me with any news whatsoever."

"Isn't it weird Walter didn't show up last night?" each of them said.

"What's going on there?"

"Apparently, he left her a note and two voice mails saying at first, he'd be home around seven thirty and then changed it to an hour later, but he never showed up at any of the ferries. So strange," Janice said, keeping her voice down.

CHAPTER 92

Edgartown, Thursday, October 29, 2015, 10:00 a.m.

Right before the FBI was to have flown in from Boston, Charlie and Huck got word that Walter had been on the LATAM flight Tuesday night to Sao Paolo. He would have landed early yesterday morning and certainly not stayed around the airport. So, he had at least a twenty-four-hour head start to disappear.

"Jesus!" said Charlie. "I can't believe it. I never even thought of him being capable of getting out of the country. I assumed Maria just overdosed on the anxiety pills and the drinking. He really delayed us looking for him by all his belongings he left at their house and the note and the voice mails he left her. Without these red herrings, we would have started to look for him immediately after finding her body. We just assumed what he wanted us to assume: that he was in his car coming back to Woods Hole. Those notes and voice mails cost us six or more hours before even starting to look for him. More than enough time for him to walk on that plane and clear out of here. Jesus Christ! I don't believe it. I just don't believe it!" Charlie repeated, shaking his head. "I just don't fucking believe it!"

Huck said, "My guys are picking up the Feds at the airport, and I'll clue them in about Walter flying to Brazil. This is more than we've ever seen here on this island, that's for sure." He picked up his phone and made the call.

PART 5

Edgartown, late October, 2015

Chapter 93

Edgartown, Thursday, October 29, 2015, late morning

Rick was at his desk, reviewing a divorce agreement that he and Mary Anne hammered out, to neither of their clients' benefit. They'd already worked out how each attorney would posture to their clients about how they were going "to nail" the other spouse and get the best for their clients. Of course, it was all a game. They couldn't care less and just wanted an easy time. Neither attorney was suited for trial, so, long ago, they had worked out a dog and pony show that appeared to make each side think their lawyer was doing the best job.

Janet's voice said, "Hello? This is Janet Maron speaking."

The other voice said, "Hello, Janet, this is Robin Rebello down at the courthouse. How are you doing?"

"Oh, fine, thank you, Robin, and you? I'm surprised to hear from you today! It's been quite a while," said Janet.

"Can't complain, m'dear. Older and wiser as they say." She chuckled. "The reason I'm calling is that Judge Mayhew just told us that he wants your grand jury to sit Monday morning. He apologizes for the lack of notice, but it can't be helped, he said."

"Monday? Are you kidding? Oh, no…I'm in the middle trying to get my gala committee to get off their you-know-what, and Monday is a full workday. Too late to call them off now, so I'll have to get Kate to try to lead them to make some decisions. What timing! But I know I can't do a thing about it. Okay, I'll be there. What time? Nine o'clock?"

"Yes, dear. You as the foreman and James Bilodeau as the clerk may want to come in about 8:45 a.m. to get settled, but you don't technically need to. I just know Judge Mayhew likes a little time to meet the two of you before everyone else piles in. The judge says to plan a full day and to expect this to be a fairly lengthy number of days, so you might want to clear your calendar now of anything important. It appears you have about another six weeks of possible service, but other than that, I have no idea of how long you're all going to need. I know you know this, Janet, but I have to say it anyway. You are not to discuss any information with anyone, including your husband and family and friends, with the exception of saying you've been called back to serve Monday."

"Oh, I know, Robin, but thank you for telling me again. I understand completely. I'll be there about 8:45 a.m., first thing Monday. Hope to say hi to you then! Bye for now."

Rick heard the receiver put back into place. He got up from his desk and went out the back door to the house and entered the kitchen where Janet was standing looking at the refrigerator contents. She was so absorbed that she didn't hear him come in and jumped when he said, "So, I hear you're going back to the grand jury Monday!"

She turned around and said, "However did you know? I just this minute got a call from Robin telling me the same thing!"

"I know everything around here. I've got my sources, you know," Rick said, scoffing at her. "You think you're so smart all the time, but you're not. Anyway, what's for dinner tonight?"

She was mystified at how he always seemed to know everything about everyone, and especially about her, her friends and conversations with them and family. But she dismissed this as quickly as it flitted across her mind.

"I'm thinking of the *shish taouk* with falafel and baba ghanoush I got from Shawarma Falafel when I was up in Boston last Sunday. And I still have some grape leaves that your mother put up."

Rick softened his demeanor a bit when he heard what dinner would be. He wouldn't of course comment on his pleasure at hearing the news of what was for dinner, that would be weak, and instead only said "Gotta go" and walked back out the door to his office.

Sitting at his desk, he went through the events of the past few days. "Wow. Charlie isn't waiting for anything. He's jumping right on it. Unbelievable what happened in the last couple of days. Unbelievable. Thank God I acted when I did with Maria giving Matt that money, and at least I got my first amount from her. Too bad about the second amount I was going to ask for yesterday but at least I covered myself regarding the 'retainer' she gave me for 'something' she was going to speak to me about. One day later, all her assets would have been tied up until complete restitution, and that would have been impossible, given the way they were spending."

He closed the door and called Charlie. "Hey, Charlie, my man! What's new? I just heard the grand jury has been reconvened. Can't imagine what that's about, ha ha."

"Yeah. I was all ready to go ahead with evidence and reconvene the grand jury anyway. Unbelievable timing, huh? But something new just happened. However, Judge Mayhew said to go ahead anyway. They will both be tried now *in absentia* even if we don't have either of them."

"Are you talking of Walter's disappearance? He's probably by now in some Caribbean island with some babe. I knew she couldn't possibly keep him. I just knew it."

"And, you're right! Or almost right!" Charlie said. "We *just* learned that Walter is now in Brazil. Now, it's true that with Walter's escape, he might have been enabling her with booze and pills, getting her to a state where she might easily overdose, but that doesn't make him a murderer. But what he did share with her was greed. She attracted him to her by her successful real estate career, but once she got him, she realized it wasn't enough to keep him forever. So finally, she let him know what she was doing and how they both could profit from this, and this really attracted him. He was in it with her for good. We'll have to see what the grand jury does Monday," Charlie said.

"Well, good luck, m'boy. I can't imagine what you've already dug up on her—or should I now say them? I'm sure there's more than meets the eye when clients start coming out of the woodwork after the *Gazette* runs the story of her death today. Of that, I'm sure," said Rick, a bit mysteriously.

"Yeah, me too," said Charlie. "Gotta go, my assistant just brought in the latest revisions to the indictment being presented Monday. See ya." Charlie hung up. Rick then dialed Matt to fill him in.

Chapter 94

Edgartown, Thursday, October 29, 2015, early afternoon

Janet had immediately called her board and staff and told them it was likely she wouldn't be available for some time—weeks maybe. She asked if the staff could meet on Saturdays and take Mondays off during this unknown but very busy period of time, which they agreed to do. They were all great people, she thought.

At the time the grand jury was first named, just three weeks before Maria's death, eighteen people were called to serve for the fourth quarter of the year, meeting for the first time on Thursday, October 1. At that time, there weren't any cases to hear, so all they had done was to elect the foreperson and the clerk from the final thirteen who were chosen to be the jury, while an additional five alternates were also named. They were told that in Massachusetts, a grand jury typically sits for three months. Occasionally, they may serve longer if a specific indictment has not yet been resolved.

Right after they all had been selected upstairs in the courtroom, they began to receive their instructions.

Judge Mayhew had said then, "The first order of business is for the grand jury to elect its foreman and clerk. For example, you might want to consider someone like Janet Maron. She's the executive director of the Vineyard Arts Society and has lived on the island for the past fifteen years. She's also an elected town official and has been appointed by the selectmen to the Regional Transit Authority. You certainly can elect anyone you want to elect. I'm just mentioning her as an example of what you might want to consider in naming your foreperson.

You will recall when you all first were sworn in at the beginning of your term, you were told you sit at the pleasure of the court for a three-month term. If need be, that period can be extended if a case is still being presented. You were also told that because there were not any cases being presented to you then by the prosecutor, you could wait to see if you were called back on an active case and then elect the foreperson and clerk, but you decided to elect your foreperson and clerk back then. You may remember your oath, but I will read it again so you recall exactly what you are to do or not to do.

"You, as grand jurors of this County of Dukes County, solemnly swear that you will diligently inquire and true presentment make of all matters and things given you in charge. The state's counsel, your fellows and your own, you shall keep secret. You shall present no man for envy, hatred, or malice, nor leave any man unpresented for love, fear, favor, affection, or hope of reward, but you shall present things truly as they come to your knowledge, according to the best of your understanding. So help you God."

After he reread their oath, he continued talking to them, "You will recall that your sole responsibility is to hear the prosecution's case or cases and determine whether or not there is enough evidence to bring this person or persons to trial. It is not your responsibility to determine their guilt or innocence: that will be done by another jury, *if* you determine there is to be a trial. This is the reason you will only hear evidence today presented by the prosecution—you will not hear or see any defense then. Once again, that will wait until trial, if you so decide that the prosecution has presented enough facts and accusations to make you concur that this person or persons should be brought to trial. Your duty involves deciding whether or not there is to be a formal accusation: it is not a finding. The guilt or innocence of these people will *not* be determined by you—that will be left to the trial jury itself when both the prosecution and the defense will present their cases. Is that clear?"

Judge Mayhew had belabored this point because in his experience, no matter what the judge advised the grand jury, there were always people who didn't understand the difference between a trial jury and a grand jury.

The eighteen people assembled nodded their heads and muttered "yes" or "understood" or "uh-huh." Five of them would be alternates, who would sit in on the entire proceeding but to listen only and not to participate in discussions or votes, unless one of the thirteen was recused.

"Thank you, ladies and gentlemen. You may now go down to the jury room we have set aside for you and your deliberations. Court Officer Amaral will take you there now. Let me warn you again: no one who enters that jury room may ever tell anyone—husband, lawyer, friend, daughter, son—what you will read, hear, and discuss there. Never ever and going into the future. There will be absolutely no discussion of who, what, when, why, how of those being accused of a crime and those who may have been wronged by this person or persons. If you discuss this outside of your official duties as grand jury members, and only in this building when you are all meeting together, you will bear the consequences. This is a punishable offence—both fines and jail time. This is not an idle warning. I cannot stress this confidentiality enough.

"The foreperson you elect will keep you on track, make sure all points are thoroughly explained and discussed, and eventually call for a vote or votes," he said, putting down his glasses and looking directly at Janet and then at the jury. He then stood up.

At the direction of the court officer, they all stood in unison and then followed Officer Amaral down the stairs to the jury room, marked Private. The alternates were again told to sit quietly on the side and to pay attention but not talk. They elected Janet Maron as foreperson and Jim Bilodeau as clerk. And that was a month ago.

CHAPTER 95

Edgartown, Monday, November 2, 2015, 9:00 a.m.

And here they were again, the same group, in the same room below the courtroom, but this time it was Monday, November 2, a little more than four weeks later, and they now had two new cases in front of them. The two bills were brought into the grand jury room by the district attorney and delivered to Janet, the foreman. The district attorney had already signed the indictment bills.

As foreperson, Janet received the indictment documents—the first for Maria Almeida Da Costa Keller and the second for Walter Adam Keller. Janet tried to keep her face impassive as she quickly scanned both documents before she gave each one to her clerk, Jim Bilodeau, who stamped each. Janet was shocked to read the outline of the things both Maria and Walter were said to have done.

The district attorney stepped up in front of the jury and introduced himself.

"Good morning, ladies and gentlemen. My name is Charles O'Brien, and I'm the district attorney for this county. I'm originally from Mashpee on the Cape and went to UMass Boston as an undergrad. After graduation I got a job in the State House with the Secretary of the Commonwealth Michael Connolly in the Registry of Deeds Division. You will come to see how my first job out of college is of particular importance in these two cases before you today. Working for the secretary, I knew then I wanted to be a lawyer, and after eighteen months with that job, I went down the hill to Suffolk Law School and graduated in 1995. I immediately went in to public service and eventually was elected as the Cape and Islands' district attorney serving Barnstable, Nantucket, and here, Dukes County. I am the chief prosecutor in this district and one of eleven DAs in the Commonwealth. My wife and I and our three children now live in Hyannisport."

He continued, "I'm pleased to be here today to present one of the more interesting cases I have ever encountered serving as DA. If you all decide to indict one or both of these two people, I fully expect this to become news. Not just local news, but national news. Knowing this, and knowing you are bound by law to never speak about what you have heard in this room, and I mean never, I am formally warning you that a grand jury is sworn forever to absolute secrecy. You cannot say anything at all of anything you hear or read or discuss in this room to your best friend, your spouse, your parents, or siblings—no one. Never. Or, you will face a severe penalty. In 1994, a former grand juror who leaked secret details was sentenced to the maximum eight years and one month in prison by a federal judge who said he would have given him more if he could. More recently a lawyer was sentenced to two and one half years in prison. I think you know just how we will proceed if any of you discuss anything whatsoever about these two cases or any others that may come before you in the weeks to come that you are still serving on this grand jury.

"These are two of the most unusual cases I have ever seen in all my years as a prosecutor. Some of you have heard what has happened to these two individuals in the past several days and others have not yet heard. You will be shocked, but you will not let yourselves be influenced by rumors and reports you may have already heard on this small island, but only by knowledge acquired from the evidence before you or from your own observations. While you are inquiring as to one offence, another and different offence may be proved, or witnesses before you may, in testifying, commit the crime of perjury."

He continued, "Some of you will know the accused, Maria and Walter Keller, and some of you will know the people who are said to be the victims. Maria has been found dead of an apparent accidental death, and Walter is no longer in this country. This particular case is not about her death or his disappearance, but instead it's about whether or not these two people, husband and wife as coconspirators or as individuals acting alone, were involved together, or separately, in their real estate business that they used to defraud would-be buyers on property the so-called buyers thought was for sale, and for which they signed over 'earnest money,' also called a down payment, to Maria Keller, believing the property was soon to be legally in their hands. They were told a closing date would be set in the next several months, in time to occupy the property for next year's 2016 summer season. Additional monies, other than the down payment, sometimes were also given to Maria for interior decorations, additional construction, landscape design, and so on. She is the legal owner and principal of the well-respected Baldwin Real Estate Agency, and Walter is not officially listed as an employee or principal, nor were client checks written out to him, nor was he a signatory on the real estate accounts. However, we believe he was fully informed about all transactions, and we know he interacted with the clients during house tours and social dinners."

He took a sip of water and continued, "Nothing seemed amiss on the surface. This was the island's premiere real estate agency run by a local woman of solid background and family without any trace of malpractice. In fact, the true owners of these properties that were supposedly for sale—whether the owners were alive or not, and I'll get to that later—were totally unaware of such promises and transactions and had never given their houses to the Kellers to be put on the market. The true owners never knew about the so-called *buyers*, and the so-called *buyers* never knew these weren't legitimate real estate transactions. This is because the Kellers chose their 'buyers' and 'sellers' purposely."

He continued, sipping water once again. "Both the buyers and sellers lived off-island, far enough away to ensure neither would come here in the off-season, and thus blow up their scam. Only Maria and Walter knew the whole story, and they made sure neither of the parties, the 'buyer' and the 'seller,' ever knew of the existence of the other party. The Kellers alone controlled the scheme."

One juror, Laura Alley, a woman who worked for the Chilmark School in a clerical capacity, asked, "Then how did the 'buyers' hear of the property if it wasn't advertised, and how come the 'sellers' didn't find out their property was supposedly for sale? It doesn't make sense."

Charlie continued, "Like all good real estate brokers, Maria knew people all over the island. She was now the owner of the Baldwin Real Estate Agency, by far the biggest firm on the island and the most successful in terms of representing expensive properties. If you had money, and wanted to buy, she'd be the one you'd be directed to if you hadn't been here for very long and the one to go to if you come here and rent big houses every summer and then decided to buy. And, if you had owned property here for generations, like so many wealthy families did, she'd most likely be your caretaker during the off-season. She had their keys, regularly checked on their property, alerted them to discovered problems, called in the tradesmen to fix the issue, oversaw any construction or interior decorations, and reported back to the owners. For these services, she was paid handsomely, three hundred dollars a month from each owner. She had at least a hundred and fifty to two hundred properties, so that alone is about half a million dollars, not counting her legitimate real estate commissions.

"Had Maria and Walter been able to get away and leave the island intact, it would have taken time for the real owners and the 'fake' owners to discover what had been going on behind the scenes. And then all hell would break out. But something went wrong, and the house of cards fell down now as opposed to in a few more months. The plan had been to continue until February or March and then pull out, having swindled even more money than they had already accumulated. Most swindlers try to grab as much cash as they can before they call it quits, and the timing of Walter's disappearance doesn't make sense, as no one was really on to them—yet. There was still money to be made. We don't know enough yet, but are guessing that something—some outside force—spooked them, and we believe both Maria and Walter decided to leave now, rather than run the risk of being exposed by whoever might have been onto them. One Keller was able to escape, but the other wasn't. But maybe Walter figured he had enough to live on himself and he so might as well 'get out of

Dodge' now, leaving Maria behind. We'll probably never know. All we *do* know is that Walter did not kill Maria. Maria OD'd herself.

"The obvious question we all have is, how did she and he, or she or he, think they could get away with this? Summer comes every year. When the real owners or the new 'owners' arrived or arrived back on the island, what would happen? How would the Kellers tell the new owners that their hundreds of thousands of down payment money was for nothing?"

Before he could continue, Stu Bishop interjected and said, "It's unbelievable that no one discovered anything until just now! Didn't anyone have questions or concerns or anything? Whatta bunch of a-holes these people are—too much money for their own good. That's what my father always used to say, 'They have too much money for their own good,' that's what he'd say. That's just what he said. And, he was right! Maybe he didn't have the college education they had, but he was a damn bit smarter than any of these a-holes." Stu believed that one had to repeat things four or five times in a row if the others are to comprehend what he said. It was more like the inverse.

That pretty much summed up everyone's feelings in the room; everyone murmured, "Yeah," "Uh-huh," "You're right," or "Unbelievable!"

Janet took over and continued, "District Attorney O'Brien is going to go over what happened in each instance. It's not my role to present the case, but it's important we all understand what a Ponzi scheme is so we can grasp the facts."

Charlie thanked her and thought she's a good foreperson. He'd let Rick know she was doing a good job.

He said, "To answer Juror Bishop's question, it would go like this. Maria had earlier explained to the new 'buyers' that on the Vineyard, deeds for property that went back to the 1650s were extremely difficult to trace to get a 'clear title,' and therefore this tedious process would take an inordinate amount of time and one had to be patient. However, over the coming winter months, if the new 'owner' started wondering why the closing date *still* hadn't been set, and they started complaining about this enough to worry Maria, she would quickly set a 'closing date' and call the 'buyers,' saying, "I just got word that the registry has cleared the title, and we can proceed!' That would stop their complaints as it seemed to them that all was in order."

"If they continued to complain and threaten her thereafter as the spring approached, she would offer to return their earnest money so they could start a new real estate search when they returned that summer. Most people wanted the property, because it was below market value, so they often stayed put with her, saying to themselves, 'Well, she did offer to return our money, so everything must be okay. It's just that stupid backward island and these islanders.'"

Charlie looked around to see if he had lost them or if they were still paying attention. Some of the islanders were of marginal intelligence, at best, he thought.

"At some point in the process, Maria would have them assign her a power of attorney so she could represent them at the official 'closing' that was soon taking place at an attorney's office here on the island so they wouldn't have to come back in the winter. Once that was done, just before the 'closing,' they would wire the remainder of the purchase funds into her escrow account, and the 'closing' would take place on the date Maria had given them. She'd call them afterward to confirm this and say it'd most likely be 'a little while' before the Registry of Deeds would formally record the deed, and she would say, with a laugh, that being the county government on the island, everyone knew they marched to 'island time,' not 'real time.'

"On the other hand, if the new 'owners' were really fed up waiting for their closing date, they might say, 'Forget the whole deal! We want our money back! This is crazy! Nothing should take this long, not even on that backward island of yours in the middle of the Atlantic Ocean that you can't even get to half the time! We're going to start looking in the Hamptons.'

"And so, she'd quickly send back their money, which immediately quieted them. She'd then go through her Rolodex again to try to get a new client whom she could perform a new scam on. Therefore, instead of dwindling, the pot of money kept growing with new scams, even if one or two got tired of waiting and demanded their money back. One canceled sale would not make much of an overall difference to her, as she was very good at what she was doing. The art of the scam, that's what a Ponzi is.

"Their goal was to get as much as they could this winter and escape from here in the late spring. Timing is everything." He took another sip of water and looked at the wall clock. *Not bad,* he said to himself, *only took three minutes so far.*

"Again, you are not judging the guilt or innocence of either side. That will be up to a trial jury once you decide if you believe there has been a crime here. It's my job to convince you that there *is* a crime—in fact, *multiple* crimes here. I would not be standing here today in front of you without factual proof. You will not hear from anyone who opposes the Commonwealth's position today. This is a grand jury convened to secretly hear what we, the Commonwealth, have to say. If you all conclude there hasn't been a crime, the matter is dropped. If you believe like we do that there has been a crime based on what I present to you, then you issue an indictment. The court would then arrest the perpetrators, and a trial jury would be called and a date for trial set. The trial jury then decides on the fate of each person."

The jurors all nodded their head or murmured assent that they understood. Even if they all didn't.

"One of these people before you is someone who apparently was embarrassed by her Portuguese background and working-class family, who envied others' social position that her background had denied her, who was motivated by greed and fabricated her falsehoods, who showed her lack of loyalty to family by dumping her first spouse without any warning to him, the father of her child and our local police chief, and by trading up to a more sophisticated off-islander husband.

"The other person is about the off-islander who came here to explore business opportunities and who saw the potential for easy wealth by manipulating a well-placed island girl with promises of a better life, of travel and expensive cars, and of living somewhere else once they had gained enough money to escape the very place she hated.

"Let me be clear: we believe both parties are guilty, and no one was forced into these crimes. One, Maria, had the means to make it all happen, but both Maria and Walter conspired and had the same motive—swindling victims out of their money for a better life elsewhere. One is now dead. The other has fled. So how can the Commonwealth indict one of them if either is not present or can speak for himself? The reason, once again, is that a grand jury only indicts. A trial jury, if it comes to that, and we hope it does, can convict or acquit. You have to decide if the state has enough evidence to say to the courts, 'Yes. We believe crimes were committed, and yes, each person was aware of the crimes he and she committed. They did these acts knowingly and willfully and maliciously.' It's called Malice Aforethought. Once you do this, the court will call a trial jury, and the Commonwealth will proceed."

"The other obvious question you must have is, if the two accused are not here in person, how can you indict them? The answer is, we will try them *in absentia*, meaning we will still have the trial and reach a verdict. If we all agree there is enough evidence to hand one or both of them to a trial jury, the trial jury will also try them *in absentia*. If funds can be recuperated, then victims will be able to recoup some of their losses. Without a guilty verdict, no one can recover anything.

"I also want to make certain you know that although we will present today certain of these crimes, this is a case that is still unfolding. Just yesterday we learned that another victim had left a voice mail complaining about the time it was taking to close on 'their new house.' As word spreads, we are positive that additional indictments will be required, and I can assure you today that until every victim comes forward over time, you all will be recalled into this room many times. In other words, it is unlikely that you will only serve a total of three months. I am sorry, but this is our law."

He asked if they had questions or if he could proceed with specific accusations. The jurors looked somber as they realized this was indeed a bizarre case and one that could go on for a very long time. Employers must allow a grand jury member to serve, but people like Kenny Norton, a plumber, was looking at a significant drop in business and income—he was his own employer. No one paid him for jury duty. He got money only if he was working. Cathy DeBettencourt worked for the hospital, and she'd be okay. Others thought of the sudden curtailment of freedom to come and go as they please in retirement. They weren't free any longer. They all realized what this meant to each and every one of them, and no one was happy. But there was nothing they could do.

Charlie said, "The first case is that of a Mr. Oscar Pease. He has been deceased for a number of years and last lived in a retirement home in Braintree. He has no known relatives at this time, and an attorney is trying to settle his estate that consists almost exclusively of property on Planting Field Way, Edgartown, and a small amount of cash, now being used by the attorney to pay property taxes. The house has been uninhabited for about seven years, which was when his last living relative relocated him to this retirement home to be near her. She paid the taxes on his house here, but she died about a year ago. It was the retirement home that told us he died about the same time as his cousin. He had no visitors at all except for this relative. The property's executor was Attorney Thomas Osborn, and all taxes are current, but the estate had not yet been settled, and so it sat. A real estate broker like Maria would certainly know that this property was all but forgotten. As many old properties on the island, the title is 'clouded,' meaning clear title can only be traced back to a certain time. Because it's 'clouded,' anyone who wants to buy this property is taking a risk that someone might have a valid claim to it that goes back a hundred or more years ago. And, if this were to happen, the new buyer would be out of luck. The chain of title would recognize the relative as the true owner. But many people take the chance, as the odds are very low that a 'long-lost relative' will emerge. In cases of clouded titles, the court will decide the ownership."

He put down his papers and removed his reading glasses and said, "As I said, we're getting more calls even as I now speak to you. I can tell you that Maria must have been consumed, eaten alive by fear. As with any Ponzi scheme, it's a dead end. Some liken the scheme to a house of cards: with each card you place that stays standing, you are exhilarated and on a high. But, deep down inside you, you know that with one shaky movement of your hand, the whole house of cards comes falling down. For Maria, it was exactly the same: someone, somewhere would make that fatal call to her. 'Where has all that money I put into this property gone when I don't even have the deed yet?' Or, 'This is taking too long, I want my down payment back, and you can cancel the P&S as those dates have long since expired! We've had it with you! We're contacting the authorities!'

"The first client who screams gets their money back and drops the matter, so Maria's safe for the moment. The house of cards is still standing. She then goes out and 'sells' another house and receives new money from the unsuspecting client. If a second client starts to scream, the same thing will happen. That client is also given back their money, and Maria will again replenish that amount and more with an unsuspecting new client. And so it goes, on and on, until… the next card is placed. But this time, ladies and gentleman of the jury, her hand starts to shake, and the cards all fall at once," Charlie said. "Just like that! Crash!" And he banged his hand down on the worn oak table behind which he stood.

He stopped and looked around at the faces to gauge their interest and comprehension. They got the analogy. Everyone once in their life has played that card game, and they all know the odds. He continued, "The goal of Maria's game was twofold: keep getting new money to pay off those who are screaming mad, and get out of the game before the fatal card is placed on the house. It's all a matter of timing. Nothing more. Off-island, it's called chutzpah by people of the Jewish 'persuasion' (as Charlie's father used to call them, showing he was one of the few tolerant Irishmen in Southie).

"Here, on-island," Charlie continued, "people say it's *arrogance*, *daring*, *foolhardy*, and *risky*. But, ladies and gentlemen of the jury, both of us off-island and on-island prosecutors only call this—*a felony*."

Officer Amaral, who stood outside the door, knocked. Charlie opened it. "You're wanted upstairs by the judge. Right now."

Charlie told the group to talk about what he had said and that Janet, as foreperson, should lead the discussion. He'd return as soon as he was able. And, he went out into the corridor with Officer Amaral and shut the door behind him.

Janet briefly described what she knew of Ponzis. "It's a scam. Maria gains the confidence of someone who wants to buy property at a good price, she takes down payment money, issues a phony purchase and sale, delays the closing as long as she can—or sooner, if someone starts to get antsy, sets a closing date where, with their power of attorney, she acts on their behalf, and then calls them to let them know the closing was successful and the property is now theirs. All this has to be done in the off-season, before next summer brings everyone back to the island. Maria and Walter planned to take off with the money at the last minute before people were expected to arrive on the island for the summer.

"Timing and secrecy are essential, but the critical factor lies in the con men being entirely believable. That's how con men succeed. We don't know if any of this is true, and if true, we don't know if it's Maria acting alone or Maria and Walter acting together. That's why we have two separate indictments before us today. Do you understand in general what I believe is the issue at hand?" They all nodded their head.

They were all stunned at the magnitude of Maria's and Walter's fraud. Before them, they had eight examples, and apparently there would be more.

The term *Ponzi scheme* was again explained to those who had never heard of it. Definitions were provided for *forgery*, *fraud*, *uttering*, *purchase and sale*, *recorded deed*, *clouded title*, *felony*, and so forth.

Chapter 96

Edgartown, Monday, November 2, 2015, 11:50 a.m.

It was clear some of the jurors couldn't exactly grasp the Ponzi concept presented by Charlie, who used legalese more than he realized, so it was up to Janet and a couple of the others to make it as clear as possible to islanders who hadn't had the sophisticated background the others had when it came to real estate and wealth.

Janet didn't know exactly where to begin to recap what Charlie had presented to them all. True, she was married to an attorney, but you don't learn law by osmosis, she thought as she gathered herself together.

"There is a lot here to digest. We can't discuss the whole case at once—it's too big and too complicated. I will try to give you my idea of what a Ponzi scheme is, but I am not a lawyer, and once we all agree we understand the general concept of a Ponzi scheme as it relates to real estate, that's when the district attorney will come back in to finish his presentation. After he presents his entire case, and we've only heard a smattering of what he will tell us, and we begin to deliberate the accusations, we will proceed case by case. We will not tackle the entire case or cases, as it is here, we will do this methodically. It's simply too much to do at once."

Officer Amaral came back into the jury room. "I'm sorry to interrupt, but the judge says you should all take a one-hour lunch break. There's to be no talking among you outside of this room. Absolutely, nothing at all about this case. If you decide to get lunch together, you can talk about your family, yourself—anything you want except for this case and being on the grand jury. Do you all understand completely? We start promptly at one-thirty p.m."

The jurors nodded their head and mumbled assent and filed out the door and up the stairs. Janet went to Dock Street and sat down, ordering a patty melt. She was completely floored by the news she had heard this morning and just couldn't understand how Maria had been fooling everyone. These things didn't happen on a place like this. She read an old *Cape Cod Times* that was left by someone that morning and tried to do the crossword puzzle. Normally she could do this one in a snap, but she gave up as she just couldn't concentrate. She said goodbye to Don and Mary, left a good tip, and walked back up Main Street to the courthouse. Coming in the front door, she saw Charlie talking to Officer Amaral in hushed tones. Officer Amaral came over and told her the district attorney and the judge had some new information that would be given to them in a short while.

What the jurors didn't know yet was that Maria's Boston bank account had just received the wire transfer from a Harold Strock, dba HS Fashions, in the amount of $9,050,000 for Middlemark. Although the wire transfer had been made by phone on October 26, one week ago, because of the size of the transfer, the Boston Federal Reserve had held it while they investigated it. The reserve had just released the money to the Boston bank, who in turn notified the Edgartown police, to make sure they knew one of their townspeople was dealing in an unusually large amount of money, in case there was something going on they didn't know about.

Charlie and the judge had spent the last hour researching the true owners of Middlemark, talking with them in England and had just finished amending the indictment to include both the Terrevauts and Mr. Strock as additional victims, noting Strock was probably the only one of all the people Maria and Walter had scammed who would actually get their money back, as it had come in after her death.

Charlie entered the jury room and waited until Janet had finished her talk and then told them about the new victims. He then said it was a long day; it was already 3:45 p.m. and dismissed them for the day but said to be back the next morning. Everyone filed out of the courthouse silently. They were swimming with details and overloaded with facts. And they had no one they could talk to tonight to off-load this burden. They had to keep absolutely quiet about everything they had learned.

PART 6

FLORIANOPOLIS, BRAZIL

Chapter 97

Florianopolis, Week of November 2, 2015

Walter had settled in and was finding his way around the house and gardens and the city. Constanca was a blessing—she kept to herself, made dinner whenever he wanted to eat in, and every morning prepared the best coffee and pastries he had ever eaten. They'd talk about Maria and what a sad time she was having, the alcohol and pills and the pressures she seemed to face at work and how difficult it was at the time for Walter to try to deal with her, as he loved her so. He said she had insisted she go to Canyon Ranch alone and that Walter go immediately to Brazil and await her here until her rehab was finished. She was hoping it wouldn't be more than six weeks, and then they'd be together with dear Constanca in this beautiful home.

He of course didn't mention he had left her the morning before she died, passed out on the couch, when he left for the ferry to Boston. A new laptop and an Internet search uncovered what was happening back on the island once he got safely ensconced in his new home in Florianopolis. No one asked for identification in Brazil with a proper greasing of the hand.

About ten days after arriving in Florianopolis, right after Constanca had removed his coffee cup and plate and went to the kitchen, he feigned shock and cried out to Constanca.

"Maria esta morta! Morta! Morta!" He broke down sobbing.

Constanca rushed in and at first couldn't understand what he was saying until he finally made it clear to her that Maria had left the *instalação de reabilitação* and was found dead in a bar nearby.

Constanca collapsed on the seat next to him and wailed a high-pitched, shrill, spine-chilling tone. Her keening was so loud. He hoped no one was passing by to hear this.

It was all he could do to put his arms around her and his head on her shoulders and feign sobbing. God, he hated these backward people who came out of the jungle. All he wanted to do was get out of her presence, but he knew he had to put up with this for some time. Jesus, he hated this! It made him think of how he had to comfort Maria when she was sloppily drunk and blubbering.

He finally drew himself away from Constanca and said, "I've got to go back and get Maria's ashes. She would have wanted to be buried next to her dear aunt Fernanda. Would you take care of the ceremony details while I'm away, and we will have the burial when I return in four or five days?"

She nodded, hugged him, and he went to get his suitcase. In a few minutes, he was downstairs giving her another hug and called the taxi. He waved goodbye out the window and told the driver he wanted to go to Balneário Camboriú, at the Infinity Blue Resort. He added he knew it would be about a two-hour trip, but he would pay for the return trip. He wanted no one to know of this taxi ride and winked at the man, as if it were to meet with a girlfriend. The driver gave Walter a thumbs-up and smiled in the mirror. He would be quiet. "Não se preocupe," he said, and he turned the taxi onto 101 Norte.

Walter sat back and smiled. Life was getting really good. Now all he needed to do was to arrange with the concierge for a Brazilian beauty to spend five days at this well-known resort. "I'll slip him 200 reais—$50 is nothing to get a hottie! Perfect," he said to himself.

Chapter 98

Florianopolis, Week of November 9, 2015

Walter returned a week later (he decided to stay an extra two days with Izabel—she was stunning and willing to do anything). That concierge knew his business, and he smiled graciously as Walter slipped him another 200 reais on his way out the door. "What a week!" he said to himself. His overnight bag was in the trunk along with the box and the ceramic urn he had bought. He indicated to the shopkeeper he would have the funeral home put the ashes in the urn when he got there; he told the man he didn't like the urns the funeral home had shown him—he preferred something special for his beloved wife and produced a tear, of sorts, to further emphasize his sorrow.

When he arrived at his home and saw Constanca, she burst into tears at the sight of the box he was carrying. They hugged, and he put the urn on the table next to the terrace where he liked to take his breakfast. As he climbed the stairs to his bedroom, he saw Constanca caress the urn and whisper something. Just one more thing to do and then he'd be free of Maria forever. He'd get the burial details from Constanca when he came down for a drink before dinner. *Almost there, Walter. You're almost there.*

The short ceremony at the churchyard was quick, and Constanca had brought a massive bouquet of white flowers that she kissed before laying them on top of the urn. Walter put his arm around her and walked her out of the quiet yard into street where his car was. Constanca was quiet the entire way home, for which Walter was grateful. He couldn't stand much more of this grieving. She wanted to stay in her room for the rest of the day and indicated there was food in the fridge. She hoped he'd understand her sorrow. He held her and said, "Claro." She went off to her side of the house. He went back out to the garden where he made himself a drink.

Enough is enough! She's dead. I'm alive. And, I didn't kill her. Period! Walter said to himself as he reached for another caipirinha and closed his eyes in the warm sunshine, thinking of Izabel just two hours north. It wouldn't be impossible to see her again, and he smiled and dozed off.

Chapter 99

Florianopolis, Week of November 16, 2015

As the next few days moved on, Walter and Constanca spent more time together; and one afternoon, she opened up to this dear husband of Maria and wept and wept.

She said, "I only wish Fernanda had lived that last night." She went on in her broken English, and to the best Walter could make out, she said that after the reading of the will in the attorney's office, Fernanda's attorney had told Maria and Constanca that Fernanda almost immediately regretted changing back her will to favor her children. She called the attorney right before bed to say she'd be in the day following the special outing that had been planned by Maria. Fernanda had made a foolish mistake and now wanted to revert the document in Maria's sole favor. But it was too late. Fernanda died in her sleep that night, and now Maria had only inherited the house and its endowment.

Walter couldn't believe it—Maria had been so close to inheriting everything, and that would have made them wealthier than they now were. He corrected himself and said, *Rather, that I am now*, and smiled. Damn it! Luck has a way of poking its nose in the way of destiny. Or, was luck, in fact, destiny? Although he was not a literary man, Walter did remember a saying Hunter S. Thompson coined: "Luck is a very thin wire between survival and disaster, and not many people can keep their balance on it."

Well, Hunter, my boy, I'm the one who's still on it. Walter smirked as he continued to listen to Constanca's story about Fernanda's ill-timed death.

Constanca said that the news the attorney had given Maria after the reading of the will must have had added an extra burden to Maria's unhappiness that led to her drinking and then her death. Constanca broke down again.

Walter took Constanca's hand and pressed his lips to it, with a tear in his eye, and said, "No matter how it ended, Maria was a dear soul and loved Aunt Fernanda and you more than you would ever know."

The old lady broke down again.

But days later, Constanca was happier. Walter would be here from now on—they got along so well, and he was so grateful, and she told her sister he was so appreciative of anything she did for him.

"What a fine man, that Valter is. Fernanda would have been so happy to know that Maria and he had married and that he is now here in their home. Things have a way for working out in the end. Gracas a Deus. Gracas a Deus," and she wiped her own tear from her eye.

And, meanwhile, thought Walter, *My beautiful adopted country, Brazil, has no extradition treaty with the US.* Perfeito em todos os sentidos. Walter was rather proud of how quickly he was picking up Portuguese.

Chapter 100

Florianopolis, Monday, November 23, 2015, mid-morning

One morning toward the end of November, Walter decided to empty out the documents and papers Maria had gathered thinking she was going with Walter to escape to Brazil. Before leaving the island for Boston, Walter had stuffed all of that into his own briefcase and now wanted to get rid of what he no longer might need. He hadn't bothered to read anything, but knew it was time.

When he had first arrived in Florianopolis four weeks earlier, he had stuck his leather briefcase in the back of the closet, and he now pulled it out. With a snap of the lock, the case easily opened, and he was once again surprised to see the bunch of legal-looking papers separated by a number of elastic bands, all held together by a small bungee cord.

What on earth is the meaning of all these documents? he thought. *Why had she accumulated so many?* He had so quickly shoved all those papers into his briefcase before he left, he hadn't stopped to figure it all out. All he wanted to do was get off the island and on the plane at Logan. There was no time to waste getting out of the country.

He recalled she had said she'd keep her driver's license on her and that's why he didn't see it. Her passport, birth certificate, bank statements, and a copy of the trust and her will they had made together in Thom Osborn's office were all here, of course, but... *What's all this other stuff?*

He quickly glanced at the top document and saw it was an original signed copy of Fernanda's will and last testament dated the afternoon of the day she died on July 9, 1997. The next one was dated one month after that, and the next dated one month later, etc. The last one was dated almost a year after her death, in the beginning of the following summer. He stood there stunned. "What the hell is this? This doesn't make sense," he said to himself.

He went through the briefcase in more detail and took out the copy of Fernanda's will that Maria had given him to bring to Boston to the Brazilian Consulate as verification that Maria and he owned property in Brazil and that Fernanda's trust would take care of it and them for as long as they lived. This proof enabled the consul to get their residency established right away. All the Brazilian government cared about was that they would not become wards of the state, and the will proved that.

"That checks," he said to himself. He then went through the other papers that were also wills but dated differently.

At first, Walter compared each of the other wills that had been in Maria's briefcase to the copy of the will he had brought to the consulate in Boston, which had been verified there and used to establish their Brazilian residency. Maria's wills all read exactly the same, word for word, except for the dates. Most important, these wills now named Maria as the sole heir to all of Fernanda's wealth: not only the house, but all her trust's assets. So why did she have these? It made no sense. Fernanda had died long before, and Maria hadn't contested the will that was read by Fernanda's attorney. These wills here appeared to be useless.

As he stood there puzzling over these documents, he suddenly realized there *was* something different besides the dates (and her being the sole heir). He had overlooked the attorney's signature! The differently dated "originals" that Maria had put aside to bring with her had a different attorney's and witnesses' names and signatures than the one Walter had brought to the Boston consulate. The other ones in Maria's briefcase all had been signed by a different attorney, a Notario Costas, at 4:00 p.m. on the same day Fernanda's will had been signed by her own attorney earlier that same morning.

In other words, he now could claim the will he held in his hands was in fact the valid will; it superseded the one Fernanda had made the morning before she died by several hours. It was signed after the will that Fernanda signed in her attorney's office. Consequently, the will that had been read to the family, Maria, and Constanca years before would now be invalid!

Oh my god, he thought, *I might be richer than I think!*

He immediately went to see Constanca and asked if she could make an appointment with Fernanda's attorney to see him sometime this week.

Constanca said, "Eu sinto muito—ele morreu dois anos atrás!"

Walter had picked up some Portuguese and repeated this in English to her, "He died two years ago?"

"Si, Senhor Valter. Dois anos atrás!"

"Gracas, Constanca. Nao faz mal. Gracas."

And he went to his phone and called Consul Mauricio's brother at the Banco Bradesco. Within a minute, he was on the phone.

"Yes, of course, Senhor Keller. I remember your name well. My brother the consul in Boston spoke highly of you. I'd be glad to meet with you tomorrow morning—10:00 a.m. in my office?" His English was excellent.

A few minutes later, he took the will dated late on the day Fernanda died—and destroyed all the others—and was out the door heading toward the center of town to find Notario Costas at the address on the will Maria had kept on the Vineyard.

Chapter 101

Florianopolis, Monday, November 23, 2015, 1:00 p.m.

Walter was not altogether surprised to find the office in a somewhat seedy side of the commercial sector of Florianopolis. He wanted to see if the notary recalled the person who brought in these "wills" to notarize and why he notarized a series of these same documents but with different dates. His plan was to threaten bringing the notary to the police for knowingly notarizing false documents. He thought of this as a form of cashless blackmail. "I'll not pursue this legally if you keep your mouth shut," he'd say. And then he'd offer him a token payment of $10,000 or about 40,000 BRL and have him sign a statement saying this particular will (the one dated later in the afternoon on the day before Fernanda actually died) was indeed the one that he had notarized years before and that Walter's payment today was for authenticating Fernanda's full name, her signature, the date, etc. as being *bona fide* and authentic.

At the same time, Walter would also have him "notarize" Fernanda's attorney's secretary's signature on a document, drafted by Walter himself, that confirmed the secretary did indeed take Fernanda's call later on the same day after Fernanda had signed her new will. When Fernanda called back that afternoon, she was asking for a new appointment to change back her will to favor Maria. The attorney had taken her call and then told the secretary to set up an appointment for him and Fernanda two days from then, as unfortunately, he was already late for an appointment and couldn't see Fernanda that day. She also would state that after the reading of the will, the attorney had told Maria and Constanca that Fernanda had wanted to change back her will, giving everything to Maria, but had died in the night before they could meet the next day.

The *notario* was as sleazy looking as Walter had imagined. Walter started with the copy of the will he had brought with him and then stated he knew the *notario* had signed several copies of the will each with different dates.

He looked directly at the *notario*'s eyes and said to him, "And, I know who brought these in for signature—it was not a *Fernanda Serpa*, but someone else a great deal younger than this old woman."

Walter said, "Further, I have all the other copies in my possession, and I've had given them all to my own lawyer for safekeeping along with a letter to be opened in the event of my untimely or suspicious death.

"The letter I've prepared in English that you are going to sign now will outline the fraud inherent in your having authenticated a series of—forged—signatures by a person other than the deceased and that these 'originals' all had different dates. In doing this fraudulent and criminal act, you thereby knowingly aided and abetted the person, a young woman, who had brought these false documents to you, the notary. In addition, it will state that today you have accepted a cashier's check in the amount of approximately 40,000 BRL ($10,000 USD) for these 'services.' You know full well that this is the minimum amount Brazil considers to be at a felonious level."

Walter also pointed out that on the $10,000 cashier's check he was about to hand over to the notary had Senhor Mauricio's, of the Banco Bradesco, *personal* signature and that the two of them were close personal and business friends. He continued, "As you know, the Mauricio family is a very powerful family, not only in Florianopolis but in all of Brazil," and he looked again in the eyes of the *notario.*

Walter then pulled out the document he had written for the attorney's secretary to sign and told him he had to "notarize" this too.

The *notario* understood full well what this meant and nodded. He then called in his own secretary and got another person off the street to sign their names verifying that the *notario* had signed both documents of his own free will in front of them, and they had seen identification proving that the *notario* was who he said he was. The *notario* picked up a pen and signed what Walter had prepared. For the witnesses' kindness, Walter slipped each woman 1,000 BRL (about $250, a large sum for them). "Muito obrigado, senhor. Gracas," they said.

Walter said goodbye to the *notario* and reminded him that if anything suspicious happened to him, his own attorney had Walter's letter outlining the *notario*'s illegal activity years before "authenticating" the various wills that Maria brought to him.

The *notario* sat down at his desk and shook. He knew that he had signed his life away if this man ever were to use the confession he had signed. Although he did not know this American's name, he did know he had seen that woman who had appeared in his office years ago, but more importantly, he realized that this man was very connected—the Banco Bradesco signature was enough to convince him of that. At least he got money out of it, and although it was hush money, it was something. He would never say anything about this visit to anyone, ever. He got up from his desk and let his secretary know that he was gone for the day.

He went out into the sunlight, looked down the back alley and both sides of the street before he continued toward the Praia Mole nude beach to the Bar do Deca for a few refreshing caipirinhas, his favorite drink made of lime and sugar cane brandy, so he could first relax before he'd hook up with some surfer guy for the afternoon and evening to forget the awful morning visit from that American. He was feeling better and better as he walked down the street, finding the first Banco Bradesco he could to deposit the check and then take out about 1,000 BRL to pay for the drinks, the private cabana he'd rent, and of course for the guy.

I'll be fine, he thought, *I just need to be careful and shut up.*

CHAPTER 102

Florianopolis, Tuesday morning, November 24, 2015

The next morning, after Constanca had prepared his orange juice, the *pingado* he loved—it was so simple—just some warm milk with sweetened coffee served in a glass, but so good, especially alongside the skillet-toasted French bread rolls (*pão na chapa*), he left for his meeting at the bank.

Life was looking especially good to Walter this morning and would be even better after his meeting at ten o'clock with Senhor Tomas Mauricio. He even spent a few minutes at the table to uncharacteristically look around the lush courtyard and see the brilliantly colored birds pecking at the grain Constanca faithfully scattered every morning. The sun reflected in the fountain was a harbinger of good things to come.

He softly whispered, "Thank you, dear Maria, for being even more deceptive than I had ever realized. Your forgery started much earlier than our real estate scams. In fact, I now believe you forged Matt's signature on the quickie Dominican divorce papers and probably Peg Baldwin's signature on her papers that gave you the agency outright, but I had never realized how young you started this—with your own aunt. If you were here now, I'd clink glasses in honor of your deviant behavior that defined you at an age most high school students were trying to figure out which college to attend. You, my dear, had the smarts, the wherewithal, and the daring to plot your future well ahead of anyone you ever knew. How did you even think of copying your aunt's will several times over with different dates, forging her signatures on each one, and then finding that sleazy little *notario* to validate each one? Hats off to you, my dear. It's too bad you didn't have the time to enjoy the fruits of all your long labor. But you should know, I actually have now found real, honest-to-God respect and admiration for you. I'm sorry I didn't see all this when you were alive. Thank you, my dear, thank you."

He continued sipping his *pingado* shaking his head in amazement of Maria's daring and cunning. He never really had fully appreciated her ability and thought maybe they could have gone much further? But he quickly chased that from his mind and said to himself that he was in the best possible position now.

But then, all of a sudden, something he had just whispered to himself hit him like a cold bucket of water. He then thought more about Maria's forgeries…and then, Maria and Matt's divorce in the Dominican Republic enabling Walter and Maria to get married.

Only one party needed to be there in person as long as the other party had signed the divorce agreement. It hit him again, this time like a cannonball: Matt had seemed totally surprised at the divorce and remarriage. He wasn't an urbane or sophisticated person and never questioned the divorce's validity. No one did at the time. The papers were official—no one thought to ask Matt if he had signed his approval before Maria and he left for the island. What if Maria had forged Matt's signature? Oh my god, that would mean we were never legally married. And, I wouldn't have any claim to Maria's property here per Fernanda's will. It clearly states "and future husband and children, if any." Matt and then Heather would be the heirs! Jesus Christ! I don't believe this! I've got to get things settled right now. Fuck! And he shoved the table away and got up, leaving the white linen napkin, hand-embroidered *FSC* in blue cotton thread from the island of Sao Miguel, on the chair, and quickly went to dress.

Thirty minutes later he was in a taxi going to Senhor Tomas's office in the main branch of the bank. He was welcomed into one of the most impressive private offices he had ever seen. The banker's "desk," a ten-foot slab of rare bubinga wood, was stunning. On the desk was an Azurite with Malachite desk set—he noticed the clock was a Swiza Quartz, probably costs $1,000 or more. Walter had done his homework, working his way up the wealth ladder. The photo of an attractive woman with three teenaged children was framed in gold, and it was clearly his family. Senhor Tomas let Walter take it all in before he invited him to sit down.

Walter took out the letter from the *notario* and the will itself, dated eighteen years ago on July 8, 1997, and stamped at 18:06. It was signed by Fernanda, the *notario*, and by two witnesses. It looked perfectly legal.

The banker asked about the other will, the one everyone thought was the legitimate will of Fernanda, dividing her substantial assets among her children and giving Maria the house with a permanent endowment until she died or her husband and any biological children died (Fernanda had specifically stipulated in the will, if Maria were to marry, which she hoped would happen, then both Maria and her husband and any children would inherit the property. And, Maria's spouse, if she died first, would be allowed to continue living there and use the endowment, as could her natural children, that being only Heather. However, when he and her children died, the home would be sold, and the assets and endowment would be divided between Fernanda's children).

"It's going to be a problem, Senhor Keller, as so much time has passed. It's going to take a certain type of judge to overturn the will everyone thought was Fernanda's last will. You know, someone who understands the intent of this unfortunate lady who died just hours after she had changed her mind and signed this new will. Clearly, she did not have the time to make her wishes known to everyone. I do have one question—a very important one—why had your wife kept this and not said anything? That is the question we need to answer before I contact an old and trusted friend of mine, Judge Alfredo Moreira, a revered member of one of Brazil's oldest families whose own history of wealth and power dates back four centuries to the 1500s. He's one of what Sao Paulo people say are the 'fifteenths,' these families who date back centuries. We need to answer this question if we," and he paused meaningfully looking at Walter, "if we two enter an 'understanding' and if I am to go to the judge to personally present our claim that you would indeed be the rightful heir to

Maria's aunt's fortune, since you were legally married to Maria and she died first." He stopped there and waited.

"Well," said Walter, "the first thing to note is that Fernanda's long-time attorney died several years ago. So, there is no one to deny that Fernanda did not get to change her will to the terms she actually wanted, which were her original wishes to leave everything to Maria.

"Second, the *notario* who originally signed this 'new' will is completely on board in swearing the will *was* signed by Fernanda herself in the afternoon before she died. He has signed a document that you see here attesting to this. He has also received some compensation for his trouble if he needs to verify this. But it is this letter that guarantees his cooperation."

Walter handed it to him and quietly waited while Senhor Tomas read it and reread it. He now had a slight smile on his face when he put down the letter on the desk and looked up at Walter.

Walter continued, "Constanca, who was at the reading of the first will with Maria, reported that after the family had left, the attorney told both of them that he had received a call from Fernanda after lunch that afternoon, just hours before she died, saying she had been foolish and sentimental when earlier in the day she had signed a new will in his office, giving her own children the bulk of her wealth, except for the house and endowment for Maria. Constanca will swear that the attorney had promised to meet with Fernanda the day after the outing Maria had planned for Fernanda so Fernanda could change back her will to give Maria everything. The only reason Fernanda didn't go to her attorney that afternoon was because, unfortunately, the attorney could not meet that afternoon as he was already late for another appointment. So, it was agreed that Fernanda would go to the attorney's office the day after the outing to execute a new will, giving everything back to Maria.

"Constanca will testify that Maria had said that her aunt could not rest until the will was changed, even if she had an appointment in two days with the attorney, and she begged Maria to bring her to the nearest *notario* she could find, somewhere in the business center of Florianopolis, and there, her aunt changed her will. It was late afternoon, after their special outing, she said. Fernanda was instantly relieved but was very tired and went to bed. Before she fell asleep, she asked Maria to make sure she remembered to bring the new will with her to her attorney the next morning so he could approve of the wording.

"When Maria awakened the next morning to find her aunt had died overnight, she was distraught and told the attorney of the visit to the *notario* she and Fernanda had made that afternoon, after their outing. Maria had also told me she had not been able to see the new will as the *notario* had put this in a large envelope and sealed and stamped it so it could only be opened by another attorney. Further, Fernanda had not told Maria about her changes she had the *notario* make but had mumbled something about wanting to change her will so she could give her eldest daughter the mother-daughter medal that all Azorean women passed down to their daughter. The following day was a flurry of activity, getting the body prepared for burial, contacting the priest and the cemetery, and buying a dark dress for the service. Constanca said Maria gave the *notario*'s sealed envelope to the attorney, which he opened in front of them, looked surprised, even shocked, but then quickly closed it, saying, 'It's nothing, just a minor change,' and said he would give it to his secretary to file. So, you see, Maria knew nothing definite about her aunt's change of heart. She assumed her aunt had not made the changes, after all," explained Walter.

In reality, Walter realized, Maria had been stumped. Since the envelope was sealed and intact when she handed it to the attorney, if she were to say she knew the new will named her sole beneficiary, she'd have to admit that she was in league with the *notario* and had paid him to write that fake will. By pretending to be ignorant of the contents of her aunt's new will, she at least would inherit the house and the endowment fund forever. Maria was smart enough to realize what the worth of the bird in hand is. So, she kept quiet.

Walter continued on with Senhor Tomas, "Years passed, and two years ago, the attorney died. The secretary stayed on at the firm as his son had taken over his father's practice, and his father had asked him to let the secretary stay on as long as she wanted. They had worked together for more than twenty-five years.

"A few months ago, the attorney's son decided to retire. He asked the secretary to start emptying his father's office and to attempt to return any files to the former clients, if they were still alive. Apparently, it was an almost impossible task as so many clients had died, but she plugged away at it, systematically going through the decades of papers, files, boxes, storage bins, and so forth. It was also a terrible job for this old woman to do—not only because of the sheer volume of documents but because it brought back lots of memories to people who were no longer there. However, she persisted, and just recently she started on Fernanda's files and found the sealed envelope that was in Fernanda's files, and she opened it.

"She was stunned and also frightened. She immediately understood that Maria should have been the rightful heir, not Fernanda's children. But she couldn't explain why the attorney had buried this in the files, as it clearly was very important. She realized he had acted willfully and fraudulently, and if she made this known, his name would be tarnished, and he would be prosecuted. She was in her eighties now, and had been very fond of the attorney and didn't want to sully his name now in death. So, she decided the best thing to do was to reseal the envelope with the attorney's old sealing wax, say nothing to the son, and track down Maria through Constanca and have her mail it to Maria. Maria could decide from there on what to do, if anything.

"The secretary had known Constanca from the frequent trips to the office accompanying Fernanda, and she knew that Constanca was allowed to live in Fernanda's home for the remainder of her life. So, without saying anything, she went there and visited Constanca and brought the envelope with the *notario*'s will inside and told her to please mail it to Maria back in the States, which she did. That's how Maria came by this. As you can see, it is sealed and in its original envelope, so Maria never knew she had inherited everything. She thought it was another piece of worthless junk that was sent to her from time to time by Constanca, so Maria just left it unopened among a pile of other documents she kept in her closet. I've been going through Maria's things recently, and it's where I found it and opened it, and now bring it to you.

"Along with the *notario*'s revised will that I found in Maria's briefcase was a copy of a letter the attorney had sent to Maria soon after the funeral, stating that he had reviewed the *notario*'s new will that Maria had handed to him and determined it had no validity, and it was best just to let it go as there would be a costly legal fight. Maria must have accepted that at face value as she never even told me about the newer will or the letter this attorney had sent her," said Walter.

"About ten days before Maria died, she received a large package from the attorney's office in Brazil, with a letter from the secretary saying that the attorney's son, who had taken over his father's law practice, decided to retire. I asked her what was in the package, and all she said was it was just some old files of her aunt's that the attorney's son had found in his father's old files.

"Since Maria and I were planning to move here, we had already started to gather any legal documents we might need, and these were already in my briefcase. You should know Maria had a drinking problem and, to her credit, agreed to go several weeks for to a residential treatment facility, and while I was waiting for her here to finish her time there, I learned she had relapsed and died. It was so terribly sad and hard for me to realize she was gone, and I knew I couldn't go back to the island for a funeral service. Maria would have wanted me to stay here, as our original plan was to have her come here immediately after her treatment where I'd be waiting for her, and our new life would begin, so I did. Maria had already decided to leave the United States and live here, so I requested Maria's ashes be sent here. Constanca and I had a mass at the church two weeks ago and put her ashes in an urn. I brought any legal documents and papers I found in her belongings, and I want to see if this will has validity."

"Is this person willing to attest to this under oath?" Senhor Mauricio asked.

There was a pause, and Walter answered, "Yes, Constanca will. And, so will the secretary."

Unbeknownst to Senhor Tomas, Walter had already instructed the *notario* to draft a statement that the old secretary of Fernanda's attorney could sign and then went to see her. Walter introduced himself to the secretary and thanked her for having recently sent the package to Maria. He explained that Maria had recently and unexpectedly died before they got a chance to complete their move to Brazil. He also wanted to make a small gift to the secretary to thank her for forwarding Maria's files to her.

The woman was stunned at all the news. First, Maria's death. Then, that this dear husband of Maria's was so generous as to offer her 20,000 BRL for having sent the package to Maria and to sign a paper that attested to the fact that Fernanda intended to change back her will to Maria and had the attorney not had another appointment that day, it would have been done.

"Yes, *si*, Senhor Valter," she said in broken but passable English, "I will sign paper." Walter pulled out the document, written by the *notario* when Walter had met with him earlier in the day, about the conversations regarding Fernanda having wanted to change back her will to Maria that afternoon, but instead had to make an appointment with the attorney the next morning, because he was already late for another appointment that afternoon.

"It's the truth," said the woman when she had finished reading the *notario*'s document written in Portuguese. "Si, eu juro que e verdade," nodding her head vehemently. "Si, si!"

When Walter had related the entire story to Senhor Tomas, who was listening to all this intently, Walter pulled out the secretary's document and showed it to Senhor Tomas. He read it slowly and then read it again. He put the document down on his desk, brushing off a piece of lint from his suit, and said, "What do you have in mind?"

"First, we need to know what the principal amount is still in Fernanda's children's trust. I assume you can find that out immediately without any problem?"

"Yes, just a moment. It so happens the trust is being administered here. Hold on, Senhor Keller, while I call my assistant." He dialed an extension and spoke briefly. Walter recognized part of the exchange and heard, "Senhora Fernanda Calvalho Serpa" and "estado o patrimonio." The banker put down the phone and said, "This is good news. The children have not yet invaded…how to say it…the corpse, of the *estado*, estate?"

Walter stifled a grin at the banker's English mistake and said "Yes, the corpus or principal are the terms meaning the amount Fernanda put into the trust at the time of her death," said Walter. "The heirs have apparently been using only the income generated from this amount, which is a good thing for Fernanda's very last wish that she was unable to carry out."

"The children are allowed to use the interest at the discretion of her trustee, which is this bank. They told me the amount in the trust now is now over $12 million or about 47 million BRL. That's certainly a lot of money. So, how exactly can we work together to see if my contacts, such as I have, including the esteemed judge I mentioned earlier, can reopen this case? Whereas you have the documents that may possibly point to your receiving a great deal of money, and whereas I am well-known in the community and have the contacts who will be necessary to determine if you, as the husband of the late Maria Almeida Keller, should now be named as beneficiary of the trust, instead of Fernanda's natural children."

Walter looked at him directly and said, "I've thought of this carefully and understand the importance of your help in this delicate matter. Even if Maria can't be here now, I want to do what she would want. I know you will have many important people to consult with on my behalf and that a fair compensation has to be made to you for all your good efforts. Simply put, I couldn't do this myself.

"Assuming the trustees are willing to let me invade the principal as I may propose, I would be pleased to give you 49 percent of what I, or shall I say *we*, withdraw. Again, it would be important for the bank to recognize this ability to use the principal in recognition of the many years Maria was denied her inheritance and had to work as hard as she did in life. She is a good person even if she had a serious sickness that led to her early death. Would the bank's trustees be amenable to my proposal, and would you also be amenable to your share for all the work you will do to see that justice is now given Maria?" Walter stopped and waited.

After a second, Senhor Tomas spoke and said that the bank trustees would not be a problem and agreed that some percentage of their withdrawals would be a generous but "fair" way to recognize all the background work he would have to do with his legal and banking personal contacts to assure that the courts would recognize Maria's rightful inheritance. However, they would have to modify Walter's 49–51 percent share proposal, and said that Walter and he could only share up to 80 percent of the trust's assets and they must do this within the next three years. The remaining 20 percent would be left intact, and only the income would thereafter be withdrawn. In this way, the trust would not have to be legally shut down, therefore avoiding more legal debate.

Walter responded positively and asked if Senhor Tomas might draw up a letter of understanding between Walter and the bank, specifically signed by Senhor Tomas. He called in a young man who appeared to be his assistant. He nodded and left the room, and Walter was told that he would be back in about twenty minutes with a document they both would read. "It is better we do this without legal advice, I think," Senhor Tomas said. "I think you would agree, *nao e?* Pardon me, that means 'don't you think?'" Walter agreed and nodded.

They passed the time making small talk and sipping coffee that Walter had taken a liking to—soft, nutty, with bittersweet chocolate tastes. They talked of Fernanda's business prowess and the gratitude she had with Maria in her life. "It is a shame that Fernanda's last wish was never executed at the time of her death, but we should be thankful that you found these documents. Now, Fernanda will have her last wish fulfilled. And, dear sir, despite the sorrow we all have that Maria is not here now to benefit from her aunt's largesse, she will be after this legal matter is resolved, I'm sure both ladies would have been happy with the outcome."

A knock at the door announced the assistant. He brought two copies in English to Senhor Tomas, who handed one to Walter. Both read silently. Walter nodded his assent, and Senhor Tomas thanked the assistant and asked him to notarize the documents that each now signed. The assistant left the room.

"My next steps are to contact the bank's trustees and then to talk to some people who know the Moreira family as well as the judge himself. As I'm sure you understand, I may have to advance some form of recompense to them for all the work they will do on behalf of bringing this matter before Judge Alfredo Moreira. I will use the arrangement as we just signed, of course."

"Certainly," said Walter.

"It's probably best we don't see each other until we have certainty that the judge will hear our case. I will keep in touch with you as the time nears, and if you have any need to contact me, please do so through my assistant who just prepared these papers of agreement between the two of us. Here is his business card. He will know who you are if you were to call him. Thank you, dear Senhor Keller. It is indeed a pleasure to be able to ensure Senhora Fernanda that her last wish will be fulfilled. And, of course, that your wife above may have the knowledge that you will also be a beneficiary of Fernanda's will. Fate has a strange and mysterious way to right ills. We should be thankful fate intervened. Now, goodbye for the moment, dear Senhor Keller. We will be in touch." He led Walter to the door, where they shook hands.

Walter went out of the bank and back to his home. He told Constanca that all was well, he had a good meeting with the banker, and he felt that Fernanda's wishes would be met within the next several months.

She wiped her eyes and said, "Gracas, senhor, por este dom precioso. Ela teria ficado contente!"

Walter simply gave her a hug and said, "O prazer é meu" (It's my pleasure). He then went out to the courtyard and sat next to the fountain that had a soothing sound. He put his sunglasses on his forehead to get some sun and soon was sleeping.

Constanca looked out on him from the living room and thought all was in order now. Yes, Fernanda had gone to meet the Lord, and she and Maria were now united eternally, and she, Constanca, was in good hands with Walter here on earth. He would take care of her forever here. *Senhor Valter is a wonderful man, and I will serve him as faithfully as I had served Fernanda. Life is good.* "Louve a Senhor!" And she crossed herself and said a silent prayer.

PART 7

Edgartown

CHAPTER 103

Edgartown, Week of November 9, 2015

The grand jury had been meeting daily. It was now a week since they were called, and more accusations were still being made. The latest was one that attracted national attention, just as the district attorney had predicted when the jurors first assembled in the courthouse after Maria and Walter were named as coconspirators *in absentia*.

Huck had forwarded a phone call he received today from a woman in St. Louis. She had left a voice mail for Maria just that morning to inquire what the next steps were in their purchase of the Katharine Graham estate in West Tisbury. She and her husband had been on a six-week cruise and hadn't had a chance to call her since they had returned about ten days ago. Huck was the person to return her call, and he learned of yet another allegation of Maria having talked to them about an exceptional property that was not yet on the market. They were her clients last summer but had not yet found the property they had wanted to buy, until this came up right before they were to leave on their trip.

When Huck and Charlie got a chance to talk in person, Huck explained that Maria told the couple that the estate of the late *Washington Post* heir, Katharine Graham, was selling her home, known as Mohu, along with fifty acres of her property while the remaining acres were being preserved by a trust. The house itself had access to Lambert's Cove Beach, and there were also several smaller structures, including a barn. It had been in her hands since 1972.

The wife, Mrs. Baxter, said Maria had the exclusive and could show the new property right then. However, if they were at all interested, they needed to make the trip immediately before word got out that it was coming on the market.

So, the Baxters (he was the hedge fund billionaire formerly from Chicago) then made a quick trip to the Vineyard right after Columbus Day, even though they were very busy getting ready for their long cruise. Maria met them at the airport and drove them to Lambert's Cove Road. The wife recalled a long winding dirt road and was impressed with the views of the shore, wetlands, and meadow, and what looked like a network of roads and trails that Maria said would remain in the family and be forever preserved. As Maria took out her key chain and opened the front door, she said that they probably knew this, but Mrs. Graham entertained all the time, and over the years, literary figures and heads of state had often gathered there, including Lady Diana, Jackie Onassis, Henry Kissinger, Mike Wallace, and so forth.

Mrs. Baxter told Charlie that the asking price for the house and its fifty-acre parcel would normally be in the mid-thirties, but if they acted now, Maria knew she could get it for $25,000,000. The Graham sons did not want to have an extended period of time when co-brokers and prospects would be trekking through their late mother's property and would reduce the price accordingly.

Mrs. Baxter did say that something strange happened on the way out of the house. She and her husband were standing on the front porch while Maria was shutting doors and turning off lights inside, when another car drove up the driveway.

A man got out and yelled, "Who the hell are you?" and started walking toward them.

Mr. Baxter yelled back, "We're the new owners, and who are *you*?"

Just then Maria came out the door and looked startled, but immediately started down the steps to meet him at his car and said, "Hi, Joe! Don't worry. I'm just showing them what a fabulous house this is and the area." And she quickly went down the steps and talked to him at his car, out of their hearing. He then waved and drove back down the road to his cottage on the property.

She laughed as she opened the Range Rover's door and said to the Baxters, who were inside then, "Don't worry. Joe's the live-in caretaker, and I didn't want him to get worried that Mrs. Graham was selling and he could possibly be losing his job if new owners didn't want him. Sorry about that!"

Charlie then asked her, "And then what did you and Mr. Baxter say?"

"Well," she said, "we all went back to the airport, and Ed and I signed the purchase and sales, and Ed gave her a check from his private bank. It was cashed almost immediately. I thought about checking in once or twice, but, frankly, we were on our cruise and anyway didn't think it was necessary as we know her reputation, and we certainly didn't want to get out the word that the property was for sale. That was a good price! Can't you tell us what the problem is?"

Charlie paused a moment and said, "I'm afraid, Mrs. Baxter, that although Maria has recently died, she is nevertheless under investigation along with her husband, and your money is most likely lost. You are the ninth party to come forward now, and we are afraid there may be others. I've convened a grand jury, and assuming they indict, and it goes to trial, I really can't see any way of recouping these sums. We know her husband has fled to Brazil, where we have no reciprocity and are guessing he has put their funds in offshore accounts. I am truly sorry."

He heard a gasp at the other end of the phone and said, "I need to tell my husband right now. I don't know even what to say to you except keep me posted. I am stunned. Thank you, and you can count on us to help you in any way possible. You have my contact information. Thank you," and she hung up.

It didn't take long for someone in the courthouse, most likely a secretary who had typed up the charges, to get the word out on the street that Katharine Graham's house was another victim of Maria's Ponzi scheme. So much for "secret" grand juries, even if it wasn't a member that spilled the beans.

That Friday, the *Gazette* ran a front-page major article on this story and that it was "rumored" that a grand jury was now sitting and "presumably" was considering this case. The *Washington Post* ran a small article on Sunday, not wanting to be part of a major headline (it was "distasteful" for a liberal newspaper to speak of the owners' wealth). The Boston TV stations and the *Globe* and *Herald* were on the island the following Monday. Then came CNN, CBS (Walter Cronkite's old network—he had died six years earlier, and his house on Edgartown Harbor, Green Hollow, had quickly been sold), and the *National Enquirer* were soon roaming the streets trying to interview residents about what they knew about Maria and her family. The *National Enquirer* even went the extra mile and sent a reporter to Brazil, but other than learning that Walter had landed in Sao Paolo, which was already known to the DA, they couldn't locate him after his flight landed. Finally, *48 Hours* and HLN ran programs on the possible causes of Maria's death...it certainly looked like Walter was a prime suspect, although the media had no idea she died of "natural" causes, meaning she had OD'd.

The jury members now didn't mind the time they were spending in session. They were famous. One or two of them thought maybe they'd get on the *Today Show*, having forgotten the admonishments of utter secrecy. Small towns don't often get this attention, and it was thrilling to most. To one person, Rick Maron, it was terrifying. The FBI was still in town, and it was only a matter of time before their forensic accountant started asking questions about the large "retainer" fees Maria had recently given him. Then what?

Chapter 104

Edgartown and Fall River, Wednesday, November 25, 2015, 9:00 a.m.

Thanksgiving was a needed respite from the last few weeks in the grand jury and of the constant talk in town about Maria's death and Walter's disappearance. Although only the Katharine Graham "sale" had made national headlines and news on the local island streets, the rest of Maria's Ponzi scheme remained a secret. The grand jury was keeping their word.

Half of the island had already left for the long weekend on the Steamship ferries from Vineyard Haven, and the other half stayed put, welcoming their own families back on the island for a "real" Thanksgiving. Morning Glory Farms was busy slaughtering turkeys and roasting them to a golden brown and making sides of butternut squash, brussels sprouts, and selling cranberries, apples, and their muffins and breads. Your Market was selling more cases of beer and wine than they had since Labor Day. Driving down Main Street in Edgartown, one could see the first signs of Christmas lights. Donaroma's Nursery was a dazzling display of red, green, and white mini string lights, and in front of the main greenhouse was a miniature picket fence behind which Santa sat in his overloaded sleigh with the reindeer perched, ready to take off. The little kids loved it.

As one moved down Main Street into the Historic District, twinkling lights on the white picket fences hid the shriveled dead leaf or two that remained on those rosebushes that had been resplendent in the summer, but now were dried up and their sharp twigs and thorns poked through the slats, catching on passersby's woolen coats and gloves in an annoying way. The gas streetlights were entwined in balsam greens and red and green lights, and the town hall was decked out more than any other building. It was a magical sight and did such a good job of hiding what really lay behind those little white pristine fences that gave Edgartown its unique character on the island.

Rick and Janet were on the 8:05 a.m.; this run—it was the older, single-ended ferry *Martha's Vineyard*, which held to its schedule even as winds blew between thirty and forty miles per hour. Rick was expected, as were his brothers and sister, to be in Fall River well before noon. The boys would watch television in the den with their father, and his sister and sisters-in-law would be in the kitchen with Ma. Janet loathed the name *Ma*. It was so "common." She called her parents *Mum* and *Dad*.

Rick has hoped for a quiet moment with his father to sound him out about the retainers Maria had given him (without saying anything about the wiretapping or blackmail of course), but the Celtics game took on a life of its own. Boston Celtics were at home, and the Philadelphia 76ers got into a shoving match that carried into the TD Garden crowd—fighting, screaming, commotion, pushing; managers, referees, fans, everyone involved. The Maron men were all yelling at the TV and rooting for Isaiah Thomas, who scored thirty points, oblivious to the thought of the women mashing potatoes, stirring gravy, and the steam in the old kitchen. If it weren't for the individuals, it would be a scene out of Norman Rockwell.

Janet hated being stuck there, even for lunch. Rick's mother was odd and had some sort of mental problems, laughing one moment and angry the next, and her sisters-in-law were a throwback to the '50s. These people had no idea what a profession was—their schooling was minimal, and they were at-home moms, talking about the latest sale at Penny's or a new way to slow-cook lamb shanks. Thanksgiving was the only time that Janet would ever see a real "American" dinner at the Morans' house, and not the Lebanese fare his mother was so proud of churning out.

In the dining room, a dark area off the "parlor" that was reserved for guests (who were nonexistent), the Victorian brown and maroon damask wallpaper was faded and corners were peeling. The heavy oak dining table had four lions with paw feet, and the oak sideboard carried the lion's head theme in the center crest. Rick's father, "the Godfather of Fall River," as the Lebanese population called him, had obtained this dining room set from one of the widows when it came time to put her in the church nursing home. A framed portrait of Saint Maron with his swarthy olive skin and a full gray beard, his black monastic habit with a hanging *stole*, and holding a long crosier, completed the funereal tableau. Janet half expected a mortician to emerge from behind a velvet curtain and come forward to whisper something to the family about the service that was now ready to begin.

As executive director of the Vineyard Arts Society, and a product of one of New England's best girls boarding schools and independent women's colleges, Janet couldn't stand the family's lack of taste and status quo life. Not one of the women ever thought of "bettering" herself. And the "boys" were content with owning fast-food and car wash franchises. She often wondered if the two brothers were laundering money. This type of business was done in cash. It was so outdated, used, and depressing. She hated coming here.

The meal went exactly how she knew it would go. People reaching over others, gravy on Rick's stubble ("It's a holiday. I don't need to shave."), his mother constantly asking if the stuffing was good ("I used frozen apricots. The fresh ones at DeMoula's Market were too expensive. Can you believe people will pay $4.99 a pound? They think money grows on trees! Why, I remember when…") Janet ate little and glanced at her Fitbit every now and then to see how much longer she had to be here.

On the way back to Woods Hole, Rick asked her, "What's going on with Maria's case?" He commented, "It's taking longer than I would have thought. Are there any new things that are making it so long?"

"Rick, you know I can't talk about it."

"Oh, come on. You know I know everyone, and Charlie, Huck, and I found Maria's body. I technically shouldn't have been there, so I don't want to get Charlie and Huck in trouble. Therefore, I'm asking you, not them, what's taking so long. That's all. I've heard some rumors that there's some others involved, and I just wanted to find out if that's bullshit or correct. That's all."

"All I can say is that we may be ending the discovery and just proceed with deciding on whether or not to indict. I'm sick of this process, and every time we seem ready to wrap it up, something new pops up. Apparently, there's something new again, but we won't know until Monday."

Rick scowled and sped up.

"Rick, be careful. Don't drive like this. It scares me," she said.

"Just shut up. I can't stand your yapping. That's all you do, all day long. Yap. Yap. Yap."

She knew better than to respond. He was such an asshole. She couldn't stand him or that awful family. What the hell had she ever been thinking! She wished she dared to divorce him. But the island was so confining, and the pressures of being the executive director of a feel-good nonprofit, that it made thoughts like this useless.

Chapter 105

Edgartown, Monday, November 30, 2015, 9:00 a.m.

When Janet came into the courthouse Monday morning following Thanksgiving, she saw Charlie talking intently with a man in a suit, carrying a briefcase. Charlie seemed surprised at what was being told to him. He saw Janet and nodded, and then both men went quickly up the back stairs, two at a time.

She saw another juror, and they chatted for a moment, and then the bailiff came over and said the grand jury has been asked to meet upstairs in the main courtroom for a brief chat with the judge before they went into session downstairs. When they all had arrived, they went upstairs to wait for the judge. Five minutes later, the judge was announced, and everyone stood up. He looked at Janet and nodded and then proceeded.

"Ladies and gentlemen, the superior court will begin in a few minutes, but before this, I want to meet alone with the grand jury in their room downstairs." He rapped the gavel, everyone stood, and he exited the courtroom, followed by Charlie and the man with the briefcase. Janet thought this was strange, but along with the others on her jury, she followed the three men, and they exited the back of the courtroom and went down the stairwell to the basement level.

Once the grand jury had seated themselves inside the jury room, Judge Mayhew and the other two entered the room. The door was shut. Charlie looked nervous, and Janet noticed he did not look her way. *What's going on?* she wondered. *This is so strange, all of this.*

Judge Mayhew addressed the group, "What I'm going to say will be surprising to all of you. And, I'm making it very clear right now that although I'm going to recuse one of you, this has nothing to do with integrity. None of you has done anything wrong in the eyes of the law, and this decision is totally outside those parameters. You may wonder, as we have too, how the Katharine Graham house news was leaked to the public, but this has nothing to do with the action we are about to take. The Cape and Islands' district attorney, Mr. O'Brien, and I were informed over the weekend of a new development in the case, and we agreed that one person here needs to be recused. Again, I am stressing this person has done nothing wrong in the eyes of the law. Nothing. Do you all understand?"

The members all nodded their head.

"Good, now don't you forget this: I will use all my powers to prosecute anyone of you if I hear rumors that you have said anything disparaging about this person. Is this understood?"

They all nodded again.

"For reasons I cannot discuss, Mrs. Maron, the foreperson of your jury, and who has done an admirable job from what District Attorney has told me, will have to be recused now. I am sorry we have to do this, as both Mr. O'Brien and I have the utmost regard for her, both as a community member and in her role as foreperson with you. However, there is nothing we can do, and I am giving you all a second to thank her for her service." Charlie started clapping, and the others followed suit.

Judge Mayhew walked over to her and shook her hand and thanked her and then brought her over to Charlie, who also did the same. The others continued clapping. The man in the suit stood silently in the background and did not clap.

Janet was stunned. She couldn't focus on what just happened. She had to find out. When the door shut behind her, before she could say anything, Judge Mayhew said, "My dear. This has nothing at all to do with you. Nothing! Neither Charlie nor I can say anything to you, as this is a grand jury matter, you know, and since you are no longer sitting on it, you cannot be privy to any such information. I'm indeed very sorry. You are exactly what we needed here."

Charlie came over and gave her a hug and said the same. "Thank you, Janet. Please remember you can't discuss this with anyone, not even your husband. We suggest you tell him that there had been a technicality with the way you were elected and that we thought it best that you be removed to avoid one of the other jurors complaining to the point we'd have to call a new grand jury. The judge and I will back you up with this story. Take care, and thank you for understanding."

Janet started to tear up, and her voice trembled. She felt as if she *had* done something wrong, despite how nice they were being. "Thank you. You have my word I won't say anything other than what you just put forth," and she put on her coat and turned away and went up the stairs to the courthouse entrance and out the door onto Main Street. The day was brisk, just above freezing, and cloudy. She didn't know the reason, but something was terribly wrong. She could "feel it in her bones," as her mother would say. She started up Main Street and then stopped and did a U-turn toward the harbor. There were people out on the street doing early Christmas shopping, and as she approached Dock Street, she saw Trey come out of the Yacht Club. Too late to turn around.

"Janet! Hi!" yelled Trey. "How are you? I haven't seen you for a while. What's up?"

Oh, shit, she said to herself, *I don't want to see anyone right now.*

She approached him and waved. "Hi, Trey, good to see you!"

"Where've you been? I'm thinking of getting a coffee at Rosewater. Want to come with me?"

"Oh, that's nice, but no, I'm on my way to take a walk up North Water Street to the lighthouse. It's a good day for a walk, and Lord knows I can use it." She laughed.

"You look great as always. Wasn't that bizarre about Maria and Walter? The phones haven't stopped ringing. Some want the nominating committee to be replaced saying they didn't do due diligence in checking them out to begin with. Others say the Club is going downhill and 'people like that wouldn't have been admitted before now' and 'we need a better system.' I'm sick of it—and them! Thank God, it's not summer as they'd be in town and at my office."

Janet said she was sorry he was going through all this and made a move to continue her walk. But Trey started in again, and she couldn't break away.

"Can you believe Walter skipped town and Maria's dead? And her Ponzi scheme affected some of our members who suddenly learned their house was 'sold.' Unreal. It's worthy of a televised *Whodunnit?* Actually, I wouldn't be surprised if *60 Minutes* came to town. You know, Jeff what's his name who's the head of it is on Chappy. I bet he's already on it. What a mess!"

"Yes," she said, "it is all shocking," and she made another move to break away.

"I bet Rick knows a lot. Has he said anything about all this—probably some of his clients were victims," Trey asked, not wanting to leave.

"You know, we didn't even talk about it after her arrest. I think this is all cloaked in secrecy, but the truth will come out—eventually." And Janet gave a wave and continued on her walk, around Dock Street, past the On Time three-car ferry across to Chappy, and then up Daggett onto North Water.

She was deep in thought. Normally, the grandiose whaling captains' homes standing tall would capture her attention as she walked by them and their pristine white picket fences, like sentry guards standing at attention. The brick sidewalks added to the New England coastal charm but were often raised unevenly by the trunks of the stately trees—once elms, but those had since died of disease—and now their substitutes were as tenacious as their predecessors' roots in uplifting the bricks.

Just as she neared the old Wakeman House, Janet tripped on the vines' overgrown and twisted roots that were emerging from the picket fence and put her left arm out against the fence to break her fall. In doing so, two of the old pickets cracked and broke, jagging into her wrist. "Ouch! Shit! This hurts!" she said as she tried to regain her bearing. "Damn vines! What a tangled mess! Someone's going to get really hurt one day!" Nothing was going right today, and she didn't know why everything had come cascading down on her. She picked out a large splinter and squeezed her wrist until blood flowed, and then started to cry. She couldn't stop.

A car coming up North Water slowed down, and the man lowered his window. "Are you all right?" he asked.

"Yes, I'm fine. Just hurt my wrist a little. I'm okay. Thank you anyway," she responded. She tried to put back the tops of the two broken pickets and then said, "Fuck it."

She looked ahead at the Harbor View Hotel, vacant over the cold months, just as were these magnificent North Water Street whaling mansions. These properties that were the epitome of care and attention in the summer were now largely unkempt and brown. The vines had once again begun to take over the pickets where the roses had flourished last summer. Instead of the July's warm breezes and clear skies, it was gray and cold. She looked up at the tree whose trunk had raised the bricks on the sidewalk and noticed the tangled masses of vines, which grew insidiously up the trunk, strangling the tree in their unrelenting ascent to reach the top. *Just like some of the people here*, she thought. The Vineyarders were like a mass of tangled vines strangling anything in their way to get to the top. She'd had it.

A half hour later in her kitchen, she called her father. "Dad, it's Janet. I have something I need to ask of you. Don't say anything. Just listen. And above all, I don't want you saying anything to anyone. I'm serious.

"I need you to ask your lawyer for the names of three good Boston divorce lawyers. He needs to make sure they do not know Rick and they haven't had any divorces on the island or even on the Cape. I don't want Rick to know either so don't leave voice mails on my machine."

Her father was silent and then said simply, "I understand. I'll get back to you as soon as possible."

A minute later, Rick burst into the kitchen. "Are you home? What happened—I thought you had grand jury? I understand you've been talking to your father too."

"I was recused. There was some problem with the selection process, and Charlie and Judge Mayhew thought it best I recused myself rather than have some complaint filed later and all this work was for nothing. Anyway, I'm glad, it was going on and on, and I wanted out."

"That's it? Nothing else you want to tell me?" he said sneeringly.

"No, what are you talking about? I just told you—you can check with Charlie if you want. He'll tell you the same thing. You know I can't say anything about the jury."

And he slammed the door and went back to his office where he again slammed his office door shut. He rewound the taped and listened again. "Bitch! You'll be sorry! Think you're so smart, don't you? Ha!"

Chapter 106

Edgartown, Monday, November 30, 2015, mid-morning

After Janet had left, the grand jury were cautioned not to talk among themselves about the recusal of Janet and were told to continue to discuss the posthumous Ponzi charges they had been presented, once they had elected their new foreman (James Bilodeau). In the courthouse upstairs, Charlie, the judge, and the man with the briefcase met privately in the judge's chambers.

Charlie introduced him to the judge. "Your Honor, this is Daniel I. Little, who is a retired FBI agent, now in private practice in an international forensic firm specializing in white-collar crime. Mr. Little was a prosecutor for the US Department of Justice, during which time he successfully tried RICO, corruption, financial and regulatory cases associated with the Boston Mafia family, namely the Francis 'Cadillac Frank' Salemme, alleged mobster you've been reading about for years. Today Attorney Little is concentrating on white-collar crimes and is both a certified document examiner and certified in financial forensics (CFF). An added bonus to us, although it may not be apparent now, is that besides determining the authenticity of documents or authorship of handwriting, Mr. Little has expertise in all criminal forensic matters, including telephone forensics…and extortion."

"Good morning, Your Honor," said Little. "I am pleased to be here. I'd like to give you a brief overview of what I would like to apply my time to in this unusual case. The forgery and uttering issues of the case are easy to determine. I've already looked at several of Mrs.

Keller's purchase and sales agreements, and it's a straightforward case requiring little of my time. However, there appears to be another aspect to this case about which I've already had a conversation with DA O'Brien, and I understand you yourself are now apprised of this further possible criminal activity." He paused.

Judge Mayhew looked up from under his glasses and said, "Yes, Charlie here talked to me late last week about this possibility, and it's why we immediately recused our foreperson, Janet Maron—an upstanding citizen—pending on what we unfold going forward. It seems incredulous to me that this second crime could be true, but we need you to ascertain whether or not there is substance here. Can you tell me what this particular aspect of your work will entail?"

"The first order of business will be a forensic audit performed by me and my team of professionals who have skill sets in both criminology and accounting. This entails following a money trail and checking for inaccuracies in overall and detailed reports of income or expenditures. If they find discrepancies, it will be my job as a separate financial investigator to determine the origin of these funds." Dan paused.

Charlie nodded to Dan to continue.

"The second task relates directly to forensic accounting discoveries, but is entirely separate from the real estate fraud and theft. Again, I haven't had the opportunity to delve into this area, but it appears to me that extortion may be an additional factor here in the Keller Ponzi scheme case. At the moment, and before further analysis, I believe there may be two types of extortion that have gone on: blackmail, when a person threatens to disclose another person's or organization's secret, causing damage; and second, bribery, another form of extortion, attempting to influence a person by giving money or items of value. In other words, I believe the Ponzi schemes conducted by Mrs. Keller, and possibly her second husband, came into the hands of someone else who bribed and blackmailed Mrs. Keller.

"I further believe that the extorter committed a third crime here: wiretapping. Only several States require, under most circumstances, the consent of all parties to a conversation. In other words, no party can be unaware that his or her conversations are being taped. And luckily, Massachusetts is one of these States. All parties need to consent to recording or eavesdropping." He stopped and looked at the judge.

The judge cried out, "This is all unbelievable. In all my career, largely in the superior court system of Massachusetts, in small cities and towns like this, I have never encountered such cases. A top real estate broker dealing with the rich and famous, and a small-town attorney who usually handles domestic disputes, small divorces, and OUI arrests! I've had Mr. Maron come before me numerous times and find him not to be the brightest bulb on the tree and inconsequential. That you have reason to believe that he had the wherewithal to become suspicious enough of Mrs. Keller and had the idea to extort is, in some ways, more surprising than her greed." He shook his head and seemed baffled by all this, but he clearly realized the attorney's expertise far outweighed his own in these matters.

"Okay," the judge continued, "I'm authorizing you to proceed with your investigations that include, but will not be limited to—if other types of crimes are discovered—the Keller fraud (including forgery, uttering, and grand theft) and the possible Maron extortion case (including wiretapping, bribery, and blackmail). I fully realize the Maron matter may only be the tip of the iceberg and that more will come out of this. But we shall see. For the moment, we will continue with the Keller cases and not introduce anything about the Maron subject. This is indeed serious. I feel sorry for Janet. She's an upstanding person and respected member of the community. God bless her as she goes forward in this tiny town. It won't be easy," and he shook his head, pushing back his chair as he stood up. "It won't be easy for her, poor thing."

Judge Mayhew looked despondent. He came around to the front of his desk and thanked Charlie for having found Dan and told Dan that the town was lucky to have him step in here now for what appeared to be complicated felonies that were linked, although not one and the same. The two men said their goodbyes to the judge and left the chambers together and went down the stairs and out onto Main Street, leaving the judge alone.

Alone in his chambers, Mayhew went back to his seat, disheartened, and looked out the second-story window toward the harbor. The sky was gray but calm. In fact, everything looked calm. There was no hint of what was roiling under this community. He said to himself, *Who would ever have thought that this little spit of sand just a few miles off the mainland, surrounded by the Atlantic Ocean, could harbor such corruption, crime, and greed. In the city, yes, of course. It happens daily. But, here, in this beautiful little town with tree-lined lanes and rose-covered picket fences with neighbors saying hello to each other as they walk in town? It can't be. It just can't be. How can greed and corruption have spread to here?* he asked himself, shaking his head.

"Was it due to the wealthy off-islanders coming here for respite, thereby disrupting the status quo of life here and bringing along with them the diseases of the real world? Was that what happened? Or, was it always here, just masked by people not wanting to disrupt their peaceful lives and a 'live and let live' way of life?"

He stood up from his desk and looked out the window in the other direction and noticed the old, neglected, and dying linden tree near the back of the parking lot, its trunk and branches without leaves in the winter sun. *That old tree doesn't have much life in it, does it?* he mused. He looked closer and noticed the trunk and branches. *It's all covered in vines. Why doesn't the town cut them down? It's killing that old tree.*

And then, it came to him; he got his answer.

In the off-season, when the town is not manicured or tended to as in the summer months when the visitors return, the wild grapevines, now left alone, resume their quest for sunlight.

Wild grapevines need full sunlight to continue to grow, and they are predetermined to climb toward light. On good growing sites, they can grow several feet per year and quickly overtop other vegetation. Once grapevines (and ivy too) get into tree crowns, especially in young stands, the potential for the tree to thrive is severely reduced. Their tendrils wrap tightly around anything they can reach, and the vine grows so quickly and densely that in a matter of just a couple of years, it can envelop trees, suffocating them from light and killing them. Strangling and entangling the stems and branches with its thin tendrils, the wild grapes can damage trees by covering the leaves of the tree with its own, reducing the growth rate of the tree or even causing death. The weight of grapevines can break branches or cause entire trees to topple under the weight of wind, ice, and snow.

Left to get out of hand, like this poor linden here, the judge thought, these invasive and deadly vines will spread from tree to tree or along phone wires at heights impossible to reach, so the only point of attack is from the ground.

The judge knew the only ways to stop this parasitic overgrowth frenzy are by mechanical means, cutting back the stems and attempting to uproot the vines (almost impossible), or by chemical means, using herbicides or poison in a more efficient and deadly manner, but not always fatal.

In the two cases now before him, he realized that Maria's and Walter's vines had been poisoned, while Rick's vines would soon have to be uprooted. In either case, the judge thought, with this island so overgrown with the wild grapevines that prompted Bartholomew Gosnold to name the place Martha's Vineyard, no one ever could eradicate all these tangled vines once and for all...either by chemical or manual ways. These insidious roots were deeper than poison or axes could ever reach. The island sits on top of rock and sand, and the grapevines' roots are the underpinnings of the soil that holds the landmass together, allowing life to inhabit this isolated place.

"The wild grapes of Martha's Vineyard are here to stay," he concluded out loud and then went back to his philosophizing. *Some of the wild grapes will be content to live where they've always been, in open spaces in the sun and where the ocean breezes are, while others will never be satisfied with this. The latter are the parasitic ones, programmed to unflinchingly advance along invasive and deadly paths that will enable them to entangle their tendrils and leaves on the picket fences and the trees, suffocating or destroying their hosts, twisting and tangling, climbing and twisting again to strangle them more, stopping at nothing to conquer their prey in their wild quest to reach the sunlit top.*

Judge Mayhew came out of his reveries by a knock on the door.

"Your Honor, the next case is ready to be heard."

As he got up from his chair, he thought of the stanzas:

> O, what a tangled web we weave,
> When first we practise to deceive

He put on his robe and mused to himself, *Had Walter Scott lived here, the poem would have read:*

> *O, what tangled vines they weave…*

And he went out through his chamber's door, closing it quietly behind him, shaking his head while letting out a soft sigh. He knew this was not the end of the saga. He knew this Boston attorney would present more—in fact, *way* more—than Maria's and Walter's forgery and Ponzi real estate schemes. He thought to himself, *Attorney Little's discovery*—or, as he quickly corrected himself—*"suspicions" of extortion were based on wiretapping. Wiretapping! In this little town in the middle of nowhere! By someone who was known not to be sharp enough to conceive of this, much less carry it all out!*

He had just reached the courtroom door, and with his hand on the knob, he said to himself, *It was almost as if Walter Scott had instead penned:*

> O, what tangled wires we weave,
> When first we liars do deceive.

The Bailiff opened the door wide: "All rise!"

The judge took his seat. *I just might write a book about all this. No one would ever believe it.*

He began to talk. He explained that since deliberations had not yet begun, they could install a new juror. He pointed to Isabella in the front row and announced that she had been selected from the original pool to replace the recused member, and Ms. Isabella Stewart would be sworn in now.

When that was done, he once again read the instructions, and the grand jury filed downstairs, now with Isabella in tow. What the judge and others didn't yet know was that Isabella had been interviewing for the opening at the island's weekly newspaper, *The Grapevine*, as the community reporter, and she had just accepted it. They also didn't know that one of Isabella's favorite poems was Scott's "Marmion."

O what tangled thoughts we weave…

About the Author

Isabella Stewart is active in her town and county affairs, a supporter of animal rescue groups, and, above all, is a keen observer of life on that spit of sand in the Atlantic Ocean named Martha's Vineyard, where she lives happily year-round. She also wanted you to know that she is a licensed real estate broker.

CPSIA information can be obtained
at www.ICGtesting.com
Printed in the USA
LVHW051821270721
693844LV00003B/219

9 781648 019494